Kim Stanley Robinson was born in 1952 and, after travelling and working around the world, has now settled in his beloved California. He is the award-winning author of *The Orange County Trilogy*, *The Mars Trilogy (Red Mars, Green Mars* and *Blue Mars)*, *Antarctica* and a number of highly-praised short story collections. His most recent novel, *The Years of Rice and Salt*, recounts seven hundred years of alternative history.

Voyager

KIM STANLEY ROBINSON

Vinland the Dream

and Other Stories

HarperCollins*Publishers*

Voyager
An Imprint of HarperCollins*Publishers*
77–85 Fulham Palace Road,
Hammersmith, London W6 8JB

www.voyager-books.com

A Paperback Original 2002
1 3 5 7 9 8 6 4 2

'Venice Drowned', 'Mercurial', 'Ridge Running', 'The Disguise', 'The
Lucky Strike', 'Coming Back to Dixieland', 'Stone Eggs' and 'Black Air'
previously published in the collection *The Planet on the Table*, first
published in The United States in 1986 by Tom Doherty Associates,
and first published in Great Britain in 1987 by Futura Publications.

'Vinland the Dream', 'A History of the Twentieth Century, with
Illustrations', 'Remaking History', 'Muir on Shasta' and 'A Sensitive
Dependence on Initial Conditions' previously published in the
collection *Remaking History*, published in the United States by
Tom Doherty Associates Inc, 1991.

A catalogue record for this book
is available from the British Library

ISBN 0 00 713404 5

Typeset in Trump Mediaeval by
Palimpsest Book Production Limited, Polmont, Stirlingshire

Printed and bound in Great Britain by
Clays Ltd, St Ives plc

Contents

Acknowledgements

'Vinland the Dream' originally published in *Remaking History*, copyright © 1991 Kim Stanley Robinson

'A History of the Twentieth Century, with Illustrations' originally published in *Isaac Asimov's Science Fiction Magazine*, copyright © 1991. The story was revised for *Remaking History*.

'Remaking History' originally published in *What Might Have Been*, edited by Gregory Benford and Martin H. Greenberg, copyright © 1989

'The Lucky Strike' originally published in *Universe 14*, copyright © 1984, Terry Carr

'A Sensitive Dependence on Initial Conditions' originally published in *Author's Choice Monthly: Kim Stanley Robinson*, copyright © 1991

'Discovering Life' originally published in Voyager 5 Collector's Edition, copyright © 2000

'Venice Drowned' originally published in *Universe 11*, copyright © 1981, Terry Carr

'The Disguise' originally published in *Orbit 19*, copyright © 1977, Damon Knight

'Mercurial' originally published in *Universe 15*, copyright © 1981, Terry Carr

'Coming Back to Dixieland' originally published in *Orbit 18*, copyright © 1976, Damon Knight

'Stone Eggs' originally published in *Universe 13*, copyright © 1983, Terry Carr

'Ridge Running' originally published in *The Magazine of Fantasy and Science Fiction*, copyright © 1984, The Mercury Press

'Muir on Shasta' originally published in *Author's Choice Monthly: Kim Stanley Robinson*, copyright © 1991

'Black Air' originally published in *The Magazine of Science Fiction and Fantasy*, copyright © 1983, The Mercury Press

Vinland the Dream

ABSTRACT. IT WAS sunset at L'Anse aux Meadows. The water of the bay was still, the boggy beach was dark in the shadows. Flat arms of land pointed to flat islands offshore; beyond these a taller island stood like a loaf of stone in the sea, catching the last of the day's light. A stream gurgled gently as it cut through the beach bog. Above the bog, on a narrow grassy terrace, one could just make out a pattern of low mounds, all that remained of sod walls. Next to them were three or four sod buildings, and beyond the buildings, a number of tents.

A group of people – archaeologists, graduate students, volunteer labourers, visitors – moved together onto a rocky ridge overlooking the site. Some of them worked at starting a campfire in a ring of blackened stones; others began to unpack bags of food, and cases of beer. Far across the water lay the dark bulk of Labrador.

Kindling caught and their fire burned, a spark of yellow in the dusk's gloom.

Hot dogs and beer, around a campfire by the sea; and yet it was strangely quiet. Voices were subdued. The people on the hill glanced down often at the site, where the head of their dig, a lanky man in his early fifties, was giving a brief tour to their distinguished guest. The distinguished guest did not appear pleased.

Introduction. The head of the dig, an archaeology professor from McGill University, was looking at the distinguished guest with the expression he wore when confronted by an aggressive undergraduate. The distinguished guest, Canada's Minister of Culture, was asking question after question. As she did, the professor took her to look for herself, at the forge, and the slag pit, and the little midden beside Building E. New trenches were cut across the mounds and depressions, perfect rectangular cuts in the black peat; they could tell the minister nothing of what they had revealed. But she had insisted on seeing them, and now she was asking questions that got right to the point, although they could have been asked and answered just as well in Ottawa. Yes, the professor explained, the fuel for the forge was wood charcoal, the temperature had gotten to around twelve hundred degrees Celsius, the process was direct reduction of bog ore, obtaining about one kilogram of iron for every five kilograms of slag. All was as it was in other Norse forges – except that the limonites in the bog ore had now been precisely identified by spectroscopic analysis; and that analysis had revealed that the bog iron smelted here had come from northern Quebec, near Chicoutimi. The Norse explorers, who had supposedly smelted the bog ore, could not have obtained it.

There was a similar situation in the midden; rust migrated in peat at a known rate, and so it could be determined that the many iron rivets in the midden had only been there a hundred and forty years, plus or minus fifty.

'So,' the minister said, in English with a Francophone lilt. 'You have proved your case, it appears?'

The professor nodded wordlessly. The minister watched him, and he couldn't help feeling that despite the nature of the news he was giving her, she was somewhat amused. By him? By his scientific terminology? By his obvious (and growing) depression? He couldn't tell.

The minister raised her eyebrows. 'L'Anse aux Meadows, a hoax. Parcs Canada will not like it at all.'

'No one will like it,' the professor croaked.

'No,' the minister said, looking at him. 'I suppose not. Particularly as this is part of a larger pattern, yes?'

The professor did not reply.

'The entire concept of Vinland,' she said. 'A hoax!'

The professor nodded glumly.

'I would not have believed it possible.'

'No,' the professor said. 'But –' He waved a hand at the low mounds around them – 'So it appears.' He shrugged. 'The story has always rested on a very small body of evidence. Three sagas, this site, a few references in Scandinavian records, a few coins, a few cairns . . .' He shook his head. 'Not much.' He picked up a chunk of dried peat from the ground, crumbled it in his fingers.

Suddenly the minister laughed at him, then put her hand to his upper arm. Her fingers were warm. 'You must remember it is not your fault.'

He smiled wanly. 'I suppose not.' He liked the look on her face; sympathetic as well as amused. She was about his age, perhaps a bit older. An attractive and sophisticated Quebecois. 'I need a drink,' he confessed.

'There's beer on the hill.'

'Something stronger. I have a bottle of cognac I haven't opened yet . . .'

'Let's get it and take it up there with us.'

Experimental Methods. The graduate students and volunteer labourers were gathered around the fire, and the smell of roasting hot dogs filled the air. It was nearly eleven, the sun a half-hour gone, and the last light of the summer dusk slowly leaked from the sky. The fire burned like a beacon. Beer had been flowing freely, and the party was beginning to get a little more boisterous.

The minister and the professor stood near the fire, drinking cognac out of plastic cups.

'How did you come to suspect the story of Vinland?' the minister asked as they watched the students cook hot dogs.

A couple of the volunteer labourers, who had paid good money to spend their summer digging trenches in a bog, heard the question and moved closer.

The professor shrugged. 'I can't quite remember.' He tried to laugh. 'Here I am an archaeologist, and I can't remember my own past.'

The minister nodded as if that made sense. 'I suppose it was a long time ago?'

'Yes.' He concentrated. 'Now what was it. Someone was following up the story of the Vinland map, to try and figure out who had done it. The map showed up in a bookstore in New Haven in the 1950s – as you may know?'

'No,' the minister said. 'I hardly know a thing about Vinland, I assure you. Just the basics that anyone in my position would have to know.'

'Well, there was a map found in the 1950s called the Vinland map, and it was shown to be a hoax soon after its discovery. But when this investigator traced the map's history, she found that the book it had been in was accounted for all the way back to the 1820s, map and all. It meant the hoaxer had lived longer ago than I had expected.' He refilled his cup of cognac, then the minister's. 'There were a lot of Viking hoaxes in the nineteenth century, but this one was so early. It surprised me. It's generally thought that the whole phenomenon was stimulated by a book that a Danish scholar published in 1837, containing translations of the Vinland sagas and related material. The book was very popular among the Scandinavian settlers in America, and after that, you know . . . a kind of twisted patriotism, or the response of an ethnic group that had been made fun of too often . . . So we got the Kensington stone, the halberds, the mooring holes, the coins. But if a hoax predated *Antiquitates Americanae* . . . it made me wonder.'

'If the book itself were somehow involved?'

'Exactly,' the professor said, regarding the minister with pleasure. 'I wondered if the book might not incorporate, or have been inspired by, hoaxed material. Then one day I was reading a description of the field work here, and it occurred to me that this site was a bit too pristine. As if it had been built but never lived in. Best estimates for its occupation were as low as one summer, because they couldn't find any trash middens to speak of, or graves.'

'It could have been occupied very briefly,' the minister pointed out.

'Yes, I know. That's what I thought at the time. But then I heard from a colleague in Bergen that the *Gronlendinga Saga* was apparently a forgery, at least in the parts referring to the discovery of Vinland. Pages had been inserted that dated back to the 1820s. And after that, I had a doubt that wouldn't go away.'

'But there are more Vinland stories than that one, yes?'

'Yes. There are three main sources. The *Gronlendinga Saga, The Saga of Erik the Red*, and the part of *The Hauksbók* that tells about Thorfinn Karlsefni's expedition. But with one of those questioned, I began to doubt them all. And the story itself. Everything having to do with the idea of Vinland.'

'Is that when you went to Bergen?' a graduate student asked.

The professor nodded. He drained his plastic cup, felt the alcohol rushing through him. 'I joined Nielsen there and we went over *Erik the Red* and *The Hauksbók*, and damned if the pages in those concerning Vinland weren't forgeries too. The ink gave it away – not its composition, which was about right, but merely how long it had been on that paper. Which was thirteenth century paper, I might add! The forger had done a super job. But

6

the sagas had been tampered with sometime in the early nineteenth century.'

'But those are masterpieces of world literature,' a volunteer labourer exclaimed, round-eyed; the ads for volunteer labour had not included a description of the primary investigator's hypothesis.

'I know,' the professor said irritably, and shrugged.

He saw a chunk of peat on the ground, picked it up and threw it on the blaze. After a bit it flared up.

'It's like watching dirt burn,' he said absently, staring into the flames.

Discussion. The burnt garbage smell of peat wafted downwind, and offshore the calm water of the bay was riffled by the same gentle breeze. The minister warmed her hands at the blaze for a moment, then gestured at the bay. 'It's hard to believe they were never here at all.'

'I know,' the professor said. 'It looks like a Viking site, I'll give him that.'

'Him,' the minister repeated.

'I know, I know. This whole thing forces you to imagine a man in the eighteen twenties and thirties, travelling all over – Norway, Iceland, Canada, New England, Rome, Stockholm, Denmark, Greenland . . . Crisscrossing the North Atlantic, to bury all these signs.' He shook his head. 'It's incredible.'

He retrieved the cognac bottle and refilled. He was, he had to admit, beginning to feel drunk. 'And so many parts of the hoax were well hidden! You can't assume we've found them all. This place had two butternuts buried in the midden, and butternuts only grow down

7

below the St Lawrence, so who's to say they aren't clues, indicating another site down there? That's where grapevines actually grow, which would justify the name Vinland. I tell you, the more I know about this hoaxer, the more certain I am that other sites exist. The tower in Newport, Rhode Island, for instance – the hoaxer didn't build that, because it's been around since the seventeenth century – but a little work out there at night, in the early nineteenth century . . . I bet if it were excavated completely, you'd find a few Norse artefacts.'

'Buried in all the right places,' the minister said.

'Exactly.' The professor nodded. 'And up the coast of Labrador, at Cape Porcupine where the sagas say they repaired a ship. There too. Stuff scattered everywhere, left to be discovered or not.'

The minister waved her plastic cup. 'But surely this site must have been his masterpiece. He couldn't have done too many as extensive as this.'

'I shouldn't think so.' The professor drank deeply, smacked his numbed lips. 'Maybe one more like this, down in New Brunswick. That's my guess. But this was surely one of his biggest projects.'

'It was a time for that kind of thing,' the volunteer labourer offered. 'Atlantis, Mu, Lemuria . . .'

The minister nodded. 'It fulfils a certain desire.'

'Theosophy, most of that,' the professor muttered. 'This was different.'

The volunteer wandered off. The professor and the minister looked into the fire for a while.

'You are *sure*?' the minister asked.

The professor nodded. 'Trace elements show the ore came from upper Quebec. Chemical changes in the peat weren't right. And nuclear resonance dating methods show that the bronze pin they found hadn't been buried long enough. Little things like that. Nothing obvious. He was amazingly meticulous, he really thought it out. But the nature of things tripped him up. Nothing more than that.'

'But the effort!' the minister said. 'This is what I find hard to believe. Surely it must have been more than one man! Burying these objects, building the walls – surely he would have been noticed!'

The professor stopped another swallow, nodded at her as he choked once or twice. A broad wave of the hand, a gasping recovery of breath:

'Fishing village, kilometre north of here. Boarding house in the early nineteenth century. A crew of ten rented rooms in the summer of 1842. Bills paid by a Mr Carlsson.'

The minister raised her eyebrows. 'Ah.'

One of the graduate students got out a guitar and began to play. The other students and the volunteers gathered around her.

'So,' the minister said, 'Mr Carlsson. Does he show up elsewhere?'

'There was a Professor Ohman in Bergen. A Dr Bergen in Reykjavik. In the right years, studying the sagas. I presume they were all him, but I don't know for sure.'

'What do you know about him?'

'Nothing. No one paid much attention to him. I've got him on a couple transatlantic crossings, I think, but he used aliases, so I've probably missed most of them. A Scandinavian-American, apparently Norwegian by birth. Someone with some money – someone with

9

patriotic feelings of some kind – someone with a grudge against a university – who knows? All I have are a few signatures, of aliases at that. A flowery handwriting. Nothing more. That's the most remarkable thing about him! You see, most hoaxers leave clues to their identities, because a part of them wants to be caught. So their cleverness can be admired, or the ones who fell for it embarrassed, or whatever. But this guy didn't want to be discovered. And in those days, if you wanted to stay off the record . . .' He shook his head.

'A man of mystery.'

'Yeah. But I don't know how to find out anything more about him.'

The professor's face was glum in the firelight as he reflected on this. He polished off another cup of cognac. The minister watched him drink, then said kindly, 'There is nothing to be done about it, really. That is the nature of the past.'

'I know.'

Conclusions. They threw the last big logs on the fire, and flames roared up, yellow licks breaking free among the stars. The professor felt numb all over, his heart was cold, the firelit faces were smeary primitive masks, dancing in the light. The songs were harsh and raucous, he couldn't understand the words. The wind was chilling, and the hot skin of his arms and neck goosepimpled uncomfortably. He felt sick with alcohol, and knew it would be a while before his body could overmaster it.

The minister led him away from the fire, then up the rocky ridge. Getting him away from the students and labourers, no doubt, so he wouldn't embarrass himself. Starlight illuminated the heather and broken granite under their feet. He stumbled. He tried to explain to her what it meant, to be an archaeologist whose most important work was the discovery that a bit of their past was a falsehood.

'It's like a mosaic,' he said, drunkenly trying to follow the fugitive thought. 'A puzzle with most of the pieces gone. A tapestry. And if you pull a thread out . . . it's ruined. So little lasts! We need every bit we can find!'

She seemed to understand. In her student days, she told him, she had waitressed at a café in Montreal. Years later she had gone down the street to have a look, just for nostalgia's sake. The café was gone. The street was completely different. And she couldn't remember the names of any of the people she had worked with. 'This was my own past, not all that many years ago!'

The professor nodded. Cognac was rushing through his veins, and as he looked at the minister, so beautiful in the starlight, she seemed to him a kind of muse, a spirit sent to comfort him, or frighten him, he couldn't tell which. Clio, he thought. The muse of history. Someone he could talk to.

She laughed softly. 'Sometimes it seems our lives are much longer than we usually think. So that we live through incarnations, and looking back later we have nothing but . . .' She waved a hand.

'Bronze pins,' the professor said. 'Iron rivets.'

'Yes.' She looked at him. Her eyes were bright in the starlight. 'We need an archaeology for our own lives.'

Acknowledgements. Later he walked her back to the

fire, now reduced to banked red coals. She put her hand to his upper arm as they walked, steadying herself, and he felt in the touch some kind of portent; but couldn't understand it. He had drunk so much! Why be so upset about it, why? It was his job to find the truth; having found it, he should be happy! Why had no one told him what he would feel?

The minister said good-night. She was off to bed; she suggested he do likewise. Her look was compassionate, her voice firm.

When she was gone he hunted down the bottle of cognac, and drank the rest of it. The fire was dying, the students and workers scattered – in the tents, or out in the night, in couples.

He walked by himself back down to the site.

Low mounds, of walls that had never been. Beyond the actual site were rounded buildings, models built by the park service, to show tourists what the 'real' buildings had looked like. When Vikings had camped on the edge of the new world. Repairing their boats. Finding food. Fighting among themselves, mad with epic jealousies. Fighting the dangerous Indians. Getting killed, and then driven away from this land, so much lusher than Greenland.

A creak in the brush and he jumped, startled. It would have been like that: death in the night, creeping up on you – he turned with a jerk, and every starlit shadow bounced with hidden skraelings, their bows drawn taut, their arrows aimed at his heart. He quivered, hunched over.

But no. It hadn't been like that. Not at all. Instead, a man with spectacles and a bag full of old junk, directing some unemployed sailors as they dug. Nondescript, taciturn, nameless; one night he would have wandered back there into the forest, perhaps fallen or had a heart attack – become a skeleton wearing leathers and sword-belt, with spectacles over the skull's eyesockets, the anachronism that gave him away at last ... The professor staggered over the low mounds towards the trees, intent on finding that inadvertent grave ...

But no. It wouldn't be there. The taciturn figure hadn't been like that. He would have been far away when he died, nothing to show what he had spent years of his life doing. A man in a hospital for the poor, the bronze pin in his pocket overlooked by the doctor, stolen by an undertaker's assistant. An anonymous figure, to the grave and beyond. The creator of Vinland. Never to be found.

The professor looked around, confused and sick. There was a waist-high rock, a glacial erratic. He sat on it. Put his head on his hands. Really quite unprofessional. All those books he had read as a child. What would the minister think! Grant money. No reason to feel so bad!

At that latitude midsummer nights are short, and the party had lasted late. The sky to the east was already grey. He could see down onto the site, and its long sod roofs. On the beach, a trio of long narrow high-ended ships. Small figures in furs emerged from the longhouses and went down to the water, and he walked among them and heard their speech, a sort of dialect of Norwegian that he could mostly understand. They would leave that day, it was time to load the ships. They were going to take everything with them, they didn't plan to return. Too many skraelings in the forest, too many quick arrow deaths. He walked among them, helping them load stores. Then a little man in a black coat scurried behind the forge, and he roared and took off after him, scooping up a rock on the way, ready to deal out a skraeling death to that black intruder.

The minister woke him with a touch of her hand. He almost fell off the rock. He shook his head; he was still drunk. The hangover wouldn't begin for a couple more hours, though the sun was already up.

'I should have known all along,' he said to her angrily. 'They were stretched to the limit in Greenland, and the climate was worsening. It was amazing they got that far. Vinland' – he waved a hand at the site – 'was just some dreamer's story.'

Regarding him calmly, the minister said, 'I am not sure it matters.'

He looked up at her. 'What do you mean?'

'History is made of stories people tell. And fictions, dreams, hoaxes – they also are made of stories people tell. True or false, it's the stories that matter to us. Certain qualities in the stories themselves make them true or false.'

He shook his head. 'Some things really happened in the past. And some things didn't.'

'But how can you know for sure which is which? You can't go back and see for yourself. Maybe Vinland was the invention of this mysterious stranger of yours; maybe the Vikings came here after all, and landed somewhere else. Either way it can never be anything more than a story to us.'

'But . . .' He swallowed. 'Surely it matters whether it is a true story or not!'

She paced before him. 'A friend of mine once told me something he had read in a book,' she said. 'It was by a man who sailed the Red Sea, long ago. He told of a servant boy on one of the dhows, who could not remember ever having been cared for. The boy had become a sailor at age three – before that, he had been a beachcomber.' She stopped pacing and looked at the beach below them. 'Often I imagined that little boy's life. Surviving alone on a beach, at that age – it astonished me. It made me . . . happy.'

She turned to look at him. 'But later I told this story to an expert in child development, and he just shook his head. "It probably wasn't true," he said. Not a lie, exactly, but a . . .'

'A stretcher,' the professor suggested.

'A stretcher, exactly. He supposed that the boy had been somewhat older, or had had some help. You know.'

The professor nodded.

'But in the end,' the minister said, 'I found this judgment did not matter to me. In my mind I still saw that toddler, searching the tidepools for his daily food. And so for me the story lives. And that is all that matters. We judge all the stories from history like that – we value them according to how much they spur our imaginations.'

The professor stared at her. He rubbed his jaw, looked around. Things had the sharp-edged clarity they sometimes get after a sleepness night, as if glowing with internal light. He said, 'Someone with opinions like yours probably shouldn't have the job that you do.'

'I didn't know I had them,' the minister said. 'I only just came upon them in the last couple hours, thinking about it.'

The professor was surprised. 'You didn't sleep?'

She shook her head. 'Who could sleep on a night like this?'

'My feeling exactly!' He almost smiled. 'So. A *nuit blanche*, you call it?'

'Yes,' she said. 'A *nuit blanche* for two.' And she looked down at him with that amused glance of hers, as if . . . as if she understood him.

She extended her arms towards him, grasped his hands, helped pull him to his feet. They began to walk back towards the tents, across the site of L'Anse aux Meadows. The grass was wet with dew, and very green.

'I still think,' he said as they walked together, 'that we want more than stories from the past. We want something not easily found – something, in fact, that the past doesn't have. Something secret, some secret meaning . . . something that will give our lives a kind of sense.'

She slipped a hand under his arm. 'We want the Atlantis of childhood. But, failing that . . .' She laughed and kicked at a clump of grass; a spray of dew flashed ahead of them, containing, for just one moment, a bright little rainbow.

'A History of the Twentieth Century, with Illustrations'

> 'If truth is not to be found on the shelves of
> the British Museum, where, I asked myself,
> picking up a notebook and a pencil, is truth?'
> — VIRGINIA WOOLF

DAILY DOSES OF bright light markedly improve the mood of people suffering from depression, so every day at eight in the evening Frank Churchill went to the clinic on Park Avenue, and sat for three hours in a room illuminated with sixteen hundred watts of white light. This was not exactly like having the sun in the room, but it was bright, about the same as if sixteen bare lightbulbs hung from the ceiling. In this case the bulbs were probably long tubes, and they were hidden behind a sheet of white plastic, so it was the whole ceiling that glowed.

He sat at a table and doodled with a purple pen on

a pad of pink paper. And then it was eleven and he was out on the windy streets, blinking as traffic lights swam in the gloom. He walked home to a hotel room in the west Eighties. He would return to the clinic at five the next morning for a predawn treatment, but now it was time to sleep. He looked forward to that. He'd been on the treatment for three weeks, and he was tired. Though the treatment did seem to be working – as far as he could tell; improvement was supposed to average twenty per cent a week, and he wasn't sure what that would feel like.

In his room the answering machine was blinking. There was a message from his agent, asking him to call immediately. It was now nearly midnight, but he push-buttoned the number and his agent answered on the first ring.

'You have DSPS,' Frank said to him.

'What? What?'

'Delayed sleep phase syndrome. I know how to get rid of it.'

'Frank! Look, Frank, I've got a good offer for you.'

'Do you have a lot of lights on?'

'What? Oh, yeah, say, how's that going?'

'I'm probably sixty per cent better.'

'Good, good. Keep at it. Listen, I've got something should help you a hundred per cent. A publisher in London wants you to go over there and write a book on the twentieth century.'

'What kind of book?'

'Your usual thing, Frank, but this time putting together the big picture. Reflecting on all the rest of your books, so to speak. They want to bring it out in time for the turn of the century, and go oversize, use lots of illustrations, big print run –'

'A coffee table book?'

'People'll want it on their coffee tables, sure, but it's not –'

'I don't want to write a coffee table book.'

'Frank –'

'What do they want, ten thousand words?'

'They want thirty thousand words, Frank. And they'll pay a hundred thousand pound advance.'

That gave him pause.

'Why so much?'

'They're new to publishing, they come from computers and this is the kind of numbers they're used to. It's a different scale.'

'That's for sure. I still don't want to do it.'

'Frank, come on, you're the one for this! The only successor to Barbara Tuchman!' That was a blurb found on paperback editions of his work. 'They want you in particular – I mean, Churchill on the twentieth century, ha ha. It's a natural.'

'I don't want to do it.'

'Come on, Frank. You could use the money, I thought you were having trouble with the payments –'

'Yeah yeah.' Time for a different tack. 'I'll think it over.'

'They're in a hurry, Frank.'

'I thought you said turn of the century!'

'I did, but there's going to be a lot of this kind of book then, and they want to beat the rush. Set the standard and then keep it in print for a few years. It'll be great.'

'It'll be remaindered within a year. Remaindered before it even comes out, if I know coffee table books.'

His agent sighed. 'Come on, Frank. You can use the money. As for the book, it'll be as good as you make it, right? You've been working on this stuff your whole career, and here's your chance to sum up. And you've got a lot of readers, people will listen to you.' Concern made him shrill: 'Don't let what's happened get you so down that you miss an opportunity like this! Work is the best cure for depression anyway. And this is your chance to influence how we think about what's happened!'

'With a coffee table book?'

'God damn it, don't think of it that way!'

'How should I think of it.'

His agent took a deep breath, let it out, spoke very slowly. 'Think of it as a hundred thousand pounds, Frank.'

His agent did not understand.

Nevertheless, the next morning as he sat under the bright white ceiling, doodling with a green pen on yellow paper, he decided to go to England. He didn't want to sit in that room anymore; it scared him, because he suspected it might not be working. He was not sixty per cent better. And he didn't want to shift to drug therapy. They had found nothing wrong with his brain, no physical problems at all, and though that meant little, it did make him resistant to the idea of drugs. He had his reasons and he wanted his feelings!

The light room technician thought that this attitude was a good sign in itself. 'Your serotonin level is normal, right? So it's not that bad. Besides London's a lot farther north than New York, so you'll pick up the light you lose here. And if you need more you can always head north again, right?'

He called Charles and Rya Dowland to ask if he could stay with them. It turned out they were leaving for Florida the next day, but they invited him to stay anyway; they liked having their flat occupied while they were gone. Frank had done that before, he still had the key on his key-ring. 'Thanks,' he said. It would be better this way, actually. He didn't feel like talking.

So he packed his backpack, including camping gear with the clothes, and the next morning flew to London. It was strange how one travelled these days: he got into a moving chamber outside his hotel, then shifted from one chamber to the next for several hours, only stepping outdoors again when he emerged from the Camden tube station, some hundred yards from Charles and Rya's flat.

The ghost of his old pleasure brushed him as he crossed Camden High Street and walked by the cinema, listening to London's voices. This had been his method for years: come to London, stay with Charles and Rya until he found digs, do his research and writing at the British Museum, visit the used bookstores at Charing Cross, spend the evenings at Charles and Rya's, watching TV and talking. It had been that way for four books, over the course of twenty years.

The flat was located above a butcher shop. Every wall in it was covered with stuffed bookshelves, and there were shelves nailed up over the toilet, the bath, and the head of the guest bed. In the unlikely event of an earthquake the guest would be buried in a hundred histories of London.

Frank threw his pack on the guest bed and went past the English poets downstairs. The living room was nearly filled by a table stacked with papers and books. The side street below was an open-air produce market, and he could hear the voices of the vendors as they packed up for the day. The sun hadn't set, though it was past nine; these late May days were already long. It was almost like still being in therapy.

He went downstairs and bought vegetables and rice, then went back up and cooked them. The kitchen windows were the colour of sunset, and the little flat glowed, evoking its owners so strongly that it was almost as if they were there. Suddenly he wished they were.

After eating he turned on the CD player and put on some Handel. He opened the living room drapes and settled into Charles's armchair, a glass of Bulgarian wine in his hand, an open notebook on his knee. He watched salmon light leak out of the clouds to the north, and tried to think about the causes of the First World War.

In the morning he woke to the dull *thump thump thump* of frozen slabs of meat being rendered by an axe. He went downstairs and ate cereal while leafing through the *Guardian*, then took the tube to Tottenham Court Road and walked to the British Museum.

Because of *The Belle Epoque* he had already done his research on the pre-war period, but writing in the British Library was a ritual he didn't want to break; it made him part of a tradition, back to Marx and beyond. He showed his still-valid reader's ticket to a librarian and

then found an empty seat in his usual row; in fact he
had written much of *Entre Deux Guerres* in that very
carrel, under the frontal lobes of the great skull dome.
He opened a notebook and stared at the page. Slowly
he wrote, *1900 to 1914*. Then he stared at the page.

His earlier book had tended to focus on the sumptu-
ous excesses of the pre-war European ruling class, as a
young and clearly leftist reviewer in the *Guardian* had
rather sharply pointed out. To the extent that he had
delved into the causes of the Great War, he had subscribed
to the usual theory; that it had been the result of rising
nationalism, diplomatic brinksmanship, and several
deceptive precedents in the previous two decades. The
Spanish-American War, the Russo-Japanese War, and the
two Balkan wars had all remained localized and non-
catastrophic; and there had been several 'incidents', the
Moroccan affair and the like, that had brought the two
great alliances to the brink, but not toppled them over.
So when Austria-Hungary made impossible demands to
Serbia after the assassination of Ferdinand, no one could
have known that the situation would domino into the
trenches and their slaughter.

History as accident. Well, no doubt there was a lot
of truth in that. But now he found himself thinking of
the crowds in the streets of all the major cities, cheering the news of the war's outbreak; of the disappear-
ance of pacifism, which had seemed such a force; of, in
short, the apparently unanimous support for war among
the prosperous citizens of the European powers. Support
for a war that had no real reason to be!

There was something irreducibly mysterious about
that, and this time he decided he would admit it, and

discuss it. That would require a consideration of the preceding century, the *Pax Europeana*; which in fact had been a century of bloody subjugation, the high point of imperialism, with most of the world falling to the great powers. These powers had prospered at the expense of their colonies, who had suffered in abject misery. Then the powers had spent their profits building weapons, and used the weapons on each other, and destroyed themselves. There was something weirdly just about that development, as when a mass murderer finally turns the gun on himself. Punishment, an end to guilt, an end to pain. Could that really explain it? While staying in Washington with his dying father, Frank had visited the Lincoln Memorial, and there on the right hand wall had been Lincoln's Second Inaugural Address, carved in capital letters with the commas omitted, an oddity which somehow added to the speech's Biblical massiveness, as when it spoke of the ongoing war: 'YET IF GOD WILLS THAT IT CONTINUE UNTIL ALL THE WEALTH PILED BY THE BONDSMAN'S TWO HUNDRED AND FIFTY YEARS OF UNREQUITED TOIL SHALL BE SUNK AND UNTIL EVERY DROP OF BLOOD DRAWN WITH THE LASH SHALL BE PAID BY ANOTHER DRAWN WITH THE SWORD AS WAS SAID THREE THOUSAND YEARS AGO SO STILL IT MUST BE SAID "THE JUDGEMENTS OF THE LORD ARE TRUE AND RIGHTEOUS ALTOGETHER."'

A frightening thought, from that dark part of Lincoln that was never far from the surface. But as a theory of the Great War's origin it still struck him as inadequate. It was possible to believe it of the kings and presidents, the generals and diplomats, the imperial officers around the world; they had known what they were doing, and so might have been impelled by unconscious guilt to mass suicide. But the common citizen at home, ecstatic in the streets at the outbreak of general war? That seemed more likely to be just another manifestation of the hatred of the other. All my problems are your fault! He and Andrea had said that to each other a lot. Everyone did.

And yet . . . it still seemed to him that the causes were eluding him, as they had everyone else. Perhaps it was a simple pleasure in destruction. What is the primal response to an edifice? Knock it down. What is the primal response to a stranger? Attack him.

But he was losing his drift, falling away into the metaphysics of 'human nature'. That would be a constant problem in an essay of this length. And whatever the causes, there stood the year 1914, irreducible, inexplicable, unchangeable. 'AND THE WAR CAME.'

In his previous books he had never written about the wars. He was among those who believed that real history occurred in peacetime, and that in war you might as well roll dice or skip ahead to the peace treaty. For anyone but a military historian, what was interesting would begin again only when the war ended.

Now he wasn't so sure. Current views of the Belle Epoque were distorted because one only saw it through the lens of the war that ended it; which meant that the Great War was somehow more powerful than the Belle Epoque, or at least more powerful than he had thought. It seemed he would have to write about it, this time, to make sense of the century. And so he would have to research it.

He walked up to the central catalogue tables. The room darkened as the sun went behind clouds, and he felt a chill.

For a long time the numbers alone staggered him. To overwhelm trench defences, artillery bombardments of the most astonishing size were brought to bear: on the Somme the British put a gun every twenty yards along a fourteen-mile front, and fired a million and a half shells. In April 1917 the French fired six million shells. The Germans' Big Bertha shot shells seventy-five miles high, essentially into space. Verdun was a 'battle' that lasted ten months, and killed almost a million men.

The British section of the front was ninety miles long. Every day of the war, about seven thousand men along that front were killed or wounded – not in any battle in particular, but just as the result of incidental sniper fire or bombardment. It was called 'wastage'.

Frank stopped reading, his mind suddenly filled with the image of the Vietnam Memorial. He had visited it right after leaving the Lincoln Memorial, and the sight of all those names engraved on the black granite plates had powerfully affected him. For a moment it had seemed possible to imagine all those people, a little white line for each.

But at the end of every month or two of the Great War, the British had had a whole Vietnam Memorial's worth of dead. Every month or two, for fifty-one months.

He filled out book request slips and gave them to the librarians in the central ring of desks, then picked up the books he had requested the day before, and took them back to his carrel. He skimmed the books and took notes, mostly writing down figures and statistics. British factories produced two hundred and fifty million shells. The major battles all killed a half million or more. About ten million men died on the field of battle, ten million more by revolution, disease, and starvation.

Occasionally he would stop reading and try to write; but he never got far. Once he wrote several pages on the economy of the war. The organization of agriculture and business, especially in Germany under Rathenau and England under Lloyd George, reminded him very strongly of the postmodern economy now running things. One could trace the roots of late capitalism to Great War innovations found in Rathenau's *Kriegsrohstoffabteilung* (the 'War Raw Stuff Department'), or in his *Zentral Einkaufs-Gesellschaft*. All business had been organized to fight the enemy; but when the war was over and the enemy vanquished, the organization remained. People continued to sacrifice the fruits of their work, but now they did it for the corporations that had taken the wartime governments' positions in the system.

So much of the twentieth century, there already in the Great War. And then the Armistice was signed, at eleven a.m. on November 11th, 1918. That morning at the front the two sides exchanged bombardments as usual, so that by eleven a.m. many people had died.

That evening Frank hurried home, just beating a thundershower. The air was as dark as smoky glass.

And the war never ended.

This idea, that the two world wars were actually one,

was not original to him. Winston Churchill said it at the time, as did the Nazi Alfred Rosenburg. They saw the twenties and thirties as an interregnum, a pause to regroup in the middle of a two-part conflict. The eye of a hurricane.

Nine o'clock one morning and Frank was still at the Dowlands', lingering over cereal and paging through the *Guardian*, and then through his notebooks. Every morning he seemed to get a later start, and although it was May, the days didn't seem to be getting any longer. Rather the reverse.

There were arguments against the view that it was a single war. The twenties did not seem very ominous, at least after the Treaty of Locarno in 1925: Germany had survived its financial collapse, and everywhere economic recovery seemed strong. But the thirties showed the real state of things: the depression, the new democracies falling to fascism, the brutal Spanish Civil War; the starvation of the kulaks; the terrible sense of fatality in the air. The sense of slipping on a slope, falling helplessly back into war.

But this time it was different. *Total·War*. German military strategists had coined the phrase in the 1890s, while analysing Sherman's campaign in Georgia. And they felt they were waging total war when they torpedoed neutral ships in 1915. But they were wrong; the Great War was not total war. In 1914 the rumour that German soldiers had killed eight Belgian nuns was enough to shock all civilization, and later when the *Lusitania* was sunk, objections were so fierce that the Germans agreed to leave passenger ships alone. This could only happen in a world where people still held the notion that in war armies fought armies and soldiers killed soldiers, while civilians suffered privation and perhaps got killed accidentally, but were never deliberately targeted. This was how European wars had been fought for centuries: diplomacy by other means.

In 1939, this changed. Perhaps it changed only because the capability for total war had emerged from the technological base, in the form of mass long-range aerial bombardment. Perhaps on the other hand it was a matter of learning the lessons of the Great War, digesting its implications. Stalin's murder of the kulaks, for instance: five million Ukrainian peasants, killed because Stalin wanted to collectivize agriculture. Food was deliberately shipped out of that bread-basket region, emergency supplies withheld, hidden stockpiles destroyed, and several thousand villages disappeared as all their occupants starved. This was total war.

Every morning Frank leafed around in the big catalogue volumes, as if he might find some other twentieth century. He filled out his slips, picked up the books requested the previous day, took them back to his carrel. He spent more time reading than writing. The days were cloudy, and it was dim under the great dome. His notes were getting scrambled. He had stopped working in chronological order, and kept returning compulsively to the Great War, even though the front wave of his reading was well into World War Two.

Twenty million had died in the first war, fifty million in the second. Civilian deaths made the bulk of the difference. Near the end of the war, thousands of bombs were dropped on cities in the hope of starting firestorms, in which the atmosphere itself was in effect ignited, as in Dresden, Berlin, Tokyo. Civilians were the target now, and strategic bombing made them easy to hit. Hiroshima and Nagasaki were in that sense a kind of exclamation point, at the end of a sentence which the war had been saying all along: we will kill your families at home. War is war, as Sherman said; if you want peace, surrender! And they did.

After two bombs. Nagasaki was bombed three days after Hiroshima, before the Japanese had time to understand the damage and respond. Dropping the bomb on Hiroshima was endlessly debated in the literature, but Frank found few who even attempted a defence of Nagasaki. Truman and his advisors did it, people said, to a) show Stalin they had more than one bomb, and b) show Stalin that they would use the bomb even as a threat or warning only, as Nagasaki demonstrated. A Vietnam Memorial's worth of civilians in an instantaneous flash, just so Stalin would take Truman seriously. Which he did.

When the crew of the *Enola Gay* landed, they celebrated with a barbeque.

In the evenings Frank sat in the Dowland flat in silence. He did not read, but watched the evening summer light leak out of the sky to the north. The days were getting shorter. He needed the therapy, he could feel it. More light! Someone had said that on their death-bed – Newton, Galileo, Spinoza, someone like that. No doubt they had been depressed at the time.

He missed Charles and Rya. He would feel better, he

was sure, if he had them there to talk with. That was the thing about friends, after all: they lasted and you could talk. That was the definition of friendship.

But Charles and Rya were in Florida. And in the dusk he saw that the walls of books in the flat functioned like lead lining in a radioactive environment, all those recorded thoughts forming a kind of shield against poisonous reality. The best shield available, perhaps. But now it was failing, at least for him; the books appeared to be nothing more than their spines.

And then one evening in a premature blue sunset it seemed that the whole flat had gone transparent, and that he was sitting in an armchair, suspended over a vast and shadowy city.

The Holocaust, like Hiroshima and Nagasaki, had precedents. Russians with Ukrainians, Turks with Armenians, white settlers with native Americans. But the mechanized efficiency of the Germans' murder of the Jews was something new and horrible. There was a book in his stack on the designers of the death camps, the architects, engineers, builders. Were these functionaries less or more obscene than the mad doctors, the sadistic guards? He couldn't decide.

And then there was the sheer number of them, the six million. It was hard to comprehend it. He read that there was a library in Jerusalem where they had taken on the task of recording all they could find about every one of the six million. Walking up Charing Cross Road that afternoon he thought of that and stopped short. All those names in one library, another transparent room, another memorial. For a second he caught a glimpse of how many people that was, a whole London's worth. Then it faded and he was left on a street corner, looking both ways to make sure he didn't get run over.

As he continued walking he tried to calculate how many Vietnam Memorials it would take to list the six million. Roughly two per hundred thousand; thus twenty per million. So, one hundred and twenty. Count them one by one, step by step.

He took to hanging out through the evenings in pubs. The Wellington was as good as any, and was frequented occasionally by some acquaintances he had met through Charles and Rya. He sat with them and listened to them talk, but often he found himself distracted by his day's reading. So the conversations tumbled along without him, and the Brits, slightly more tolerant than Americans of eccentricity, did not make him feel unwelcome.

The pubs were noisy and filled with light. Scores of people moved about in them, talking, smoking, drinking. A different kind of lead-lined room. He didn't drink beer, and so at first remained sober; but then he discovered the hard cider that pubs carried. He liked it and drank it like the others drank their beer, and got quite drunk. After that he sometimes became very talkative, telling the rest things about the twentieth century that they already knew, and they would nod and contribute some other bit of information, to be polite, then change the subject back to whatever they had been discussing before, gently and without snubbing him.

But most of the time when he drank he only got more remote from their talk, which jumped about faster than he could follow. And each morning after, he would wake late and slow, head pounding, the day already there and a lot of the morning light missed in sleep. Depressives were not supposed to drink at all. So finally he quit going to the Wellington, and instead ate at the pubs closest to the Dowlands'. One was called The Halfway House, the other World's End, a poor choice as far as names were concerned, but he ate at World's End anyway, and afterwards would sit at a corner table and nurse a whisky and stare at page after page of notes, chewing the end of a pen to plastic shrapnel.

The Fighting Never Stopped, as one book's title put it. But the atomic bomb meant that the second half of the century looked different than the first. Some, Americans for the most part, called it the *Pax Americana*. But most called it the Cold War, 1945–1989. And not that cold, either. Under the umbrella of the superpower stalemate local conflicts flared everywhere, wars which compared to the two big ones looked small; but there had been over a hundred of them all told, killing about 350,000 people a year, for a total of around fifteen million, some said twenty; it was hard to count. Most occurred in the big ten: the two Vietnam wars, the two Indo-Pakistan wars, the Korean war, the Algerian war, the civil war in Sudan, the massacres in Indonesia in 1965, the Biafran war, and the Iran-Iraq war. Then another ten million civilians had been starved by deliberate military action; so that the total for the period was about the equal of the Great War itself. Though it had taken ten times as long to compile. Improvement of a sort.

And thus perhaps the rise of atrocity war, as if the horror of individualized murders could compensate for the lack of sheer number. And maybe it could; because now his research consisted of a succession of accounts and colour photos of rape, dismemberment, torture – bodies of individual people, in their own clothes, scattered on the ground in pools of blood. Vietnamese villages, erupting in napalm. Cambodia, Uganda, Tibet – Tibet was genocide again, paced to escape the world's notice, a few villages destroyed every year in a process called *thamzing*, or reeducation: the villages seized by the Chinese and the villagers killed by a variety of methods, 'burying alive, hanging, beheading, disembowelling, scalding, crucifixion, quartering, stoning, small children forced to shoot their parents; pregnant women given forced abortions, the fetuses piled in mounds on the village squares.'

Meanwhile power on the planet continued to shift into fewer hands. The Second World War had been the only thing to successfully end the Depression, a fact leaders remembered; so the economic consolidation begun in the First War continued through the Second War and the Cold War, yoking the whole world into a war economy.

At first 1989 had looked like a break away from that. But now, just seven years later, the Cold War losers all looked like Germany in 1922, their money worthless, their shelves empty, their democracies crumbling to juntas. Except this time the juntas had corporate sponsors; multinational banks ran the old Soviet bloc just as they did the Third World, with 'austerity measures' enforced in the name of 'the free market', meaning half the world went to sleep hungry every night to pay off debts to millionaires. While temperatures still rose, populations still soared, 'local conflicts' still burned in twenty different places.

One morning Frank lingered over cereal, reluctant to leave the flat. He opened the *Guardian* and read that the year's defence budgets worldwide would total around a trillion dollars. 'More light,' he said, swallowing hard. It was a dark, rainy day. He could feel his pupils enlarging, making the effort. The days were surely getting shorter, even though it was May; and the air was getting darker, as if London's Victorian fogs had returned, coal smoke in the fabric of reality.

He flipped the page and started an article on the conflict in Sri Lanka. Singhalese and Tamils had been fighting for a generation now, and some time in the previous week, a husband and wife had emerged from their house in the morning to find the heads of their six sons arranged on their lawn. He threw the paper aside and walked through soot down the streets.

He got to the British Museum on automatic pilot. Waiting for him at the top of the stack was a book containing estimates of total war deaths for the century. About a hundred million people.

He found himself on the dark streets of London again, thinking of numbers. All day he walked, unable to gather his thoughts. And that night as he fell asleep the calculations returned, in a dream or a hypnogogic vision: it would take two thousand Vietnam Memorials to list the century's war dead. From above he saw himself walking the Mall in Washington, DC, and the whole park from the Capitol to the Lincoln Memorial was dotted with the black Vs of Vietnam Memorials, as if a flock of giant stealth birds had landed on it. All night he walked past black wing walls, moving west towards the white tomb on the river.

The next day the first book on the stack concerned the war between China and Japan, 1931–1945. Like most of Asian history this war was poorly remembered in the West, but it had been huge. The whole Korean nation became in effect a slave labour camp in the Japanese war effort, and the Japanese concentration camps in Manchuria had killed as many Chinese as the Germans had killed Jews. These deaths included thousands in the style of Mengele and the Nazi doctors, caused by 'scientific' medical torture. Japanese experimenters had for instance performed transfusions in which they drained Chinese prisoners of their blood and replaced it with horses' blood, to see how long the prisoners would live. Survival rates varied from twenty minutes to six hours, with the subjects in agony throughout.

Frank closed that book and put it down. He picked the next one out of the gloom and peered at it. A heavy old thing, bound in dark green leather, with a dull gold pattern inlaid on the spine and boards. *A History of the Nineteenth Century, with Illustrations* – the latter tinted photos, their colours faded and dim. Published in 1902 by George Newnes Ltd; last century's equivalent of his own project, apparently. Curiosity about that had caused him to request the title. He opened it and thumbed through, and on the last page the text caught his eye: 'I believe that Man is good. I believe that we stand at the dawn of a century that will be more peaceful and prosperous than any in history.'

He put down the book and left the British Museum. In a red phone box he located the nearest car rental agency, an Avis outlet near Westminster. He took the Tube and walked to this agency, and there he rented a blue Ford Sierra station wagon. The steering wheel was on the right, of course. Frank had never driven in Great Britain before, and he sat behind the wheel trying to hide his uneasiness from the agent. The clutch, brake, and gas pedal were left-to-right as usual, thank God. And the gear shift was arranged the same, though one did have to operate it with the left hand.

Awkwardly he shoved the gear shift into first and drove out of the garage, turning left and driving down the left side of the street. It was weird. But the oddity of sitting on the right ensured that he wouldn't forget the necessity of driving on the left. He pulled to the kerb and perused the Avis street map of London, plotted a course, got back in traffic, and drove to Camden High Street. He parked below the Dowlands' and went upstairs and packed, then took his backpack down to the car. He returned to leave a note: *Gone to the land of the midnight sun*. Then he went down to the car and drove north, onto the highways and out of London.

It was a wet day, and low full clouds brushed over the land, dropping here a black broom of rain, there a Blakean shaft of sunlight. The hills were green, and the fields yellow or brown or lighter green. At first there were a lot of hills, a lot of fields. Then the highway swung by Birmingham and Manchester, and he drove by fields of rowhouses, line after line after line of them, on narrow treeless streets – all orderly and neat, and yet still among the bleakest human landscapes he had ever seen. Streets like trenches. Certainly the world was being overrun. Population densities must be near the levels set in those experiments on rats which had caused the rats to go insane. It was as good an explanation as any. Mostly males affected, in both cases: territorial hunters, bred to kill for food, now trapped in little boxes. They had gone mad. 'I believe that Man is this or that,' the Edwardian author had written, and why not; it couldn't be denied that it was mostly men's doing. The planning, the diplomacy, the fighting, the raping, the killing.

The obvious thing to do was to give the running of the world over to women. There was Thatcher in the Falklands and Indira Gandhi in Bangladesh, it was true; but still it would be worth trying, it could hardly get worse! And given the maternal instinct, it would probably be better. Give every first lady her husband's job. Perhaps every woman her man's job. Let the men care for the children, for five thousand years or fifty thousand, one for every year of murderous patriarchy.

North of Manchester he passed giant radio towers, and something that looked like nuclear reactor stacks. Fighter jets zoomed overhead. The twentieth century. Why hadn't that Edwardian author been able to see it coming? Perhaps the future was simply unimaginable, then and always. Or perhaps things hadn't looked so bad in 1902. The Edwardian, looking forward in a time of prosperity, saw more of the same; instead there had followed a century of horrors. Now one looked forward from a time of horrors; so that by analogy, what was implied for the next century was grim beyond measure. And with the new technologies of destruction, practically anything was possible: chemical warfare, nuclear terrorism, biological holocaust; victims killed by nano-assassins flying through them, or by viruses in their drinking supply, or by a particular ringing of their telephone; or reduced to zombies by drugs or brain implants, torture or nerve gas; or simply dispatched with bullets, or starved; hi tech, low tech, the methods were endless. And the motivations would be stronger than ever; with populations rising and resources depleted, people were going to be fighting not to rule, but to survive. Some little country threatened with defeat could unleash an epidemic against its rival and accidentally kill off a continent, or everyone, it was entirely possible. The twenty-first century might make the twentieth look like nothing at all.

He would come to after reveries like that and realize that twenty or thirty or even sixty miles had passed without him seeing a thing of the outside world. Automatic pilot, on roads that were reversed! He tried to concentrate.

He was somewhere above Carlisle. The map showed two possible routes to Edinburgh: one left the highway just below Glasgow, while a smaller road left sooner and was much more direct. He chose the direct route and took an exit into a roundabout and onto the A702, a two-lane road heading northeast. Its black asphalt was wet with rain, and the clouds rushing overhead were dark. After several miles he passed a sign that said 'Scenic Route', which suggested he had chosen the wrong road, but he was unwilling to backtrack. It was probably as fast to go this way by now, just more work: frequent roundabouts, villages with traffic lights, and narrow stretches where the road was hemmed by hedges or walls. Sunset was near, he had been driving for hours; he was tired, and when black trucks rushed at him out of the spray and shadows it looked like they were going to collide with him head-on. It became an effort to stay to the left rather than the right where his instincts shrieked he should be. Right and left had to be reversed on that level, but kept the same at foot level – reversed concerning which hand went on the gearshift, but not reversed for what the gearshift did – and it all began to blur and mix, until finally a huge lorry rushed head first at him and he veered left, but hit the gas rather than the brakes. At the unexpected lurch forward he swerved farther left to be safe, and that ran his left wheels off the asphalt and into a muddy gutter, causing the car to bounce back onto the road. He hit the brakes hard and the lorry roared by his ear. The car skidded over the wet asphalt to a halt.

He pulled over and turned on the emergency blinker. As he got out of the car he saw that the driver's side mirror was gone. There was nothing there but a rectangular depression in the metal, four rivet holes slightly flared to the rear, and one larger hole for the mirror adjustment mechanism, missing as well.

He went to the other side of the car to remind himself

what the Sierra's side mirrors looked like. A solid metal and plastic mounting. He walked a hundred yards back down the road, looking through the dusk for the missing one, but he couldn't find it anywhere. The mirror was gone.

Outside Edinburgh he stopped and called Alec, a friend from years past.

'What? Frank Churchill? Hello! You're here? Come on by, then.'

Frank followed his directions into the city centre, past the train station to a neighbourhood of narrow streets. Reversed parallel parking was almost too much for him; it took four tries to get the car next to the kerb. The Sierra bumped over paving stones to a halt. He killed the engine and got out of the car, but his whole body continued to vibrate, a big tuning fork humming in the twilight. Shops threw their illumination over passing cars. Butcher, baker, Indian deli.

Alec lived on the third floor. 'Come in, man, come in.' He looked harried. 'I thought you were in America! What brings you here?'

'I don't know.'

Alec glanced sharply at him, then led him into the flat's kitchen and living area. The window had a view across rooftops to the castle. Alec stood in the kitchen, uncharacteristically silent. Frank put down his backpack and walked over to look out at the castle, feeling awkward. In the old days he and Andrea had trained up several times to visit Alec and Suzanne, a primatologist. At that time those two had lived in a huge three-storeyed flat in the New Town, and when Frank and

Andrea had arrived the four of them would stay up late into the night, drinking brandy and talking in a high-ceilinged Georgian living room. During one stay they had all driven into the Highlands, and another time Frank and Andrea had stayed through a festival week, the four attending as many plays as they could. But now Suzanne and Alec had gone their ways, and Frank and Andrea were divorced, and Alec lived in a different flat; and that whole life had disappeared.

'Did I come at a bad time?'

'No, actually.' A clatter of dishes as Alec worked at the sink. 'I'm off to dinner with some friends, you'll join us – you haven't eaten?'

'No. I won't be –'

'No. You've met Peg and Rog before, I think. And we can use the distraction, I'm sure. We've all been to a funeral this morning. Friends of ours, their kid died. Crib death, you know.'

'Jesus. You mean it just . . .'

'Sudden infant death syndrome, yeah. Dropped him off at day care and he went off during his nap. Five months old.'

'Jesus.'

'Yeah.' Alec went to the kitchen table and filled a glass from a bottle of Laphroaig. 'Want a whisky?'

'Yes, please.'

Alec poured another glass, drank his down. 'I suppose the idea these days is that a proper funeral helps the parents deal with it. So Tom and Elyse came in carrying the coffin, and it was about this big.' He held his hands a foot apart.

'No.'

'Yeah. Never seen anything like it.'

They drank in silence.

The restaurant was a fashionably bohemian seafood place, set above a pub. There Frank and Alec joined Peg and Rog, another couple, and a woman named Karen. All animal behaviourists, and all headed out to Africa in the next couple of weeks – Rog and Peg to Tanzania, the rest to Rwanda. Despite their morning's event the talk was quick, spirited, wide-ranging; Frank drank wine and listened as they discussed African politics, the problems of filming primates, rock music. Only once did the subject of the funeral come up, and then they shook their heads; there wasn't much to say. Stiff upper lip.

Frank said, 'I suppose it's better it happened now than when the kid was three or four.'

They stared at him. 'Oh no,' Peg said. 'I don't think so.'

Acutely aware that he had said something stupid, Frank tried to recover: 'I mean, you know, they've more time to . . .' He shook his head, foundering.

'It's rather comparing absolutes, isn't it,' Rog said gently.

'True,' he said. 'It is.' And he drank his wine. He wanted to go on: True, he wanted to say, any death is an absolute disaster, even that of an infant too young to know what was happening; but what if you had spent your life raising six such children and then went out one morning and found their heads on your lawn? Isn't the one more absolute than the other? He was drunk, his head hurt, his body still vibrated with the day's drive, and the shock of the brush with the lorry; and it seemed likely that the dyslexia of exhaustion had invaded all his thinking, including his moral sense, making everything backward. So he clamped his teeth together and concentrated on the wine, his fork humming in his hand, his glass chattering against his teeth. The room was dark.

Afterwards Alec stopped at the door to his building and shook his head. 'Not ready for that yet,' he said. 'Let's try Preservation Hall, it's your kind of thing on Wednesday nights. Traditional jazz.'

Frank and Andrea had been fans of traditional jazz. 'Any good?'

'Good enough for tonight, eh?'

The pub was within walking distance, down a wide cobblestone promenade called the Grassmarket, then up Victoria Street. At the door of the pub they were stopped; there was a cover charge, the usual band had been replaced by a buffet dinner and concert, featuring several different bands. Proceeds to go to the family of a Glasgow musician, recently killed in a car crash. 'Jesus Christ,' Frank exclaimed, feeling like a curse. He turned to go.

'Might as well try it,' Alec said, and pulled out his wallet. 'I'll pay.'

'But we've already eaten.'

Alec ignored him and gave the man twenty pounds. 'Come on.'

Inside, a very large pub was jammed with people, and an enormous buffet table stacked with meats, breads, salads, seafood dishes. They got drinks from the bar and sat at the end of a crowded picnic table. It was noisy, the Scots accents so thick that Frank understood less than half of what he heard. A succession of local acts took the stage: the traditional jazz band that usually played, a stand-up comedian, a singer of Forties' music hall songs, a country-western group. Alec and Frank took turns going to the bar to get refills. Frank watched the bands and the crowd. All ages and types were represented. Each band said something about the late musician, who apparently had been well-known, a young rocker and quite a hellion from the sound of it. Crashed driving home drunk after a gig, and no one a bit surprised.

About midnight an obese young man seated at their table, who had been stealing food from all the plates around him, rose whalelike and surged to the stage. People cheered as he joined the band setting up. He picked up a guitar, leaned into the mike, and proceeded to rip into a selection of r&b and early rock and roll. He and his band were the best group yet, and the pub went wild. Most of the crowd got to their feet and danced in place. Next to Frank a young punk had to lean over the table to answer a grey-haired lady's questions about how he kept his hair spiked. A Celtic wake, Frank thought, and downed his cider and howled with the rest as the fat man started up Chuck Berry's 'Rock And Roll Music'.

So he was feeling no pain when the band finished its last encore and he and Alec staggered off into the night, and made their way home. But it had gotten a lot colder while they were inside, and the streets were dark and empty. Preservation Hall was no more than a small wooden box of light, buried in a cold stone city. Frank looked back in its direction and saw that a streetlight reflected off the black cobblestones of the Grassmarket in such a way that there were thousands of brief white squiggles underfoot, looking like names engraved on black granite, as if the whole surface of the earth were paved by a single memorial.

The next day he drove north again, across the Forth Bridge and then west along the shores of a loch to Fort William, and north from there through the Highlands. Above Ullapool steep ridges burst like fins out of boggy treeless hillsides. There was water everywhere, from puddles to lochs, with the Atlantic itself visible from most high points. Out to sea the tall islands of the Inner Hebrides were just visible.

He continued north. He had his sleeping bag and foam pad with him, and so he parked in a scenic overlook, and cooked soup on his Bluet stove, and slept in the back of the car. He woke with the dawn and drove north. He talked to nobody.

Eventually he reached the northwest tip of Scotland and was forced to turn east, on a road bordering the North Sea. Early that evening he arrived in Scrabster, at the northeast tip of Scotland. He drove to the docks, and found that a ferry was scheduled to leave for the Orkney Islands the next day at noon. He decided to take it.

There was no secluded place to park, so he took a room in a hotel. He had dinner in the restaurant next door, fresh shrimp in mayonnaise with chips, and went to his room and slept. At six the next morning the ancient crone who ran the hotel knocked on his door and told him an unscheduled ferry was leaving in forty minutes: did he want to go? He said he did. He got up and dressed, then felt too exhausted to continue. He decided to take the regular ferry after all, took off his clothes and returned to bed. Then he realized that exhausted or not, he wasn't going to be able to fall back asleep. Cursing, almost crying, he got up and put his clothes back on. Downstairs the old woman had fried bacon and made him two thick bacon sandwiches, as he was going to miss her regular breakfast. He ate the sandwiches sitting in the Sierra, waiting to get the car into the ferry. Once in the hold he locked the car and went up to the warm stuffy passenger cabin, and lay on padded vinyl seating and fell back asleep.

He woke when they docked in Stromness. For a moment he didn't remember getting on the ferry, and he couldn't understand why he wasn't in his hotel bed in Scrabster. He stared through salt-stained windows at fishing boats, amazed, and then it came to him. He was in the Orkneys.

Driving along the southern coast of the main island, he found that his mental image of the Orkneys had been entirely wrong. He had expected an extension of the Highlands; instead it was like eastern Scotland, low, rounded, and green. Most of it was cultivated or used for pasture. Green fields, fences, farmhouses. He was a bit disappointed.

Then in the island's big town of Kirkwall he drove past a Gothic cathedral – a very little Gothic cathedral, a kind of pocket cathedral. Frank had never seen anything like it. He stopped and got out to have a look.

Cathedral of St Magnus, begun in 1137. So early, and this far north! No wonder it was so small. Building it would have required craftsmen from the continent, shipped up here to a rude fishing village of drywall and turf roofs; a strange influx it must have been, a kind of cultural revolution. The finished building must have stood out like something from another planet.

But as he walked around the bishop's palace next door, and then a little museum, he learned that it might not have been such a shock for Kirkwall after all. In those days the Orkneys had been a crossroads of a sort, where Norse and Scots and English and Irish had met, infusing an indigenous culture that went right back to the Stone Age. The fields and pastures he had driven by had been worked, some of them, for five thousand years!

And such faces walking the streets, so intent and vivid. His image of the local culture had been as wrong as his image of the land. He had thought he would find decrepit fishing villages, dwindling to nothing as people moved south to the cities. But it wasn't like that in Kirkwall, where teenagers roamed in self-absorbed talky gangs, and restaurants open to the street were packed for lunch. In the bookstores he found big sections on local topics: nature guides, archaeological guides, histories, sea tales, novels. Several writers, obviously popular, had as their entire subject the islands. To the locals, he realized, the Orkneys were the centre of the world.

He bought a guidebook and drove north, up the east coast of Mainland to the Broch of Gurness, a ruined fort and village that had been occupied from the time of Christ to the Norse era. The broch itself was a round stone tower about twenty feet tall. Its wall was at least ten feet thick, and was made of flat slabs, stacked so carefully that you couldn't have stuck a dime in the cracks. The walls in the surrounding village were much thinner; if attacked, the villagers would have retired into the broch. Frank nodded at the explanatory sentence in the guidebook, reminded that the twentieth century had had no monopoly on atrocities. Some had happened right here, no doubt. Unless the broch had functioned as a deterrent.

Gurness overlooked a narrow channel between Mainland and the smaller island of Rousay. Looking out at the channel, Frank noticed white ripples in its blue water; waves and foam were pouring past. It was a tidal race, apparently, and at the moment the entire contents of the channel were rushing north, as fast as any river he had ever seen.

Following suggestions in the guidebook, he drove across the island to the neolithic site of Brodgar, Stenness, and Maes Howe. Brodgar and Stenness were two rings of standing stones; Maes Howe was a nearby chambered tomb.

The Ring of Brodgar was a big one, three hundred and forty feet across. Over half of the original sixty stones were still standing, each one a block of roughly dressed sandstone, weathered over the millennia into shapes of great individuality and charisma, like Rodin figures. Following the arc they made, he watched the sunlight break on them. It was beautiful.

Stenness was less impressive, as there were only four

stones left, each tremendously tall. It roused more curiosity than awe: how had they stood those monsters on end? No one knew for sure.

From the road, Maes Howe was just a conical grass mound. To see the inside he had to wait for a guided tour, happily scheduled to start in fifteen minutes.

He was still the only person waiting when a short stout woman drove up in a pickup truck. She was about twenty-five, and wore Levi's and a red windbreaker. She greeted him and unlocked a gate in the fence surrounding the mound, then led him up a gravel path to the entrance on the southwest slope. There they had to get on their knees and crawl, down a tunnel three feet high and some thirty feet long. Midwinter sunsets shone directly down this entryway, the woman looked over her shoulder to tell him. Her Levi's were new.

The main chamber of the tomb was quite tall. 'Wow,' he said, standing up and looking around.

'It's big isn't it,' the guide said. She told him about it in a casual way. The walls were made of the ubiquitous sandstone slabs, with some monster monoliths bracketing the entryway. And something unexpected: a group of Norse sailors had broken into the tomb in the twelfth century (four thousand years after the tomb's construction!) and taken shelter in it through a three-day storm. This was known because they had passed the time carving runes on the walls, which told their story. The woman pointed to lines and translated: '"Happy is he who finds the great treasure." And over here: "Ingrid is the most beautiful woman in the world."'

'You're kidding.'

'That's what it says. And look here, you'll see they did some drawing as well.'

She pointed out three graceful line figures, cut presumably with axe blades: a walrus, a narwhale, and a dragon. He had seen all three in the shops of Kirkwall, reproduced in silver for earrings and pendants. 'They're beautiful,' he said.

'A good eye, that Viking.'

He looked at them for a long time, then walked around the chamber to look at the runes again. It was a suggestive alphabet, harsh and angular. The guide seemed in no hurry, she answered his questions at length. She was a guide in the summer, and sewed sweaters and quilts in the winter. Yes, the winters were dark. But not very cold. Average temperature around thirty.

'That warm?'

'Aye it's the Gulf Stream you see. It's why Britain is so warm, and Norway too for that matter.'

Britain so warm. 'I see,' he said carefully.

Back outside he stood and blinked in the strong after-noon light. He had just emerged from a five-thousand-year-old tomb. Down by the loch the standing stones were visible, both rings. Ingrid is the most beautiful woman in the world. He looked at Brodgar, a circle of black dots next to a silver sheen of water. It was a memorial too, although what it was supposed to make its viewers remember was no longer clear. A great chief; the death of one year, birth of the next; the planets, moon and sun in their courses. Or something else, something simpler. *Here we are.*

*   *   *

It was still midafternoon judging by the sun, so he was surprised to look at his watch and see it was six o'clock. Amazing. It was going to be just like his therapy! Only better because outdoors, in the sunlight and the wind. Spend summer in the Orkneys, winter in the Falklands, which were said to be very similar . . . He drove back to Kirkwall and had dinner in a hotel restaurant. The waitress was tall, attractive, about forty. She asked him where he was from, and he asked her when it would get busy (July), what the population of Kirkwall was (about ten thousand, she guessed) and what she did in the winter (accounting). He had broiled scallops and a glass of white wine. Afterwards he sat in the Sierra and looked at his map. He wanted to sleep in the car, but hadn't yet seen a good place to park for the night.

The northwest tip of Mainland looked promising, so he drove across the middle of the island again, passing Stenness and Brodgar once more. The stones of Brodgar stood silhouetted against a western sky banded orange and pink and white and red.

At the very northwest tip of the island, the Point of Buckquoy, there was a small parking lot, empty this late in the evening. Perfect. Extending west from the point was a tidal causeway, now covered by the sea; a few hundred yards across the water was a small island called the Brough of Birsay, a flat loaf of sandstone tilted up to the west, so that one could see the whole grass top of it. There were ruins and a museum at the near end, a small lighthouse on the west point. Clearly something to check out the next day.

South of the point, the western shore of the island curved back in a broad, open bay. Behind its beach stood the well-preserved ruins of a sixteenth century palace. The bay ended in a tall sea cliff called Marwick Head, which had a tower on its top that looked like another broch, but was, he discovered in his guidebook, the Kitchener Memorial. Offshore in 1916 the HMS *Hampshire* had hit a mine and sunk, and six hundred men, including Kitchener, had drowned.

Odd, to see that. A couple of weeks ago (it felt like years) he had read that when the German front lines had been informed of Kitchener's death, they had started ringing bells and banging pots and pans in celebration; the noisemaking had spread up and down the German trenches, from the Belgian coast to the Swiss frontier.

He spread out his sleeping bag and foam pad in the back of the station wagon, and lay down. He had a candle for reading, but he did not want to read. The sound of the waves was loud. There was still a bit of light in the air, these northern summer twilights were really long. The sun had seemed to slide off to the right rather than descend, and suddenly he understood what it would be like to be above the Arctic Circle in midsummer: the sun would just keep sliding off to the right until it brushed the northern horizon, and then it would slide up again into the sky. He needed to live in Ultima Thule.

The car rocked slightly on a gust of wind. It had been windy all day; apparently it was windy all the time here, the main reason the islands were treeless. He lay back and looked at the roof of the car. A car made a good tent: flat floor, no leaks . . . As he fell asleep he thought, it was a party a mile wide and a thousand miles long.

*   *   *

He woke at dawn, which came just before five a.m. His shadow and the car's shadow were flung out towards the brough, which was an island still, as the tidal bar was covered again. Exposed for only two hours each side of low tide, apparently.

He ate breakfast by the car, and then rather than wait for the causeway to clear he drove south, around the Bay of Birsay and behind Marwick Head, to the Bay of Skaill. It was a quiet morning, he had the one-lane track to himself. It cut through green pastures. Smoke rose from farmhouse chimneys and flattened out to the east. The farmhouses were white, with slate roofs and two white chimneys, one at each end of the house. Ruins of farmhouses built to the same design stood nearby, or in back pastures.

He came to another parking lot, containing five or six cars. A path had been cut through tall grass just behind the bay beach, and he followed it south. It ran nearly a mile around the curve of the bay, past a big nineteenth century manor house, apparently still occupied. Near the south point of the bay stretched a low concrete seawall and a small modern building, and some interruptions in the turf above the beach. Holes, it looked like. The pace of his walk picked up. A few people were bunched around a man in a tweed coat. Another guide?

Yes. It was Skara Brae.

The holes in the ground were the missing roofs of Stone Age houses buried in the sand; their floors were about twelve feet below the turf. The interior walls were made of the same slab as everything else on the island, stacked with the same precision. Stone hearths,

stone bedframes, stone dressers: because of the islands'
lack of wood, the guide was saying, and the ready avail-
ability of the slabs, most of the houses' furniture had
been made of stone. And so it had endured.

Stacks of slabs held up longer ones, making shelves
in standard college student bricks-and-boards style.
Cupboards were inset in the walls. There was a kind
of stone kitchen cabinet, with mortar and pestle
beneath. It was instantly obvious what everything was
for; everything looked deeply familiar.

Narrow passageways ran between houses. These too
had been covered; apparently driftwood or whale rib
beams had supported turf roofs over the entire village,
so that during bad storms they need never go out. The
first mall, Frank thought. The driftwood had included
pieces of spruce, which had to have come from North
America. The Gulf Stream again.

Frank stood at the back of a group of seven, listening to the guide as he looked down into the homes. The
guide was bearded, stocky, fiftyish. Like the Maes Howe
guide he was good at his work, wandering about with
no obvious plan, sharing what he knew without memorized speeches. The village had been occupied for about
six hundred years, beginning around 3000 BC. Brodgar
and Maes Howe had been built during those years, so
probably people from here had helped in their construction. The bay had likely been a fresh-water lagoon at
that time, with a beach separating it from the sea.
Population about fifty or sixty. A heavy dependence on
cattle and sheep, with lots of seafood as well. Sand filled
in the homes when the village was abandoned, and turf
grew over it. In 1850 a big storm tore the turf off and

exposed the homes, completely intact except for the roofs . . .

Water seepage had rounded away every edge, so that each slab looked sculpted, and caught at the light. Each house a luminous work of art. And five thousand years old, yet *so* familiar: the same needs, the same thinking, the same solutions . . . A shudder ran through him, and he noticed that he was literally slack-jawed. He closed his mouth and almost laughed aloud. Open-mouthed astonishment could be so natural sometimes, so physical, unconscious, genuine.

When the other tourists left, he continued to wander around. The guide, sensing another enthusiast, joined him.

'It's like the Flintstones,' Frank said, and laughed.

'The what?'

'You expect to see stone TVs and the like.'

'Oh aye. It's very contemporary, isn't it.'

'It's marvellous.'

Frank walked from house to house, and the guide followed, and they talked. 'Why is this one called the chief's house?'

'It's just a guess, actually. Everything in it is a bit bigger and better, that's all. In our world a chief would have it.'

Frank nodded. 'Do you live out here?'

'Aye.' The guide pointed at the little building beyond the site. He had owned a hotel in Kirkwall, but sold it; Kirkwall had been too hectic for him. He had gotten the job here and moved out, and was very happy with it. He was getting a degree in archaeology by correspondence. The more he learned, the more amazed he was to be here; it was one of the most important archaeological sites in the world, after all. There wasn't a better one. No need to imagine furnishings and implements, 'and to see so clearly how much they thought like we do.'

Exactly. 'Why did they leave, in the end?'

'No one knows.'

'Ah.'

They walked on.

'No sign of a fight, anyway.'

'Good.'

The guide asked Frank where he was staying, and Frank told him about the Sierra.

'I see!' the man said. 'Well, if you need the use of a bathroom, there's one here at the back of the building. For a shave, perhaps. You look like you haven't had the chance in a while.'

Frank rubbed a hand over his stubble, blushing. In fact he hadn't thought of shaving since well before leaving London. 'Thanks,' he said. 'Maybe I'll take you up on that.'

They talked about the ruins a while longer, and then the guide walked out to the seawall, and let Frank wander in peace.

He looked down in the rooms, which still glowed as if lit from within. Six hundred years of long summer days, long winter nights. Perhaps they had set sail for the Falklands. Five thousand years ago.

He called good-bye to the guide, who waved. On the way back to the car park he stopped once to look back. Under a carpet of cloud the wind was thrashing the tall beach grass, every waving stalk distinct, the clouds' underside visibly scalloped; and all of it touched with a silvery edge of light.

He ate lunch in Stromness, down by the docks, watching the fishing boats ride at anchor. A very practical-looking fleet, of metal and rubber and bright plastic buoys. In the afternoon he drove the Sierra around Scapa Flow and over a bridge at the east channel, the one Winston had ordered blocked with sunken ships. The smaller island to the south was covered with green fields and white farmhouses.

Late in the afternoon he drove slowly back to the Point of Buckquoy, stopping for a look in the nearby ruins of the sixteenth century earl's palace. Boys were playing soccer in the roofless main room.

The tide was out, revealing a concrete walkway set on a split bed of wet brown sandstone. He parked and walked over in the face of a stiff wind, onto the Brough of Birsay.

Viking ruins began immediately, as erosion had dropped part of the old settlement into the sea. He climbed steps into a tight network of knee-high walls. Compared to Skara Brae, it was a big town. In the middle of all the low foundations rose the shoulder-high walls of a church. Twelfth century, ambitious Romanesque design: and yet only fifty feet long, and twenty wide! Now this was a pocket cathedral. It had had a monastery connected to it, however; and some of the men who worshipped in it had travelled to Rome, Moscow, Newfoundland.

Picts had lived here before that; a few of their ruins lay below the Norse. Apparently they had left before the Norse arrived, though the record wasn't clear. What was clear was that people had been living here for a long, long time.

After a leisurely exploration of the site Frank walked west, up the slope of the island. It was only a few hundred yards to the lighthouse on the cliff, a modern white building with a short fat tower.

Beyond it was the edge of the island. He walked towards it and emerged from the wind shelter the island provided; a torrent of gusts almost knocked him back. He reached the edge and looked down.

At last something that looked like he thought it would! It was a long way to the water, perhaps a hundred and fifty feet. The cliff was breaking off in great stacks, which stood free and tilted out precariously, as if they were going to fall at any moment. Great stone cliffs, with the sun glaring directly out from them, and the surf crashing to smithereens on the rocks below: it was so obviously, grandiloquently the End of Europe that he had to laugh. A place made to cast oneself from. End the pain and fear, do a Hart Crane off the stern of Europe . . . except this looked like the bow, actually. The bow of a very big ship, crashing westward through the waves; yes, he could feel it in the soles of his feet. And foundering, he could feel that too, the shudders, the rolls, the last sluggish list. So jumping overboard would be redundant at best. The end would come, one way or another. Leaning out against the gale, feeling like a Pict or Viking, he knew he stood at the end – end of a continent, end of a century; end of a culture.

*　　*　　*

And yet there was a boat, coming around Marwick Head from the south, a little fishing tub from Stromness, rolling horribly in the swell. Heading northwest, out to – out to where? There were no more islands out there, not until Iceland anyway, or Greenland, Spitsbergen . . . where was it going at this time of day, near sunset and the west wind tearing in?

He stared at the trawler for a long time, rapt at the sight, until it was nothing but a black dot near the horizon. Whitecaps covered the sea, and the wind was still rising, gusting really hard. Gulls skated around on the blasts, landing on the cliffs below. The sun was very near the water, sliding off to the north, the boat no more than flotsam: and then he remembered the causeway and the tide.

He ran down the island and his heart leaped when he saw the concrete walkway washed by white water, surging up from the right. Stuck here, forced to break into the museum or huddle in a corner of the church . . . but no; the concrete stood clear again. If he ran –

He pounded down the steps and ran over the rough concrete. There were scores of parallel sandstone ridges still exposed to the left, but the right side was submerged already, and as he ran a broken wave rolled up onto the walkway and drenched him to the knees, filling his shoes with seawater and scaring him much more than was reasonable. He ran on cursing.

Onto the rocks and up five steps. At his car he stopped, gasping for breath. He got in the passenger side and took off his boots, socks, and pants. Put on dry pants, socks, and running shoes.

He got back out of the car.

The wind was now a constant gale, ripping over the car and the point and the ocean all around. It was going to be tough to cook dinner on his stove; the car made a poor windbreak, wind rushing under it right at stove level.

He got out the foam pad, and propped it with his boots against the lee side of the car. The pad and the car's bulk gave him just enough wind shelter to keep the little Bluet's gas flame alive. He sat on the asphalt behind the stove, watching the flames and the sea. The wind was tremendous, the Bay of Birsay riven by white-caps, more white than blue. The car rocked on its shock absorbers. The sun had finally slid sideways into the sea, but clearly it was going to be a long blue dusk.

When the water was boiling he poured in a dried Knorr's soup and stirred it, put it back on the flame for a few more minutes, then killed the flame and ate, spooning split pea soup straight from the steaming pot into his mouth. Soup, bit of cheese, bit of salami, red wine from a tin cup, more soup. It was absurdly satis-fying to make a meal in these conditions: the wind was in a fury!

When he was done eating he opened the car door and put away his dinner gear, then got out his windbreaker and rain pants and put them on. He walked around the carpark, and then up and down the low cliffy edges of the point of Buckquoy, watching the North Atlantic get torn by a full force gale. People had done this for thou-sands of years. The rich twilight blue looked like it would last forever.

Eventually he went to the car and got his notebooks.

He returned to the very tip of the point, feeling the wind like slaps on the ear. He sat with his legs hanging over the drop, the ocean on three sides of him, the wind pouring across him, left to right. The horizon was a line where purest blue met bluest black. He kicked his heels against the rock. He could see just well enough to tell which pages in the notebooks had writing on them; he tore these from the wire spirals, and bunched them into balls and threw them away. They flew off to the right and disappeared immediately in the murk and whitecaps. When he had disposed of all the pages he had written on he cleared the long torn shreds of paper out of the wire rings, and tossed them after the rest.

It was getting cold, and the wind was a constant kinetic assault. He went back to the car and sat in the passenger seat. His notebooks lay on the driver's seat. The western horizon was a deep blue, now. Must be eleven at least.

After a time he lit the candle and set it on the dash. The car was still rocking in the wind, and the candle flame danced and trembled on its wick. All the black shadows in the car shivered too, synchronized perfectly with the flame.

He picked up a notebook and opened it. There were a few pages left between damp cardboard covers. He found a pen in his daypack. He rested his hand on the page, the pen in position to write, its tip in the quivering shadow of his hand. He wrote, 'I believe that man is good. I believe we stand at the dawn of a century that will be more peaceful and prosperous than any in history.' Outside it was dark, and the wind howled.

Remaking History

'T'HE POINT IS *not* to make an exact replica of the Teheran embassy compound.' Exasperated, Ivan Venutshenko grabbed his hair in one hand and pulled up, which gave him a faintly Oriental look. 'It's the *spirit* of the place that we want to invoke here.'

'This has the spirit of our storage warehouse, if you ask me.'

'This *is* our storage warehouse, John. We make all our movies here.'

'But I thought you said we were going to correct all the lies of the first movie,' John Rand said to their director. 'I thought you said *Escape From Teheran* was a dumb TV docudrama, only worth remembering because of De Niro's performance as Colonel Jackson. We're going to get the true story on film at last, you said.'

Ivan sighed. 'That's right, John. Admirable memory.

But what you must understand is that when making a film, *true* doesn't mean an absolute fidelity to the real.'

'I'll bet that's just what the director of the docudrama said.'

Ivan hissed, which he did often while directing their films, to show that he was letting off steam, and avoiding an explosion. 'Don't be obstructionist, John. We're not doing anything like that hackwork, and you know it. Lunar gravity alone makes it impossible for us to make a completely realist film. We are working in a world of dream, in a surrealist intensification of what really happened. Besides, we're doing these movies for our own entertainment up here! Remake bad historical films! Have a good time!'

'Sure, Ivan. Sure. Except the ones *you've* directed have been getting some great reviews downside. They're saying you're the new Eisenstein and these little remakes are the best thing to hit the screen since *Kane*. So now the pressure is on and it's not just a game anymore, right?'

'Wrong!' Ivan karate-chopped the air. 'I refuse to believe that. When we stop having fun doing this' – nearly shouting – 'I quit!'

'Sure, Sergei.'

'Don't call me that!'

'Okay, Orson.'

'JOHN!'

'But that's *my* name. If I call you that we'll all get confused.'

Melina Gourtsianis, their female lead, came to Ivan's rescue. 'Come on, John, you'll give him a heart attack, and besides it's late. Let's get on with it.'

Ivan calmed down, ran his hands through his hair. He loved doing his maddened director routine, and John loved maddening him. As they disagreed about nearly everything, they made a perfect team. 'Fine,' Ivan said. 'Okay. We've got the set ready, and it may not be an *exact* replica of the compound –' fierce glare at John – 'but it's good enough.

'Now, let's go through it one more time. It's night in Teheran. This whole quarter of the city has been gassed with a paralysing nerve gas, but there's no way of telling when the Revolutionary Guards might come barrelling in from somewhere else with gas masks or whatever, and you can't be sure some of them haven't been protected from the gas in sealed rooms. Any moment they might jump out firing. Your helicopters are hovering just overhead, so it's tremendously noisy. There's a blackout in the compound, but searchlights from other parts of the city are beginning to pin the choppers. They've been breaking like cheap toys all the way in, so now there are only five left, and you have no assurances that they will continue to work, especially since twice that number have already broken. You're all wearing gas masks and moving through the rooms of the compound, trying to find and move all fifty-three of the hostages – it's dark and most of the hostages are knocked out like the guards, but some of the rooms were well-sealed, and naturally these hostages are shouting for help. For a while – and this is the effect I want to emphasize more than any other – for a while, things inside are absolutely chaotic. No one can find Colonel Jackson, no one knows how many of the hostages are recovered and how many are still in the embassy, it's dark, it's noisy, there are shots in the distance. I want an effect like the scene at the end of *The Lady from Shanghai*, when they're in the carnival's house of mirrors shooting at each other. Multiplied by ten. Total chaos.'

'Now hold on just a second here,' John said, exaggerating his Texas accent, which came and went according to his convenience. 'I like the chaos bit, and the allusion to Welles, but let's get back to this issue of the facts. Colonel Jackson was the hero of this whole thing! He was the one that decided to go on with all them helicopters busting out in the desert, and he was the one that found Annette Bellows in the embassy to lead them around, and all in all he was on top of every minute of it. That's why they gave him all them medals!'

Ivan glared. 'What part are you playing, John?'

'Why, Colonel Jackson.' John drew himself up. 'Natch.'

'However.' Ivan tapped the side of his head, to indicate thought. 'You don't just want to do a bad imitation of the De Niro performance, do you? You want to do a new interpretation, don't you? Besides, it seems to me a foolish idea to try an imitation of De Niro.'

'I like the idea, myself,' John said. 'Show him how.'

Ivan waved him away. 'You got all you know about this affair from that stupid TV movie, just like everyone else. I, however, have been reading the accounts of the hostages and the Marines on those helicopters, and the truth is that Colonel Jackson's best moment was out there in the desert, when he decided to go on with the mission even though only five helicopters were still functioning. That was his peak of glory, his moment of heroism. And you did a perfectly adequate job of conveying that when we filmed the scene. We could see every little gear in there, grinding away.' He tapped his skull.

'De Niro would have been proud,' Melina said.

John pursed his lips and nodded. 'We need great men like that. Without them history would be dead. It'd be nothing but a bunch of broken-down helicopters out in a desert somewhere.'

'A trenchant image of history,' Ivan said. 'Too bad Shelley got to it first. Meanwhile, the truth is that after making the decision to go on with the raid, Colonel Jackson appeared, in the words of his subordinates, somewhat stunned. When they landed on the embassy roof he led the first unit in, and when they got lost inside, the whole force was effectively without leadership for most of the crucial first half-hour. All the accounts of this period describe it as the utmost chaos, saved only when Sergeant Payton – not Colonel Jackson; the TV movie lied about that – when Payton found Ms Bellows, and she led them to all the hostage rooms they hadn't found.'

'All right, all right.' John frowned. 'So I'm supposed to be kind of spaced out in this scene.'

'Don't go for too deep an analysis, John, you might strain something. But essentially you have it. Having committed the force to the raid, even though you're vastly undermanned because of the damned helicopters breaking down, you're a bit frozen by the risk of it. Got that?'

'Yeah. But I don't believe it. Jackson was a hero.'

'Fine, a hero, lots of medals. Roomfuls of medals. If

he pinned them on he'd look like the bride after the dollar dance. He'd collapse under their weight. But now let's try showing what really happened.'

'All right.' John drew himself up. 'I'm ready.'

The shooting of the scene was the part they all enjoyed the most; this was the heart of the activity, the reason they kept making movies to occupy their free hours at Luna Three. Ivan and John and Melina and Pierre-Paul, the theoreticians who traded directing chores from project to project, always blocked the scenes very loosely, allowing a lot of room for improvisation. Thus scenes like this one, which were supposed to be chaotic, were played out with a manic gusto. They were good at chaos.

And so for nearly a half-hour they rushed about the interior of their Teheran embassy compound – the base storage warehouse, with its immense rows of boxes arranged behind white panels of plywood to resemble the compound's buildings and their interiors. Their shouts were nearly drowned by the clatter of recorded helicopters, while intermittent lights flashed in the darkness. Cutouts representing the helicopters were pasted to the clear dome overhead, silhouetted against the unearthly brilliance of the stars – these last had become a trademark of Luna Three Productions, as their frequent night scenes always had these unbelievably bright stars overhead, part of the films' dreamlike effect.

The actors playing Marines bounded about the compound in their gas masks, looking like aliens descended to ravage a planet; the actors playing hostages and Revolutionary Guards lay scattered on the floor, except for a few in protected rooms, who fought or cried for help. John and Pierre-Paul and the rest hunted the compound for Melina, playing Annette Bellows. For a while it looked as if John would get to her first, thus repeating the falsehood of the De Niro film. But eventually Pierre-Paul, playing Sergeant Payton, located her room, and he and his small unit rushed about after the clear-headed Bellows, who, as she wrote later, had spent most of her months in captivity planning what she should do if this moment ever came. They located the remaining comatose hostages and lugged them quickly to the plywood helicopter on the compound roof. The sound of shots punctuated the helicopters' roar. They leaped through the helicopter's door, shafts of white light stabbing the air like Islamic swords.

That was it; the flight away would be filmed in their little helicopter interior. Ivan turned off the helicopter noise, shouted 'Cut!' into a megaphone. Then he shut down all the strategically placed minicams, which had been recording every minute of it.

'What bothers me about your movies, Ivan,' John said, 'is that you always take away the hero. Always!'

They were standing in the shallow end of the base pool, cooling off while they watched the day's rushes on a screen filling one wall of the natatorium. Many of the screens showed much the same result: darkness, flickering light, alien shapes moving in the elongated dance-like way that audiences on Earth found so surreal, so mesmerizing. There was little indication of the pulsing rhythms and wrenching suspense that Ivan's editing would create from this material. But the actors were happy, seeing arresting images of desperation, of risk, of heroism in the face of a numbingly loud confusion.

Ivan was not as pleased. 'Shit!' he said. 'We're going to have to do it again.'

'Looks okay to me,' John remarked. 'Son of Film Noir Returns From the Grave. But really, Ivan, you've got to do something about this prejudice against heroes. I saw *Escape From Teheran* when I was a kid, and it was an inspiration to me. It was one of the big reasons I got into engineering.'

Pierre-Paul objected. 'John, just how did seeing a commando film get you interested in engineering?'

'Well,' John replied, frowning, 'I thought I'd design a better helicopter, I guess.' He ignored his friends' laughter. 'I was pretty shocked at how unreliable they were. But the way old De Niro continued on to Teheran! The way he extricated all the hostages and got them back safely, even with the choppers dropping like flies. It was great! We need heroes, and history tells the story of the few people who had what it takes to be one. But you're always downplaying them.'

'The Great Man Theory of History,' Pierre-Paul said scornfully.

'Sure!' John admitted. 'Great Woman too, of course,' nodding quickly at the frowning Melina. 'It's the great leaders who make the difference. They're special people, and there aren't many of them. But if you believe Ivan's films, there aren't any at all.'

With a snort of disgust, Ivan took his attention from the rushes. 'Hell, we are going to have to do that scene again. As for my theory of history, John, you both have it and you don't. As far as I understand you.' He cocked his head and looked at his friend attentively. On the set they both played their parts to the teeth: Ivan the tormented, temperamental director, gnashing his teeth and ordering people about; John the stubborn, temperamental star, questioning everything and insisting on his preeminence. Mostly this was role-playing, part of the game, part of what made their hobby entertaining to them. Off the set the roles largely disappeared, except to make a point, or have some fun. Ivan was the base's head of computer operations, while John was an engineer involved in the Mars voyage; they were good friends, and their arguments had done much to shape Ivan's ideas for his revisionist historical films, which were certainly the ones from their little troupe making the biggest splash downside – though John claimed this was because of the suspenseful plots and the weird low-gee imagery, not because of what they were saying about history. '*Do* I understand you?' Ivan asked curiously.

'Well,' John said, 'take the one you did last time, about the woman who saved John Lennon's life. Now that was a perfect example of heroic action, as the 1982 docudrama made clear. There she was, standing right next to a man who had pulled out a damn big gun, and quicker than he could pull the trigger she put a foot in his crotch and a fist in his ear. But in your remake, all we concentrated on was how she had just started the karate class that taught her the moves, and how her husband encouraged her to take the class, and how that cabbie stopped for her even though she was going the other direction, and how that other cabbie told her that Lennon had just walked into his apartment lobby, and all that. You made it seem like it was just a coincidence!'

Ivan took a mouthful of pool water and spurted it at the spangled dome, looking like a fountain statue. 'It took a lot of coincidences to get Margaret Arvis into the Dakota lobby at the right time,' he told John. 'But some of them weren't coincidences – they were little acts of generosity or kindness or consideration, that put her where she could do what she did. I didn't take the heroism away. I just spread it around to all the places it belonged.'

John grimaced, drew himself up into his star persona. 'I suppose this is some damn Commie notion of mass social movements, sweeping history along in a consensus direction.'

'No, no,' Ivan said. 'I always concentrate on individuals. What I'm saying is that all our individual actions add up to history, to the big visible acts of our so-called "leaders". You know what I mean; you hear people saying all the time that things are better now because John Lennon was such a moral force, travelling everywhere, Nobel Peace Prize, secular pope, the conscience of the world or whatnot.'

'Well, he *was* the conscience of the world!'

'Sure, sure, he wrote great songs. And he got a lot of antagonists to talk. But without Margaret Arvis he would have been killed at age forty. And without Margaret Arvis's husband, and her karate instructor, and a couple cabbies in New York, and so on, she wouldn't have been there to save his life. So we all become part of it, see? The people who say it was all because of Lennon, or Carter, or Gorbachev – they're putting on a few people what we *all* did.'

John shook his head, scattering water everywhere.

'Very sophisticated, I'm sure! But in fact it was precisely Lennon and Carter and Gorbachev who made huge differences, all by themselves. Carter started the big swing towards human rights. Palestine, the new Latin America, the American Indian nations – none of those would have existed without him.'

'In fact,' Melina added, glancing mischievously at Pierre-Paul, 'if I understand the Margaret Arvis movie correctly, if she hadn't been going to see Carter thank his New York campaign workers for the 1980 victory, she wouldn't have been in the neighbourhood of the Dakota, and so she wouldn't have had the chance to save Lennon's life.'

John rose up like a whale breaching. 'So it's Carter we have to thank for that, too! As for Gorbachev, well, I don't have to tell you what all he did. That was a hundred-eighty degree turnaround for you Russkies, and no one can say it would have happened without him.'

'Well – he was an important leader, I agree.'

'Sure was! And Carter was just as crucial. Their years were the turning point, when the world started to crawl out from under the shadow of World War Two. And that was their doing. There just aren't many people who could've done it. Most of us don't have it in us.'

Ivan shook his head. 'Carter wouldn't have been able to do what he did unless Colonel Ernest Jackson had saved the rescue mission to Teheran, by deciding to go on.'

'So Jackson is a hero too!'

'But then Jackson wouldn't have been a hero if the officer back in the Pentagon hadn't decided at the last minute to send sixteen helicopters instead of eight.'

'And,' Melina pointed out quickly, 'if Annette Bellows hadn't spent most of a year daydreaming about what she would do in a rescue attempt, so that she knew blindfolded where every other hostage was being kept. They would have left about half the hostages behind without her, and Carter wouldn't have looked so good.'

'Plus they needed Sergeant Payton to find Bellows,' Ivan added.

'Well shit!' John yelled defensively, which was his retort in any tight spot. He changed tack. 'I ain't so sure that Carter's reelection hinged on those hostages anyway. He was running against a flake, I can't remember the guy's name, but he was some kind of idiot.'

'So?' Melina said. 'Since when has that made any difference?'

With a roar John dove at her, making a big splash. She was much faster than he was, however, and she evaded him easily as he chased her around the pool; it looked like a whale chasing a dolphin. He was reduced to splashing at her from a distance, and the debate quickly degenerated into a big splash fight, as it often did.

'Oh well,' John declared, giving up the attack and floating in the shallow end. 'I love watching Melina swim the butterfly. In this gravity it becomes a godlike act. Those muscular arms, that sinuous dolphin motion . . .'

Pierre-Paul snorted. 'You just like the way the butterfly puts her bottom above water so often.'

'No way! Women are just more hydrodynamic than men, don't you think?'

'Not the way you like them.'

'Godlike. Gods and goddesses.'

'You look a bit godlike yourself,' Melina told him. 'Bacchus, for instance.'

'Hey.' John waved her off, jabbed a finger at the screens. 'I note that all this mucho sophisticated European theorizing has been sunk. Took a bit of Texas logic, is all.'

'Only Texas logic could do it,' Pierre-Paul said.

'Right. You admit my point. In the end it's the great leaders who have to act, the rare ones, no matter if we ordinary folks help them into power.'

'When you revise your proposition like that,' Ivan said, 'you turn it into mine. Leaders are important, but they are leaders because we made them leaders. They are a collective phenomenon. They are expressions of us.'

'Now wait just a minute! You're going over the line again! You're talking like heroic leaders are a dime a dozen, but if that were true it wouldn't matter if Carter had lost in 1980, or if Lennon had been killed by that guy. But look at history, man! Look what happened when we did lose great leaders! Lincoln was shot; did they come up with another leader comparable to him? No way! Same with Gandhi, and the Kennedys, and King, and Sadat, and Olof Palme. When those folks were killed their countries suffered the lack of them, because they were special.'

'They *were* special,' Ivan agreed, 'and obviously it was a bad thing they were killed. And no doubt there was a short-term change for the worse. But they're not irreplaceable, because they're human beings just like us. None of them, except maybe Lincoln or Gandhi, was any kind of genius or saint. It's only afterwards we think of them that way, because we want heroes so much. But we're the heroes. All of us put them in place. And there are a lot of capable, brilliant people out there to replace the loss of them, so that in the long run we recover.'

'The *real* long run,' John said darkly. 'A hundred years or more, for the South without Lincoln. They just aren't that common. The long run proves it.'

'Speaking of the long run,' Pierre-Paul said, 'is anyone getting hungry?'

They all were. The rushes were over, and Ivan had dismissed them as unusable. They climbed out of the pool and walked towards the changing room, discussing restaurants. There were a considerable number of them in the station, and new ones were opening every week. 'I just tried the new Hungarian restaurant,' Melina said. 'The food was good, but we had trouble, when the meal was over, finding someone to give us the check!'

'I thought you said it was a Hungarian restaurant,' John said.

They threw him back in the pool.

The second time they ran through the rescue scene in the compound, Ivan had repositioned most of the mini-cams, and many of the lights; his instructions to the actors remained the same. But once inside the hallways of the set, John Rand couldn't help hurrying in the general direction of Annette Bellows's room.

All right, he thought. Maybe Colonel Jackson had been a bit hasty to rush into the compound in search of hostages, leaving the group without a commander. But his heart had been in the right place, and the truth was, he had found a lot of the hostages without any help from Bellows at all. It was easy; they were scattered in ones and twos on the floor of almost every room he and his commandos entered, and stretched out along with the guards in the rooms and in the halls, paralysed by the nerve gas. Damn good idea, that nerve gas. Guards and hostages, tough parts to play, no doubt, as they were getting kicked pretty frequently by commandos running by. He hustled his crew into room after room, then sent them off with hostages draped over their shoulders, pretending to stagger down the halls, banging into walls – *really* tough part to play, hostage – and clutching at gas masks and such; great images for the minicams, no doubt about it.

When all his commandos had been sent back, he ran around a corner in what he believed to be the direction of Annette Bellows's room. Over the racket of the helicopters, and the occasional round of automatic fire, he thought he could make out Melina's voice, shouting hoarsely. So Pierre-Paul hadn't gotten to her yet. Good. Now he could find her and be the one to follow her around rescuing the more obscurely housed hostages, just as De Niro had in the docudrama. It would give Ivan fits, but they could argue it out afterwards. No way of telling what had really happened in that compound twenty years before, after all; and it made a better *story* his way.

Their set was only one storey tall, which was one of the things that John had objected to; the compound in Teheran had been four storeys high, and getting up stairs had been part of the hassle. But Ivan was going to play with the images and shoot a few stair scenes later on, to achieve the effect of multiple floors. Fine, it meant he had only to struggle around a couple of narrow corners, jumping comatose Revolutionary Guards, looking fierce for the minicams wherever they were. It was really loud this time around; *really* loud.

Then one of the walls fell over on him, the plywood pinning him to the ground, the boxes behind it tumbling down and filling the hallway. 'Hey!' he cried out, shocked. This wasn't the way it had happened. What was going on? The noise of the helicopters cut off abruptly, replaced by a series of crashes, a whooshing sound. That sound put a fine electric thrill down his spine; he had heard it before, in training routines. Air leaving the chamber. The dome must have been breached.

He heaved up against the plywood. Stuck. Flattening himself as much as possible he slithered forward, under the plywood and out into a small space among fallen boxes. Hard to tell where the hallway had been, and it was pitch-dark. There wouldn't be too much time left. He thought of his little gas mask, then cursed; it wasn't connected to a real oxygen supply. That's what comes from using fake props! he thought angrily. A gas mask with nothing attached to it. Open to the air, which was departing rapidly. Not much time.

He found room among the boxes to stand, and he was about to run over them to the door leading out of the warehouse – assuming the whole station hadn't been breached – when he remembered Melina. Stuck in her embassy room down the hall, wouldn't she still be there? Hell. He groped along in the dark, hearing shouts in the distance. He saw lights, too. Good. He was holding his breath, for what felt like minutes at a time, though it was probably less than thirty seconds. Every time he sucked in a new breath he expected it to be the freezing vacuum, but the supply of rushing, cold – very cold – air continued to fill him. Emergency supply pouring out into the breach, actually a technique he had helped develop himself. Seemed to be working, at least for the moment.

He heard a muffled cry to one side, began to pull at the boxes before him. Squeak in the gloom, ah-ha, there she was. Not fully conscious. Legs wet, probably blood, uh-oh. He pulled hard at boxes, lifted her up. Adrenaline and lunar gravity made him feel like Superman with that part of things, but there didn't seem to be anywhere near as much air as before, and what was left was damned cold. Hurt to breathe. And harder than hell to balance as he hopped over objects with Melina in his arms. Feeling faint, he climbed over a row of boxes and staggered towards a distant light. A sheet of plywood smacked his shin and he cried out, then fell over. 'Hey,' he said. The air was gone.

When he came to he was lying in a bed in the station hospital. 'Great,' he muttered. 'Whole station wasn't blown up.'

His friends laughed, relieved to hear him speak. The whole film crew was in there, it seemed. Ivan, standing next to the bed, said, 'It's okay.'

'What the hell happened?'

'A small meteor, apparently. Hit out in our sector,

in the shuttle landing chambers, ironically. But it wrecked our storage space as well, as you no doubt noticed.'

John nodded painfully. 'So it finally happened.'

'Yes.' This was one of the great uncontrollable dangers of the lunar stations; meteors small and large were still crashing down onto the moon's airless surface, by the thousands every year. Odds were poor that any one would hit something as small as the surface parts of their station, but coming down in such numbers . . . In the long run they were reduced to a safety status somewhat equivalent to that of mountain climbers. Rockfall could always get you.

'Melina?' John said, jerking up in his bed.

'Over here,' Melina called. She was a few beds down, and had one leg in a cast. 'I'm fine, John.' She got out of bed to prove it, and came over to kiss his cheek. 'Thanks for the rescue!'

John snorted. 'What rescue?'

They laughed again at him. Pierre-Paul pointed a forefinger at him. 'There are heroes everywhere, even among the lowest of us. Now you have to admit Ivan's argument.'

'The hell I do.'

'You're a hero,' Ivan said to him, grinning. 'Just an ordinary man, so to speak. Not one of the great leaders at all. But by saving Melina, you've changed history.'

'Not unless she becomes president,' John said, and laughed. 'Hey Melina! Go out and run for office! Or save some promising song-writer or something.'

Ivan just shook his head. 'Why are you so stubborn? It's not so bad if I'm right, John. Think about it. If I am right, then we aren't just sitting around waiting for leaders to guide us.' A big grin lit his face. 'We become the masters of our fate, we make our own decisions and act on them – we choose our leaders, and instruct them by consensus, so that we can take history any direction we please! Just as you did in the warehouse.'

John lay back in his bed and was silent. Around him his friends grinned; one of them was bringing up a big papier-mâché medal, which vaguely resembled the one the Wizard of Oz pins to the Cowardly Lion. 'Ah hell,' John said.

'When the expedition reaches Mars, they'll have to name something after you,' Melina said.

John thought about it for a while. He took the big medal, held it limply. His friends watched him, waiting for him to speak.

'Well, I still say it's bullshit,' he told Ivan. 'But if there is any truth to what you say, it's just the good old spirit of the Alamo you're talking about, anyway. We've been doing it like that in Texas for years.'

They laughed at him.

He rose up from the bed again, swung the medal at them furiously. 'I swear it's true! Besides, it's all Robert De Niro's fault, anyway! I was *imitating* the real heroes, don't you see? I was crawling around in there all dazed, and then I saw De Niro's face when he was playing Colonel Jackson in the Teheran embassy, and I said to myself, well hell, what would he have done in this here situation? And that's just what I did.'

The Lucky Strike

WAR BREEDS STRANGE pastimes. In July of 1945 on Tinian Island in the North Pacific, Captain Frank January had taken to piling pebble cairns on the crown of Mount Lasso – one pebble for each B-29 takeoff, one cairn for each mission. The largest cairn had four hundred stones in it. It was a mindless pastime, but so was poker. The men of the 509th had played a million hands of poker, sitting in the shade of a palm around an upturned crate sweating in their skivvies, swearing and betting all their pay and cigarettes, playing hand after hand after hand, until the cards got so soft and dog-eared you could have used them for toilet paper. Captain January had gotten sick of it, and after he lit out for the hilltop a few times some of his crewmates started trailing him. When their pilot Jim Fitch joined them it became an official pastime, like throwing flares into the compound or going hunting for stray

83

Japs. What Captain January thought of the development he didn't say. The others grouped near Captain Fitch, who passed around his battered flask. 'Hey, January,' Fitch called. 'Come have a shot.'

January wandered over and took the flask. Fitch laughed at his pebble. 'Practising your bombing up here, eh, Professor?'

'Yah,' January said sullenly. Anyone who read more than the funnies was Professor to Fitch. Thirstily January knocked back some rum. He could drink it any way he pleased up here, out from under the eye of the group psychiatrist. He passed the flask on to Lieutenant Matthews, their navigator.

'That's why he's the best,' Matthews joked. 'Always practising.'

Fitch laughed. 'He's best because I make him be best, right, Professor?'

January frowned. Fitch was a bulky youth, thick-featured, pig-eyed – a thug, in January's opinion. The rest of the crew were all in their mid-twenties like Fitch, and they liked the captain's bossy roughhouse style. January, who was thirty-seven, didn't go for it. He wandered away, back to the cairn he had been building. From Mount Lasso they had an overview of the whole island, from the harbour at Wall Street to the north field in Harlem. January had observed hundreds of B-29s roar off the four parallel runways of the north field and head for Japan. The last quartet of this particular mission buzzed across the width of the island, and January dropped four more pebbles, aiming for crevices in the pile. One of them stuck nicely.

'There they are!' said Matthews. 'They're on the taxi-ing strip.'

January located the 509th's first plane. Today, the first of August, there was something more interesting to watch than the usual Superfortress parade. Word was out that General Le May wanted to take the 509th's mission away from it. Their commander Colonel Tibbets had gone and bitched to Le May in person, and the general had agreed the mission was theirs, but on one condition: one of the general's men was to make a test flight with the 509th, to make sure they were fit for combat over Japan. The general's man had arrived, and now he was down there in the strike plane, with Tibbets and the whole first team. January sidled back to his mates to view the takeoff with them.

'Why don't the strike plane have a name, though?' Haddock was saying.

Fitch said, 'Lewis won't give it a name because it's not his plane, and he knows it.' The others laughed. Lewis and his crew were naturally unpopular, being Tibbets' favourites.

'What do you think he'll do to the general's man?' Matthews asked.

The others laughed at the very idea. 'He'll kill an engine at takeoff, I bet you anything,' Fitch said. He pointed at the wrecked B-29s that marked the end of every runway, planes whose engines had given out on takeoff. 'He'll want to show that he wouldn't go down if it happened to him.'

'Course he wouldn't!' Matthews said.

'You hope,' January said under his breath.

'They let those Wright engines out too soon,'

85

Haddock said seriously. 'They keep busting under the takeoff load.'

'Won't matter to the old bull,' Matthews said. Then they all started in about Tibbets' flying ability, even Fitch. They all thought Tibbets was the greatest. January, on the other hand, liked Tibbets even less than he liked Fitch. That had started right after he was assigned to the 509th. He had been told he was part of the most important group in the war, and then given a leave. In Vicksburg a couple of fliers just back from England had bought him a lot of whiskies, and since January had spent several months stationed near London they had talked for a good long time and gotten pretty drunk. The two were really curious about what January was up to now, but he had stayed vague on it and kept returning the talk to the blitz. He had been seeing an English nurse, for instance, whose flat had been bombed, family and neighbours killed . . . But they had really wanted to know. So he had told them he was onto something special, and they had flipped out their badges and told him they were Army Intelligence, and that if he ever broke security like that again he'd be transferred to Alaska. It was a dirty trick. January had gone back to Wendover and told Tibbets so to his face, and Tibbets had turned red and threatened him some more. January despised him for that. The upshot was that January was effectively out of the war, because Tibbets really played his favourites. January wasn't sure he really minded, but during their year's training he had bombed better than ever, as a way of showing the old bull he was wrong to write January off. Every time their eyes had met it was clear what was going on. But

Tibbets never backed off no matter how precise January's bombing got. Just thinking about it was enough to cause January to line up a pebble over an ant and drop it.

'Will you cut that out?' Fitch complained. 'I swear you must hang from the ceiling when you take a shit so you can practise aiming for the toilet.' The men laughed.

'Don't I bunk over you?' January asked. Then he pointed. 'They're going.'

Tibbets' plane had taxied to runway Baker. Fitch passed the flask around again. The tropical sun beat on them, and the ocean surrounding the island blazed white. January put up a sweaty hand to aid the bill of his baseball cap.

The four props cut in hard, and the sleek Superfortress quickly trundled up to speed and roared down Baker. Three-quarters of the way down the strip the outside right prop feathered.

'Yow!' Fitch crowed. 'I told you he'd do it!'

The plane nosed off the ground and slewed right, then pulled back on course to cheers from the four young men around January. January pointed again. 'He's cut number three, too.'

The inside right prop feathered, and now the plane was pulled up by the left wing only, while the two right props windmilled uselessly. 'Holy smoke!' Haddock cried. 'Ain't the old bull something?'

They whooped to see the plane's power, and Tibbets' nervy arrogance.

'By God, Le May's man will remember this flight,' Fitch hooted. 'Why, look at that! He's banking!'

Apparently taking off on two engines wasn't enough for Tibbets; he banked the plane right until it was standing on its dead wing, and it curved back towards Tinian.

Then the inside left engine feathered.

War tears at the imagination. For three years Frank January had kept his imagination trapped, refusing to give it any play whatsoever. The dangers threatening him, the effects of the bombs, the fate of the other participants in the war, he had refused to think about any of it. But the war tore at his control. That English nurse's flat. The missions over the Ruhr. The bomber just below him blown apart by flak. And then there had been a year in Utah, and the vicelike grip that he had once kept on his imagination had slipped away.

So when he saw the number two prop feather, his heart gave a little jump against his sternum and helplessly he was up there with Ferebee, the first team bombardier. He would be looking over the pilots' shoulders . . .

'Only one engine?' Fitch said.

'That one's for real,' January said harshly. Despite himself he *saw* the panic in the cockpit, the frantic rush to power the two right engines. The plane was dropping fast and Tibbets levelled it off, leaving them on a course back towards the island. The two right props spun, blurred to a shimmer. January held his breath. They needed more lift; Tibbets was trying to pull it over the island. Maybe he was trying for the short runway on the south half of the island.

But Tinian was too tall, the plane too heavy. It roared right into the jungle above the beach, where 42nd Street met their East River. It exploded in a bloom of fire. By the time the sound of the explosion struck them they knew no one in the plane had survived.

Black smoke towered into white sky. In the shocked silence on Mount Lasso insects buzzed and creaked. The air left January's lungs with a gulp. He had been with Ferebee there at the end, he had heard the desperate shouts, seen the last green rush, been stunned by the dentist-drill-all-over pain of the impact.

'Oh my God,' Fitch was saying. 'Oh my God.' Matthews was sitting. January picked up the flask, tossed it at Fitch.

'C-come on,' he stuttered. He hadn't stuttered since he was sixteen. He led the others in a rush down the hill. When they got to Broadway a jeep careened towards them and skidded to a halt. It was Colonel Scholes, the old bull's exec. 'What happened?'

Fitch told him.

'Those damned Wrights,' Scholes said as the men piled in. This time one had failed at just the wrong moment; some welder stateside had kept flame to metal a second less than usual – or something equally minor, equally trivial – and that had made all the difference.

They left the jeep at 42nd and Broadway and hiked east over a narrow track to the shore. A fairly large circle of trees was burning. The fire trucks were already there.

Scholes stood beside January, his expression bleak. 'That was the whole first team,' he said.

'I know,' said January. He was still in shock, in imagination crushed, incinerated, destroyed. Once as a kid he had tied sheets to his arms and waist, jumped off the roof and landed right on his chest; this felt like that had. He had no way of knowing what would come of this crash, but he had a suspicion that he had indeed smacked into something hard.

Scholes shook his head. A half hour had passed, the fire was nearly out. January's four mates were over chattering with the Seabees. 'He was going to name the plane after his mother,' Scholes said to the ground. 'He told me that just this morning. He was going to call it *Enola Gay*.'

At night the jungle breathed, and its hot wet breath washed over the 509th's compound. January stood in the doorway of his Quonset barracks hoping for a real breeze. No poker tonight. Voices were hushed, faces solemn. Some of the men had helped box up the dead crew's gear. Now most lay on their bunks. January gave up on the breeze, climbed onto his top bunk to stare at the ceiling.

He observed the corrugated arch over him. Cricketsong sawed through his thoughts. Below him a rapid conversation was being carried on in guilty undertones, Fitch at its centre.

'January is the best bombardier left,' he said. 'And I'm as good as Lewis was.'

'But so is Sweeney,' Matthews said. 'And he's in with Scholes.'

They were figuring out who would take over the strike. January scowled. Tibbets and the rest were less than twelve hours dead, and they were squabbling over who would replace them.

January grabbed a shirt, rolled off his bunk, put the shirt on.

'Hey, Professor,' Fitch said. 'Where you going?'

'Out.'

Though midnight was near it was still sweltering. Crickets shut up as he walked by, started again behind him. He lit a cigarette. In the dark the MPs patrolling their fenced-in compound were like pairs of walking armbands. The 509th, prisoners in their own army. Fliers from other groups had taken to throwing rocks over the fence. Forcefully January expelled smoke, as if he could expel his disgust with it. They were only kids, he told himself. Their minds had been shaped in the war, by the war, and for the war. They knew you couldn't mourn the dead for long; carry around a load like that and your own engines might fail. That was all right with January. It was an attitude that Tibbets had helped to form, so it was what he deserved. Tibbets would *want* to be forgotten in favour of the mission, all he had lived for was to drop the gimmick on the Japs, he was oblivious to anything else, men, wife, family, anything.

So it wasn't the lack of feeling in his mates that bothered January. And it was natural of them to want to fly the strike they had been training a year for. Natural, that is, if you were a kid with a mind shaped by fanatics like Tibbets, shaped to take orders and never imagine consequences. But January was not a kid, and he wasn't going to let men like Tibbets do a thing to his mind. And the gimmick . . . the gimmick was not natural. A chemical bomb of some sort, he guessed. Against the Geneva Convention. He stubbed his cigarette against the sole of his sneaker, tossed the butt over the fence. The tropical night breathed over him. He had a headache.

For months now he had been sure he would never fly a strike. The dislike Tibbets and he had exchanged in their looks (January was acutely aware of looks) had been real and strong. Tibbets had understood that January's record of pinpoint accuracy in the runs over the Salton Sea had been a way of showing contempt, a way of saying *you can't get rid of me even though you hate me and I hate you.* The record had forced Tibbets to keep January on one of the four second-string teams, but with the fuss they were making over the gimmick January had figured that would be far enough down the ladder to keep him out of things.

Now he wasn't so sure. Tibbets was dead. He lit another cigarette, found his hand shaking. The Camel tasted bitter. He threw it over the fence at a receding armband, and regretted it instantly. A waste. He went back inside.

Before climbing onto his bunk he got a paperback out of his footlocker. 'Hey, Professor, what you reading now?' Fitch said, grinning.

January showed him the blue cover. *Winter's Tales*, by an Isak Dinesen. Fitch examined the little wartime edition. 'Pretty racy, eh?'

'You bet,' January said heavily. 'This guy puts sex on every page.' He climbed onto his bunk, opened the book. The stories were strange, hard to follow. The voices below bothered him. He concentrated harder.

As a boy on the farm in Arkansas, January had read everything he could lay his hands on. On Saturday afternoons he would race his father down the muddy lane to the mailbox (his father was a reader too), grab *The Saturday Evening Post* and run off to devour every word of it. That meant he had another week with nothing new to read, but he couldn't help it. His favourites were the Hornblower stories, but anything would do. It was a way off the farm, a way into the world. He had become a man who could slip between the covers of a book whenever he chose.

But not on this night.

The next day the chaplain gave a memorial service, and on the morning after that Colonel Scholes looked in the door of their hut right after mess. 'Briefing at eleven,' he announced. His face was haggard. 'Be there early.' He looked at Fitch with bloodshot eyes, crooked a finger. 'Fitch, January, Matthews – come with me.'

January put on his shoes. The rest of the men sat on their bunks and watched them wordlessly. January followed Fitch and Matthews out of the hut.

'I've spent most of the night on the radio with General Le May,' Scholes said. He looked them each in the eye. 'We've decided you're to be the first crew to make a strike.'

Fitch was nodding, as if he had expected it.

'Think you can do it?' Scholes said.

'Of course,' Fitch replied. Watching him January understood why they had chosen him to replace Tibbets: Fitch was like the old bull, he had that same ruthlessness. The young bull.

'Yes, sir,' Matthews said.

Scholes was looking at him. 'Sure,' January said, not wanting to think about it. 'Sure.' His heart was pounding directly on his sternum. But Fitch and Matthews looked serious as owls, so he wasn't going to stick out by looking odd. It was big news, after all; anyone would be taken aback by it. Nevertheless, January made an effort to nod.

'Okay,' Scholes said. 'McDonald will be flying with you as copilot.' Fitch frowned. 'I've got to go tell those British officers that Le May doesn't want them on the strike with you. See you at the briefing.'

'Yes, sir.'

As soon as Scholes was around the corner Fitch swung a fist at the sky. 'Yow!' Matthews cried. He and Fitch shook hands. 'We did it!' Matthews took January's hand and wrung it, his face plastered with a goofy grin. 'We did it!'

'Somebody did it, anyway,' January said.

'Ah, Frank,' Matthews said. 'Show some spunk. You're always so cool.'

'Old Professor Stoneface,' Fitch said, glancing at January with a trace of amused contempt. 'Come on, let's get to the briefing.'

The briefing hut, one of the longer Quonsets, was completely surrounded by MPs holding carbines. 'Gosh,' Matthews said, subdued by the sight. Inside it was already smoky. The walls were covered by the usual maps of Japan. Two blackboards at the front were draped with sheets. Captain Shepard, the naval officer who worked with the scientists on the gimmick, was in back with his assistant Lieutenant Stone, winding a reel of film onto a projector. Dr Nelson, the group psychiatrist, was already seated on a front bench near the wall. Tibbets had recently sicced the psychiatrist on the group – another one of his great ideas, like the spies in the bar. The man's questions had struck January as stupid. He hadn't even been able to figure out that Easterly was a flake, something that was clear to anybody who flew with him, or even played him in a single round of poker. January slid onto a bench beside his mates.

The two Brits entered, looking furious in their stiff-upper-lip way. They sat on the bench behind January. Sweeney's and Easterly's crews filed in, followed by the other men, and soon the room was full. Fitch and the rest pulled out Lucky Strikes and lit up; since they had named the plane only January had stuck with Camels.

Scholes came in with several men January didn't recognize, and went to the front. The chatter died, and all the smoke plumes ribboned steadily into the air.

Scholes nodded, and two intelligence officers took the sheets off the blackboards, revealing aerial reconnaissance photos.

'Men,' Scholes said, 'these are the target cities.'

Someone cleared his throat.

'In order of priority they are Hiroshima, Kokura, and Nagasaki. There will be three weather scouts: *Straight Flush* to Hiroshima, *Strange Cargo* to Kokura, and *Full House* to Nagasaki. *The Great Artiste* and *Number 91* will be accompanying the mission to take photos. And *Lucky Strike* will fly the bomb.'

There were rustles, coughs. Men turned to look at January and his mates, and they all sat up straight. Sweeney stretched back to shake Fitch's hand, and there were some quick laughs. Fitch grinned.

'Now listen up,' Scholes went on. 'The weapon we are going to deliver was successfully tested stateside a couple of weeks ago. And now we've got orders to drop it on the enemy.' He paused to let that sink in. 'I'll let Captain Shepard tell you more.'

Shepard walked to the blackboard slowly, savouring his entrance. His forehead was shiny with sweat, and January realized he was excited or nervous. He wondered what the psychiatrist would make of that.

'I'm going to come right to the point,' Shepard said. 'The bomb you are going to drop is something new in history. We think it will knock out everything within four miles.'

Now the room was completely still. January noticed that he could see a great deal of his nose, eyebrows, and cheeks; it was as if he were receding back into his body, like a fox into its hole. He kept his gaze rigidly on Shepard, steadfastly ignoring the feeling. Shepard pulled a sheet back over a blackboard while someone else turned down the lights.

'This is a film of the only test we have made,' Shepard said. The film started, caught, started again. A wavery cone of bright cigarette smoke speared the length of the room, and on the sheet sprang a dead grey landscape: a lot of sky, a smooth desert floor, hills in the distance. The projector went *click-click-click-click, click-click-click-click.* 'The bomb is on top of the tower,' Shepard said, and January focused on the pinlike object sticking out of the desert floor, off against the hills. It was between eight and ten miles from the camera, he judged; he had gotten good at calculating distances. He was still distracted by his face.

Click-click-click-click, click – then the screen went white for a second, filling even their room with light. When the picture returned the desert floor was filled with a white bloom of fire. The fireball coalesced and then quite suddenly it leaped off the earth all the way into the *stratosphere*, by God, like a tracer bullet leaving a machine gun, trailing a whitish pillar of smoke behind it. The pillar gushed up and a growing ball of smoke billowed outward, capping the pillar. January calculated the size of the cloud, but was sure he got it wrong. There it stood. The picture flickered, and then the screen went white again, as if the camera had melted or that part of the world had come apart. But the flapping from the projector told them it was the end of the film.

January felt the air suck in and out of his open mouth. The lights came on in the smoky room and for a second he panicked, he struggled to shove his features into an accepted pattern, the psychiatrist would be looking around at them all – and then he glanced around and realized he needn't have worried, that he wasn't alone. Faces were bloodless, eyes were blinky or bug-eyed with shock, mouths hung open or were clamped whitely shut. For a few moments they all had to acknowledge what they were doing. January, scaring himself, felt an urge to say, 'Play it again, will you?' Fitch was pulling his curled black hair off his thug's forehead uneasily. Beyond him January saw that one of the Limeys had already reconsidered how mad he was about missing the flight. Now he looked sick. Someone let out a long *whew*, another whistled. January looked to the front again, where the psychiatrist watched them, undisturbed.

Shepard said, 'It's big, all right. And no one knows what will happen when it's dropped from the air. But the mushroom cloud you saw will go to at least thirty thousand feet, probably sixty. And the flash you saw at the beginning was hotter than the sun.'

Hotter than the sun. More licked lips, hard swallows, readjusted baseball caps. One of the intelligence officers passed out tinted goggles like welder's glasses. January took his and twiddled the opacity dial.

Scholes said, 'You're the hottest thing in the armed forces, now. So no talking, even among yourselves.' He took a deep breath. 'Let's do it the way Colonel Tibbets would have wanted us to. He picked every one of you because you were the best, and now's the time to show he was right. So – so let's make the old man proud.'

The briefing was over. Men filed out into the sudden sunlight. Into the heat and glare. Captain Shepard approached Fitch. 'Stone and I will be flying with you to take care of the bomb,' he said.

Fitch nodded. 'Do you know how many strikes we'll fly?'

'As many as it takes to make them quit.' Shepard stared hard at all of them. 'But it will only take one.'

War breeds strange dreams. That night January writhed over his sheets in the hot wet vegetable darkness, in that frightening half sleep when you sometimes know you are dreaming but can do nothing about it, and he dreamed he was walking . . .

. . . *walking through the streets when suddenly the sun swoops down, the sun touches down and everything is instantly darkness and smoke and silence, a deaf roaring. Walls of fire. His head hurts and in the middle of his vision is a bluewhite blur as if God's camera went off in his face. Ah – the sun fell, he thinks. His arm is burned. Blinking is painful. People stumbling by, mouths open, horribly burned –*

He is a priest, he can feel the clerical collar, and the wounded ask him for help. He points to his ears, tries to touch them but can't. Pall of black smoke over everything, the city has fallen into the streets. Ah, it's the end of the world. In a park he finds shade and cleared ground. People crouch under bushes like frightened animals. Where the park meets the river red and black figures crowd into steaming water. A figure gestures from a copse of bamboo. He enters it, finds five or six faceless soldiers huddling. Their eyes have melted, their mouths are holes. Deafness spares him their words. The sighted soldier mimes drinking. The soldiers are thirsty. He nods and goes to the river in search of a container. Bodies float downstream.

Hours pass as he hunts fruitlessly for a bucket. He pulls people from the rubble. He hears a bird screeching and he realizes that his deafness is the roar of the city burning, a roar like the blood in his ears but he is not deaf, he only thought he was deaf because there are no human cries. The people are suffering in silence. Through the dusky night he stumbles back to the river, pain crashing through his head. In a field men are pulling potatoes out of the ground that have been baked well enough to eat. He shares one with them. At the river everyone is dead –

– and he struggled out of the nightmare drenched in rank sweat, the taste of dirt in his mouth, his stomach knotted with horror. He sat up and the wet rough sheet clung to his skin. His heart felt crushed between lungs desperate for air. The flowery rotting jungle smell filled him and images from the dream flashed before him so vividly that in the dim hut he saw nothing else. He grabbed his cigarettes and jumped off the bunk, hurried out into the compound. Trembling he lit up, started pacing around. For a moment he worried that the idiot psychiatrist might see him, but then he dismissed the idea. Nelson would be asleep. They were all asleep. He shook his head, looked down at his right arm and almost dropped his cigarette – but it was just his stove scar, an old scar, he'd had it most of his life, since the day he'd pulled the frypan off the stove and onto his arm, burning it with oil. He could still remember the round O of fear that his mother's mouth had made as she rushed in to see what was wrong. Just an old burn scar, he thought, let's not go overboard here. He pulled his sleeve down.

For the rest of the night he tried to walk it off, cigarette after cigarette. The dome of the sky lightened until all the compound and the jungle beyond it was visible. He was forced by the light of day to walk back into his hut and lie down as if nothing had happened.

Two days later Scholes ordered them to take one of Le May's men over Rota for a test run. This new lieutenant colonel ordered Fitch not to play with the engines on takeoff. They flew a perfect run. January put the dummy gimmick right on the aiming point just as he had so often in the Salton Sea, and Fitch powered the plane down into the violent bank that started their 150-degree turn and flight for safety. Back on Tinian the lieutenant colonel congratulated them and shook each of their hands. January smiled with the rest, palms cool, heart steady. It was as if his body were a shell, something he could manipulate from without, like a bombsight. He ate well, he chatted as much as he ever had, and when the psychiatrist ran him to earth for some questions he was friendly and seemed open.

'Hello, doc.'

'How do you feel about all this, Frank?'

'Just like I always have, sir. Fine.'

'Eating well?'

'Better than ever.'

'Sleeping well?'

'As well as I can in this humidity. I got used to Utah, I'm afraid.' Dr Nelson laughed. Actually January had hardly slept since his dream. He was afraid of sleep. Couldn't the man see that?

'And how do you feel about being part of the crew chosen to make the first strike?'

'Well, it was the right choice, I reckon. We're the b – the best crew left.'

'Do you feel sorry about Tibbets' crew's accident?'

'Yes, sir, I do.' You better believe it.

After the jokes and firm handshakes that ended the interview January walked out into the blaze of the tropical noon and lit a cigarette. He allowed himself to feel how much he despised the psychiatrist and his blind profession at the same time he was waving good-bye to the man. Ounce brain. Why couldn't he have seen? Whatever happened it would be his fault ... With a rush of smoke out of him January realized how painfully easy it was to fool someone if you wanted to. All action was no more than a mask that could be perfectly manipulated from somewhere else. And all the while in that somewhere else January lived in a *click-click-click* of film, in the silent roaring of a dream, struggling against images he couldn't dispel. The heat of the tropical sun – ninety-three million miles away, wasn't it? – pulsed painfully on the back of his neck.

As he watched the psychiatrist collar their tail-gunner Kochenski, he thought of walking up to the man and saying *I quit*. I don't want to do this. In imagination he saw the look that would form in the man's eye, in Fitch's eye, in Tibbets' eye, and his mind recoiled from the idea. He felt too much contempt for them. He wouldn't for anything give them a means to despise him, a reason to call him coward. Stubbornly he banished the whole complex of thought. Easier to go along with it.

And so a couple of disjointed days later, just after midnight of August 9th, he found himself preparing for the strike. Around him Fitch and Matthews and Haddock were doing the same. How odd were the every-day motions of getting dressed when you were off to demolish a city, to end a hundred thousand lives! January found himself examining his hands, his boots, the cracks in the linoleum. He put on his survival vest, checked the pockets abstractedly for fishhooks, water kit, first aid package, emergency rations. Then the para-chute harness, and his coveralls over it all. Tying his bootlaces took minutes; he couldn't do it when watch-ing his fingers so closely.

'Come on, Professor!' Fitch's voice was tight. 'The big day is here.'

He followed the others into the night. A cool wind was blowing. The chaplain said a prayer for them. They took jeeps down Broadway to runway Able. *Lucky Strike* stood in a circle of spotlights and men, half of them with cameras, the rest with reporter's pads. They surrounded the crew; it reminded January of a Hollywood premiere. Eventually he escaped up the hatch and into the plane. Others followed. Half an hour passed before Fitch joined them, grinning like a movie star. They started the engines, and January was thankful for their vibrating, thought-smothering roar. They taxied away from the Hollywood scene and January felt relief for a moment until he remembered where they were going. On runway Able the engines pitched up to their twenty-three hundred rpm whine, and looking out the clear windscreen he saw the runway paint-marks move by ever faster. Fitch kept them on the runway till Tinian had run out from under them, then quickly pulled up. They were on their way.

When they got to altitude January climbed past Fitch and McDonald to the bombardier's seat and placed his parachute on it. He leaned back. The roar of the four engines packed around him like cotton batting. He was on the flight, nothing to be done about it now. The heavy vibration was a comfort, he liked the feel of it there in the nose of the plane. A drowsy, sad acceptance hummed through him.

Against his closed eyelids flashed a black eyeless face and he jerked awake, heart racing. He was on the flight, no way out. Now he realized how easy it would have been to get out of it. He could have just said he didn't want to. The simplicity of it appalled him. Who gave a damn what the psychiatrist or Tibbets or anyone else thought, compared to this? Now there was no way out. It was a comfort, in a way. Now he could stop worrying, stop thinking he had any choice.

Sitting there with his knees bracketing the bomb-sight January dozed, and as he dozed he daydreamed his way out. He could climb the step to Fitch and McDonald and declare he had been secretly promoted to major and ordered to redirect the mission. They were to go to Tokyo and drop the bomb in the bay. The Jap War Cabinet had been told to watch this demonstration of the new weapon, and when they saw that fireball boil the bay and bounce into heaven they'd run and sign surrender papers as fast as they could write, kamikazes or not. They weren't crazy, after all. No need to murder a whole city. It was such a good plan that the generals back home were no doubt changing the mission at this very minute, desperately radioing their instructions to Tinian, only to find out it was too late . . . so that when they returned to Tinian January would become a hero for guessing what the generals really wanted, and for risking all to do it. It would be like one of the Hornblower stories in *The Saturday Evening Post*.

Once again January jerked awake. The drowsy pleasure of the fantasy was replaced with desperate scorn. There wasn't a chance in hell that he could convince Fitch and the rest that he had secret orders superseding theirs. And he couldn't go up there and wave his pistol around and *order* them to drop the bomb in Tokyo Bay, because he was the one who had to actually drop it, and he couldn't be down in front dropping the bomb and up ordering the others around at the same time. Pipe dreams.

Time swept on, slow as a second hand. January's thoughts, however, matched the spin of the props; desperately they cast about, now this way now that, like an animal caught by the leg in a trap. The crew was silent. The clouds below were a white scree on the black ocean. January's knee vibrated against the squat stand of the bombsight. He was the one who had to drop the bomb. No matter where his thoughts lunged they were brought up short by that. He was the one, not Fitch or the crew, not Le May, not the generals and scientists back home, not Truman and his advisors. Truman – suddenly January hated him. Roosevelt would have done it differently. If only Roosevelt had lived! The grief that had filled January when he learned of Roosevelt's death reverberated through him again, more strongly than ever. It was unfair to have worked so hard and then not see the war's end. And FDR would have ended it differently. Back at the start of it all he had declared that civilian centres were never to be bombed, and if he had lived, if, if, if. But he hadn't. And now it was smiling bastard Harry Truman, ordering *him*, Frank January, to drop the sun on two hundred thousand women and children. Once his father had taken him to see the Browns play before twenty thousand, a giant crowd – 'I never voted for you,' January whispered viciously, and jerked to realize he had spoken aloud. Luckily his microphone was off. But Roosevelt would have done it differently, he *would have*.

The bombsight rose before him, spearing the black sky and blocking some of the hundreds of little cruciform stars. *Lucky Strike* ground on towards Iwo Jima, minute by minute flying four miles closer to their target. January leaned forward and put his face in the cool headrest of the bombsight, hoping that its grasp might hold his thoughts as well as his forehead. It worked surprisingly well.

His earphones crackled and he sat up. 'Captain January.' It was Shepard. 'We're going to arm the bomb now, want to watch?'

'Sure thing.' He shook his head, surprised at his own duplicity. Stepping up between the pilots, he moved stiffly to the roomy cabin behind the cockpit. Matthews was at his desk taking a navigational fix on the radio signals from Iwo Jima and Okinawa, and Haddock stood beside him. At the back of the compartment was a small circular hatch, below the larger tunnel leading to the rear of the plane. January opened it, sat down and swung himself feet first through the hole.

The bomb bay was unheated, and the cold air felt good. He stood facing the bomb. Stone was sitting on the floor of the bay; Shepard was laid out under the bomb, reaching into it. On a rubber pad next to Stone were tools, plates, several cylindrical blocks. Shepard pulled back, sat up, sucked a scraped knuckle. He shook his head ruefully: 'I don't dare wear gloves with this one.'

'I'd be just as happy myself if you didn't let something slip,' January joked nervously. The two men laughed.

'Nothing can blow till I change those green wires to the red ones,' Stone said.

'Give me the wrench,' Shepard said. Stone handed it to him, and he stretched under the bomb again. After some awkward wrenching inside it he lifted out a cylindrical plug. 'Breech plug,' he said, and set it on the mat.

January found his skin goose-pimpling in the cold air. Stone handed Shepard one of the blocks. Shepard extended under the bomb again. 'Red ends towards the breech.' 'I know.' Watching them January was reminded of auto mechanics on the oily floor of a garage, working under a car. He had spent a few years doing that himself, after his family moved to Vicksburg. Hiroshima was a river town. One time a flatbed truck carrying bags of cement powder down Fourth Street hill had lost its brakes and careened into the intersection with River Road, where despite the driver's efforts to turn it smashed into a passing car. Frank had been out in the yard playing, had heard the crash and saw the cement dust rising. He had been one of the first there. The woman and child in the passenger seat of the Model T had been killed. The woman driving was okay. They were from Chicago. A group of folks subdued the driver of the truck, who kept trying to help at the Model T, though he had a bad cut on his head and was covered with white dust.

'Okay, let's tighten the breech plug.' Stone gave Shepard the wrench. 'Sixteen turns exactly,' Shepard said. He was sweating even in the bay's chill, and he paused to wipe his forehead. 'Let's hope we don't get hit by lightning.' He put the wrench down and shifted onto his knees, picked up a circular plate. Hubcap, January thought. Stone connected wires, then helped Shepard install two more plates. Good old American know-how, January thought, goose pimples rippling across his skin like cat's paws over water. There was Shepard, a scientist, putting together a bomb like he was an auto mechanic changing oil and plugs. January felt a tight rush of rage at the scientists who had designed the bomb. They had worked on it for over a year down there in New Mexico, had none of them in all that time ever stopped to think what they were doing?

But none of them had to drop it. January turned to hide his face from Shepard, stepped down the bay. The bomb looked like a big long trash can, with fins at one end and little antennae at the other. Just a bomb, he thought, damn it, it's just another bomb.

Shepard stood and patted the bomb gently. 'We've got a live one now.' Never a thought about what it would do. January hurried by the man, afraid that hatred would crack his shell and give him away. The pistol strapped to his belt caught on the hatchway and he imagined shooting Shepard – shooting Fitch and McDonald and plunging the controls forward so that *Lucky Strike* tilted and spun down into the sea like a spent tracer bullet, like a plane broken by flak, following the arc of all human ambition. Nobody would ever know what had happened to them, and their trash can would be dumped at the bottom of the Pacific where it belonged. He could even shoot everyone and parachute out, and perhaps be rescued by one of the Superdumbos following them . . .

The thought passed and remembering it January squinted with disgust. But another part of him agreed that it was a possibility. It could be done. It would solve his problem. His fingers explored his holster snap.

'Want some coffee?' Matthews asked.

'Sure,' January said, and took his hand from the gun to reach for the cup. He sipped: hot. He watched Matthews and Benton tune the loran equipment. As the beeps came in Matthews took a straightedge and drew lines from Okinawa and Iwo Jima on his map table. He tapped a finger on the intersection. 'They've taken the art out of navigation,' he said to January. 'They might as well stop making the navigator's dome,' thumbing up at the little Plexiglas bubble over them.

'Good old American know-how,' January said.

Matthews nodded. With two fingers he measured the distance between their position and Iwo Jima. Benton measured with a ruler.

'Rendezvous at five thirty-five, eh?' Matthews said. They were to rendezvous with the two trailing planes over Iwo.

Benton disagreed: 'I'd say five-fifty.'

'What? Check again, guy, we're not in no tugboat here.'

'The wind —'

'Yah, the wind. Frank, you want to add a bet to the pool?'

'Five thirty-six,' January said promptly.

They laughed. 'See, he's got more confidence in me,' Matthews said with a dopey grin.

January recalled his plan to shoot the crew and tip the plane into the sea, and he pursed his lips, repelled. Not for anything would he be able to shoot these men, who, if not friends, were at least companions. They passed for friends. They meant no harm.

Shepard and Stone climbed into the cabin. Matthews offered them coffee. 'The gimmick's ready to kick their ass, eh?' Shepard nodded and drank.

January moved forward, past Haddock's console. Another plan that wouldn't work. What to do? All the flight engineer's dials and gauges showed conditions were normal. Maybe he could sabotage something? Cut a line somewhere?

Fitch looked back at him and said, 'When are we due over Iwo?'

'Five-forty, Matthews says.'

'He better be right.'

A thug. In peacetime Fitch would be hanging around a pool table giving the cops trouble. He was perfect for war. Tibbets had chosen his men well – most of them, anyway. Moving back past Haddock, January stopped to stare at the group of men in the navigation cabin. They joked, drank coffee. They were all a bit like Fitch: young toughs, capable and thoughtless. They were having a good time, an adventure. That was January's dominant impression of his companions in the 509th; despite all the bitching and the occasional moments of overmastering fear, they were having a good time. His mind spun forward and he saw what these young men would grow up to be like as clearly as if they stood before him in businessmen's suits, prosperous and balding. They would be tough and capable and thoughtless, and as the years passed and the great war receded in time they would look back on it with ever-increasing nostalgia, for they would be the survivors and not the dead. Every year of this war would feel like ten in their memories, so that the war would always remain the central experience of their lives – a time when history lay palpable in their hands, when each of their daily acts affected it, when moral issues were simple, and others told them what to do – so that as more years passed and the survivors aged, bodies falling apart, lives in one rut or another, they would unconsciously push harder and harder to thrust the world into war again, thinking somewhere inside themselves that if they could only return to world war then they would magically be again as they were in the last one – young, and free, and happy. And by that time they would hold the positions of power, they would be capable of doing it.

So there would be more wars, January saw. He heard it in Matthews' laughter, saw it in their excited eyes. 'There's Iwo, and it's five thirty-one. Pay up! I win!' And in future wars they'd have more bombs like the gimmick, hundreds of them no doubt. He saw more planes, more young crews like this one, flying to Moscow no doubt or to wherever, fireballs in every capital, why not? And to what end? To what end? So that the old men could hope to become magically young again. Nothing more sane than that.

They were over Iwo Jima. Three more hours to Japan. Voices from *The Great Artiste* and *Number 91* crackled on the radio. Rendezvous accomplished, the three planes flew northwest, towards Shikoku, the first Japanese island in their path. January went aft to use the toilet. 'You okay, Frank?' Matthews asked. 'Sure. Terrible coffee, though.' 'Ain't it always.' January tugged at his baseball cap and hurried away. Kochenski and the other gunners were playing poker. When he was done he returned forward. Matthews sat on the stool before his maps, readying his equipment for the constant monitoring of drift that would now be required. Haddock and Benton were also busy at their stations. January manoeuvred between the pilots down into the nose. 'Good shooting,' Matthews called after him.

Forward it seemed quieter. January got settled, put his headphones on and leaned forward to look out the ribbed Plexiglas.

Dawn had turned the whole vault of the sky pink. Slowly the radiant shade shifted through lavender to blue, pulse by pulse a different colour. The ocean below was a glittering blue plane, marbled by a pattern of puffy pink cloud. The sky above was a vast dome, darker above than on the horizon. January had always thought that dawn was the time when you could see most clearly how big the earth was, and how high above it they flew. It seemed they flew at the very upper edge of the atmosphere, and January saw how thin it was, how it was just a skin of air really, so that even if you flew up to its top the earth still extended away infinitely in every direction. The coffee had warmed January, he was sweating. Sunlight blinked off the Plexiglas. His watch said six. Plane and hemisphere of blue were split down the middle by the bombsight. His earphones crackled and he listened in to the reports from the lead planes flying over the target cities. Kokura, Nagasaki, Hiroshima, all of them had six-tenths cloud cover. Maybe they would have to cancel the whole mission because of weather. 'We'll look at Hiroshima first,' Fitch said. January peered down at the fields of miniature clouds with renewed interest. His parachute slipped under him. Readjusting it he imagined putting it on, sneaking back to the central escape hatch under the navigator's cabin, opening the hatch . . . he could be out of the plane and gone before anyone noticed. Leave it up to them. They could bomb or not but it wouldn't be January's doing. He could float down onto the world like a puff of dandelion, feel cool air rush around him, watch the silk canopy dome hang over him like a miniature sky, a private world.

An eyeless black face. January shuddered; it was as though the nightmare could return any time. If he jumped nothing would change, the bomb would still fall – would he feel any better, floating on his Inland Sea? Sure, one part of him shouted; maybe, another conceded; the rest of him saw that face . . .

Earphones crackled. Shepard said, 'Lieutenant Stone has now armed the bomb, and I can tell you all what we are carrying. Aboard with us is the world's first atomic bomb.'

Not exactly, January thought. Whistles squeaked in his earphones. The first one went off in New Mexico. Splitting atoms: January had heard the term before. Tremendous energy in every atom, Einstein had said. Break one, and – he had seen the result on film. Shepard was talking about radiation, which brought back more to January. Energy released in the form of X rays. Killed by X rays! It would be against the Geneva Convention if they had thought of it.

Fitch cut in. 'When the bomb is dropped Lieutenant Benton will record our reaction to what we see. This recording is being made for history, so watch your language.' Watch your language! January choked back a laugh. Don't curse or blaspheme God at the sight of the first atomic bomb incinerating a city and all its inhabitants with X rays!

Six-twenty. January found his hands clenched together on the headrest of the bombsight. He felt as if he had a fever. In the harsh wash of morning light the skin on the backs of his hands appeared slightly translucent. The whorls in the skin looked like the delicate patterning of waves on the sea's surface. His hands were made of atoms. Atoms were the smallest building block of matter, it took billions of them to make those tense, trembling hands. Split one atom and you had the fireball. That meant that the energy contained in even one hand ... he turned up a palm to look at the lines and the mottled flesh under the transparent skin. A person was a bomb that could blow up the world. January felt that latent power stir in him, pulsing with every hard heart-knock. What beings they were, and in what a blue expanse of a world! – And here they spun on to drop a bomb and kill a hundred thousand of these astonishing beings.

When a fox or raccoon is caught by the leg in a trap, it lunges until the leg is frayed, twisted, perhaps broken, and only then does the animal's pain and exhaustion force it to quit. Now in the same way January wanted to quit. His mind hurt. His plans to escape were so much crap – stupid, useless. Better to quit. He tried to stop thinking, but it was hopeless. How could he stop? As long as he was conscious he would be thinking. The mind struggles longer in its traps than any fox.

Lucky Strike tilted up and began the long climb to bombing altitude. On the horizon the clouds lay over a green island. Japan. Surely it had gotten hotter, the heater must be broken, he thought. Don't think. Every few minutes Matthews gave Fitch small course adjustments. 'Two seventy-five, now. That's it.' To escape the moment January recalled his childhood. Following a mule and plough. Moving to Vicksburg (rivers). For a while there in Vicksburg, since his stutter made it hard to gain friends, he had played a game with himself. He had passed the time by imagining that everything he did was vitally important and determined the fate of the world. If he crossed a road in front of a certain car, for instance, then the car wouldn't make it through the next intersection before a truck hit it, and so the man driving would be killed and wouldn't be able to invent the flying boat that would save President Wilson from kidnappers – so he had to wait for that car because everything afterward depended on it. Oh damn it, he thought, damn it, think of something *different*. The last Hornblower story he had read – how would *he* get out of this? The round O of his mother's face as she ran in and saw his arm – The Mississippi, mud-brown behind its levees – Abruptly he shook his head, face twisted in frustration and despair, aware at last that no possible avenue of memory would serve as an escape for him now, for now there was no part of his life that did not apply to the situation he was in, and no matter where he cast his mind it was going to shore up against the hour facing him.

Less than an hour. They were at thirty thousand feet, bombing altitude. Fitch gave him altimeter readings to dial into the bombsight. Matthews gave him wind-speeds. Sweat got in his eye and he blinked furiously. The sun rose behind them like an atomic bomb, glinting off every corner and edge of the Plexiglas, illuminating his bubble compartment with a fierce glare. Broken plans jumbled together in his mind, his breath was short, his throat dry. Uselessly and repeatedly he damned the scientists, damned Truman. Damned the Japanese for causing the whole mess in the first place, damned yellow killers, they had brought this on themselves. Remember Pearl. American men had died under bombs when no war had been declared; they had started it and now it was coming back to them with a vengeance. And they deserved it. And an invasion of Japan would take years, cost millions of lives – end it now, end it, they deserved it, they deserved it steaming river full of charcoal people silently dying damned stubborn race of maniacs!

'There's Honshu,' Fitch said, and January returned to the world of the plane. They were over the Inland Sea. Soon they would pass the secondary target, Kokura, a bit to the south. Seven-thirty. The island was draped more heavily than the sea by clouds, and again January's heart leaped with the idea that weather would cancel the mission. But they did deserve it. It was a mission like any other mission. He had dropped bombs on Africa, Sicily, Italy, all Germany . . . He leaned forward to take a look through the sight. Under the X of the crosshairs was the sea, but at the lead edge of the sight was land. Honshu. At two hundred and thirty miles an hour that gave them about a half hour to Hiroshima. Maybe less. He wondered if his heart could beat so hard for that long.

Fitch said, 'Matthews, I'm giving over guidance to you. Just tell us what to do.'

'Bear south two degrees,' was all Matthews said. At last their voices had taken on a touch of awareness, even fear.

'January, are you ready?' Fitch asked.

'I'm just waiting,' January said. He sat up, so Fitch could see the back of his head. The bombsight stood between his legs. A switch on its side would start the bombing sequence; the bomb would not leave the plane immediately upon the flick of the switch, but would drop after a fifteen-second radio tone warned the following planes. The sight was adjusted accordingly.

'Adjust to a heading of two sixty-five,' Matthews said. 'We're coming in directly upwind.' This was to make any side-drift adjustments for the bomb unnecessary. 'January, dial it down to two hundred and thirty-one miles per hour.'

'Two thirty-one.'

Fitch said, 'Everyone but January and Matthews, get your goggles on.'

January took the darkened goggles from the floor. One needed to protect one's eyes or they might melt. He put them on, put his forehead on the headrest. They were in the way. He took them off. When he looked through the sight again there was land under the crosshairs. He checked his watch. Eight o'clock. Up and reading the papers, drinking tea.

'Ten minutes to AP,' Matthews said. The aiming point was Aioi Bridge, a T-shaped bridge in the middle of the delta-straddling city. Easy to recognize.

'There's a lot of cloud down there,' Fitch nodded. 'Are you going to be able to see?'

'I won't be sure until we try it,' January said.

'We can make another pass and use radar if we need to,' Matthews said.

Fitch said. 'Don't drop it unless you're sure, January.'

'Yes, sir.'

Through the sight a grouping of rooftops and grey roads was just visible between broken clouds. Around it green forest. 'All right,' Matthews exclaimed, 'here we go! Keep it right on this heading, Captain! January, we'll stay at two thirty-one.'

'And same heading,' Fitch said. 'January, she's all yours. Everyone make sure your goggles are on. And be ready for the turn.'

January's world contracted to the view through the bombsight. A stippled field of cloud and forest. Over a small range of hills and into Hiroshima's watershed. The broad river was mud brown, the land pale hazy green, the growing network of roads flat grey. Now the tiny rectangular shapes of buildings covered almost all the land, and swimming into the sight came the city proper, narrow islands thrusting into a dark blue bay. Under the crosshairs the city moved island by island, cloud by cloud. January had stopped breathing, his fingers were rigid as stone on the switch. And there was Aioi Bridge. It slid right under the crosshairs, a tiny T right in a gap in the clouds. January's fingers crushed the switch. Deliberately he took a breath, held it. Clouds swam under the crosshairs, then the next island. 'Almost there,' he said calmly into his microphone. 'Steady.' Now that he was committed his heart was humming like the Wrights. He counted to ten. Now flowing under the crosshairs were clouds alternating with green forest, leaden roads. 'I've turned the switch, but I'm not getting a tone!' he croaked into the mike. His right hand held the switch firmly in place. Fitch was shouting something – Matthews' voice cracked across it – 'Flipping it b-back and forth,' January shouted, shielding the bombsight with his body from the eyes of the pilots. 'But *still* – wait a second –'

He pushed the switch down. A low hum filled his ears. 'That's it! It started!'

'But where will it land?' Matthews cried.

'Hold steady!' January shouted.

Lucky Strike shuddered and lofted up ten or twenty feet. January twisted to look down and there was the bomb, flying just below the plane. Then with a wobble it fell away.

The plane banked right and dove so hard that the centrifugal force threw January against the Plexiglas. Several thousand feet lower Fitch levelled it out and they hurtled north.

'Do you see anything?' Fitch cried.

From the tailgun Kochenski gasped 'Nothing.' January struggled upright. He reached for the welder's goggles, but they were no longer on his head. He couldn't find them. 'How long has it been?' he said.

'Thirty seconds,' Matthews replied.

January clamped his eyes shut.

The blood in his eyelids lit up red, then white.

On the earphones a clutter of voices: 'Oh my God. Oh my God.' The plane bounced and tumbled, metallically shrieking. January pressed himself off the Plexiglas. ''Nother shockwave!' Kochenski yelled. The plane rocked again, bounced out of control, this is it, January thought, end of the world, I guess that solves my problem.

He opened his eyes and found he could still see. The engines still roared, the props spun. 'Those were the shockwaves from the bomb,' Fitch called. 'We're okay now. Look at that! Will you look at that sonofabitch go!'

January looked. The cloud layer below had burst apart, and a black column of smoke billowed up from a core of red fire. Already the top of the column was at their height. Exclamations of shock clattered painfully in January's ears. He stared at the fiery base of the cloud, at the scores of fires feeding into it. Suddenly he could see past the cloud, and his fingernails cut into his palms. Through a gap in the clouds he saw it clearly, the delta, the six rivers, there off to the left of the tower of smoke: the city of Hiroshima, untouched.

'We missed!' Kochenski yelled. 'We missed it!'

January turned to hide his face from the pilots; on it was a grin like a rictus. He sat back in his seat and let the relief fill him.

Then it was back to it. 'God damn it!' Fitch shouted down at him. McDonald was trying to restrain him. 'January, get up here!'

'Yes, sir.' Now there was a new set of problems.

January stood and turned, legs weak. His right fingertips throbbed painfully. The men were crowded forward to look out the Plexiglas. January looked with them.

The mushroom cloud was forming. It roiled out as if it might continue to extend forever, fed by the inferno and the black stalk below it. It looked about two miles wide, and a half mile tall, and it extended well above the height they flew at, dwarfing their plane entirely. 'Do you think we'll all be sterile?' Matthews said.

'I can taste the radiation,' McDonald declared. 'Can you? It tastes like lead.'

Bursts of flame shot up into the cloud from below, giving a purplish tint to the stalk. There it stood: lifelike, malignant, sixty thousand feet tall. One bomb. January shoved past the pilots into the navigation cabin, overwhelmed.

'Should I start recording everyone's reactions, Captain?' asked Benton.

'To hell with that,' Fitch said, following January back. But Shepard got there first, descending quickly from the navigation dome. He rushed across the cabin, caught January on the shoulder, 'You bastard!' he screamed as January stumbled back. 'You lost your nerve, coward!'

January went for Shepard, happy to have a target at last, but Fitch cut in and grabbed him by the collar, pulled him around until they were face to face –

'Is that right?' Fitch cried, as angry as Shepard. 'Did you screw up on purpose?'

'No,' January grunted, and knocked Fitch's hands away from his neck. He swung and smacked Fitch on the mouth, caught him solid. Fitch staggered back, recovered, and no doubt would have beaten January up, but Matthews and Benton and Stone leaped in and held him back, shouting for order. 'Shut up! Shut up!' McDonald screamed from the cockpit, and for a moment it was bedlam, but Fitch let himself be restrained, and soon only McDonald's shouts for quiet were heard. January retreated to between the pilot seats, right hand on his pistol holster.

'The city was in the crosshairs when I flipped the switch,' he said. 'But the first couple of times I flipped it nothing happened –'

'That's a lie!' Shepard shouted. 'There was nothing wrong with the switch, I checked it myself. Besides, the bomb exploded *miles* beyond Hiroshima, look for yourself! That's *minutes*.' He wiped spit from his chin and pointed at January. 'You did it.'

'You don't know that,' January said. But he could see the men had been convinced by Shepard, and he took a step back. 'You just get me to a board of inquiry, quick.

And leave me alone till then. If you touch me again,' glaring venomously at Fitch and then Shepard, 'I'll shoot you.' He turned and hopped down to his seat, feeling exposed and vulnerable, like a treed raccoon.

'They'll shoot *you* for this,' Shepard screamed after him. 'Disobeying orders – treason –' Matthews and Stone were shutting him up.

'Let's get out of here,' he heard McDonald say. 'I can taste the lead, can't you?'

January looked out the Plexiglas. The giant cloud still burned and roiled. One atom . . . Well, they had really done it to that forest. He almost laughed but stopped himself, afraid of hysteria. Through a break in the clouds he got a clear view of Hiroshima for the first time. It lay spread over its islands like a map, unharmed. Well, that was that. The inferno at the base of the mushroom cloud was eight or ten miles around the shore of the bay and a mile or two inland. A certain patch of forest would be gone, destroyed – utterly blasted from the face of the earth. The Japs would be able to go out and investigate the damage. And if they were told it was a demonstration, a warning – and if they acted fast – well, they had their chance. Maybe it would work.

The release of tension made January feel sick. Then he recalled Shepard's words and he knew that whether his plan worked or not he was still in trouble. In trouble! It was worse than that. Bitterly he cursed the Japanese, he even wished for a moment that he *had* dropped it on them. Wearily he let his despair empty him.

A long while later he sat up straight. Once again he was a trapped animal. He began lunging for escape, casting about for plans. One alternative after another. All during the long grim flight home he considered it, mind spinning at the speed of the props and beyond. And when they came down on Tinian he had a plan. It was a long shot, he reckoned, but it was the best he could do.

The briefing hut was surrounded by MPs again. January stumbled from the truck with the rest and walked inside. He was more than ever aware of the looks given him, and they were hard, accusatory. He was too tired to care. He hadn't slept in more than thirty-six hours, and had slept very little since the last time he had been in the hut, a week before. Now the room quivered with the lack of engine vibration to stabilize it, and the silence roared. It was all he could do to hold on to the bare essentials of his plan. The glares of Fitch and Shepard, the hurt incomprehension of Matthews, they had to be thrust out of his focus. Thankfully he lit a cigarette.

In a clamour of question and argument the others described the strike. Then the haggard Scholes and an intelligence officer led them through the bombing run. January's plan made it necessary to hold to his story: '. . . and when the AP was under the crosshairs I pushed down the switch, but got no signal. I flipped it up and down repeatedly until the tone kicked in. At that point there was still fifteen seconds to the release.'

'Was there anything that may have caused the tone to start when it did?'

'Not that I noticed immediately, but –'

'It's impossible,' Shepard interrupted, face red. 'I

checked the switch before we flew and there was nothing wrong with it. Besides, the drop occurred over a minute –'

'Captain Shepard,' Scholes said. 'We'll hear from you presently.'

'But he's obviously lying –'

'Captain Shepard! It's not at all obvious. Don't speak unless questioned.'

'Anyway,' January said, hoping to shift the questions away from the issue of the long delay, 'I noticed something about the bomb when it was falling that could explain why it stuck. I need to discuss it with one of the scientists familiar with the bomb's design.'

'What was that?' Scholes asked suspiciously.

January hesitated. 'There's going to be an inquiry, right?'

Scholes frowned. 'This is the inquiry, Captain January. Tell us what you saw.'

'But there will be some proceeding beyond this one?'

'It looks like there's going to be a court-martial, yes, Captain.'

'That's what I thought. I don't want to talk to anyone but my counsel, and some scientist familiar with the bomb.'

'*I'm* a scientist familiar with the bomb,' Shepard burst out. 'You could tell me if you really had anything, you –'

'I said I need a scientist!' January exclaimed, rising to face the scarlet Shepard across the table. 'Not a G-God damned mechanic.' Shepard started to shout, others joined in and the room rang with argument. While Scholes restored order January sat down, and he refused to be drawn out again.

'I'll see you're assigned counsel, and initiate the court-martial,' Scholes said, clearly at a loss. 'Meanwhile you are under arrest, on suspicion of disobeying orders in combat.' January nodded, and Scholes gave him over to the MPs.

'One last thing,' January said, fighting exhaustion. 'Tell General Le May that if the Japs are told this drop was a warning, it might have the same effect as –'

'I told you!' Shepard shouted. 'I told you he did it on purpose!'

Men around Shepard restrained him. But he had convinced most of them, and even Matthews stared at him with surprised anger.

January shook his head wearily. He had the dull feeling that his plan, while it had succeeded so far, was ultimately not a good one. 'Just trying to make the best of it.' It took all of his remaining will to force his legs to carry him in a dignified manner out of the hut.

His cell was an empty NCO's office. MPs brought his meals. For the first couple of days he did little but sleep. On the third day he glanced out the office's barred window, and saw a tractor pulling a tarpaulin-draped trolley out of the compound, followed by jeeps filled with MPs. It looked like a military funeral. January rushed to the door and banged on it until one of the young MPs came.

'What's that they're doing out there?' January demanded.

Eyes cold and mouth twisted, the MP said, 'They're making another strike. They're going to do it right this time.'

'No!' January cried. 'No!' He rushed the MP, who

knocked him back and locked the door. '*No!*' He beat the door until his hands hurt, cursing wildly. 'You don't *need* to do it, it isn't *necessary*.' Shell shattered at last, he collapsed on the bed and wept. Now everything he had done would be rendered meaningless. He had sacrificed himself for nothing.

A day or two after that the MPs led in a colonel, an iron-haired man who stood stiffly and crushed January's hand when he shook it. His eyes were a pale, icy blue.

'I am Colonel Dray,' he said. 'I have been ordered to defend you in court-martial.' January could feel the dislike pouring from the man. 'To do that I'm going to need every fact you have, so let's get started.'

'I'm not talking to anybody until I've seen an atomic scientist.'

'I am your *defence* counsel –'

'I don't care who you are,' January said. 'Your defence of me depends on you getting one of the scientists *here*. The higher up he is, the better. And I want to speak to him alone.'

'I will have to be present.'

So he would do it. But now January's lawyer, too, was an enemy.

'Naturally,' January said. 'You're my lawyer. But no one else. Our atomic secrecy may depend on it.'

'You saw evidence of sabotage?'

'Not one word more until that scientist is here.'

Angrily the colonel nodded and left.

Late the next day the colonel returned with another man. 'This is Dr Forest.'

'I helped develop the bomb,' Forest said. He had a crew cut and dressed in fatigues, and to January he looked more Army than the colonel. Suspiciously he stared back and forth at the two men.

'You'll vouch for this man's identity on your word as an officer?' he asked Dray.

'Of course,' the colonel said stiffly, offended.

'So,' Dr Forest said. 'You had some trouble getting it off when you wanted to. Tell me what you saw.'

'I saw nothing,' January said harshly. He took a deep breath; it was time to commit himself. 'I want you to take a message back to the scientists. You folks have been working on this thing for years, and you must have had time to consider how the bomb should have been used. You know we could have convinced the Japs to surrender by showing them a demonstration –'

'Wait a minute,' Forest said. 'You're saying you didn't see anything? There wasn't a malfunction?'

'That's right,' January said, and cleared his throat. 'It wasn't *necessary*, do you understand?'

Forest was looking at Colonel Dray. Dray gave him a disgusted shrug. 'He told me he saw evidence of sabotage.'

'I want you to go back and ask the scientists to intercede for me,' January said, raising his voice to get the man's attention. 'I haven't got a chance in that court-martial. But if the scientists defend me then maybe they'll let me live, see? I don't want to get shot for doing something every one of you scientists would have done.'

Dr Forest had backed away. Colour rising, he said, 'What makes you think that's what we would have done? Don't you think we considered it? Don't you think men better qualified than you made the decision?' He waved a hand – 'God damn it – what made you think you were competent to decide something as important as that!'

January was appalled at the man's reaction; in his plan it had gone differently. Angrily he jabbed a finger at Forest. 'Because *I* was the man doing it, *Doctor* Forest. You take even one step back from that and suddenly you can pretend it's not your doing. Fine for you, but *I was there.*'

At every word the man's colour was rising. It looked like he might pop a vein in his neck. January tried once more. 'Have you ever tried to imagine what one of your bombs would do to a city full of people?'

'I've had enough!' the man exploded. He turned to Dray. 'I'm under no obligation to keep what I've heard here confidential. You can be sure it will be used as evidence in Captain January's court-martial.' He turned and gave January a look of such blazing hatred that January understood it. For these men to admit he was right would mean admitting that they were wrong – that every one of them was responsible for his part in the construction of the weapon January had refused to use. Understanding that, January knew he was doomed.

The bang of Dr Forest's departure still shook the little office. January sat on his cot, got out a smoke. Under Colonel Dray's cold gaze he lit one shakily, took a drag. He looked up at the colonel, shrugged. 'It was my best chance,' he explained. That did something – for the first and only time the cold disdain in the colonel's eyes shifted to a little, hard, lawyerly gleam of respect.

*   *   *

The court-martial lasted two days. The verdict was guilty of disobeying orders in combat and of giving aid and comfort to the enemy. The sentence was death by firing squad.

For most of his remaining days January rarely spoke, drawing ever further behind the mask that had hidden him for so long. A clergyman came to see him, but it was the 509th's chaplain, the one who had said the prayer blessing the *Lucky Strike*'s mission before they took off. Angrily January sent him packing.

Later, however, a young Catholic priest dropped by. His name was Patrick Getty. He was a little pudgy man, bespectacled and, it seemed, somewhat afraid of January. January let the man talk to him. When he returned the next day January talked back a bit, and on the day after that he talked some more. It became a habit.

Usually January talked about his childhood. He talked of ploughing mucky black bottom land behind a mule. Of running down the lane to the mailbox. Of reading books by the light of the moon after he had been ordered to sleep, and of being beaten by his mother for it with a high-heeled shoe. He told the priest the story of the time his arm had been burnt, and about the car crash at the bottom of Fourth Street. 'It's the truck driver's face I remember, do you see, Father?'

'Yes,' the young priest said. 'Yes.'

And he told him about the game he had played in which every action he took tipped the balance of world affairs. 'When I remembered that game I thought it was dumb. Step on a sidewalk crack and cause an earthquake

– you know, it's stupid. Kids are like that.' The priest
nodded. 'But now I've been thinking that if everybody
were to live their whole lives like that, thinking that
every move they made really was important, then . . .
it might make a difference.' He waved a hand vaguely,
expelled cigarette smoke. 'You're accountable for what
you do.'

'Yes,' the priest said. 'Yes, you are.'

'And if you're given orders to do something wrong,
you're still accountable, right? The orders don't change
it.'

'That's right.'

'Hmph.' January smoked a while. 'So they say,
anyway. But look what happens.' He waved at the office.
'I'm like the guy in a story I read – he thought everything in books was true, and after reading a bunch of
westerns he tried to rob a train. They tossed him in
jail.' He laughed shortly. 'Books are full of crap.'

'Not all of them,' the priest said. 'Besides, you weren't
trying to rob a train.'

They laughed at the notion. 'Did you read that story?'

'No.'

'It was the strangest book – there were two stories in
it, and they alternated chapter by chapter, but they didn't
have a thing to do with each other! I didn't get it.'

'. . . Maybe the writer was trying to say that everything connects to everything else.'

'Maybe. But it's a funny way to say it.'

'I like it.'

And so they passed the time, talking.

So it was the priest who was the one to come by and

tell January that his request for a Presidential pardon had been refused. Getty said awkwardly, 'It seems the President approves the sentence.'

'That bastard,' January said weakly. He sat on his cot.

Time passed. It was another hot, humid day.

'Well,' the priest said. 'Let me give you some better news. Given your situation I don't think telling you matters, though I've been told not to. The second mission – you know there was a second strike?'

'Yes.'

'Well, they missed too.'

'What?' January cried, and bounced to his feet. 'You're kidding!'

'No. They flew to Kokura, but found it covered by clouds. It was the same over Nagasaki and Hiroshima, so they flew back to Kokura and tried to drop the bomb using radar to guide it, but apparently there was a – a genuine equipment failure this time, and the bomb fell on an island.'

January was hopping up and down, mouth hanging open, 'So we n-never –'

'We never dropped an atom bomb on a Japanese city. That's right.' Getty grinned. 'And get this – I heard this from my superior – they sent a message to the Japanese government telling them that the two explosions were warnings, and that if they didn't surrender by September first we would drop bombs on Kyoto and Tokyo, and then wherever else we had to. Word is that the Emperor went to Hiroshima to survey the damage, and when he saw it he ordered the Cabinet to surrender. So . . .'

'So it worked,' January said. He hopped around, 'It worked, it worked!'

'Yes.'

'Just like I said it would!' he cried, and hopping before the priest he laughed.

Getty was jumping around a little too, and the sight of the priest bouncing was too much for January. He sat on his cot and laughed till the tears ran down his cheeks.

'So –' he sobered quickly. 'So Truman's going to shoot me anyway, eh?'

'Yes,' the priest said unhappily. 'I guess that's right.'

This time January's laugh was bitter. 'He's a bastard, all right. And proud of being a bastard, which makes it worse.' He shook his head. 'If Roosevelt had lived . . .'

'It would have been different,' Getty finished. 'Yes. Maybe so. But he didn't.' He sat beside January. 'Cigarette?' He held out a pack, and January noticed the white wartime wrapper. He frowned.

'You haven't got a Camel?'

'Oh. Sorry.'

'Oh well. That's all right.' January took one of the Lucky Strikes, lit up. 'That's awfully good news.' He breathed out. 'I never believed Truman would pardon me anyway, so mostly you've brought good news. Ha. They *missed*. You have no idea how much better that makes me feel.'

'I think I do.'

January smoked the cigarette.

'. . . So I'm a good American after all. I *am* a good American,' he insisted, 'no matter what Truman says.'

'Yes,' Getty replied, and coughed. 'You're better than Truman any day.'

'Better watch what you say, Father.' He looked into

the eyes behind the glasses, and the expression he saw there gave him pause. Since the drop every look directed at him had been filled with contempt. He'd seen it so often during the court-martial that he'd learned to stop looking; and now he had to teach himself to see again. The priest looked at him as if he were . . . as if he were some kind of hero. That wasn't exactly right. But seeing it . . .

January would not live to see the years that followed, so he would never know what came of his action. He had given up casting his mind forward and imagining possibilities, because there was no point to it. His planning was ended. In any case he would not have been able to imagine the course of the post-war years. That the world would quickly become an armed camp pitched on the edge of atomic war, he might have predicted. But he never would have guessed that so many people would join a January Society. He would never know of the effect the Society had on Dewey during the Korean crisis, never know of the Society's successful campaign for the test ban treaty, and never learn that thanks in part to the Society and its allies, a treaty would be signed by the great powers that would reduce the number of atomic bombs year by year, until there were none left.

Frank January would never know any of that. But in that moment on his cot looking into the eyes of young Patrick Getty, he guessed an inkling of it – he felt, just for an instant, the impact on history.

And with that he relaxed. In his last week everyone who met him carried away the same impression, that of a calm, quiet man, angry at Truman and others, but in a withdrawn, matter-of-fact way. Patrick Getty, a strong force in the January Society ever after, said January was talkative for some time after he learned of the missed attack on Kokura. Then he became quieter and quieter, as the day approached. On the morning that they woke him at dawn to march him out to a hastily constructed execution shed, his MPs shook his hand. The priest was with him as he smoked a final cigarette, and they prepared to put the hood over his head. January looked at him calmly. 'They load one of the guns with a blank cartridge, right?'

'Yes,' Getty said.

'So each man in the squad can imagine he may not have shot me?'

'Yes. That's right.'

A tight, unhumorous smile was January's last expression. He threw down the cigarette, ground it out, poked the priest in the arm. 'But I *know*.' Then the mask slipped back into place for good, making the hood redundant, and with a firm step January went to the wall. One might have said he was at peace.

A Sensitive Dependence on
Initial Conditions

THE COVERING LAW model of historical explanation states that an event is explained if it can be logically deduced from a set of initial conditions, and a set of general historical laws. These sets are the *explanans*, and the event is the *explanandum*. The general laws are applied to the initial conditions, and the explanandum is shown to be the inevitable result. An explanation, in this model, has the same structure as a prediction.

On the morning of August 6th, 1945, Colonel Paul Tibbetts and his crew flew the *Enola Gay* from Tinian Island to Hiroshima, and dropped an atomic bomb on the city. Approximately a hundred thousand people died. Three days later, another crew dropped a bomb on the outskirts of Nagasaki. Approximately seventy thousand people died. The Japanese surrendered.

President Harry Truman, in consultation with his

advisors, decided to drop the bombs. Why did he make these decisions? Because the Japanese had fiercely defended many islands in the South Pacific, and the cost of conquering them had been high. Kamikaze attacks had sunk many American ships, and it was said that the Japanese would stage a gigantic kamikaze defence of the home islands. Estimated American casualties resulting from an invasion of the home islands ranged as high as a million men.

These were the conditions. General laws? Leaders want to end wars as quickly as possible, with a minimum of bloodshed. They also like to frighten potential postwar enemies. With the war in Europe ended, the Soviet Army stood ready to go wherever Stalin ordered it. No one could be sure where Stalin might want to go. An end to the Japanese war that frightened him would not be a bad thing.

But there were more conditions. The Japanese were defenceless in the air and at sea. American planes could bomb the home islands at will, and a total naval blockade of Japan was entirely possible. The Japanese civilian population was already starving; a blockade, combined with bombing of military sites, could very well have forced the Japanese leaders to surrender without an invasion.

But Truman and his advisors decided to drop the bombs. A complete explanation of the decision, omitted here due to considerations of length, would have to include an examination of the biographies of Truman, his advisors, the builders of the bomb, and the leaders of Japan and the Soviet Union; as well as a detailed analysis of the situation in Japan in 1945, and of

American intelligence concerning that situation.

President Truman was re-elected in 1948, in an upset victory over Thomas Dewey. Two years later the United States went to war in Korea, to keep that country from being overrun by Communists supported by the Soviet Union and China. It was only one of many major wars in the second half of the twentieth century; there were over sixty, and although none of them were nuclear, approximately fifty million people were killed.

Heisenberg's uncertainty principle says that we cannot simultaneously determine both the velocity and the position of a particle. This not a function of human perception, but a basic property of the universe. Thus it will never be possible to achieve a deterministic prediction of the movement of all particles throughout spacetime. Quantum mechanics, which replaced classical mechanics as the best description of these events, can only predict the probabilities among a number of possible outcomes.

The covering law model of historical explanation asserts that there is no logical difference between historical explanation and scientific explanation. But the model's understanding of scientific explanation is based on classical mechanics. In quantum reality, the covering law model breaks down.

The sufficient conditions model of historical explanation is a modification of the covering law model; it states that if one can describe a set of initial conditions that are sufficient (but not necessary) for the event to occur, then the event can be said to be explained. Deduction from general law is not part of this model, which is descriptive rather than prescriptive, and 'seeks only to achieve an acceptable degree of coherent narrative.'

In July of 1945, Colonel Tibbetts was ordered to demonstrate his crew's ability to deliver an atomic weapon, by flying a test mission in the western Pacific. During the takeoff Tibbetts shut down both propellors on the right wing, to show that if this occurred during an armed takeoff, he would still be able to control the plane. The strain of this manoeuvre, however, caused the inboard left engine to fail, and in the emergency return to Tinian the *Enola Gay* crashed, killing everyone aboard.

A replacement crew was chosen from Tibbetts' squadron, and was sent to bomb Hiroshima on August 9th, 1945. During the run over Hiroshima the bombardier, Captain Frank January, deliberately delayed the release of the bomb, so that it missed Hiroshima by some ten miles. Another mission later that week encountered cloud cover, and missed Kokura by accident. January was court-martialled and executed for disobeying orders in battle. The Japanese, having seen the explosions and evaluated the explosion sites, surrendered.

January decided to miss the target because: he had a visionary dream in which he saw the results of the bombing; he had not been in combat for over a year; he was convinced the war was over; he had been in London during the Blitz; he disliked his plane's pilot; he hated Paul Tibbetts; he was a loner, older than his fellow squadron members; he had read the Hornblower stories in the *Saturday Evening Post*; he once saw a truck crash into a car, and watched the truck driver in the aftermath; he was burned on the arm by stove oil when a child; he had an imagination.

The inboard left engine on the *Enola Gay* failed because a worker at the Wright manufacturing plant had failed to keep his welding torch flame on a weld for the required twenty seconds. He stopped three seconds too soon. He stopped three seconds too soon because he was tired. He was tired because the previous night he had stayed up late, drinking with friends.

In 1948, President Truman lost to Thomas Dewey in a close election that was slightly influenced by a political group called the January Society. The Korean conflict was settled by negotiation, and in February of 1956 a treaty was signed in Geneva, banning the use and manufacture of nuclear weapons.

Light behaves like either wave or particle, depending on how it is observed. The famous two-slit experiment, in which interference in wave patterns causes light shining through two slits in a partition to hit a screen in a pattern of light and dark bars, is a good example of this. Even when photons are sent at the slits one at a time, the pattern of light and dark bars still appears, implying that the single quantum of light is passing through both slits at the same time, creating an interference pattern with itself.

History is an interference pattern, says the covering law model. The conditions are particles; the laws are waves.

The necessary conditions model states that historical explanation requires merely identifying the kind of historical event being explained, and then locating among its initial conditions some that seem necessary for the event to take place. No general laws of history can help; one can only locate more necessary conditions. As William Dray writes in *Laws and Explanation in History*, an explanandum is explained when we 'can trace the course of events by which it came about.'

Tibbetts and his crew died in a training flight crash, and the *Lucky Strike* was sent in the *Enola Gay*'s place. The bombardier, Captain Frank January, after much frantic thought on the flight there, performed just as Tibbetts' bombardier would have, and dropped the bomb over the T-shaped Aioi Bridge in Hiroshima. Approximately a hundred thousand people died. Three days later Nagasaki was bombed. The Japanese surrendered. Truman was re-elected. The Korean War led to the Cold War, the assassination of Kennedy on November 22nd, 1963, the Vietnam War, the collapse of the Soviet bloc in the fall of 1989. Replacing one crew with another made no larger difference.

Richard Feynman's notion of a 'sum over histories' proposes that a particle does not move from point A to point B by a single path, as in classical mechanics, but rather by every possible path within the wave. Two numbers describe these possible paths, one describing the size of the wave, the other the path's position in the crest-to-trough cycle. When Pauli's exclusion principle, which states that two particles cannot occupy the same position at the same velocity within the mathematical limits of the uncertainty principle, is applied to the sum over histories, it indicates that some possible paths cause interference patterns, and cancel each other out; other paths are phased in a reinforcing way, which makes their occurrence more probable.

Perhaps history has its own sum over histories, so that all possible histories resemble ours. Perhaps every possible bombardier chooses Hiroshima.

The weak covering law model attempts to rescue the notion of general historical laws by relaxing their rigour, to the point where one can no longer deduce the explanandum from the explanans alone; the laws become not laws but tendencies, which help historians by providing 'guiding threads' between events and their initial conditions. Thus the uncertainty principle is acknowledged, and the covering law model brought into the twentieth century.

But can any historical model explain the twentieth century? Tibbetts crashed, the *Lucky Strike* flew to Hiroshima, and Captain January chose to spare the city. He was executed, the war ended, Dewey won the 1948 election; the Korean conflict was resolved by negotiation; and nuclear weapons were banned by treaty in February of 1956.

But go on. In November of 1956, conflict broke out in the Middle East between Egypt and Israel, and Britain and France quickly entered the conflict to protect their interests in the Suez Canal. President Dewey, soon to be replaced by President-elect Dwight Eisenhower, asked Britain and France to quit the conflict; his request was ignored. The war spread through the Middle East. In December the Soviet Army invaded West Germany. The United States declared war on the Soviet Union. China launched assaults in Indochina, and the Third

World War was under way. Both the United States and the Soviet Union quickly assembled a number of atomic bombs, and in the first week of 1957, Jerusalem, Berlin, Bonn, Paris, London, Warsaw, Leningrad, Prague, Budapest, Beirut, Amman, Cairo, Moscow, Vladivostok, Tokyo, Peking, Los Angeles, Washington, DC and Princeton, New Jersey (hit by a bomb targeted for New York) were destroyed. Loss of life in that week and the year following was estimated at a hundred million people.

At normal energies, the strong nuclear force has a property called confinement, which binds quarks tightly together. At the high energies achieved in particle accelerators, however, the strong nuclear force becomes much weaker, allowing quarks and gluons to jet away almost like free particles. This property of dispersion at high energies is called 'asymptotic freedom'.

History is a particle accelerator. Energies are not always normal. We live in a condition of asymptotic freedom, and every history is possible. Each bombardier has to choose.

In *The Open Society and Its Enemies* Karl Popper writes: 'If two armies are equally well-led and well-armed, and one has an enormous numerical superiority, the other will never win.' Popper made this proposition to demonstrate that any historical law with broad explanatory power would become so general as to be trivial. For the school of thought that agrees with him, there can be no covering laws.

In June of 1945, seven of the scientists who had worked on the Manhattan Project submitted a document called the Franck Report to the Scientific Panel of the Interim Committee, which was overseeing the progress of the bomb. The Franck Report called for a demonstration of the bomb before observers from many countries, including Japan. The Scientific Panel decided this was a possible option and passed the Report on to the Committee, which passed it on to the White House. 'The Buck Stops Here.' Truman read the Report and decided to invite James Franck, Leo Szilard, Niels Bohr, and Albert Einstein to the White House to discuss the issue. Final consultations included Oppenheimer, Secretary of War Stimson, and the military head of the Manhattan Project, General Leslie Groves. After a week's intense debate Truman instructed Stimson to contact the Japanese leadership and arrange a demonstration drop, to be made on one of the uninhabited islands in the Izu Shichito archipelago, south of Tokyo Bay. An atomic bomb was exploded on Udone Shima on August 24th, 1945; the mushroom cloud was visible from Tokyo. Films of the explosion were shown to Emperor Hirohito. The Emperor instructed his government to surrender, which it did on August 31st, one day before Truman had declared he was going to begin bombing Japanese cities.

Truman won the election of 1948. In 1950 north Korean troops invaded the south, until a series of six so-called Shima blasts, each closer to the north's advance forces, stopped them at the 38th parallel. In 1952 Adlai Stevenson became president, and appointed Leo Szilard the first presidential science advisor. In 1953 Stalin died, and in 1956 Szilard was sent to Moscow for a consultation with Khrushchev. This meeting led to the founding of the

International Peace Brigade, which sent internationally integrated teams of young people to work in underdeveloped countries and in countries still recovering from World War Two. In 1960 John Kennedy was elected president, and he was succeeded in 1968 by his brother Robert. In 1976, in the wake of scandals in the administration, Richard Nixon was elected. At this point in time the postwar period is usually considered to have ended. The century itself came to a close without any further large wars. Though there had been a number of local conflicts, the existence of nuclear weapons had ended war as practised in the first half of the century. In the second half, only about five million people died in war.

The great man theory considers particles; historical materialism considers waves. The wave/particle duality, confirmed many times by experiment, assures us that neither theory can be the complete truth. Neither theory will serve as the covering law.

The defenders of the covering law model reply to its various critiques by stating that it is irrelevant whether historians actually use the model or not; the fact remains that they *should*. If they do not, then an event like 'the bottle fell off the table' could be explained by either 'the cat's tail brushed it', or 'the cat looked at it cross-eyed', and there would be no basis for choosing between the two explanations. Historical explanation is not just a matter of the practice of historians, but of the nature of reality. And in reality, physical events are constrained by general laws – or if they are not laws, they are at least extraordinarily detailed descriptions of the links between an event and those that follow it, allowing predictions that, if not deterministically exact, are still accurate enough to give us enormous power over physical reality. That, for anyone but followers of David Hume, serves as law enough. And humans, as part of the stuff of the universe, are subject to the same physical laws that control all the rest of it. So it makes sense to seek a science of history, and to try to formulate some general historical laws.

What would these general laws look like? Some examples:

If two armies are equally well-led and well-armed, and one has an enormous numerical superiority, the other will never win.

A privileged group will never relinquish privilege voluntarily.

Empires rise, flourish, fall and are replaced, in a cyclical pattern.

A nation's fortunes depend on its success in war.

A society's culture is determined by its economic system.

Belief systems exist to disguise inequality.

Lastly, unparalleled in both elegance and power, subsuming many of the examples listed above: power corrupts.

So there do seem to be some quite powerful laws of historical explanation. But consider another:

For want of a nail, the battle was lost.

For instance: on July 29th, 1945, a nomad in Kirgiz walked out of his yurt and stepped on a butterfly. For lack of the butterfly flapping its wings, the wind in the area blew slightly less. A low pressure front therefore moved over east China more slowly than it would have.

And so on August 6th, when the *Enola Gay* flew over Hiroshima, it was covered by ninety per cent cloud cover, instead of fifty per cent. Colonel Tibbetts flew to the secondary target, Nagasaki; it was also covered. The *Enola Gay* had little fuel left, but its crew was able to fly over Kokura on the way back to Tinian, and taking advantage of a break in the clouds, they dropped the bomb there. Ninety thousand people died in Kokura. The *Enola Gay* landed at Tinian with so little fuel left in its tanks that what remained 'wouldn't have filled a cigarette lighter.' On August 9th a second mission tried Hiroshima again, but the clouds were still there, and the mission eventually dropped the bomb on the less heavily clouded secondary target, Nagasaki, missing the city centre and killing only twenty thousand people. The Japanese surrendered a week later.

On August 11th, 1945, a child named Ai Matsui was born in Hiroshima. In 1960 she began to speak in local meetings on many topics, including Hiroshima's special position in the world. Its citizens had escaped annihilation, she said, as if protected by some covering angel (or law); they had a responsibility to the dead of Kokura and Nagasaki, to represent them in the world of the living, to change the world for the good. The Hiroshima Peace Party quickly grew to become the dominant political movement in Hiroshima, and then, in revulsion at the violence of the 1960s in Vietnam and elsewhere, all over Japan. In the 1970s the party became a worldwide movement, gaining the enthusiastic support of ex-President Kennedy, and President Babbitt. Young people from every country joined it as if experiencing a religious conversion. In 1983 Japan began its Asian Assistance League. One of its health care programmes saved the life of a young woman in India, sick with malaria. The next year she had a child, a woman destined to become India's greatest leader. In 1987, the nation of Palestine raised its flag over the West Bank and parts of Jordan and Lebanon; a generation of camp children moved into homes. A child was born in Galilee. In 1990 Japan started its African Assistance League. The Hiroshima Peace Party had a billion members.

And so on; so that by July 29th, 2045, no human on Earth was the same as those who would have lived if the nomad in Kirgiz had not stepped on the butterfly a century before.

This phenomenon is known as the butterfly effect, and it is a serious problem for all other models of historical explanation; meaning trouble for you and for me. The scientific term for it is 'sensitive dependence on initial conditions'. It is an aspect of chaos theory first studied by the meteorologist Edward Lorenz, who, while running computer simulations of weather patterns, discovered that the slightest change in the initial conditions of the simulation would quickly lead to completely different weather.

So the strong covering law model said that historical explanation should equal the rigour of scientific explanation. Then its defenders, bringing the model into the quantum world, conceded that predictions can never be anything but probabilistic at best. The explanandum was no longer deducible from the explanans; one could only suggest probabilities.

Now chaos theory has added new problems. And yet

consider: Captain Frank January chose to miss Hiroshima. Ten years later, nuclear weapons were universally banned. Eleven years later, local conflicts in the Middle East erupted into general war, and nuclear weapons were quickly reassembled and used. For it is not easy to forget knowledge, once it is learned; symmetry T, which says that physical laws are the same no matter which way the time arrow is pointed, does not actually exist in nature. There is no going back.

And so by 1990, in this particular world, the bombed cities were rebuilt. The Western industrial nations were rich, the southern developing nations were poor. Multinational corporations ruled the world's economy. The Soviet bloc was falling apart. Gigantic sums of money were spent on armaments. By the year 2056, there was very little to distinguish this world from the one in which January had dropped the bomb, in which Tibbetts had bombed Hiroshima, in which Tibbetts had made a demonstration, in which Tibbetts bombed Kokura.

Perhaps a sum over histories had bunched the probabilities. Is this likely? We don't know. We are particles, moving in a wave. The wave breaks. No maths can predict which bubbles will appear where. But there is a sum over histories. Chaotic systems fall into patterns, following the pull of strange attractors. Linear chaotic figures look completely non-repetitive, but slice them into Poincaré sections and they reveal the simplest kinds of patterns. There is a tide, and we float in it; perhaps it is the flux of the cosmos itself; swim this way or that, the tide still carries us to the same destination. Perhaps.

*   *   *

So the covering law model is amended yet again. Explanations still require laws, but there are not laws for every event. The task of historical explanation becomes the act of making distinctions, between those parts of an event that can be explained by laws, and those that cannot. The component events that combine to create an explanandum are analysed each in turn, and the historian then concentrates on the explicable components.

Paul Tibbetts flies towards Hiroshima. The nomad steps out of his yurt.

Lyapunov exponents are numbers that measure the conflicting effects of stretching, contracting, and folding in the phase space of an attractor. They set the topological parameters of unpredictability. An exponent greater than zero means stretching, so that each alternative history moves farther and farther apart as time passes. An exponent smaller than zero means contraction, so that alternatives tend to come back together. When the exponent equals zero, a periodic orbit results.

What is history's Lyapunov exponent? This is the law that no one can know.

Frank January flies towards Hiroshima. The nomad stops in his yurt.

It is said that the historian's task requires an imaginative reconstruction of the thinking of people who acted in the past, and of the circumstances in which they acted. 'An explanation is said to be successful when the historian gets the sense of reliving the past which he is trying to explain.'

You are flying towards Hiroshima. You are the

bombardier. You have been given the assignment two days before. You know what the bomb will do. You do not know what you will do. You have to decide.

There are a hundred billion neurons in the brain. Some of the neurons have as many as eighty thousand synaptic endings. During thought, neurotransmitter chemicals flow across the synaptic clefts between one neuron's synaptic knobs and another's dendritic spines, reversing a slight electric charge, which passes on a signal. The passage of a signal often leaves changes in the synapses and dendrites along the way, forever altering the structure of the brain. This plasticity makes memory and learning possible. Brains are always growing; intensely in the first five years, then steadily thereafter.

At the moment of choice, then, signals fly through a neural network that has been shaped over a lifetime into a particular and unique structure. Some signals are conscious, others are not. According to Roger Penrose, during the process of decision quantum effects in the brain take over, allowing a great number of parallel and simultaneous computations to take place; the number could be extraordinarily large, 10^{21} or more. Only at the intrusion of the 'observation', that is to say a decision, do the parallel computations resolve back into a single conscious thought.

And in the act of deciding, the mind attempts the work of the historian: breaking the potential events down into their component parts, enumerating conditions, seeking covering laws that will allow a prediction of what will follow from the variety of possible choices. Alternative futures branch like dendrites away from the present moment, shifting chaotically, pulled this way and that by attractors dimly perceived. Probable outcomes emerge from those less likely.

And then, in the myriad clefts of the quantum mind, a mystery: the choice is made. We have to choose, that is life in time. Some powerful selection process, perhaps aesthetic, perhaps moral, perhaps practical (survival of the thinker), shoves to consciousness those plans that seem safest, or most right, or most beautiful, we do not know; and the choice is made. And at the moment of this observation the great majority of alternatives disappear without trace, leaving us in our asymptotic freedom to act, uncertainly, in time's assymetrical flow.

There are few covering laws. Initial conditions are never fully known. The butterfly may be on the wing, it may be crushed underfoot. You are flying towards Hiroshima.

Discovering Life

THE FINAL APPROACH to the Jet Propulsion Laboratory, a narrow road running up the flank of the ugly brown mountains overlooking Los Angeles, is a fine road in ordinary circumstances, but when something newsworthy occurs it is inadequate to handle the influx of media visitors. On this morning the line of cars and trailers extended down from the security gate almost to the freeway offramp, and Bill Dawkins watched the temperature gauge of his old Ford Escort rise as he inched forward, all the vehicles adding to the smog that already made the air a tangible grey mist. Eventually he passed the security guards and drove up to the employee parking lot, then walked down past the guest parking lot, overflowing with TV trailers topped by satellite dishes. Surely every language and nation in the world was represented, all bringing their own equipment of course.

Inside the entry building Bill turned right and looked in the press conference room, also jammed to overflowing. A row of Bill's colleagues sat up on the stage behind a long table crowded with mikes, facing the cameras and lights and reporters. Bill's friend Mike Collinsworth was answering a question about contamination, trying to look like he was enjoying himself. But very few scientists like other scientists listening in on them when they are explaining things to non-scientists, because then there is someone there to witness just how gross their gross simplifications are; so an affair like this was in its very nature embarrassing. And to complicate the situation this press corps was a very mixed crowd, ranging from experts who in some senses (social context, historical background) knew more than the scientists themselves, all the way to TV faces who could barely read their prompters. That, plus the emotional load of the subject matter amounting almost to hysteria, gave the event an excruciating quality that Bill found perversely fascinating to watch.

A telegenic young woman got the nod from John and took the radio mike being passed around. 'What does this discovery mean to you?' she said. 'What do you think the meaning of this discovery will be?'

The seven men on stage looked at each other, and the crowd laughed. John said, 'Mike?' and Mike made a face that got another laugh. But John knew his crew; Mike was a smartass in real life, indeed Bill could imagine some of his characteristic answers scorching the air: it means I have to answer stupid questions in front of billions of people, it means I can stop working eighty-hour weeks and see what a real life is like again; but

Mike was also good at the PR stuff, and with a straight face he answered the second of the questions, which Bill would have thought was the harder of the two.

'Well, the meaning of it depends, to some extent, on what the exobiologists find out when they investigate the organisms more fully. If the organisms follow the same biochemical principles as life on Earth, then it's possible they are a kind of cousin to Terran life, bounced on meteorites from Mars to here, or here to Mars. If that's the case then it's possible that DNA analysis will even be able to determine about when the two families parted company, and which planet has the older population. We may find out that we're all Martians originally.'

He waited for the obligatory laugh. 'On the other hand, the investigation may show a completely alien biochemistry, indicating a separate origin. That's a very different scenario.' Now Mike paused, realizing he was at the edge of his soundbite envelope, also of deep waters. He decided to cut it short: 'Either way that turns out, we'll know that life is very adaptable, and that it can either cross space between planets, or begin twice in the same solar system, so either way we'll be safer in assuming that life is fairly widespread in the universe.'

Bill smiled. Mike was good; the answer provided a quick summary of the situation, bullet points, potential headlines: 'Bacteria On Mars Proves Life is Common in the Universe.' Which wasn't exactly true, but there was no winning the soundbite game.

Bill left the room and crossed the little plaza, then entered the big building forming the north flank of the compound. Upstairs the little offices and cubicles all had their doors open and portable TVs on, all tuned to the press conference just a hundred yards away; there was a holiday atmosphere, including streamers and balloons, but Bill couldn't feel it somehow. There on the screens under the CNN logo his friends were being played up as heroes, young devoted rocket scientists replacing astronauts by necessity as the exploration of Mars proceeded robotically – silly, but very much preferable to the situation when things went wrong, when they were portrayed as harried geek rocket scientists not quite up to the task, the extremely important (though underfunded) task of teleoperating the exploration of the cosmos from their desks. They had played both roles several times at JPL, and had come to understand that for the media, and perhaps the public, there was no middle ground, no recognition that they were just people doing their jobs, difficult but interesting jobs in difficult but not intolerable circumstances. No, for the world they were a biannual nine-hours' wonder, either nerdy heroes or nerdy goats, and the next day forgotten. That was just the way it was, and not what was bothering Bill. He felt at loose ends. Mission accomplished, his TO DO list almost empty; it left him feeling somewhat empty; but that was not it either. He still had phone and e-mail media questions waiting, and he worked through those on automatic pilot, his answers honed by the previous week's work. The lander had drilled down and secured a soil sample from under the sands at the mouth of Shalbatana Vallis, where thermal sensors had detected heat from a volcanic vent, which meant the permafrost ice in that region had liquid percolations in it. The sample had been placed in a metal sphere which had been hermetically sealed and boosted to Martian orbit. After a rendezvous with an orbiter it had been flown back to Earth and been released in such a manner that it had dropped into Earth's atmosphere without orbiting at all, and slammed into Utah's Dugway Proving Grounds a mere ten yards from its target. An artificial meteorite, yes. No, the ball could not have broken on impact, it had been engineered for that impact, indeed could have withstood striking a sidewalk or a wall of steel, and had been recovered intact in the little crater it had made – recovered by robot and flown robotically to Johnson Space Center in Houston, where it had been placed inside hermetically sealed chambers in sealed labs in sealed buildings before being opened, everything having been designed for just this purpose. No, they did not need to sterilize Dugway, or all of Utah, they did not need to nuke Houston (not to kill Martian bacteria anyway), and all was well; the alien life was safely locked away and could not get out. People were safe.

Bill answered a lot of questions like these, feeling that there were many people out there who badly needed a better education in risk assessment. They got in their cars and drove on freeways, smoking cigarettes and holding high-energy radio transmitters against their heads, in order to get to newsrooms where they were greatly concerned to find out if they were in danger from microbacteria locked away behind triple hermetic seals in Houston. By the time Bill broke for lunch he was feeling more depressed than irritated. People were ignorant, short-sighted, poorly educated, fearful, superstitious;

deeply meshed in magical thinking of all kinds. And yet that too was not really what was bothering him.

Mike was in the cafeteria, hungrily downing his lunchtime array of flavinoids and anti-oxidants, and Bill joined him, feeling cheered. Mike was giving them a low-voiced recap of the morning's press conference (many journalists were in the JPL cafeteria on guest passes), 'What is the meaning of life?' Mike whispered urgently, 'it means metabolism, it means hunger at lunchtime, please God let us eat, that's what it means.' Then the TVs overhead began to show the press conference in Houston, and like everyone else they watched and listened to the tiny figures on the screen. The exobiologists at Johnson Space Center were making their initial report: the Martian bacteria were around one hundred nanometres long, bigger than the fossil nanobacteria tentatively identified in ALH 84001, but smaller than most Terran bacteria; they were single-celled, they contained proteins, ribosomes, DNA strands composed of base pairs of adenine, thymine, guanine, and cytosine –

'Cousins,' Mike declared.

– the DNA resembled certain Terran organisms like the Columbia Basement archaea *Methanospirillum jacobii*, thus possibly they were the descendant of a common ancestor . . .

'Cousins!'

– very possibly mitochondrial DNA analysis would reveal when the split had happened. 'Separated at birth,' one of the Johnson scientists offered, to laughter. They were just like the JPL scientists in their on-screen performances. Spontaneous generation versus panspermia, frequent transpermia between Earth and Mars; all these concepts poured out in a half-digested rush, and people would still be calling for the nuclear destruction of Houston and Utah in order to save the world from alien infection, from andromeda strains, from fictional infections – infictions, as Mike said with a grin.

The Johnson scientists nattered on solemnly, happy still to be in the limelight; it had been an oddity of NASA policy to place the Mars effort so entirely at JPL, in effect concentrating one of the major endeavours of human history into one small university lab, with many competing labs out there like baby birds in the federal nest, ready to peck JPL's eyes out if given the chance. Now the exobiology teams at Johnson and AMES were finally involved, and it was no longer just JPL's show, although they were still headquarters and had engineered the sample-return operation just as they had all the previous Martian landers. This diffusion of the project was a relief of course, but could also be seen as a disappointment – the end of an era. But no – watching the TV Bill could tell that wasn't what was bothering him either.

Mike returned with Bill and Nassim to their offices, and they continued to watch the Johnson press conference on a desk TV in Nassim's. Apparently the sample contained more than one species, perhaps as many as five, maybe more. They just didn't know yet. They thought they could keep them all alive in Mars jars, but weren't sure. They were sure that they had the organisms contained, and that there was no danger.

Someone asked about ramifications for the human exploration of Mars, and the answers were scattered.

'Very severely problematized,' someone said; it would be a matter for discussion at the very highest levels, NASA of course but also NSF, the National Academy of Sciences, the International Astronomical Union, various UN bodies – in short, the scientific government of the world.

Mike laughed. 'The human mission people must be freaking out.'

Nassim nodded. 'The Ad Martem Club has already declared that these things are only bacteria, like bathroom scum, we kill billions of them every day, they're no impediment to us conquering Mars.'

'They can't be serious.'

'They are serious, but crazy. We won't be setting foot there for a very long time. If ever.'

Suddenly Bill understood. 'That would be sad,' he said. 'I'm a humans-to-Mars guy myself.'

Mike grinned and shook his head. 'You better not be in too much of a hurry.'

Bill went back in his office. He cleaned up a little, then called Eleanor's office, wanting to talk to her, wanting to say We did it, the mission is a success and the dream has therefore been shattered, but she wasn't in. He left a message that he would be home around the usual time, then concentrated on his TO DO list, no longer adding things to the bottom faster than he took them off at the top, trying to occupy his mind but failing. The realization was sinking in that he had always thought that their work was about going to Mars, about making a better world there; this was how he had justified everything about his life, the killing hours of the job, the looks on his family's faces, Eleanor's fully sympathetic but disappointed, frustrated that it had turned out this way, the two of them caught despite their best efforts in a kind of 1950s marriage, the husband gone all day every day – except of course that Eleanor worked long hours too, so that their kids had always been daycare and after-school care kids, all day every weekday. Once Bill had dropped Joe, their younger one, off at daycare on a Monday morning, and looking back in through the window he had seen an expression on the boy's face – of abandonment and stoic solitude, of facing another ten hours at the same old place, to be gotten through somehow like everyone else – a look which on the face of a three-year-old had pierced Bill to the heart. And all that – all the time he had put in, all those days and years, had been so that one day humans would inhabit Mars and make a decent civilization at last; his whole life burned in a cubicle because the start of this great project was so tenuous, because so few people believed or understood, so that it was down to them, one little lab trying its best to execute the 'faster better cheaper' plan which contained within it (as they often pointed out) a contradiction of the second law of thermodynamics among other problems, a plan that they knew could only really achieve two out of the three qualities in any real-world combination, but making the attempt anyway, finding that the only true 'cheaper' involved was the cost of their own labour and the quality of their own lives, rocket scientists running like squirrels in cages to make the inhabitation of Mars a reality – a project which only the future Martians of some distant century would truly appreciate and honour. Except now there weren't going to be any future Martians.

Then it was after six, and he was out in the evening smog with Mike and Nassim, carpooling home. They got on the 210 freeway and rolled along quite nicely until the carpool lane stalled with all the rest, because of the intersection of 210 and 110; and then they were into stop-and-go like everyone else, the long lines of cars brake-lighting forward in that accordion pattern of acceleration and deceleration so familiar to them all. The average speed on the LA freeway system was now eleven miles per hour, low enough to make them and many other Angelenos try the surface streets instead, but Nassim's computer modelling and their empirical trials had made it clear that for any drive over five miles long the clogged freeways were still faster than the clogged streets.

'Well, another red letter day,' Mike announced, and pulled a bottle of Scotch from his daypack. He snapped open the cap and took a swig, then passed the bottle to Bill and Nassim. This was something he did on ceremonial occasions, after all the great JPL successes or disasters, and though both Bill and Nassim found it alarming, they did not refuse quick pulls. Mike took another one before twisting the cap very tightly on the bottle and stuffing it back inside his daypack, actions which appeared to give him the feeling he had returned the bottle to a legally sealed state. Bill and Nassim had mocked him before for this belief, and now Nassim said,

'Why don't you just carry a little soldering iron with you so you can reseal it properly.'

'Ha ha.'

'Or adopt the NASA solution,' Bill said, 'take your swigs and then throw the bottle overboard.'

'Ha ha, now don't be biting the hand that feeds you.'

'That's the hand people always bite.'

Mike stared at him. 'You're not happy about this big discovery, are you, Bill.'

'No!' Bill said, sitting there with his foot on the brake. 'No! I always thought we were the, the bringing of the inhabitation of Mars. I thought that people would go on to live there, and terraform the planet, you know, establish a whole world there, a second strand of history, and we would always be back at the start of it all. And now these damn bacteria are there already, and we may never land there at all. We'll stay here and leave Mars to the Martians, the bacterial Martians –'

'The little red natives –'

'And so we're at the start of nothing! We're the start of a dead end.'

'Balderdash,' Mike said.

And Bill's spirits rose a bit; he felt a glow like the Scotch run through him; he may have slaved away in a cubicle burning ten years of his life on the start of a dead-end project, a project that would never be enacted, but at least he had been able to work on it with people like these, like brothers to him now after all the years, brilliant weird guys who would use the word 'balderdash' in conversation in all seriousness, because (in Mike's case) he read Victorian boy's literature for his entertainment, among other odd habits, a guy who had not in the slightest way appeared on TV while playing the Earnest Rocket Scientist, playing a stupid role created by the media's questions and expectations, all of them playing their stupid roles in precisely the stupid soap opera that Bill had dreamed they were going to escape someday, What does life mean to you, Dr Labcoat, what does this discovery mean, Well, it means we have burned up our lives on a dead-end project, 'What do you mean balderdash!' Bill exclaimed. 'They'll make Mars a nature preserve! a bacterial nature preserve, for God's sake! No one will risk even landing there, much less terraforming the place!'

'Sure they will,' Mike said. 'People will go there. Eventually. They'll settle, they'll terraform – just like you've been dreaming. It might take longer than you were thinking, but you were never going to be one of the ones going anyway, so what's the rush? It'll happen.'

'I don't think so,' Bill said.

'Sure it will. Whichever way it happens it'll happen.'

'Oh thank you! Thank you very much! Whichever way it happens it'll happen? That's so very helpful!'

'Not your most testable hypothesis,' Nassim noted.

Mike grinned. 'You don't have to test it, it's that good.'

Harshly, Bill laughed, 'Too bad you didn't tell the reporter that! Whatever happens will happen! This discovery means whatever it means!' and then they were all cackling, 'This discovery means that there's life on Mars!' 'This discovery means whatever you want it to mean!' 'That's how meaning always means!'

Their mirth subsided. They were still stuck in stop-and-go traffic, in the rows of red blinks on the vast viaduct slashing through the city, under a sour milk sky.

'Well, shit,' Mike said, waving at the view. 'I guess we'll just have to terraform Earth instead.'

Venice Drowned

BY THE TIME Carlo Tafur struggled out of sleep, the baby was squalling, the teapot whistled, the smell of stove smoke filled the air. Wavelets slapped the walls of the floor below. It was just dawn. Reluctantly he untangled himself from the bedsheets and got up. He padded through the other room of his home, ignoring his wife and child, and walked out the door onto the roof.

Venice looked best at dawn, Carlo thought as he pissed into the canal. In the dim mauve light it was possible to imagine that the city was just as it always had been, that hordes of visitors would come flooding down the Grand Canal on this fine summer morning ... Of course, one had to ignore the patchwork constructions built on the roofs of the neighbourhood to indulge the fancy. Around the church – San Giacomo du Rialto – all the buildings had even their top floors awash, and so it had been necessary to break up the tile roofs, and erect shacks on the roofbeams made of materials fished up from below: wood, brick, lath, stone, metal, glass. Carlo's home was one of these shacks, made of a crazy combination of wood beams, stained glass from San Giacometta, and drainpipes beaten flat. He looked back at it and sighed. It was best to look off over the Rialto, where the red sun blazed over the bulbous domes of San Marco.

'You have to meet those Japanese today,' Carlo's wife, Luisa, said from inside.

'I know.' Visitors still came to Venice, that was certain.

'And don't go insulting them and rowing off without your pay,' she went on, her voice sounding clearly out of the doorway, 'like you did with those Hungarians. It really doesn't matter what they take from under the water, you know. That's the past. That old stuff isn't doing anyone any good under there, anyway.'

'Shut up,' he said wearily. 'I know.'

'I have to buy stovewood and vegetables and toilet paper and socks for the baby,' she said. 'The Japanese are the best customers you've got; you'd better treat them well.'

Carlo reentered the shack and walked into the bedroom to dress. Between putting on one boot and the next he stopped to smoke a cigarette, the last one in the house. While smoking he stared at his pile of books on the floor, his library as Luisa sardonically called the collection: all books about Venice. They were tattered, dog-eared, mildewed, so warped by the damp that none of them would close properly, and each mouldy page was as wavy as the Lagoon on a windy day. They were a miserable sight, and Carlo gave the closest stack a kick with his cold boot as he returned to the other room.

'I'm off,' he said, giving his baby and then Luisa a kiss. 'I'll be back late – they want to go to Torcello.'

'What could they want up there?'

He shrugged. 'Maybe just to see it.' He ducked out the door.

Below the roof was a small square where the boats of the neighbourhood were moored. Carlo slipped off the tile onto the narrow floating dock he and the neighbours had built, and crossed to his boat, a wide-beamed sailboat with a canvas deck. He stepped in, unmoored it, and rowed out of the square onto the Grand Canal.

Once on the Grand Canal he tipped the oars out of the water and let the boat drift downstream. The big canal had always been the natural course of the channel through the mud flats of the Lagoon; for a while it had been tamed, but now it was a river again, its banks made of tile rooftops and stone palaces, with hundreds of tributaries flowing into it. Men were working on roof-houses in the early morning light. Those who knew Carlo waved, hammers or rope in hand, and shouted hello. Carlo wiggled an oar perfunctorily before he was swept past. It was foolish to build so close to the Grand Canal, which now had the strength to knock the old structures down, and often did. But that was their business. In Venice they were all fools, if one thought about it.

Then he was in the Basin of San Marco, and he rowed through the Piazzetta beside the Doges' Palace, which was still imposing at two storeys high, to the Piazza. Traffic was heavy as usual. It was the only place in Venice that still had the crowds of old, and Carlo enjoyed it for that reason, though he shouted curses as loudly as anyone when gondolas streaked in front of him. He jockeyed his way to the basilica window and rowed in.

Under the brilliant blue and gold of the domes it was noisy. Most of the water in the rooms had been covered with a floating dock. Carlo moored his boat to it, heaved his four scuba tanks on, and clambered up after them. Carrying two tanks in each hand he crossed the dock, on which the fish market was in full swing. Displayed for sale were flats of mullet, lagoon sharks, tunny, skates, and flatfish. Clams were piled in trays, their shells gleaming in the shaft of sunlight from the stained-glass east window; men and women pulled live crabs out of holes in the dock, risking fingers in the crab-jammed traps; fishermen bawled out prices, and insulted the freshness of their neighbours' product.

In the middle of the fish market, Ludovico Salerno, one of Carlo's best friends, had his stalls of scuba gear. Carlo's two Japanese customers were there. He greeted them and handed his tanks to Salerno, who began refilling them from his machine. They conversed in quick, slangy Italian while the tanks filled. When they were done, Carlo paid him and led the Japanese back to his boat. They got in and stowed their backpacks under the canvas decking while Carlo pulled the scuba tanks on board.

'We are ready to voyage at Torcello?' one asked, and the other smiled and repeated the question. Their names

were Hamada and Taku. They had made a few jokes
concerning the latter name's similarity to Carlo's own,
but Taku was the one with less Italian, so the sallies
hadn't gone on for long. They had hired him four days
before, at Salerno's stall.

'Yes,' Carlo said. He rowed out of the Piazza and up
back canals past Campo San Maria Formosa, which was
nearly as crowded as the Piazza. Beyond that the canals
were empty, and only an occasional roof-house marred
the look of flooded tranquillity.

'That part of city Venice here not many people live,'
Hamada observed. 'Not houses on houses.'

'That's true,' Carlo replied. As he rowed past San
Zanipolo and the hospital, he explained, 'It's too close
to the hospital here, where many diseases were
contained. Sicknesses, you know.'

'Ah, the hospital!' Hamada nodded, as did Taku. 'We
have swam hospital in our Venice voyage previous to
that one here. Salvage many fine statues from lowest
rooms.'

'Stone lions,' Taku added. 'Many stone lions with
wings in room below Twenty-forty waterline.'

'Is that right,' Carlo said. Stone lions, he thought, set
up in the entryway of some Japanese businessman's
expensive home around the world . . . He tried to divert
his thoughts by watching the brilliantly healthy, mask-
like faces of his two passengers as they laughed over
their reminiscences.

Then they were over the Fondamente Nuova, the
northern limit of the city, and on the Lagoon. There
was a small swell from the north. Carlo rowed out a
way and then stepped forward to raise the boat's single

sail. The wind was from the east, so they would make good time north to Torcello. Behind them Venice looked beautiful in the morning light, as if they were miles away, and a watery horizon blocked their full view of it.

The two Japanese had stopped talking and were looking over the side. They were over the cemetery of San Michele, Carlo realized. Below them lay the island that had been the city's chief cemetery for centuries; they sailed over a field of tombs, mausoleums, gravestones, obelisks that at low tide could be a navigational hazard ... Just enough of the bizarre white blocks could be seen to convince one that they were indeed the result of the architectural thinking of fishes. Carlo crossed himself quickly to impress his customers, and sat back down at the tiller. He pulled the sail tight and they heeled over slightly, slapped into the waves.

In no more than twenty minutes they were east of Murano, skirting its edge. Murano, like Venice an island city crossed with canals, had been a quaint little town before the flood. But it didn't have as many tall buildings as Venice, and it was said that an underwater river had undercut its islands. In any case, it was a wreck. The two Japanese chattered with excitement.

'Can we visit to that city here, Carlo?' asked Hamada.

'It's too dangerous,' Carlo answered. 'Buildings have fallen into the canal.'

They nodded, smiling. 'Are people live here?' Taku asked.

'A few, yes. They live in the highest buildings on the floors still above water, and work in Venice. That way they avoid having to build a roof-house in the city.'

The two faces of his companions expressed incomprehension.

'They avoid the housing shortage in Venice,' Carlo said. 'There's a certain housing shortage in Venice, as you may have noticed.' His listeners caught the joke this time and laughed.

'Could live on floors below if owning scuba such as that here,' Hamada said, gesturing at Carlo's equipment.

'Yes,' he replied. 'Or we could grow gills.' He bugged his eyes out and wiggled his fingers at his neck to indicate gills. The Japanese loved it.

Past Murano the Lagoon was clear for a few miles, a sunbeaten blue covered with choppy waves. The boat tipped up and down, the wind tugged at the sail cord in Carlo's hand. He began to enjoy himself. 'Storm coming,' he volunteered to the others, and pointed at the black line over the horizon to the north. It was a common sight; short, violent storms swept over Brenner Pass from the Austrian Alps, dumping on the Po Valley and the Lagoon before dissipating in the Adriatic ... once a week, or more, even in the summer. That was one reason the fish market was held under the domes of San Marco; everyone had gotten sick of trading in the rain.

Even the Japanese recognized the clouds. 'Many rain fall soon here,' Taku said.

Hamada grinned and said, 'Taku and Tafur, weather prophets no doubt, make big company!'

They laughed. 'Does he do this in Japan, too?' Carlo asked.

'Yes, indeed, surely. In Japan rains every day – Taku says, "It rains tomorrow for surely." Weather prophet!'

After the laughter receded, Carlo said, 'Hasn't all the rain drowned some of your cities too?'

'What's that here?'

'Don't you have some Venices in Japan?'

But they didn't want to talk about that. 'I don't understand . . . No, no Venice in Japan,' Hamada said easily, but neither laughed as they had before. They sailed on. Venice was out of sight under the horizon, as was Murano. Soon they would reach Burano. Carlo guided the boat over the waves and listened to his companions converse in their improbable language, or mangle Italian in a way that alternately made him want to burst with hilarity or bite the gunwale with frustration.

Gradually Burano bounced over the horizon, the campanile first, followed by the few buildings still above water. Murano still had inhabitants, a tiny market, even a midsummer festival; Burano was empty. Its campanile stood at a distinct angle, like the mast of a foundered ship. It had been an island town, before 2040; now it had 'canals' between every rooftop. Carlo disliked the town intensely and gave it a wide berth. His companions discussed it quietly in Japanese.

Just beyond it was Torcello, another island ghost town. The campanile could be seen from Burano, tall and white against the black clouds to the north. They approached in silence. Carlo took down the sail, set Taku in the bow to look for snags, and rowed cautiously to the edge of town. They moved between rooftops and walls that stuck up like reefs or like old foundations out of the earth. Many of the roof tiles and beams had been taken for use in construction back in Venice. This had happened to Torcello before. During the Renaissance it had been a little rival of Venice, boasting a population of twenty thousand, but during the sixteenth and seventeenth centuries it had been entirely deserted. Builders from Venice had come looking in the ruins for good marble or a staircase of the right dimensions . . . Briefly a tiny population had returned, to make lace and host those tourists who wanted to be melancholy; but the waters rose, and Torcello died for good. Carlo pushed off a wall with his oar, and a big section of it tilted over and sank. He tried not to notice.

He rowed them to the open patch of water that had been the Piazza. Around them stood a few intact rooftops, no taller than the mast of their boat; broken walls of stone or rounded brick; the shadowy suggestion of walls just underwater. It was hard to tell what the street plan of the town would have been. On one side of the Piazza was the cathedral of Santa Maria Assunta, however, still supporting the white campanile that stood square and solid, as if over a living community.

'That here is the church we desire to dive,' Hamada said.

Carlo nodded. The amusement he had felt during the sail was entirely gone. He rowed around the Piazza looking for a flat spot where they could stand and put on the scuba gear. The church outbuildings – it had been an extensive structure – were all underwater. At one point the boat's keel scraped the ridge of a roof. They rowed down the length of the barnlike nave, looked in the high windows: floored with water. No surprise. One of the small windows in the side of the campanile had been widened with sledgehammers. Directly inside it was the stone staircase and, a few steps up, a stone floor. They hooked the boat to the wall and moved their gear up to the floor. In the dim midday light the stone of the interior was pocked with shadows. It had a rough-hewn look. The citizens of Torcello had built the campanile in a hurry, thinking that the world would end at the millennium, the year 1000. Carlo smiled to think how much longer they had had than that. They climbed the steps of the staircase, up to the sudden sunlight of the bell chamber, to look around; viewed Burano, Venice in the distance ... to the north, the shallows of the Lagoon, and the coast of Italy. Beyond that, the black line of clouds was like a wall nearly submerged under the horizon, but it was rising; the storm would come.

They descended, put on the scuba gear, and flopped into the water beside the campanile. They were above the complex of church buildings, and it was dark. Carlo slowly led the two Japanese back into the Piazza and swam down. The ground was silted, and Carlo was careful not to step on it. His charges saw the great stone chair in the centre of the Piazza (it had been called the Throne of Attila, Carlo remembered from one of his mouldy books, and no one had known why), and waving to each other they swam to it. One of them made ludicrous attempts to stand on the bottom and walk around in his fins; he threw up clouds of silt. The other joined him. They each sat in the stone chair, columns of bubbles rising from them, and snapped pictures of each other with their underwater cameras. The silt would ruin the shots, Carlo thought. While they cavorted, he wondered sourly what they wanted in the church.

Eventually, Hamada swam up to him and gestured at the church. Behind the mask his eyes were excited. Carlo pumped his fins up and down slowly and led them around to the big entrance at the front. The doors were gone. They swam into the church.

Inside it was dark, and all three of them unhooked their big flashlights and turned them on. Cones of murky water turned to crystal as the beams swept about. The interior of the church was undistinguished, the floor thick with mud. Carlo watched his two customers swim about and let his flashlight beam rove the walls. Some of the underwater windows were still intact, an odd sight. Occasionally the beam caught a column of bubbles, transmuting them to silver.

Quickly enough the Japanese went to the picture at the west end of the nave, a tile mosaic. Taku (Carlo guessed) rubbed the slime off the tiles, vastly improving their colour. They had gone to the big one first, the one portraying the Crucifixion, the Resurrection of the Dead, and the Day of Judgement. A busy mural. Carlo swam over to have a better look. But no sooner had the Japanese wiped the wall clean than they were off to the other end of the church, where above the stalls of the apse was another mosaic. Carlo followed.

It didn't take long to rub this one clean; and when the water had cleared, the three of them floated there, their flashlight beams converged on the picture revealed.

It was the Teotaca Madonna, the God-bearer. She stood against a dull gold background, holding the Child in her arms, staring out at the world with a sad and knowing gaze. Carlo pumped his legs to get above the Japanese, holding his light steady on the Madonna's face. She looked as though she could see all time: all her child's short life, all the terror and calamity after that . . . There were mosaic tears on her cheeks. At the sight of them, Carlo could barely check tears of his own from joining the general wetness on his face. He felt that he had suddenly been transposed to a church on the deepest floor of the ocean, the pressure of his feelings threatened to implode him, he could scarcely hold them off. The water was freezing, he was shivering, sending up a thick, nearly continuous stream of bubbles . . . and the Madonna watched. With a kick he turned and swam away. Like startled fish his two companions followed him. Carlo led them out of the church into murky light, then up to the surface, to the boat and the window casement.

Fins off, Carlo sat on the staircase and dripped. Taku and Hamada scrambled through the window and joined him. They conversed for a moment in Japanese, clearly excited. Carlo stared at them blackly.

Hamada turned to him. 'That here is the picture we desire,' he said. 'The Madonna with Child.'

'What?' Carlo cried.

Hamada raised his eyebrows. 'We desire taking home that here picture to Japan.'

'But it's impossible! The picture is made of little tiles stuck to the wall – there's no way to get them off!'

'Italy government permits,' Taku said, but Hamada silenced him with a gesture.

'Mosaic, yes. We use instruments we take here – water torch. Archaeology method, you understand. Cut blocks out of wall, bricks, number them – construct on new place in Japan. Above water.' He flashed his pearly smile.

'You can't do that,' Carlo stated, deeply affronted.

'I don't understand,' Hamada said. But he did. 'Italian government permits us that.'

'This isn't Italy,' Carlo said savagely, and in his anger stood. What good would a Madonna do in Japan, anyway? They weren't even Christian. 'Italy is over there,' he said, in his excitement mistakenly waving to the southeast, no doubt confusing his listeners even more. 'This has never been Italy! This is Venice! The Republic!'

'I don't understand.' He had that phrase down pat. 'Italian government has giving permit us.'

'Christ,' Carlo said. After a disgusted pause: 'Just how long will this take?'

'Time? We work that afternoon, tomorrow; place the bricks here, go hire Venice barge to carry bricks to Venice –'

'Stay here overnight? I'm not going to stay here overnight, God damn it!'

'We bring sleeping bag for you –'

'No!' Carlo was furious. 'I'm not staying, you miserable heathen hyenas –' He pulled off his scuba gear.

'I don't understand.'

Carlo dried off, got dressed. 'I'll let you keep your scuba tanks, and I'll be back for you tomorrow afternoon, late. *Understand?*'

'Yes,' Hamada said, staring at him steadily, without expression. 'Bring barge?'

'What? – yes, yes, I'll bring your barge, you miserable slime-eating catfish. Vultures . . .' He went on for a while, getting the boat out of the window.

'Storm coming!' Taku said brightly, pointing to the north.

'To hell with you!' Carlo said, pushing off and beginning to row. 'Understand?'

He rowed out of Torcello and back onto the Lagoon. Indeed, a storm was coming. He would have to hurry. He put up the sail and pulled the canvas decking back until it covered everything but the seat he was sitting on. The wind was from the north now, strong but fitful. It pulled the sail taut, and the boat bucked over the choppy waves, leaving behind a wake that was bright white against the black of the sky. The clouds were drawing over the sky like a curtain, covering half of it: half black, half colourless blue, and the line of the edge was solid. It resembled that first great storm of 2040, Carlo guessed, that had pulled over Venice like a black wool blanket and dumped water for forty days. And it had never been the same again, not anywhere in the world . . .

Now he was beside the wreck of Burano. Against the black sky he could see only the drunken campanile, and suddenly he realized why he hated the sight of this abandoned town: it was a vision of the Venice to come, a cruel model of the future. If the water level rose even three metres, Venice would become nothing but a big Burano. Even if the water didn't rise, more people were leaving Venice every year . . . One day it would be empty. Once again the sadness he had felt looking at the Teotaca filled him, a sadness become a bottomless despair. 'God damn it,' he said, staring at the crippled campanile; but that wasn't enough. He didn't know words that were enough. 'God *damn* it.'

Just beyond Burano the squall hit. It almost blew the sail out of his hand; he had to hold on with a fierce clench, tie it to the stern, tie the tiller in place, and scramble over the pitching canvas deck to lower the sail, cursing all the while. He brought the sail down to its last reefing, which left a handkerchief-sized patch exposed to the wind. Even so, the boat yanked over the waves and the mast creaked as if it would tear loose . . . The choppy waves had become white-caps, in the screaming wind their tops were tearing loose and flying through the air, white foam in the blackness . . .

Best to head for Murano for refuge, Carlo thought. Then the rain started. It was colder than the Lagoon water and fell almost horizontally. The wind was still picking up. His handkerchief sail was going to pull the mast out. 'Madonna,' he said. He got onto the decking again, slid up to the mast, took down the sail with cold and disobedient fingers. He crawled back to his hole in the deck, hanging on desperately as the boat yawed. It was almost broadside to the waves and hastily he grabbed the tiller and pulled it around, just in time to meet a large wave stern-on. He shuddered with relief. Each wave seemed bigger than the last; they picked up quickly on the Lagoon. Well, he thought, what now? Get out the oars? No, that wouldn't do; he had to keep stern-on to the waves, and besides, he couldn't row effectively in this chop. He had to go where the waves were going, he realized; and if they missed Murano and Venice, that meant the Adriatic.

As the waves lifted and dropped him, he grimly contemplated the thought. His mast alone acted like a sail in a wind of this force; and the wind seemed to be blowing from a bit to the west of north. The waves – the biggest he had ever seen on the Lagoon, perhaps the

biggest *ever* on the Lagoon – pushed in about the same
direction as the wind, naturally. Well, that meant he
would miss Venice, which was directly south, maybe
even a touch west of south. Damn, he thought. And all
because he had been angered by those two Japanese and
the Teotaca. What did he care what happened to a
sunken mosaic from Torcello? He had helped foreign-
ers find and cart off the one bronze horse of San Marco
that had fallen ... more than one of the stone lions of
Venice, symbol of the city ... the entire Bridge of Sighs,
for Christ's sake! What had come over him? Why should
he have cared about a forgotten mosaic?

Well, he had done it; and here he was. No altering
it. Each wave lifted his boat stern first and slid under
it until he could look down in the trough, if he cared
to, and see his mast nearly horizontal, until he rose
over the broken, foaming crest, each one of which
seemed to want to break down his little hole in the
decking and swamp him – for a second he was in midair,
the tiller free and useless until he crashed into the next
trough. Every time at the top he thought, this wave will
catch us, and so even though he was wet and the wind
and rain were cold, the repeated spurts of fear adrenaline and his thick wool coat kept him warm. A hundred
waves or so served to convince him that the next one
would probably slide under him as safely as the last,
and he relaxed a bit. Nothing to do but wait it out, keep
the boat exactly stern-on to the swell ... and he would
be all right. Sure, he thought, he would just ride these
waves across the Adriatic to Trieste or Rijeka, one of
those two tawdry towns that had replaced Venice as
Queen of the Adriatic ... the princesses of the Adriatic,

so to speak, and two little sluts they were, too . . . Or ride the storm out, turn around, and sail back in, better yet . . .

On the other hand, the Lido had become a sort of reef, in most places, and waves of this size would break over it, capsizing him for sure. And, to be realistic, the top of the Adriatic was wide. Just one mistake on the top of these waves (and he couldn't go on forever) and he would be broached, capsized, and rolled down to join all the other Venetians who had ended up on the bottom of the Adriatic. And all because of that damn Madonna. Carlo sat crouched in the stern, adjusting the tiller for the particulars of each wave, ignoring all else in the howling, black, horizonless chaos of water and air around him, pleased in a grim way that he was sailing to his death with such perfect seamanship. But he kept the Lido out of mind.

And so he sailed on, losing track of time as one does when there is no spatial referent. Wave after wave after wave. A little water collected at the bottom of his boat, and his spirits sank. That was no way to go, to have the boat sink by degrees under him . . .

Then the high-pitched, airy howl of the wind was joined by a low booming, a bass roar. He looked over his shoulder in the direction he was being driven and saw a white line, stretching from left to right; his heart jumped, fear exploded through him. This was it. The Lido, now a barrier reef tripping the waves. They were smashing down on it, he could see white sheets bouncing skyward and blowing to nothing. He was terrifically frightened. It would have been so much easier to founder at sea.

But there – among the white breakers, off to the right – a grey finger pointing up at the black –

A campanile. Carlo was forced to look back at the wave he was under, to straighten the boat, but when he looked back it was still there. A campanile, standing there like a dead lighthouse. 'Jesus!' he said aloud. It looked as if the waves were pushing him a couple hundred metres to the north of it. As each wave lifted him he had a moment when the boat was sliding down the face of the wave as fast as it was moving under him; during these moments he shifted the tiller a bit and the boat turned and surfed across the face, to the south, until the wave rose up under him to the crest, and he had to straighten it out. He repeated the delicate operation time after time, sometimes nearly broaching the boat in his impatience. But that wouldn't do – just take as much from each wave as it will give you, he thought. And pray it will add up to enough.

The Lido got closer, and it looked as if he was directly upwind of the campanile. It was the one at the Lido channel entrance, or perhaps the one at Pellestrina, farther south; he had no way of knowing, and at the moment didn't care. He was just happy that his ancestors had seen fit to construct such solid bell towers. In between waves he reached under the decking and by touch found his boat hook and the length of rope he carried. It was going to be a problem, actually, when he got to the campanile – it would not do to pass it helplessly by a few metres. On the other hand he couldn't smash into it and expect to survive either, not in these waves. In fact the more he considered it, the more exact and difficult he realized the approach would have to be, and fearfully he stopped thinking about it and concentrated on the waves.

The last one was the biggest. As the boat slid down its face, the face got steeper, until it seemed they would be swept on by this wave forever. The campanile loomed ahead, big and black. Around it waves pitched over and broke with sharp, deadly booms; from behind Carlo could see the water sucked over the breaks, as if over short but infinitely broad waterfalls. The noise was tremendous. At the top of the wave it appeared he could jump in the campanile's top windows – he got out the boat hook, shifted the tiller a touch, took a deep breath. Amid the roaring, the wave swept him just past the stone tower, smacking against it and splashing him; he pulled the tiller over hard, the boat shot into the wake of the campanile – he stood and swung the boat hook over a window casement above him. It caught, and he held on hard.

He was in the lee of the tower. Broken water rose and dropped under the boat, hissing, but without violence, and he held. One-handed, he wrapped the end of his rope around the sail-cord bolt in the stern, tied the other end to the boat hook. The hook held pretty well. He took a risk and reached down to tie the rope firmly to the bolt. Then another risk: when the boiling soupy water of another broken wave raised the boat, he leaped off his seat, grabbed the stone windowsill, which was too thick to get his fingers over – for a moment he hung by his fingertips. With desperate strength he pulled himself up, reached in with one hand and got a grasp on the inside of the sill, and pulled himself in and over. The stone floor was about four feet below the window.

Quickly he pulled the boat hook in, put it on the floor, and took up the slack in the rope.

He looked out the window. His boat rose and fell, rose and fell. Well, it would sink or it wouldn't. Meanwhile, he was safe. Realizing this, he breathed deeply, let out a shout. He remembered shooting past the side of the tower, face no more than two metres from it – getting drenched by the wave slapping the front of it – why, he had done it perfectly! He couldn't do it again like that in a million tries. Triumphant laughs burst out of him, short and sharp: 'Ha! Ha! Ha! Jesus Christ! Wow!'

'Whoooo's theeeerre?' called a high scratchy voice, floating down the staircase from the floor above. 'Whooooooooo's there? . . .'

Carlo froze. He stepped lightly to the base of the stone staircase and peered up. Through the hole to the next floor flickered a faint light. To put it better, it was less dark up there than anywhere else. More surprised than fearful (though he was afraid), Carlo opened his eyes as wide as he could –

'Whoooooo's theeeeeerrrrrrre? . . .'

Quickly he went to the boat hook, untied the rope, felt around on the wet floor until he found a block of stone that would serve as anchor for his boat. He looked out the window: boat still there; on both sides, white breakers crashing over the Lido. Taking up the boat hook, Carlo stepped slowly up the stairs, feeling that after what he had been through he could slash any ghost in the ether to ribbons.

It was a candle lantern, flickering in the disturbed air – a room filled with junk –

'Eeek! Eeek!'

'Jesus!'

'Devil! Death, away!' A small black shape rushed at him, brandishing sharp metal points.

'Jesus!' Carlo repeated, holding the boat hook out to defend himself. The figure stopped.

'Death comes for me at last,' it said. It was an old woman, he saw, holding lace needles in each hand.

'Not at all,' Carlo said, feeling his pulse slow back down. 'Swear to God, Grandmother, I'm just a sailor, blown here by the storm.'

The woman pulled back the hood of her black cape, revealing braided white hair, and squinted at him.

'You've got the scythe,' she said suspiciously. A few wrinkles left her face as she unfocused her gaze.

'A boat hook only,' Carlo said, holding it out for her inspection. She stepped back and raised the lace needles threateningly. 'Just a boat hook, I swear to God. To God and Mary and Jesus and all the saints, Grandmother. I'm just a sailor, blown here by the storm from Venice.' Part of him felt like laughing.

'Aye?' she said. 'Aye, well then, you've found shelter. I don't see so well anymore, you know. Come in, sit down, then.' She turned around and led him into the room. 'I was just doing some lace for penance, you see . . . though there's scarcely enough light.' She lifted a tomboli with the lace pinned to it. Carlo noticed big gaps in the pattern, as in the webs of an injured spider. 'A little more light,' she said and, picking up a candle, held it to the lit one. When it was fired, she carried it around the chamber and lit three more candles in lanterns that stood on tables, boxes, a wardrobe. She motioned for him to sit in a heavy chair by her table, and he did so.

As she sat down across from him, he looked around the chamber. A bed piled high with blankets, boxes and tables covered with objects . . . the stone walls around, and another staircase leading up to the next floor of the campanile. There was a draught. 'Take off your coat,' the woman said. She arranged the little pillow on the arm of her chair and began to poke a needle in and out of it, pulling the thread slowly.

Carlo sat back and watched her. 'Do you live here alone?'

'Always alone,' she replied. 'I don't want it otherwise.' With the candle before her face, she resembled Carlo's mother or someone else he knew. It seemed very peaceful in the room after the storm. The old woman bent in her chair until her face was just above her tomboli; still, Carlo couldn't help noticing that her needle hit far outside the apparent pattern of lace, striking here and there randomly. She might as well have been blind. At regular intervals Carlo shuddered with excitement and tension. It was hard to believe he was out of danger. More infrequently they broke the silence with a short burst of conversation, then sat in the candlelight absorbed in their own thoughts, as if they were old friends.

'How do you get food?' Carlo asked, after one of these silences had stretched out. 'Or candles?'

'I trap lobsters down below. And fishermen come by and trade food for lace. They get a good bargain, never fear. I've never given less, despite what he said –' Anguish twisted her face as the squinting had, and she stopped. She needled furiously, and Carlo looked away. Despite the draught, he was warming up (he hadn't removed his coat, which was wool, after all), and he was beginning to feel drowsy . . .

'He was my spirit's mate, do you comprehend me?'

Carlo jerked upright. The old woman still looked at her tomboli.

'And – and he left me here, here in this desolation when the floods began, with words that I'll remember forever and ever and ever. Until death comes . . . I wish you *had* been death!' she cried. 'I wish you had.'

Carlo remembered her brandishing the needles. 'What is this place?' he asked gently.

'What?'

'Is this Pellestrina? San Servolo?'

'This is Venice,' she said.

Carlo shivered convulsively, stood up.

'I'm the last one of them,' the woman said. 'The waters rise, the heavens howl, love's pledges crack and lead to misery. I – I live to show what a person can bear and not die. I'll live till the deluge drowns the world as Venice is drowned; I'll live till all else living is dead; I'll live . . .' Her voice trailed off; she looked up at Carlo curiously. 'Who are you, really? Oh, I know. I know. A sailor.'

'Are there floors above?' he asked, to change the subject.

She squinted at him. Finally she spoke. 'Words are vain. I thought I'd never speak again, not even to my own heart, and here I am, doing it again. Yes, there's a floor above intact; but above that, ruins. Lightning blasted the bell chamber apart, while I lay in that very bed.' She stood up. 'Come on, I'll show you.' Under her cape she was tiny.

She picked up the candle lantern beside her, and Carlo followed her up the stairs, stepping carefully in the shifting shadows.

On the floor above, the wind swirled, and through the stairway to the floor above that, he could distinguish black clouds. The woman put the lantern on the floor, started up the stairs. 'Come.'

Once through the hole they were in the wind, out under the sky. The rain had stopped. Great blocks of stone lay about the floor, and the walls broke off unevenly.

'I thought the whole campanile would fall,' she shouted at him over the whistle of the wind. He nodded, and walked over to the west wall, which stood chest high. Looking over it, he could see the waves approaching, rising up, smashing against the stone below, spraying back and up at him. He could feel the blows in his feet. Their force frightened him; it was hard to believe he had survived them and was now out of danger. He shook his head violently. To his right and left the white lines of crumbled waves marked the Lido, a broad swath of them against the black. The old woman was speaking, he saw; he walked back to her side and listened.

'The waters yet rise,' she shouted. 'See? And the lightning . . . you can see the lightning breaking the Alps to dust. It's the end, child. Every island fled away, and the mountains were not found . . . the second angel poured out his vial upon the sea, and it became as the blood of a dead man: and every living thing died in the sea.' On and on she spoke, her voice mingling with the sound of the gale and the boom of the waves, just carrying over it all . . . until Carlo, cold and tired, filled with pity and a black anguish like the clouds rolling over them, put his arm around her thin shoulders and turned her around. They descended to the floor below, picked up the extinguished lantern, and descended to her chamber, which was still lit. It seemed warm, a refuge. He could hear her still speaking. He was shivering without pause.

'You must be cold,' she said in a practical tone. She pulled a few blankets from her bed. 'Here, take these.' He sat down in the big heavy chair, put the blankets around his legs, put his head back. He was tired. The old woman sat in her chair and wound thread onto a spool. After a few minutes of silence she began talking again, and as Carlo dozed and shifted position and nodded off again, she talked and talked, of storms, and drownings, and the world's end, and lost love . . .

In the morning when he woke up, she was gone. Her room stood revealed in the dim morning light: shabby, the furniture battered, the blankets worn, the knick-knacks of Venetian glass ugly, as Venetian glass always was . . . but it was clean. Carlo got up and stretched his stiff muscles. He went up to the roof; she wasn't there. It was a sunny morning. Over the east wall he saw that his boat was still there, still floating. He grinned – the first one in a few days; he could feel that in his face.

The woman was not on the floors below, either. The lowest one served as her boathouse, he could see. In it were a pair of decrepit rowboats and some lobster pots. The biggest 'boatslip' was empty. She was probably out checking pots. Or perhaps she hadn't wanted to talk with him in the light of day.

From the boathouse he could walk around to his craft, through water only knee-deep. He sat in the stern, reliving the previous afternoon, and grinned again at being alive.

He took off the decking and bailed out the water on the keel with his bailing can, keeping an eye out for the old woman. Then he remembered the boat hook and went back upstairs for it. When he returned there was still no sight of her. He shrugged. He'd come back and say good-bye another time. He rowed around the campanile and off the Lido, pulled up the sail, and headed northwest, where he presumed Venice was.

The Lagoon was as flat as a pond this morning, the sky cloudless, like the blue dome of a great basilica. It was amazing, but Carlo was not surprised. The weather was like that these days. Last night's storm, however, had been something else. That was the mother of all squalls, those were the biggest waves in the Lagoon ever, without a doubt. He began rehearsing his tale in his mind, for wife and friends.

Venice appeared over the horizon right off his bow, just where he thought it would be: first the great campanile, then San Marco and the other spires. The campanile . . . Thank God his ancestors had wanted to get up there so close to God – or so far off the water – the urge had saved his life. In the rain-washed air, the sea approach to the city was more beautiful than ever, and it didn't even bother him as it usually did that no matter how close you got to it, it still seemed to be over the horizon. That was just the way it was, now. The Serenissima. He was happy to see it.

He was hungry, and still very tired. When he pulled

into the Grand Canal and took down the sail, he found he could barely row. The rain was pouring off the land into the Lagoon, and the Grand Canal was running like a mountain river. It was tough going. At the fire station where the canal bent back, some of his friends working on a new roof-house waved at him, looking surprised to see him going upstream so early in the day. 'You're going the wrong way!' one shouted.

Carlo waved an oar weakly before plopping it back in. 'Don't I know it!' he replied.

Over the Rialto, back into the little courtyard of San Giacometta. Onto the sturdy dock he and his neighbours had built, staggering a bit – careful there, Carlo.

'Carlo!' his wife shrieked from above. 'Carlo, Carlo, Carlo!' She flew down the ladder from the roof.

He stood on the dock. He was home.

'Carlo, Carlo, Carlo!' his wife cried as she ran onto the dock.

'Jesus,' he pleaded, 'shut up.' And pulled her into a rough hug.

'Where have you been, I was so worried about you because of the storm, you said you'd be back yesterday, oh, Carlo, I'm so glad to see you . . .' She tried to help him up the ladder. The baby was crying. Carlo sat down in the kitchen chair and looked around the little makeshift room with satisfaction. In between chewing down bites of a loaf of bread he told Luisa of his adventure: the two Japanese and their vandalism, the wild ride across the Lagoon, the madwoman on the campanile. When he had finished the story and the loaf of bread, he began to fall asleep.

'But Carlo, you have to go back and pick up those Japanese.'

'To hell with them,' he said slurrily. 'Creepy little bastards . . . They're tearing the Madonna apart, didn't I tell you? They'll take everything in Venice, every last painting and statue and carving and mosaic and all . . . I can't stand it.'

'Oh, Carlo. It's all right. They take those things all over the world and put them up and say this is from Venice, the greatest city in the world.'

'They should be here.'

'Here, here, come in and lie down for a few hours. I'll go see if Giuseppe will go to Torcello with you to bring back those bricks.' She arranged him on their bed. 'Let them have what's under the water, Carlo. Let them have it.' He slept.

He sat up struggling, his arm shaken by his wife.

'Wake up, it's late. You've got to go to Torcello to get those men. Besides, they've got your scuba gear.'

Carlo groaned.

'Maria says Giuseppe will go with you. He'll meet you with his boat on the Fondamente.'

'Damn.'

'Come on, Carlo, we need that money.'

'All right, all right.' The baby was squalling. He collapsed back on the bed. 'I'll do it. Don't pester me.'

He got up and drank her soup. Stiffly he descended the ladder, ignoring Luisa's instructions and warnings, and got back in his boat. He untied it, pushed off, let it float out of the courtyard to the wall of San Giacometta. He stared at the wall.

Once, he remembered, he had put on his scuba gear and swum down into the church. He had kneeled behind one of the stone pews in front of the altar, adjusting his weightbelts and tank to do so, and had tried to pray through his mouthpiece and the facemask. The silver bubbles of his breath had floated up through the water towards heaven; whether his prayers had gone with them, he had no idea. After a while, feeling somewhat foolish – but not entirely – he had swum out the door. Over it he had noticed an inscription and stopped to read it, facemask centimetres from the stone. *Around This Temple Let the Merchant's Law Be Just, His Weight True, and His Covenants Faithful.* It was an admonition to the old usurers of the Rialto, but he could make it his, he thought; the true weight could refer to the diving belts, not to overload his clients and sink them to the bottom . . .

The memory passed and he was on the surface again, with a job to do. He took in a deep breath and let it out, put the oars in the oarlocks and started to row.

Let them have what was under the water. What lived in Venice was still afloat.

The Disguise

I PULLED OPEN THE theatre door and stuck my foot against it to keep the wind that swirled in the street from slamming it shut. I swung my duffel bag through the doorway and followed it inside. The door closed with a forced hiss and the bright lights of the street were replaced by dim greys. The air was still.

My eyes adjusted, and slowly, as if candles were being lit, I perceived the narrow high room which was the foyer of the Rose Theatre. I crossed the room and peered in the ticket window. A thin young man, with eye sockets blacked, and white hair cropped close to his head, looked up at me. I dropped my bag, pulled my card from my pocket and handed it to him.

'Pallio,' I said.

'Very good,' he said, and looked at the card. 'Now when Velasquo arrives we'll have everyone.' He picked up a cast list and put a check beside my name. After slotting my card into the register, he touched some keys, and the square of plastic disappeared. 'The charge is twelve per cent higher now,' he murmured. 'They're trying to tax us to death.' The card reappeared and he handed it back to me. 'Let me take you to your room.'

I picked up my bag. The cashier appeared through a doorway beside the window and led me down the hall, looking back over his shoulder to talk: 'I don't trust this *Guise* play, I think that whole Aylesbury Collection is a Collier forgery . . .' I ignored him and watched the footprints he left in the thick blue-black carpet. Dull bronze-flake wallpaper shattered the light from a half-dozen gas jets. The Rose was in its full Regency splendour, for the first time in months. The halls felt as subterranean as before, however; the Rose occupied only a few bottom floors in the Barnard Tower, an eighty-storey complex.

The cashier stopped at one of a series of doors and opened it for me. Light flooded over us. We went in and were on a different set; snapping Jacob's ladders and coloured liquids bubbling up tubes made me look for a mad scientist. But it was only a white-coated techni-cian, at the computer terminal. He turned around, revealing a scrubbed, precisely shaved face. 'Whom have you brought us?' he said.

'Pallio,' replied the cashier. I dropped my bag.

'We're ready to give you your part,' the technician said.

The chair was dressed up like a chrome-and-glass version of the table Frankenstein's monster was born on. 'Does Bloomsman have to do this,' I said.

'You know our director.'

'Last time I was here it was a dentist's chair.'

'Not many liked that one, as I recall.'

I got into the chair while he tapped keys at the terminal, calling up from the artificial mind a detailed description of my brain's structure. When he was done he wrapped the pharmaceutical band around my neck. 'Ready?' he asked. He tapped a key on the chair's console and I felt the odd sensation, like flexing a stiff muscle, of the injection – a tiny witch's brew of L-dopa, bufotenine, and norepinephrine. As always my heart began hammering immediately: not because of the introduced chemicals, but because of my own adrenaline, flooding through me to combat the imagined danger of a primal violation.

We waited. The room enlarged and flattened out into a painted cylinder. 'Now for the hood,' said the technician, his voice like tin. The hood descended and it was dark. The goggles were cold against my face, and my scalp prickled as filaments touched it.

'Time for the implant,' the technician said. 'Let's have alpha waves if you please.' I started the stillness behind my nose. 'Fine. Here we go.'

In my vision a blue field flickered at around ten cycles per second, and voices chattered in both ears, creating counterpoints of blank verse. In those connected clumps known as the limbic system, scattered across the bottom of my cerebral cortex, new neural activity began. Electrical charges skipped through the precise network of neurons until they reached the edge of the familiar; synapses fired in new directions, and were forever changed. I was growing. I felt none of it.

Memories came before me in confusing abundance, passing before I could fix on them. An afternoon by the window in an Essex library, watching green hills become invisible in the grey rain. In the colony off Jamaica just after the earthquake, when everyone was silent, feeling the pressure of the hundred fathoms of water above. The run of basses in the scherzo of Beethoven's Fifth. A strong smell of disinfectant – hospital smell – and the voice of Carlos, droning quietly: 'It was in the fourth act of *Hamlet*, when I as Claudius was on my knees, attempting to pray. Hamlet was above and to one side, on the balcony, and in my peripheral vision his face distorted into a mask of fang and snout. As he finished his soliloquy he turned away from the balustrade, but his head stayed fixed, twisted entirely over one shoulder, and he continued to glare down at me. My memory flooded. The moment I understood he was the Hieronomo, he jumped the balustrade, and I leaped to my feet only to meet the falling épée blade directly in the chest. I heard the cries of shock, but nothing more . . .'

Blackness. Then the suction pulling at my eyes as the eyepieces withdrew. The hood rose and the white room reappeared. I twisted my head back and forth.

'Got it?' asked the technician. I paused and thought. Pallio . . . yes. A series of exclamations marked his entrance in the first scene, a conference with Velasquo. I knew only my first few lines, plus cue lines, and Bloomsman's laconic blocking, appropriate to the improvisational nature of the art: 'Confront Velasquo centre stage.' The rest of my part would come to me throughout the course of the play, irregularly, recalled by unknown cues. This was the minimum script that

Bloomsman allowed one to receive; it was the preferred preparation among seasoned actors.

'Backstage is that way,' the technician said. He helped me up. I swayed unsteadily. 'Break a leg,' he said brightly, and returned to his terminal. I picked up my costume bag and left the room.

The hall expanded near the gas jets and contracted in the dimmer sections. I stopped and leaned against the wall, concentrating to recover from the dissociation of the implant. The wallpaper was not actually flake – it had once been a smooth sheen, but had cracked and peeled away into thousands of bronze shavings. Chips broke off under me and floated to the carpet. I strode down the hall, uncertain how long I had stopped. My sense of estrangement was stronger than usual, as if I had learned more than a play.

The hall ended in a T and I could not remember which way to go. Acting on a dim intuition I turned right and found myself in a veritable maze of T-connections. I alternated turns, going first right, then left. One hall I followed dropped several steps, then turned and became a flight of stairs, which I descended. At the bottom of this stairway were three long, dim halls, all furnished (like the stairway) with the same dark carpet, bronze wallpaper, and gas jets. I chose the right-hand one and ventured on. Just as I began to think myself inextricably lost there was a door, recessed into the right wall. I opened it and was at the back of the theatre, looking across the audience to the curtain.

The audience was large, about forty or fifty people. Many times I had acted in plays which no one had come to see; in those the imaginary fourth wall had become real, and we had played for ourselves, aware only of the internal universe of the play. Most actors preferred it that way. But I liked the idea of an audience watching. And it was not surprising, with this play. It wasn't often that one got to see the first performance of a play four hundred years old.

An usher appeared and propped the door open for me. Behind him a fully-armed security guard looked me over. He was there, I supposed, because of Hieronomo. The usher offered me a programme and I took it. 'I need to get backstage,' I whispered.

He smiled. 'Just go through the door by the stage,' he said. 'It's easier.'

Backstage I stopped and looked at the programme in my hand. The first page listed the dramatis personae:

THE GUISE

Pallio, Duke of Naples
Velasquo, his younger brother
Donado, a Cardinal
Sanguinetto, a Sicilian count
Orcanes }
Hamond } gentlemen: followers of Donado
Mura, a priest: attendant to Donado
Ursini }
Ferrando } friends to Sanguinetto
Elazar, a supposed doctor

Caropia, sister to Pallio and Velasquo
Leontia, wife to Donado, and sister to Orcanes

Carmen, servant to Caropia

Courtiers, Masquers, Officers and Guards, Pages, Seer.

Director: Eunice Bloomsman

The opposite page was almost filled by one of Bloomsman's learned programme notes:

The Guise is one of the four previously lost plays in the Aylesbury Collection, twenty-four plays and hundreds of miscellaneous papers discovered in 2052. The invaluable books and manuscripts, found at Aylesbury Manor near Oxford, had been locked in a storage trunk for over three hundred years.

The copy of *The Guise* in the Collection is a quarto volume, published in 1628 'by N.O. for Thomas Archer.' Stage directions have been added by an unknown 17th century hand.

The text is anonymous. It was presumed that the play was by John Webster, who mentioned a work of his by the same title in the dedication to *The Devil's Law Case* (1623). But this has been questioned. Earlier references to a *Guise* play – variously spelled *The Gwuisse*, or *The Guesse* – indicate that there was probably more than one play so named. Most of these presumably concern the de Guise family, but the plot of our play was taken from an Italian novella, *Il Travestimento di Pallio*.

Critics have made cases for the authorship of Middleton, Tourneur, and Massinger. The debates continue – even the authenticity of the entire

Collection has been questioned recently. While this state of uncertainty remains, we at the Rose have thought it best not to attribute authorship.

This is the first Vancouver performance of *The Guise*.

It was less than I already knew from talking to Bloomsman. I had been one of many requesting a part; it had been worse than trying to get reservations to play Hamlet. Everyone who performed Jacobean drama had enquired, fascinated by the prospect of a new and unknown play. It had been a surprise when Bloomsman called and said, 'You'll be Pallio.'

I made my way through backstage corridors to the dressing room, found the cubicle with my name on it. My first costume – grey britches, white ruffled shirt-front, long blue coat – felt as familiar to me as my street clothes. The other costumes went on hooks. I sat down before the mirror, turned on its lights, and pulled my makeup kit from the bottom of the bag. My face was damp; the white powder stuck to it. I darkened my eyelids, exaggerated the curve of my upper lip. The sight of the stranger in the mirror, face white as a mask, quickened my pulse. I considered the many layers of his character, and played over his archaic language.

A small crystal perfume bottle rolled against my foot. I reached down, picked it up; still seated, I stuck my head around the partition separating me from the next cubicle. There was no one there. Dresses, white and scarlet and black, hung from the walls, making the cubicle seem smaller. Crystal bottles like the one in my hand reflected the blue light from the makeup mirror behind them.

Within the mirror there was movement. I turned my head and looked up at an auburn-haired actress, one I had never seen before. Her face was a narrow oval. Her eyes, grey as slate and flecked with black, surveyed me calmly. She looked into her cubicle and back, clearly framing her question. I lifted the bottle in explanation, and her mouth, which curved down sharply in repose, lifted as if propelled by the same motion, into a warm smile.

'Caropia?' I asked.

Her head turned aside. She walked past me into her cubicle without responding. A strand of her hair spiralled down; her slim back was splashed with tiny streaks of the powder that whitened her shoulders. I noticed that the grey eyes were still observing me from the mirror, and I quickly withdrew. Pallio's face mocked me in my own glass. Remember where you are, he said . . . By and large, acting was as congenial an art form as any other; friends often performed plays together. But those of us who gravitated to the world of Jacobean tragedy were not a very communicative bunch. Strangers came in, played their parts, and went their separate ways into the city, remaining strangers to each other. The Hieronomo was one of us.

The stage set was large and uncluttered. The bedroom at the rear had wide black staircases bracketing it, and a narrow balcony above, so that it was deeply recessed, like a cave. I experienced the familiar wash of *déjà vu* as I viewed it; a false one, in that I had truly *already seen* the set, as part of the implanting. Real *déjà vu* would have been an uncanny feeling, I was sure; but in a world of memory implants it was as common as recollection itself. (Still, there were people addicted to the sensation. They would implant in their memory the remembrance of a world tour and then take that very tour, in a continuous state of *déjà vu*, pulse high, adrenaline running in their arteries . . .)

In the large prop room directly behind the stage the director, Eunice Bloomsman, was holding the first and final cast meeting. Bloomsman was quite short, and very calm. Many of the players were ignoring her, expressing the common belief among them that directors were powerless lackeys, no more than the stage managers of old. But they were mistaken – directors programmed the information to be implanted in the players, and that gave them the chance to exert much subtle influence.

Bloomsman looked up at me, then continued. 'All of you but one chose minimum text, so you'll have to stay alert to keep up. I've made the cues two and sometimes three lines long, so you'll have plenty of warning. In case you get lost there will be prompters in the usual places.

'This play has an extraordinary history, as you know, and there's a large audience here to see us, so let's try to do a good job. That means an absolute ban on interpolations – agreed?' There were nods from several. 'Good. Now introduce yourselves so you'll know who's who.'

A tall man stood, dressed in the rich red robes of stage clergy. 'I'm Cardinal Donado,' he said.

Two men then rose and introduced themselves as Hamond and Orcanes, followers of Donado. I had played with them before; they always performed together.

The actor next to them tugged at his black waistcoat and looked about the chamber. 'Sanguinetto,' he said in a harsh, low voice. I had played with him before also. He always took the part of the most deranged villain the work had to offer, which in revenge tragedy was saying a great deal. I had watched him play Iago with the most chilling bitterness; and in *Edward II* he had laughed his way through the ugly part of the murderer Lightborn. This actor took the backstage convention of silence to its limit, and never said anything but his lines. Between scenes he stood wordlessly near his next entrance. This was too much for some. Once a young actor had drawn me aside and asked me if I thought he was the Hieronomo – I had laughed. No, I told him, the Hieronomo always takes the part of the hero. Besides, he always returns with a different face, and I've seen this man before.

The others rose and identified themselves. I didn't recognize any of them. Latecomers from the dressing room arrived, and the diverse mix of costumes now included every colour, creating a confusion much more plausible than any coordinated costuming could be. This was Bloomsman's idea, another of her innovations that seemed to give the players more freedom.

When the auburn-haired actress stood, she looked directly at me. Behind the mask of cosmetics (her mouth was a dangerous sickle of dark red) her grey eyes seemed colourless. 'Caropia,' she said. I remained expressionless, and she smiled.

Then there was a rustle and a man stepped out of a dim back corner of the room. He was dressed in black, and his short hair was a light, dull blond. He had thin lips, and a wide jaw that made his face look square.

My heart was thumping rapidly. Bloomsman turned to him. 'And you are?' she inquired.

'I am Velasquo,' the man said, and at that moment I felt extreme cold, as if suddenly probability had relaxed and all the air had left my side of the room. Something about the man – the turn of his nose – told me I should know him, and in my brain thoughtless energy ran through neural corridors, struggling in vain for recognition.

'That's very good,' Bloomsman was saying. Everyone else was attending to their appearance, each of them preparing for his or her five thousandth, ten thousandth entrance . . . I felt isolated. 'The whole cast is here. Is everyone familiar with the stage?' The question was ignored. Bloomsman pursed her lips into an expression of contempt. 'Let's begin.'

The curtain rose. Lights dimmed, and the audience was nothing but rows of white faces, which slowly became indistinct, like blobs of dough, then faded away in the deeper gloom. Small rustlings ended, and the little room was perfectly silent, perfectly dark.

A shaft of blue light, so faint that it first appeared to be only a seam in the blackness, gained strength and defined centre stage. Into this conjuration of blue walked Velasquo, who stopped as if snared by it. He turned to face the audience, and from my vantage point at stage right I could see his sharp profile, and the light hair, now glazed blue, and a suddenly raised hand, in which a sheet of paper fluttered. He spoke, in a nasal tenor:

'This note commands me: I must have
  revenge!'

He read the note aloud. It was a garbled, nearly incoherent document, which informed him that his father
the old Duke had been murdered, 'poison'd by a spider
in his bed,' and exhorted him to vengeance. It made
only obscure references to the identity of the killer –
'What now seems finest is most ill' – and Velasquo
threw it down in disgust.

He explained to the audience that his father's death
had been unexpected and mysterious; it had been attrib-
uted to overeating by Elazar, a doctor of doubtful reputation. He saw now that the foul play had been obvious.
Bitterly he described the corrupt court of Naples, which,
under the 'dull and amiable' hand of his elder brother
Pallio, now the Duke, had become the plaything of
riotous sycophants. Pallio was too stupid to want to
search for a murderer. (I listened with great interest.)
The rest of the court was too evil, and probably somehow implicated in the deed. Only his sister Caropia
remained untainted. As he described the rest of us, one
by one, my mind reverberated with the memory of the
play, which hovered just on the edge of consciousness.
Suddenly I knew the end of the play; the tangled plots
that led to it were still a blank, but there were tendrils
of association that linked each character with his final
fate, and I saw the culmination, the vivid murders, my
own death, the bloody, corpse-littered stage.

Shaken, I watched Velasquo walk towards me. I had
never divined the end of the play so soon before –
Velasquo raised his voice, and my attention was drawn
back to him. He vowed to look for the note's author,
who clearly knew more than he had written, and then
search for the killer:

'I'll seek him out – to do it I'll dissemble:
And if there be a murderer, let him tremble.'

That was my cue.

I walked on stage and an aura of blue light surrounded
me. Velasquo greeted me and I replied, a bit too loudly,
I thought, for the size of the room. I began concentrating, working to express naturally lines I had never
spoken, doing that improvisation of stance and gesture
which makes ours so much different from the acting in
any previous tradition.

His eyes never leaving me, Velasquo suddenly told
me of the contents of the note – 'Our poor father has
been most foully murdered!'

My mouth fell open. 'But nay,' I objected, 'he's dead.'
Velasquo ignored me and proceeded to describe the deed,
in much more elaborate detail than the mysterious
letter had, as if the bald mention of the crime had
brought the scene up full-bloom in his imagination. At
the end of the gruesome tale I said, 'That's not so well
done, brother!' and continued to make stupid exclamations of shock as Velasquo listed the rest of the potential assassins at court. Finally he exhorted me to
vengeance, and I eagerly agreed to help him. 'I'll be your
constant aid. But now, what shall we tell our holy
sister?'

'Nothing.'

With an audible snap the stage was flooded in white
and yellow light, and nearly the entire cast paraded on.

Velasquo moved away from me and drifted off through the colourful throng. The Cardinal led his retinue on, and I performed my function as Duke by calling, in a clear falsetto, for order amongst the revellers. One of the Cardinal's men proposed a masque, to be held two days hence, and I gave the idea my ducal approval. At the other side of the stage Sanguinetto voiced caustic, railing asides, which were making the audience laugh; in my peripheral vision I could see their mouths opening, faint in the wash of light from the stage. The Cardinal lost several lines by speaking too soon. I had no idea what he had said, and wondered if I had been cued. It was always at this point, in the first crowd scene, that confusions were most likely to occur . . .

Caropia entered in a white gown, holding a cross at her breast. By the obsequious gestures of the others it was clear she was revered by all. Even Sanguinetto was silent. I went to her and she held out the cross; I kissed it. Velasquo did the same, and the Cardinal bowed deeply. She went to him and they began a quick exchange that the rest of us were supposed to ignore. I remembered my blocking, voiced in Bloomsman's dry tones – 'Mime dialogue with Velasquo, far stage left.'

Velasquo grabbed my arm and pulled me there. I mouthed words and he stared at my forehead. His mustard-brown eyes were nearly crossed in their intensity. Again I had the overpowering sensation of *presque vu* which told me I *almost knew* him. He mouthed words and as my memory supplied his high, rasplike voice, the sensation of recognition grew to something like panic. Abruptly he turned and began his exit, yet he looked back at me, as if in response to my inner turmoil; his head swivelled almost completely over his right shoulder. At once I knew him.

I stepped back. He squinted slightly, surprised by the move. I turned and crossed the stage, unable to face him, and halted only when I was alone in the narrow corridor between the wings and the prop room.

He was the Hieronomo, I was certain of it. Was he?

Hieronomo is the hero of Thomas Kyd's *The Spanish Tragedie*, the first and most influential of English revenge dramas. In it Hieronomo's son is killed by noblemen of the Spanish court. Hieronomo feigns insanity to facilitate his revenge, but despair pushes the imitation into reality, and by the time he completes his vengeance he is mad.

Someone playing this role had apparently experienced a similar breakdown: the previous December, in a performance at the Kean Theatre, the actor playing Hieronomo's foe, the old Duke, had actually died, killed by a knife with a loose button-tip. By the time this was discovered, the Hieronomo had disappeared.

In the months following he had appeared six more times, perhaps ten, depending on how many rumours you believed; each time with a different face, and a different name, but the same deadly blade. In *Women Beware Women*, and *Antonio's Revenge*, and in three different *Hamlets*, the end had been disrupted by the villain's death. It was said that once he had stayed to finish *Hamlet*, and had taken a round of applause before slipping away. Others reported that another Claudius had been killed at his prayers, in act four, providing a surprise ending; I knew that one to be true; I had known the actor. The rest was hearsay and rumour, spreading at differing speeds through the strange community, so that undoubtedly each of us had heard a different selection of stories, whispered to us in dressing room or lavatory.

I was sure Velasquo was he. I scoffed at the notion, aware of the power the new legend had gained among those who played in these dramas. But once the suspicion had appeared, it was impossible to expel – it was more *certainty* than suspicion, yet I resisted it. It was as likely as not that he was just another actor, doing an excellent job. In such company, how could I tell otherwise? How could I tell anything in this theatre? I knew each player only as his part. It was impossible to know anything for sure – or if not, it would have to be cleverly learned.

Someone tapped my arm and I jumped. It was one of the prompters. 'You're on,' he said. I hurried to the stage, afraid I would have to ask him where we were, but the sight of Caropia, standing alone by the bed in the inner chamber, brought the scene to me. It was late in the act. I composed myself and walked on.

Her slim face was a shadowed mask of contemplation, and in the weak blue light she was nothing but modulations of grey. We stood frozen for long moments, until white light splashed across centre stage. Then Caropia looked up. 'Who's there?' she asked. 'Your brother Pallio,' I said, in a lower voice than I had used before, and then we rushed at each other and crashed together, to embrace and kiss with abandon. She bit at me, and I pulled my head back and laughed directly at the audience, aware of their collective gasp, which marked the pleasure of suspicions confirmed.

We desisted and I told Caropia, with suitable contempt, how Velasquo had come to me to confide that he suspected foul play in our father's death. At this her mouth set in its sharp downward curve. 'You play the fool,' she said, 'he *is* one. Make your Sanguinetto kill him, as you had him kill our odious father . . .' I explained that this was impractical, since clearly someone at the court already knew what had happened. We had to dissemble and find that person out, before we could deal with Velasquo. Caropia shrugged; it was my problem, I was to solve it as I would. I reminded her that I had had the old Duke killed at her instigation – she alone had feared his discovery of our incest – but the reminder was a mistake. In harsh and dangerous tones she asked me not to mention the matter again. I agreed, but begged her to help me find the informer, and as she walked offstage she replied that she would if it pleased her. Out of the audience's sight she turned and the faintest trace of a smile lifted her mouth. She nodded at me with approval. But I still had a short soliloquy:

'Damned bitch!' I said, 'I'd kill you too did I not lust for you.' Then I looked to the audience.

'I love her as a man holds a wolf by the ears,' I said, and launched myself with vigour into the soliloquy of the villain, the stage-Machiavel: glorying in my crimes, gleefully listing my subterfuges, basking in my own cleverness, wittily seducing the audience to my side. 'To lie upon my sister I have laid my father under earth – grave crimes,' I informed them, and their laughter was

an approval of sorts. I voiced the final couplet as a close
confidence:

> '. . . there's no one knows me.
> An honest simpleton still be my guise –
> Who does not seem a fool cannot be wise.'

The theatre blacked out and I made my way to the
staccato roll of applause. The first act was over.

I sat down on a stool just offstage and watched the
second act begin. Caropia stood before the bed. She was
dressed in red, a muted crimson with gold thread in it.
In the sharp white-yellow light it seemed the same
colour as her hair, and her mouth.

Sanguinetto entered from above. He stepped down
soundlessly, choosing the stairs to the right. His black
doublet complemented black hair and beard; his face
was powder-white. He greeted her and told her of the
arrival of the seer. 'Does he read dreams?' she asked,
and looked pleased when Sanguinetto answered that he
did.

Sanguinetto reached the stage and crossed in front
of Caropia. When he came between her and the audience it was like an eclipse; the light shifted to blue,
and when she reappeared it seemed she was dressed in
grey. Offstage in the wings opposite me, Velasquo leaned
against a wall and watched.

With contemptuous amusement, Sanguinetto was
blackmailing her. His references were vague to me;
apparently he referred to something I had missed in the
first act. Something that Caropia had done, or was doing,

had been discovered by Sanguinetto. Now he was using the information as a lever to extract sexual favours. 'Thy painted visage will be naught but candied flesh,' he told her, 'if you lie not with me.' He circled her briskly and balked her attempts to turn her back on him. She tried to forestall him by denying his accusation, but he ran his hand over her hair and mocked her; and slowly, bitterly, she acquiesced.

As they moved back to the bed, continuing the macabre dance of thrust and parry, I marvelled at their skill, at the absolute verisimilitude of their every movement and intonation. This was acting of the highest order; it was impossible for me to imagine them as anyone but Caropia and Sanguinetto.

Velasquo watched the scene without expression.

With Sanguinetto's hand at her throat, Caropia sank back on the bed. The lights dimmed with her descent and the theatre was black before Sanguinetto joined her.

I sat in the dark, and considered tests.

I was startled to attention by my cue lines. The next scene had already begun. I strode on stage and spoke to the audience:

'O excellent! By that he'll conquer Rome!'

The audience roared. I had no idea what I had referred to, having forgotten the cue. I retreated to the left staircase, in my confusion aware only of my blocking.

More characters arrived and the scene became complex. Everyone was involved in the central event (which I had not yet deciphered), but many were making

covert conversation, or uttering malicious asides. The
Cardinal spoke, and suddenly I understood the import
of the scene: he was asking Caropia to take holy orders,
to become a nun. He persisted with an icy calm that I
couldn't interpret, and her refusals became increasingly
strident. Sanguinetto, Hamond and Orcanes, Ferrando
and Ursini, all publicly encouraged her while privately
vilifying her. Only Velasquo actually meant his praise.
I could see the dim white faces of the audience breaking into laughter, and I felt Caropia's humiliation
keenly. We could make her comic for the rest of the
play, if we wanted to (I recalled once playing in a
Revenger's Tragedy in which the cast had nearly killed
themselves with mirth). Finally my cue lines arrived
and it was easy for me to feign Pallio's anger:

'They that mock her soon will lie in heaps
Of rotting flesh, all broken open to
The sun and flies and maggots,
And their half-empty eye sockets will stare
At naught but Pallio, astonish'd still by his
Abrupt revenge . . .'

The scene continued, but the laughter was greatly
diminished. Velasquo grasped me by the arm. 'Brother,
I must speak to you anon,' he said, staring at me curiously. I agreed, averting my gaze, and he slipped offstage
behind me, leaving me with my heart knocking. He
would have to be tested . . .

Now Caropia approached me, ostensibly to consult
in private about the question of holy orders. She drew
me out on the apron just above the audience, and in a

voice tight with rage demanded that I kill Sanguinetto.
I asked why, and she told me a near-truth, the best sort
of lie; Sanguinetto was blackmailing her, demanding
sexual favours in exchange for silence concerning *my*
guilt in the old Duke's death. I reacted with a lover's
anger, and as I railed against Sanguinetto she stroked
my arm, the softness of her hands belying the absolute
implacability of her intentions.

She left with a last velvet command, and I found myself
alone – the rest had exited during our dialogue. Blue light
surrounded me, as tangible as if the gel covering the bulb
had poured down into the cone of light. I collected myself
and tried to project an assured, amused control:

> 'The brother that I hate, and the sister
> That I hate and love (for there's
> Two feelings closer to each other than
> The minds of any pair of us) both press
> Me now like halves of a garotte,
> Yet I'll slip out and let them gnash together;
> I have a plot – yet soft – Velasquo –'

He entered. My back to him, and face to the audience,
I let my features slacken into those of the Pallio he
knew. There was laughter, and with a sudden leer I
encouraged it, for it was directed at Velasquo. I turned
and greeted him. He began by complaining that he had
found no clue to the murderer's identity. I informed
him that I had some news that might help him, then
answered his questions so foolishly that it took him
some time to deduce that if Sanguinetto kept spiders,
and was blackmailing Caropia, he must indeed be the

villain we were searching for. I expressed amazement
at his intelligence.

While the audience laughed at my duplicity,
Velasquo's face darkened, his jaw muscles bunched.
The laughter died away completely before he spoke:
'I'd have this be vengeance all will remember,' he said,
in a voice so harsh that it enforced belief, made one
wonder, with squeamish anticipation, what forms
revenge might take ... He spoke no more of it,
however, which made me suspect he was omitting
lines; he sent me on my way, then stalked aimlessly
around the stage. Suddenly he stopped and laughed,
first quietly, then in a sharp howl. In the midst of this
nerve-shattering mirth the blackout snapped down and
terminated both light and sound.

I was conscious of a plan that had formulated itself
sometime during Velasquo's ominous drunkard's walk.
I had a test, one that would leave me concealed; he
would know he had been tested, of course – it was an
unusual test that did not reveal that – but he would
not know by whom.

In the prop room Ferrando and Ursini were running
over an exchange of dialogue in double-time. A
prompter at the rear entrance raised a hand; they filed
on, allowing two brief bursts of yellow into the dark,
grainy green of the room. I went to the prop table and
casually scanned the small pile of stage-notes.

The top one was the one that would betray Pallio. I
picked it up, and, holding it against me, went into the
lavatory. Inside a stall I took a pencil stub from my vest
pocket (my ribs were sticky with sweat), and flattened

the vellum against the wall with my other hand. In a clumsy, rounded imitation of Bloomsman's Italianate lettering, I listed all the plays I had ever heard connected with the Hieronomo:

The Spanish Tragedie
Hamlet
Hamlet, Act Four
Antonio's Revenge
Women Beware Women
The Atheist's Tragedy

I couldn't think of a fully appropriate tag, and so finally added *manet alta mente repostum*; it remains deep in my mind. That would do.

I had just quietly replaced the note, and was turning from the prop table, when Sanguinetto appeared from the left hallway. He watched me as he picked up the sheet of vellum and put it inside his black doublet; I couldn't tell if he had seen me return it or not. His beard, rising almost to his eyes, hid all expression, and his steady stare revealed nothing but interest. He went to the curtained opening and paused for a moment. He pushed the curtain aside, allowing blue light to wash over him, and made his final entrance.

From the rear I could see only a portion of centre stage, and I feared Velasquo would be out of my sight at the crucial moment, aborting the test and leaving me with my uncertainties. Hastily I made my way through the dark to stage right, to the vantage point where I had observed most of the play.

Caropia was there; noticing my appearance, she gestured me to her and with a lift of her head directed my attention to the stage. I stood beside her and looked out, feeling her hand's pressure against my arm.

Velasquo was in disguise, wearing a black hooded cape. He was establishing his credentials – he was, he said to Sanguinetto, Pinon d'Alsquove, a fellow Sicilian, who had been forced to flee their native island because he had unfortunately murdered a gentleman of importance. Sanguinetto accepted this, exhibiting the usual Jacobean inability to see through even the simplest of disguises. They seated themselves at a dining table set out on the apron, and proceeded to drink and regale each other with tales. Strange revellers they were, both dressed in black, presented in a brilliant white-violet light that illuminated every face in the audience. They traded bloody stories, and it became clear that Pinon d'Alsquove had much in common with his fellow countryman. (There was a certain logic to this Jacobean thinking: since all Italians were depraved, it made sense that the farther south one went, the worse they became.) The crime that caused Pinon's exile had been the last in a long and gruesome series. Sanguinetto became unnaturally gay as Pinon described the various methods he had used to dispatch his enemies back in Sicily, and they quickly finished a tall, slim bottle of wine. As Sanguinetto uncorked another one Pinon spoke to the audience, in Velasquo's high voice: 'In midst of all his mirth he will meet death.' Then they were roaring with laughter again, at the champagne cascading from the bottle Sanguinetto held in his lap. As he drank and bit huge chunks from a turkey leg, Pinon described one of his weapons:

> '. . . a most ingenious toy,
> A tiny spring with rapier-pointed ends,
> Held tight by threads of lightest leather; which
> Then hidden in the victim's food, and ate,
> The threads are quick digested, and the spring
> Jumps to its fullest length, ripping great holes
> Within thy rival's guts. Thus do Moors
> Kill dogs . . .'

Sanguinetto chewed on obliviously, and everyone in the theatre watched him eat. 'Aye,' Pinon concluded,

> 'Methinks I know all of the finest ways
> To end th' existence of a foe –'

Sanguinetto swallowed and struggled to his feet. He leaned over Pinon:

> 'Thou missed a way that should be known
> To all Sicilians – I will show thee.'

He hurried to the rear exit in long strides, knocked the curtain aside and disappeared. Pinon spoke in Velasquo's voice:

> 'Now I suspect I've drawn him out like snail
> From shell, into the light where I may crush
>   him.'

Sanguinetto reappeared, holding at arm's length a tall glass box, like a candle lantern. Within it a thick-bodied, long-legged spider – a cane spider, I guessed – scrabbled

up the walls and slid down again. Pinon leaped up,
knocking his chair over. Sanguinetto pointed at the
spider and leered proudly.

> 'This spider's of a kind known but in Sicily.
> 'Tis said they come out of the sides
> Of fiery Aetna, as if escaped from hell.
> They live in fumes, feed on the fruit that's
>   killed
> By ash, and are most poisonous.'

'Tell me,' Pinon said, his voice rising uncontrollably
up to Velasquo's high tenor,

>   '... might I buy that beauty
> From thee? I have a murder would be done
> Most fitting thus, most artful ...'

Sanguinetto considered it, cocking his head drunkenly to one side.

> 'I've more of these, they breed by hundreds –
>   aye.
> Done, if you pay me well enough.'

Pinon: 'I'll pay you.'

They made the exchange, Sanguinetto accepting a
small pouch. He looked in it and grinned. Pinon was
staring with an intense frown at the spider within the
glass. Sanguinetto returned to the table and sat down,
his back to Velasquo.

Sanguin:	'We'll celebrate this sale with more revelry.'
Pinon:	'Indeed it is a glad occasion.'
Sanguin:	'I give you my assurance, who You set that tiny demon on will die Most painful –'
Pinon:	'You'd know best, I'm certain . . .'

Now Pinon was standing right behind Sanguinetto, caped arms high so that he appeared a huge shadow, holding the glass box directly over the seated man's head. (Caropia's fingers were digging into my arm.) The spider's legs struck at the glass soundlessly. Sanguinetto reached forward and grabbed the foam-streaked bottle, raised it to his lips, tilted his head back; they froze:

Pinon pulled the floor of the box away and the spider dropped onto Sanguinetto's face. He struck at it with his free hand and it jumped to the table. As it skittered across, he smashed the bottle on it, scattering green glass everywhere. He staggered to his feet and arched back; his scream and Velasquo's high staccato laugh began simultaneously. The laughter continued longer.

On the table three or four spindly legs flailed at the air, their fine articulation destroyed. With stiff, awkward movements, Sanguinetto pulled his dagger from his belt and stabbed at the legs of the beast until they were still. He left the dagger in the table and collapsed over his chair. His voice, guttural as a rasp over metal, rose from near the floor.

'Stranger, I would thy heart were that black
  corse
Upon the table: surely it resembles nothing
  closer.
You had no cause to murder me . . .'

Velasquo pushed the hood from his head, and his
face, gleaming with sweat, suffused with exhilaration,
shifted as he looked about the room. He circled the
table, leaning over Sanguinetto to shout at him, inter-
spersing his lines with bursts of strained laughter:

'I did have cause; I am Velasquo, see?
My father's murder made me seek revenge!
You murdered him, 'gainst you I had revenge!
Now all that's sweet is nothing to revenge!'

'Wrong,' croaked Sanguinetto.

                              '. . . As well might I
  commend myself
For vengeance 'gainst you, having killed that
  spider,
As you to gloat o'er me, who was no more
Than insect used to slay your father –'

Vel: 'What's this?'
Sanguin: 'I was hired, hired by Pallio –
              here's my commission –'

He pulled the note from his doublet and tossed it on
the floor, then twisted as spasms racked him.

'A cauldron churns and bubbles within my
  skull –
I see hell waiting; Death will have its fill –'

After a while he moved no more.

Velasquo kneeled at the sheet of vellum, smoothed it on his leg, read. I could feel my heart knocking at the back of my throat –

His head snapped up, his eyes, ablaze with a vicious, yellow intensity, searched from exit to exit, *looking at actors:* his expression was absolutely murderous. I wanted to flatten myself against the wall, to hide; it was difficult indeed to stand beside Caropia and feign unconcerned interest. For *his* was no acting, he had understood, he was the Hieronomo! I felt a surge of relief at the certainty of it, replaced by fear when I recalled what I was certain of. I was in mortal danger. But I *knew*.

Finally he broke the silence, in a voice that filled the room like cold air.

'Pallio. Pallio, the simpleton, the fool.
That mask conceal'd a parricide most cruel.
Though first deceiv'd by his quick cloak of
  lies –'

He paused then, so that the next line would contain his private reference, unaware how accurate it already was:

'I'll use his blood to wash away *his* guise.'

The blackout allowed me to flee to my cubicle.

*   *   *

Act four began, and with it the gradual acceleration and disintegration typical of revenge tragedy. Plots skipped and jumped and ran afoul of each other, twisting without evident logic to their conclusion; characters died . . . From my cubicle I listened to the first scenes emerging tinnily from a speaker placed in the partition. Leontia, the Cardinal's wife, whom I hadn't seen since before the play began, was being strangled by the Cardinal's men. The Cardinal entreated Caropia to leave Naples, and, perfectly aware of the danger at the court, she agreed. I felt pained at that; foolishly, I had hoped we would remain lovers until the end. Caropia was then confronted by Carmen, her maid, who had been eaves-dropping. Carmen demanded payment to keep her from informing me of the Cardinal's plan – I laughed at that – it was a strange world we existed in, where some plotted against others, who listened as they did it. Caropia agreed, and then promptly poisoned her. The maid's screams brought guards, and the doctor Elazar, who declared it a natural death. He too had blackmail in mind, and after the guards left, Caropia was forced to stab him and hide his body under the bed.

I stopped listening, and attempted to decide what I should do next. Nothing occurred to me. *Nothing*, I thought, remembering with disgust the century or two of experience I had to draw on: I recalled canoeing down the Amazon, fighting in the streets of New York, a thousand other like events . . .

But what I actually had done was difficult to distinguish from all the things I remembered doing. All I was sure of was that I had spent a lot of time in a chair, living in words; and on stages. It was as if I were driving a vehicle, and the rearview mirror had expanded to fill the windshield. Or as if I were the Angel of Time, flying backwards into the future! Metaphors came up to me like bowling balls out of an automatic return; but no plans, nothing like a decision. Who was I to decide? Who was I?

'Pallio,' said the speaker loudly. It was a prompter, calling for me. I returned to the prop room, reluctant to take to the stage again. I could no longer remember what attraction I had ever had to it.

Bloomsman herself waved at me: I was on. I stepped out upon a dark stage. There was just enough grainy, purple light leaking down to enable me to perceive the silhouettes of three men, pulling something from beneath the bed. Something about the scene – the lithe, long-limbed black figures, crouching – lacked all familiarity – *jamais vu* swept over me like nausea. I no longer understood what I saw. The dark room was a dimensionless field, and the black figures were nameless objects, ominous because they moved. Meaningless sounds rang in my ears.

I came to and found myself confronted by Ferrando and Ursini, on a brightly lit apron. Their blades were out and pointed at my throat. My first thought was that I'd left my épée in my costume bag, and was defenceless; then synapses fired, for what reason I knew not, and my lines came to me. I was safe from them.

They accused me of Sanguinetto's murder, and in a rather weak imitation of the ingenuous public Pallio I informed them that Velasquo had been the last person seen with their late master. With trembling voice I quickly shifted their suspicions to Velasquo, feeling thankful that it made sense to play Pallio as a distracted man. I left the stage, and then had to watch while Velasquo surprised them and knifed them both in the back. He did it with a verve and accuracy that left me chilled; surely their improvised blocking couldn't be so well-done: had he begun already? But in the darkness between scenes Ferrando and Ursini brushed by me, muttering and giggling together. I shook my head in hopes of clearing it, inhaled sharply, and moved back onstage.

Again the light was deep crevasse-blue. Caropia was already there: we embraced. This was to be one of our last scenes together, I knew. Surely everyone knew. I moved to the apron and saw below me, in the front row, Ferrando, Ursini, Elazar, Carmen, Leontia, and Sanguinetto. It was the custom for actors whose work was done to join the audience, but it made me uncomfortable. Given the traditions of the genre it always seemed to me that they were still in the play as ghosts, who might speak at any time. I resisted the impulse to move to the other side of the apron.

My attention shifted back to Caropia. In her slim face the pebble-grey eyes were large, and filled with pain. I had so many disparate images of her to link . . . and yet, within the play and without, I knew nothing real about her. Our backstage silence augmented the Jacobean notion that the other sex was unknowable, a different species, an alien intelligence. Still, watching her bowed head, her slender arms moving nervously, I felt Pallio's emotions as my own, and I wanted to break into the play and experience that incestuous closeness. I spoke, infusing my lines with all these illusory feelings, to the invisible actress inside her, the one who made them both a mystery. I spoke tenderly of our love, and lamented our situation: 'We are so far in blood . . .' ''Tis payment,' Caropia cried, and railed against the sequence of unchangeable events she found herself trapped in. Bitterly she blamed our incest: 'Our sin of lust has webbed these plots around us, so I've dreamt –' I interrupted:

> 'Why shouldst thou not love best the one
>   known best?
> It is no crime, and were it, it has gain'd
> Us more than lost . . .'

She spoke of the church and we argued religion. Finally I interrupted again:

> 'In this world all are quite alone,
> All efforts grasp for union. Who's succeeded
> More than thou and I? We shar'd the womb,
> The universe of childhood; lov'd
> As lovers in the lust of youth –'

And Caropia, thinking no doubt of her pact with the Cardinal, replied:

> 'Thou know'st me well as one can know
>   another.'

I smiled, a tremendous effort, and continued:

> 'Thus be calm – thy dreams are naught but
>   visions

Of thine other self, beheld while in
The timeless void of sleep. We've fears
   enough
In this world.'

I turned from her and the tone of reassurance left
me. I voiced my real concern:

                '. . . I fear Velasquo's
Found me out; his eyes shout "murderer"
With all the brutal energy of horror.
He greets me mornings, dines with me at
   noon,
And stalks the palace grounds at night,
As if he were a hungry wolf, and I
A man alone on the trackless waste –'

Velasquo entered, several lines too early. Unable to
finish in his presence, I moved to the other side of the
apron and returned his baleful glare. Below me
Sanguinetto was smiling.

There was silence. It was the first time the three of
us had been onstage by ourselves, and the triangle we
formed was the focus of all the tension we had managed
to create. Beneath our polite exchange (Velasquo was
enquiring if Caropia would accompany him to the
masque) were layers: the reality of the play, the reality
of the players . . . Velasquo's crafted jests probed at me
with an intensity I alone could understand, although
all that he did made perfect sense in the context of the
play; indeed it must have appeared that he was doing
a superb job. Only small stresses in his intonation

revealed the danger, like swirls in a river, indicating swift undercurrents. I replied with a brittle hostility that had little acting in it, and we snapped at each other like the two poles of a Jacob's ladder:

Pallio:	'She goes with me, keep you away from her –'
Vel:	'Would you be kicked?'
Pallio:	'Would you have your neck broke?'

The audience's silence was a measure of their absorption. Despite my earlier revulsion, and the blank nausea of the *jamais vu*, I felt growing within me, insidiously, the pleasure of acting, the chill tingling one feels when a scene is going very well.

This pleasure in the scene's success was soon overwhelmed by the fear which was making it succeed; Velasquo's thinly veiled attack was strengthening. His pale eyes glared at me intently, looking for some involuntary movement or expression that would show me to be the one who had recognized him. I struggled to keep only Pallio's wariness on my face, but it was a delicate distinction, one becoming more and more difficult to make . . . I exited to the sound of his high laughter.

Once off, I hurried around towards the dressing room. Caropia's was the only voice emerging from the wall-speakers in the narrow corridor, and footsteps were padding behind me. I almost ran, remembering the early death in *Hamlet*. But it was only the Cardinal, completing errands of his own.

The dressing room was momentarily empty. I took

my épée from my costume bag and once again locked myself in a lavatory stall. The steel of the blade gleamed as I pulled away the leather scabbard.

It was an old épée, once used in competitive electric fencing. I had polished the half-sphere bell and removed the plug socket from inside it to convert it to a theatre sword. The wire running down a slot in the blade was still there, as was the tip, a small spring-loaded cylinder. The blade was stiff, and curved down slightly. At the bell it was triangular in cross-section, a short, wide-based triangle, with the base uppermost. It narrowed to a short cylindrical section at the end, which screwed into the tip.

I tried to unscrew the tip, certain that what I was doing was not real, that I was acting for myself. Surely the thing to do was to stop the play (I winced) and proclaim Velasquo's identity to all. Or to slip away, out the back, and escape him entirely.

Yet naming him before all would not do – where was my proof? Even my own conviction was shaken by the question of evidence. There wasn't any. The first real *proof* I would get would be a sudden hard lunge for my throat, with a sharp blade . . .

The tip wouldn't unscrew. I twisted until my fingers and hands were imprinted with red bars and semicircles, but it felt as if tip and blade were a solid piece. I clamped the tip between two molars and turned, but succeeded only in hurting my teeth. I needed pliers. I stared at the tip.

And if I were to escape, the Hieronomo would also. Surgery would change his face and voice, and he would return. I knew that in that case I would never be able to perform again without wondering if it were him again, playing opposite me . . .

I put the tip on the floor under my boot sole. Holding it flat against the floor, I pulled up on the blade. When I lifted my foot, the tip stuck out at right angles from the blade. I put it back on the floor, and carefully stepped on the new bend until it was straight again. I repeated the operation delicately; I knew, from years of fencing, how easily the blades would snap. Presently there appeared behind the tip a ripple, a weak spot that would break when struck hard enough. I slipped the scabbard back on, satisfied that the épée could be swiftly transformed into a weapon that would kill.

At some level unknown to me I had decided. I left the stall and stared at the white face in the mirror, feeling a stranger to myself.

Back in the dressing room, Caropia and Velasquo were in earnest conference. When they saw me, Caropia returned to her cubicle and Velasquo, looking angry, crossed to the other side of the room.

I sat down beside Caropia and listened to the speaker above us. The Cardinal was arranging, with whom I could not tell, to have Hamond and Orcanes poisoned at the masque. Apparently the masque was to take place very soon. As I changed my coat I could feel my pulse throbbing in my arms.

'Disguise,' said a voice in my ear. I jumped and turned to see Velasquo, his square face set close to mine.

'It's an odd word,' he continued. 'Shouldn't it be enguise, or beguise? Doesn't *dis*guise imply the opposite of what you want it to mean?'

I stared at him, in an agony of apprehension that he might go on, that he might reveal (disguise?) himself openly, and dare me to act – '*Dis* can also be used to intensify a verb,' I finally stammered.

'You are disguised,' he said, and scrutinized me closely. Then he walked away.

In my brain a chemical typhoon whirled. The exchange had been so – dramatic ... suddenly I was stunned by the horrible suspicion that all our words were lines, all the events backstage part of a larger play ... Bloomsman, Bloomsman ... By coincidence (or perhaps not) Caropia appeared to sense this thought. She stuck her head around the partition and said, with a sardonic smile, 'You learnt it of no fencer to shake thus,' a line from a play that I myself had once spoken. I picked up my épée and strode away in agitation, all my certainties shattered.

Caropia caught up with me just outside the prop room, and touched my hand. I watched her and tried to conceal the fact that I was still trembling. She smiled and slipped her arm under mine. The archaic gesture seemed fraught with emotion. For the first time I understood that it was not just another dominant/submissive signal from the past, that it had been able to express one human's support for another. My confusion lessened. One way or other I would know, soon enough.

The prop room was filled with actors getting ready for the masque. Bloomsman had done her usual meticulous prop work; the masks were bright animal heads that covered one to the shoulders. A menagerie composed chiefly of pigs, tigers, and horses, we stared at each other and whispered with excitement.

Bloomsman handed us our masks and smiled – a smile that now seemed to be filled with ominous possibility. 'It's going fine,' she said. 'Let's do this last scene right.' She put on a mask herself, a remorselessly grinning gargoyle.

I looked at my mask: a red fox. I could guess what Velasquo's would be. Caropia's was an exact model of her own head, with holes cut out for her eyes and mouth. The result, once on, was grotesque. She looked in a wall-mirror and laughed. 'I'm animal enough already,' she said. The gargoyle shrugged and said, in Bloomsman's calm voice, 'I thought it the right thing.'

Velasquo was already on stage, announcing his plans to the audience. Somehow he had learned of the relationship between Caropia and me. Long after everyone else in the theatre, he had seen through her guise. His desire for vengeance now focused as much on her as me. She was to die of poison placed in her drinking cup. Beside me, she watched the cup, still on the prop table, and shivered. I felt fear for her then, and great affection, and heedlessly I whispered to her, 'Don't drink from it.'

She stared at me, and began to laugh. But I did not and she stopped. Her grey eyes surveyed me and slowly widened, as if in fear of me. 'I won't,' she whispered in a soothing voice. She disengaged her arm and moved away, glancing back once with an expression I could not read, but which could have been one of . . . terror.

The stage was divided by two long tables, both laden with silver and gold, fruits and meat, candles and flasks of liqueurs. As the stage filled with masquers, servants

– in masks that were faceless white blanks – continued to load the tables. The fantastic menagerie milled about slowly and randomly seating themselves. Lines were shouted simultaneously, creating a cacophony that could only have been Bloomsman's doing.

I stood behind Caropia, at one end of the front table, peering through the eyeholes of my fox-face in search of Velasquo. My black, shiny nose protruded far before me. I saw that the Cardinal was not masked – he was still in his red robes, but a papal coronet was tilted back on his head. He viewed the uproar with an indulgent smile. Around him goats in formal dress drank wine.

My eye was caught by a movement above. A tall figure dressed in black leaned over the balcony and observed the activity; his mask was a skull. I glanced into the audience, and the backwash from the multicoloured glare was enough illumination to confirm my suspicion. Sanguinetto was gone. It was he on the balcony, playing the medieval death-figure. He began to descend the stairs, pausing for several seconds after each step.

The masque gained energy. A plate piled high with meat was tipped over; people rose from their seats, shouting witticisms. A long body of glittering red liquid flashed through the air and drenched one of the Cardinal's goats. There was still no sign of Velasquo. An orange fight started between tables, and the noise reached a frantic pitch, timed by the metronome of Sanguinetto's steps. Two women, both with tiger masks, began to claw at each other.

At the height of the cacophony a long scream cut through the sound, making its ragged descant. When it ended there was silence and the company was still, forming a bizarre tableau. A man with a pig's head and red doublet staggered to the apron. He tore at his snout and pulled the mask off, to reveal Orcanes. His face was bloated and purple. He clutched his throat, sank to his knees. As he collapsed another scream ripped the air. Another player, also in pig mask, fell to the floor and drummed out his death. Sanguinetto, now on the stage, paced between tables.

The Cardinal stood, his face grim. 'Who can account for these untimely deaths?' he demanded.

'*Pallio*,' a voice behind me called. I spun around and saw the wolf's face, fangs protruding, yellow eyes agleam. I tore off my mask and stepped back to increase the distance between us.

'Who is this man?' I asked, my voice preternaturally calm. 'He must be mad.'

'Your brother I,' he said, and pulled off his mask. 'Velasquo.'

'Velasquo!' I cried, and spoke to the Cardinal:

'Why, he kill'd Sanguinetto, Ferrando
And Ursini; yea, perhaps the old Duke too.
These new deaths without doubt are also his
    devise –'

Vel: 'He's false; he is the murd'rer of our father.
    Here's proof –'

Velasquo threw Sanguinetto's note down. I picked it up and looked at it. Pencilled beneath my Latin tag, in a fine imitation of Bloomsman's hand, was another title: *The Guise*. Proof indeed.

I crumpled the sheet and tossed it to the floor. 'A forgery,' I said, voice still calm. 'He tries usurping me.'

I pulled my épée from my scabbard. Velasquo did the same. The company drew back, pulling the front table with them to make room. The Cardinal made his way forward. Sanguinetto stood beside him. The two of them linked arms, and the Cardinal spoke:

'The truth is in Fate's hands. Let them fence.'

And in my mind I heard the blocking instruction, in Bloomsman's dry voice: 'Fence.'

Finally, finally the light became red, a bright crimson glare that bathed us both in blood. We circled each other warily. I watched his wrist, his stance, and in my concentration the world contracted to the two of us. Adrenaline flooded through me and my pulse was trip-hammer fast.

His blade had a tip on it, but that meant nothing; I knew it would slide back on contact, releasing the sharp point. The Hieronomo had used it before.

We began tentatively. He lunged, I parried, and we established a simple parry-riposte pattern, often used in practice, at very high speed. The flashing blades and the rapid clicking of clean parries were highly dramatic, but meant little.

After a short pause to regain balance, Velasquo lunged again, more fully this time, and we bouted with increased speed, using the full variety of tactics. The scrape and ring of steel against steel, the wooden thumping of our footwork, our hoarse breathing were the only sounds in the theatre.

The exchange ended and we stared at each other, breathing heavily. A wrinkle of concentration appeared between his eyes. I was sure he now realized that my knowledge of fencing was not implanted, that it was learned from actual experience. Implanted fencing was adequate for theatrics, but it consisted entirely of conscious moves and strategies, it was a verbal memory. Fencing learned by experience was remembered to a large extent in the cerebellum, where movement and balance are controlled, and thus reactions were nearly reflex-fast. Velasquo was certainly aware of this, and now he knew that he had been discovered by someone capable of besting him.

Suddenly he lunged with great violence. The thrust avoided my parry and I had to leap back to dodge his blade. The real fight had begun. He lunged in straight-forward attacks that were easy enough to parry, but when I did so he remised, continued to attack. He was ignoring my tipped weapon, which was clearly harmless. When I understood this, I jumped back and slapped my épée against the floor. The tip stayed on. I had to retreat and parry for my life, watching nothing but his blade, and striking it aside desperately each time it thrust at me.

My heel hit the bottom of the left stairway and I nearly stumbled. I stepped up backward, and Velasquo followed, negating my height advantage with the energy of his attack. I turned and ran up to the balcony, swinging my épée against the bannister all the way. The tip stayed on. I turned and lunged fiercely at my pursuer. He halted, lead foot three steps above his hind foot, and we engaged in a grim slashing battle, as if we were fighting with sabres. I didn't want him to reach the balcony. It was hopeless; still unafraid of my épée, he drove me back by degrees and managed, step by step, to make his way up to my level. When he reached the balcony I turned and sprinted down the other staircase four steps at a time, spinning and slashing once to impede his pursuit, and slamming my blade viciously against the side wall all the way down.

When I got to the stage, I saw that my tip had snapped off and disappeared. Exultantly I turned, parried Velasquo's running attack, and riposted straight at his chest. He leaped to one side to avoid the thrust. Several feet separated us; we stood panting.

He saw the change in my blade, invisible from more than a few feet away, and his expression became one of alarm – the idea struck him, perhaps, that tonight we had reversed roles; tonight I had become the Hieronomo. He looked up to my face, and I smiled.

Instinctively he lunged and in a fury of desperate motion drove me back across the stage. But now we were armed evenly, he had to respect my blade, and I wasn't forced to retreat for long. We battled with a sweaty, intense, total concentration.

He stopped and our blades circled each other: mine jagged and blunt, but slender; his still tipped by the treacherous false button. He started a complicated, deceptive attack. I stole the offensive from him with a stop thrust, lunged for his chest and hit just below the sternum. Amazingly, the blade did not bend and push my hand back, as it always had before: *it slid right in*.

Velasquo dropped his épée, stumbled back and fell, tugging free of my blade. I lifted it; the steel was streaked with blood, unnaturally red in the light. It dripped like water. Velasquo rolled onto his belly.

I looked up and surveyed the stage. Most of the cast had moved into the wings, which were blocked.

Caropia stepped forward, her tall cup still in her hands. Her eyes and mouth were black holes in a face as white as the mask she had long since removed. She appeared confused, but spoke her lines nevertheless, in a dry, airy voice:

> 'There lies he, chok'd in his own blood,
> A ravenous wolf whom all the world thought
>   good.'

Velasquo rolled over. Caropia's cup toppled to the floor. Sanguinetto, his mask still on, stepped towards me. I swung my épée in his direction and he stopped. I walked towards the rear exit, keeping the blade pointed at him.

Above me on the balcony, the gargoyle waved an arm, and the curtain jerked downward. The audience leaped to their feet, and I thought *They're after me, I'm caught*; but they were clapping, cheering, it was an ovation – the gargoyle bowed – I fled.

An unfamiliar door in the dressing room gave me access to a dark storage room. I crossed it, entered another hallway. It turned and almost immediately I was lost, running without plan down hallways and through dark rooms. Muffled shouts of pursuit reverberated through the walls from time to time, spurring me on. I tried to work my way in a single direction. A short set of stairs led me up to a little closet theatre, stage no bigger than a sitting room. Hearing voices back-stage, I crouched down between two rows of seats. I looked through the slot between two seat backs and watched a red-coated guard, one of the extras from our play, run on stage and halt. I held my breath. He surveyed the room quickly, then left as quickly as he had entered. The voices receded like echoes and I got up and ran again, out the back of the theatre.

I was in a long white hallway with a very high ceiling. Green light poured from long strips in the wall. To my left, at the end of the hall, was a door. I ran for it. As I approached I saw words printed on the door, above the horizontal bar that opened it: EMERGENCY EXIT – ALARM WILL SOUND.

The moment I comprehended the words, the dry, ineffable presence of *déjà vu* filled me: *this had happened before*. In a flash I knew everything, I understood all that had occurred in the theatre, it stood before me in my mind like a crystalline sphere. But just as quickly the entire matrix of thought collapsed, leaving no trace except the memory of its existence: *presque vu*, almost seen.

I slammed into the bar crossing the door, and it flew open. To the sharp blast of a siren I leaped out into the chill air, and back into the world.

Mercurial

'She rules all of Oz,' said Dorothy, 'and so she
rules your city and you, because you are in the
Winkie Country, which is part of the Land of Oz.'
'It may be,' returned the High Coco-Lorum, 'for
we do not study geography and have never
inquired whether we live in the Land of Oz or
not. And any Ruler who rules us from a distance,
and unknown to us, is welcome to the job.'
– L. FRANK BAUM. *The Lost Princess of Oz*

I AM NOT, DESPITE the appearances, fond of crime
detection. In the past, it is true, I occasionally
accompanied my friend Freya Grindavik as she
solved her cases, and admittedly this watsoning gave
me some good material for the little tales I have written for the not-very-discriminating markets on Mars
and Titan. But after The Case of the Golden Sphere of
the Lion of Mercury, in which I ended up hung by the

feet from the clear dome of Terminator, two hundred metres above the rooftops of the city, my native lack of enthusiasm rose to the fore. And following the unfortunate Adventure of the Vulcan Accelerator, when Freya's arch-foe Jan Johannsen tied us to a pile of hay under a large magnifying glass in a survival tent, there to await Mercury's fierce dawn, I put my foot down: no more detecting. That, so to speak, was the last straw.

So when I agreed to accompany Freya to the Solday party of Heidi Van Seegeren, it was against my better judgement. But Freya assured me there would be no business involved; and despite the obvious excesses, I enjoy a Solday party as much as the next aesthete. So when she came by my villa, I was ready.

'Make haste,' she said. 'We're late, and I must be before Heidi's Monet when the Great Gates are opened. I adore that painting.'

'Your infatuation is no secret,' I said, panting as I trailed her through the crowded streets of the city. Freya, as those of you who have read my earlier tales know, is two and a half metres tall, and broad-shouldered; she barged through the shoals of Solday celebrants rather like a whale, and I, pilot-fishlike, dodged in her wake. She led me through a group of Greys, who with carpetbeaters were busy pounding rugs saturated with yellow dust. As I coughed and brushed off my fine burgundy suit, I said, 'My feeling is that you have taken me to view that antique canvas once or twice too often.'

She looked at me sternly. 'As you will see, on Solday it transcends even its usual beauty. You look like a bee drowning in pollen, Nathaniel.'

'Whose fault is that?' I demanded, brushing my suit fastidiously.

We came to the gate in the wall surrounding Van Seegeren's town villa, and Freya banged on it loudly. The gate was opened by a scowling man. He was nearly a metre shorter than Freya, and had a balding head that bulged rather like the dome of the city. In a mincing voice he said, 'Invitations?'

'What's this?' said Freya. 'We have permanent invitations from Heidi.'

'I'm sorry,' the man said coolly. 'Ms Van Seegeren has decided her Solday parties have gotten overcrowded, and this time she sent out invitations and instructed me to let in only those who have them.'

'Then there has been a mistake,' Freya declared. 'Get Heidi on the intercom, and she will instruct you to let me in. I am Freya Grindavik, and this is Nathaniel Sebastian.'

'I'm sorry,' the man said, quite unapologetically. 'Every person turned away says the same thing, and Ms Van Seegeren prefers not to be disturbed so frequently.'

'She'll be more disturbed to hear we've been held up.' Freya shifted towards the man. 'Who are you, anyway?'

'I am Sandor Musgrave, Ms Van Seegeren's private secretary.'

'How come I've never met you?'

'Ms Van Seegeren hired me two months ago,' Musgrave said, and stepped back so he could look Freya in the eye without straining his neck. 'That is immaterial, however –'

'I've been Heidi's friend for over forty years,' Freya said slowly, once again shifting forward to lean over the man. 'And I would wager she values her friends more than her secretaries . . .'

Musgrave stepped back indignantly. 'I'm sorry!' he snapped. 'I have my orders! Good day!'

But alas for him, Freya was now standing well in the gateway, and she seemed uninclined to move; she merely cocked her head at him. Musgrave comprehended his problem, and his mouth twitched uncertainly.

The impasse was broken when Van Seegeren's maid Lucinda arrived from the street. 'Oh, hello, Freya, Nathaniel. What are you doing out here?'

'This new Malvolio of yours is barring our entrance,' Freya said.

'Oh, Musgrave,' said Lucinda. 'Let these two in, or the boss will be mad.'

Musgrave retreated with a deep scowl. 'I've studied the ancients, Ms Grindavik,' he said sullenly. 'You need not insult me.'

'Malvolio was a tragic character,' Freya assured him. 'Read Charles Lamb's essay concerning the matter.'

'I certainly will,' Musgrave said stiffly, and hurried to the villa, giving us a last poisonous look.

'Of course Lamb's father,' Freya said absently, staring after the man, 'was a house servant. Lucinda, who is that?'

Lucinda rolled her eyes. 'The boss hired him to restore some of her paintings, and get the records in order. I wish she hadn't.'

The bell in the gate sounded. 'I've got it, Musgrave,' Lucinda shouted at the villa. She opened the gate, revealing the artist Harvey Washburn.

'So you do,' said Harvey, blinking. He was high again; a bottle of the White Brother hung from his hand. 'Freya! Nathaniel! Happy Solday to you – have a drink?'

We refused the offer, and then followed Harvey around the side of the villa, exchanging a glance. I felt sorry for Harvey. Most of Mercury's great collectors came to Harvey's showings, but they dissected his every brushstroke for influences, and told him what he *should* be painting, and then among themselves they called his work amateurish and unoriginal, and never bought a single canvas. I was never surprised to see him drinking.

We rounded the side of the big villa and stepped onto the white stone patio, which was made of a giant slab of England's Dover cliffs, cut out and transported to Mercury entire. Malvolio Musgrave had spoken the truth about Heidi reducing the size of her Solday party: where often the patio had been jammed, there were now less than a dozen people. I spotted George Butler, Heidi's friend and rival art collector, and Arnold Ohman, the art dealer who obtained for many of Mercury's collectors their ancient masterpieces from Earth. As I greeted them Freya led us all across the patio to the back wall of the villa, which was also fronted with white slabs of the Dover cliffs. There, all alone, hung Claude Monet's *Rouen Cathedral – Sun Effect*. 'Look at it, Nathaniel!' Freya commanded me. 'Isn't it beautiful?'

I looked at it. Now you must understand that, as owner of the Gallery Orientale, and by deepest personal aesthetic conviction, I am a connoisseur of Chinese art, a style in which a dozen artfully spontaneous brush-strokes can serve to delineate a mountain or two, several trees, a small village and its inhabitants, and perhaps some birds. Given my predilection, you will not be surprised to learn that merely to look at the antique rectangle of colour that Freya so admired was to risk damaging my eyes. Thick scumbled layers of grainy paint scarcely revealed the cathedral of the title, which wavered under a blast of light so intense that I doubted Mercury's midday could compete with it. Small blobs of every colour served to represent both the indistinct stone and a pebbly sky; both were composed of combinations principally of white, yellow, and purple, though as I say, every other colour made an appearance.

'Stunning,' I said, with a severe squint. 'Are you sure this Monet wasn't a bit nearsighted?'

Freya glared at me, ignoring Butler's chuckles. 'I suppose your comment might have been funny the first time you made it. To children, anyway.'

'But I heard it was actually *true*,' I said, shielding my eyes with one hand. 'Monet *was* nearsighted, and so like Goya his vision affected his painting –'

'I should hope so,' Harvey said solemnly.

'– so all he could see were those blobs of colour, isn't that sad?'

Freya shook her head. 'You won't get a rise out of me today, Nathaniel. You'll have to think up your dinner conversation by yourself.'

Momentarily stopped by this riposte, I retired with Arnold Ohman to Heidi's patio bar. After dialling drinks from the bartender we sat on the blocks of Dover cliffs that made up the patio's low outer wall. We toasted Solday, and contemplated the clouds of yellow talc that swirled over the orange tile rooftops below us. For those of you who have never visited it, Terminator is an oval city. The forward half of the city is flat, and projects out under the clear dome. The rear half of the oval is terraced, and rises to the tall Dawn Wall, which supports the upper rim of the dome, and shields the city from the perpetually rising sun. The Great Gates of Terminator are near the top of the Dawn Wall, and when they are opened, shafts of Sol's overwhelming light spear through the city's air, illuminating everything in a yellow brilliance. Heidi Van Seegeren's villa was about halfway up the terraced slope; we looked upon grey stone walls, orange tile roofs, and the dusty vines and lemon trees of the terrace gardens that dotted the city; outside the dome the twelve big tracks over which the city slid extended off to the horizon, circling the planet like a slender silver wedding band. It was a fine view, and I lifted my glass to the idea that Claude Monet wasn't there to paint it. For sometimes, if you ask me, reality is enough.

Ohman downed his drink in one swallow. Rumour had it that he was borrowing heavily to finance one of his big terran purchases; it was whispered he was planning to buy the closed portion of the Louvre – or the Renaissance room of the Vatican museum – or Amsterdam's Van Gogh collection. But rumours like that circulated around Arnold continuously. He was that kind of dealer. It was unlikely any of them were true; still, his silence seemed to reveal a certain tension.

'Look at the way Freya is soaking in that painting you got for Heidi,' I said, to lift his spirits. Freya's face was within centimetres of the canvas, where she could examine it blob by blob; the people behind her could see nothing but her white-blond hair. Ohman smiled at the sight. He had brought the Monet back from his most recent terran expedition, and apparently it had been a great struggle to obtain it. Both the English family that owned it and the British government had had to be paid enormous sums to secure its release, and only the fact that Mercury was universally considered humanity's greatest art museum had cleared the matter with the courts. It had been one of Arnold's finest hours. Now he said, 'Maybe we should pull her away a bit, so that others can see.'

'If both of us tug on her it may work,' I said. We stood and went to her side. Harvey Washburn, looking flushed and frazzled, joined us, and we convinced Freya to share the glory. Ohman and Butler conferred over something, and entered the villa through the big French doors that led into the concert room. Inside, Heidi's orchestra rolled up and down the scales of Mussorgsky's *Hut of Baba Yaga*. That meant it was close to the time when the Great Gates would open (Heidi always gets inside information about this). Sure enough, as Mussorgsky's composition burst from the *Hut of Baba Yaga* into the *Great Gates of Kiev*, two splinters of white light split the air under the dome. Shouts and fanfares rose everywhere, nearly drowning the amplified sound of our orchestra. Slowly the Great Gates opened, and as they did the shafts of light grew to thick buttery gold bars of air. By their rich, nearly blinding glare, Heidi Van Seegeren made her first entrance from her villa, timing her steps to the exaggerated Maazel ritard that her conductor Hiu employed every Solday when *Pictures at an Exhibition* was performed. This ritard shifted the music from the merely grandiose to the utterly bombastical, and it took Heidi over a minute to cross her own narrow patio; but I suppose it was not entirely silly, given the ritual nature of the moment, and the flood of light that was making the air appear a thick, quite tangible gel. What with the light, and the uproar created by the keening Greys and the many orchestras in the neighbourhood, each playing their own overture or fanfare (the *Coriolan* came from one side of us, the *1812* from the other), it was a complex and I might even say *noisy* aesthetic moment, and the last thing I needed was to take another look at the Monet monstrosity, but Freya would not have it otherwise.

'You've never seen it when the Great Gates are opened,' she said. 'That was the whole point in bringing you here today.'

'I see.' Actually I barely saw anything; as Freya had guided me by the arm to the painting I had accidentally looked directly at the incandescent yellow bars of sunlight, and brilliant blue afterimages bounced in my sight. I heard rather than saw Harvey Washburn join us. Many blinks later I was able to join the others in devoting my attention to the big canvas.

Well. The Monet positively *glowed* in the dense, lambent air; it gave off light like a lamp, vibrating with a palpable energy of its own. At the sight of it even I was impressed.

'Yes,' I admitted to Freya and Harvey, 'I can see how precisely he placed all those little chunks of colour, and I can see how sharp and solid the cathedral is under all that goo, but it's like Solday, you know, it's a heightened effect. The result is garish, really, it's too much.'

'But this is a painting of midday,' Harvey said. 'And as you can see, midday can get pretty garish.'

'But this is Terminator! The Greys have put a lot of talc in the air to make it look this way!'

'So what?' Freya demanded impatiently. 'Stop thinking so much, Nathaniel. Just *look* at it. *See* it. Isn't it beautiful? Haven't you felt things look that way sometimes, seeing stone in sunlight?'

'Well . . .' And, since I am a strictly honest person, if I had said anything at all I would have had to admit that it did have a power about it. It drew the eye; it poured light onto us as surely as the beams of sunlight extending from the gates in the Dawn Wall to the curved side of the clear dome.

'Well?' Freya demanded.

'Well yes,' I said, 'yes I see that cathedral front – I feel it. But there must have been quite a heat wave in old Rouen. It's as if Monet had seen Terminator on Solday, the painting fits so well with this light.'

'No,' Freya said, but her left eye was squinted, a sign she is thinking.

Harvey said, 'We make the conditions of light in Terminator, and so it is an act of the imagination, like this painting. You shouldn't be surprised if there are similarities. We value this light because the old masters created it on their canvases.'

I shook my head, and indicated the brassy bedlam around us. 'No. I believe we made this one up ourselves.'

Freya and Harvey laughed, with the giddiness that Solday inspires.

Suddenly a loud screech came from inside the villa. Freya hurried across the patio into the music room, and I followed her. Both of us, however, had forgotten the arrangements that Heidi made on Soldays to cast the brilliant light throughout her home, and as we ran past the silenced orchestra into a hallway we were blasted by light from a big mirror carefully placed in the villa's central atrium. Screams still echoed from somewhere inside, but we could only stumble blindly through bright pulsing afterimages, retinal Monets if you will, while unidentified persons bowled into us, and mirrors crashed to the floor. And the atrium was raised, so that occasional steps up in the hallway tripped us. 'Murder!' someone cried. 'Murder! There he goes!' And with that a whole group of us were off down the halls like hounds – blind hounds – baying after unknown prey. A figure leaped from behind a mirror glaring white, and Freya and I tackled it just inside the atrium.

When my vision swam back I saw it was George Butler. 'What's going on?' he asked, very politely for a man who had just been jumped on by Freya Grindavik.

'Don't ask us,' Freya said irritably.

'Murder!' shrieked Lucinda from the hallway that led from the atrium directly back to the patio. We jumped up and crowded into the hallway. Just beyond a mirror shattered into many pieces lay a man's body; apparently he had been crawling towards the patio when he collapsed, and one arm and finger extended ahead of him, pointing to the patio still.

Freya approached, gingerly turned the body's head. 'It's that Musgrave fellow,' she said, blinking to clear her sight. 'He's dead all right. Struck on the head with the mirror there, no doubt.'

Heidi Van Seegeren joined us. 'What's going on?'

'That was my question,' George Butler said.

Freya explained the situation to her.

'Call the police,' Heidi said to Lucinda. 'And I suppose no one should leave.'

I sighed.

And so crime detection ensnared me once again. I helped Freya by circulating on the patio, calming the shocked and nervous guests. 'Um, excuse me, very sorry to inform you, yes, sorry – hard to believe, yes – somebody had it in for the secretary Musgrave, it appears,' all the while watching to see if anyone would jump, or turn pale, or start to run when I told them. Then, of course, I had to lead gently to the idea that everyone had gone from guest to suspect, soon to be questioned by Freya and the police. 'No, no, of *course* you're not suspected of anything, furthest thing from our minds, it's just that Freya wants to know if there's anything you saw that would help,' and so on. Then I had to do the difficult scheduling of Freya's interviews, at the same time I was supposed to keep an eye out for anything suspicious. Oh, the watson does the dirty work, all right. No wonder we always look dense when the detective unveils the solutions; we never have the time even to get the facts straight, much less meditate on their meaning. All I got that day were fragments: Lucinda whispered to me that Musgrave had worked for George Butler before Heidi hired him. Harvey Washburn told me that Musgrave had once been an artist, and that he had only recently moved to Mercury from Earth; this was his first Solday. That didn't give him much time to be hired by Butler, fired, and then hired by Van Seegeren. But was that of significance?

Late in the day I spoke with one of the police officers handling the case. She was relieved to have the
help of Freya Grindavik; Terminator's police force is
small, and often relies on the help of the city's famous
detective for the more difficult cases. The officer gave
me a general outline of what they had learned: Lucinda
had heard a shout for help, had stepped into the atrium
and seen a bloodied figure crawling down the hallway
towards the patio. She had screamed and run for help,
but only in the hallway was clear vision possible, and
she had quickly gotten lost. After that, chaos; everyone
at the party had a different tale of confusion.

After that conversation I had nothing more to do, so
I got all the sequestered guests coffee and helped pick up
some of the broken hall mirrors and passed some time
prowling Heidi's villa, getting down on my hands and
knees with the police robots to inspect a stain or two.

When Freya was finished with her interrogations, she
promised Heidi and the police that she would see the case
to its end – at least provisionally: 'I only do this for entertainment,' she told them irritably. 'I'll stay with it as long
as it entertains me. And I shall entertain myself with it.'

'That's all right,' said the police, who had heard this
before. 'Just so long as you'll take the case.' Freya
nodded, and we left.

The Solday celebration was long since over; the Great
Gates were closed, and once again through the dome
shone the black sky. I said to Freya, 'Did you hear about
Musgrave working for Butler? And how he came from
Earth just recently?' For you see, once on the scent I
am committed to seeing a case solved.

'Please, Nathaniel,' Freya said. 'I heard all that and

more. Musgrave stole the concept of Harvey Washburn's first series of paintings; he blackmailed both Butler and our host Heidi to obtain his jobs from them – or so I deduce from their protestations and certain facts concerning their recent questionable merger that I am privy to. And he tried to assault Lucinda, who is engaged to the cook Delaurence –' She let out a long sigh. 'Motives are everywhere.'

'It seems this Musgrave was a thoroughly despicable sort,' I said.

'Yes. An habitual blackmailer.'

'Nothing *suggests* itself to you?'

'No. I don't know why I agree to solve these things. Here I am committed to this headbashing, and my best clue is something that *you* suggested.'

'I wasn't aware that I had suggested anything!'

'There is a fresh perspective to ignorance that can be very helpful.'

'So it *is* important that Musgrave just arrived from Earth?'

She laughed. 'Let's stop in the Plaza Dubrovnik and get something to eat. I'm starving.'

Almost three weeks passed without a word from Freya, and I began to suspect that she was ignoring the case. Freya has no real sense of right and wrong, you see; she regards her cases as games, to be tossed aside if they prove too taxing. More than once she has cheerfully admitted defeat, and blithely forgotten any promises she may have made. She is *not* a moral person.

So I dropped by her home near Plaza Dubrovnik one evening, to rouse her from her irresponsible indifference.

When she answered the door there were paint smudges on her face and hands.

'Freya,' I scolded her. 'How could you take up an entirely new hobby when there is a *case* to be solved?'

'Generously I allow you entrance after such a false accusation,' she said. 'But you will have to eat your words.'

She led me downstairs to her basement laboratory, which extended the entire length and breadth of her villa. There on a big white-topped table lay Heidi Van Seegeren's Monet, looking like the three-dimensional geologic map of some minerally blessed country.

'What's this?' I exclaimed. 'Why is this here?'

'I believe it is a fake,' she said shortly, returning to a computer console.

'Wait a moment!' I cried. On the table around the painting were rolls of recording chart paper, lab note-books, and what looked like black-and-white photos of the painting. 'What do you mean?'

After tapping at the console she turned to me. 'I mean, I believe it's a fake!'

'But I thought art forgery was extinct. It is too easy to discover a fake.'

'Ha!' She waved a finger at me angrily. 'You pick a bad time to say so. It is a common opinion, of course, but not necessarily true.'

I regarded the canvas more closely. 'What makes you think this a fake? I thought it was judged a masterpiece of its period.'

'Something you said first caused me to question it,' she said. 'You mentioned that the painting seemed to have been created by an artist familiar with the light of Terminator. This seemed true to me, and it caused me to reflect that one of the classic signs of a fake was anachronistic sensibility – that is to say, the forger injects into his vision of the past some element of his time that is so much a part of his sensibility that he cannot perceive it. Thus the Victorians faked Renaissance faces with a sentimentality that only they could not immediately see.'

'I see.' I nodded sagely. 'It did seem that cathedral had been struck with Solday light, didn't it.'

'Yes. The trouble is, I have been able to find no sign of forgery in the physical properties of the painting.' She shook her head. 'And after three weeks of uninterrupted chemical analysis, that is beginning to worry me.'

'But Freya,' I said, as something occurred to me. 'Does all this have a bearing on the Musgrave murder?'

'I think so,' she replied. 'And if not, it is certainly more interesting. But I believe it does.'

I nodded. 'So what, exactly, have you found?'

She smiled ironically. 'You truly want to know? Well. The best test for anachronisms is the polonium 210, radium 226 equilibrium –'

'Please, Freya. No jargon.'

'Jargon!' She raised an eyebrow to scorn me. 'There is no such thing. Intelligence is like mould in a petri dish – as it eats ever deeper into the agar of reality, language has to expand with it to describe what has been digested. Each speciality provides the new vocabulary for its area of feeding and gets accused of fabricating jargon by those who know no better. I'm surprised to hear such nonsense from you. Or perhaps not.'

'Very well,' I said, hands up. 'Still, you must communicate your meaning to me.'

'I shall. First I analysed the canvas. The material and

its weave match the characteristics of the canvas made by the factory outside Paris that provided Monet throughout the painting of the Rouen cathedral series. Both the fabric and the glue appear very old, though there is no precise dating technique for them. And there was no trace of solvents that might have been used to strip paint off a genuine canvas of the period.

'I then turned to the paint. Follow so far?' she asked sharply. 'Paint?'

'You may proceed without further sarcasm, unless unable to control yourself.'

'The palette of an artist as famous as Monet has been studied in detail, so that we know he preferred cadmium yellow to chromium yellow or Naples yellow, that he tended to use Prussian blue rather than cobalt blue, and so on.' She tapped the flecks of blue at the base of the cathedral. 'Prussian blue.'

'You've taken paint off the canvas?'

'How else test it? But I took very small samples, I assure you. Whatever the truth concerning the work, it remains a masterpiece, and I would not mar it. Besides, most of my tests were on the white paint, of which there is a great quantity, as you can see.'

'Why the white paint?' I leaned over to stare more closely at the canvas.

'Because lead white is one of the best dating tools we have. The manufacturing methods used to make it changed frequently around Monet's time, and each change in method altered the chemical composition of the paint. After 1870, for instance, the cheaper zinc white was used to adulterate lead white, so there should be over one per cent zinc in Monet's lead white.'

'And is that what you found?'

'Yes. The atomic absorption spectrum showed –' She dug around in the pile of chart paper on the table – 'Well, take my word for it –'

'I will.'

'Nearly twelve per cent. And the silver content for late nineteenth century lead white should be around four parts per million, the copper content about sixty parts per million. So it is with this paint. There is no insoluble antimony component, as there would be if the paint had been manufactured after 1940. The X-ray diffraction pattern' – she unrolled a length of chart paper and showed me where three sharp peaks in a row had been penned by the machine – 'is exactly right, and there is the proper balance of polonium 210 and radium 226. That's very important, by the way, because when lead white is manufactured the radioactive balance of some of its elements is upset, and it takes a good three hundred years for them to decay back to equilibrium. And this paint is indeed back to that equilibrium.'

'So the paints are Monet's,' I concluded. 'Doesn't that prove the work authentic?'

'Perhaps,' Freya admitted. 'But as I was doing all this analysis, it occurred to me that a modern forger has just as much information concerning Monet's palette as I do. With a modern laboratory it would be possible to use such information as a recipe, so to speak, and then to synthesize paints that would match the recipe exactly. Even the radioactively decayed lead white could be arranged, by avoiding the procedures that disrupt the radioactive balance in the first place!'

'Wouldn't that be terrifically complicated?'

Freya stared at me. '*Obviously*, Nathaniel, we are dealing with a very very meticulous faker here. But how else could it be done, in this day and age? Why else do it at all? The complete faker must take care to anticipate every test available, and then in a modern laboratory create the appropriate results for every one of them. It's admirable!'

'Assuming there ever was such a forger,' I said dubiously. 'It seems to me that what you have actually done here is prove the painting genuine.'

'I don't think so.'

'But even with these paints made by recipe, as you call them, the faker would still have to paint the painting!'

'Exactly. Conceive the painting, and execute it. It becomes very impressive, I confess.' She walked around the table to look at the work from the correct angle. 'I do believe this is one of the *best* of the Rouen cathedral series – astonishing, that a forger would be capable of it.'

'That brings up another matter,' I said. 'Doesn't this work have a five-hundred-year-old pedigree? How could a whole history have been provided for it?'

'Good question. But I believe I have discovered the way. Let's go upstairs – you interrupted my preparations for lunch, and I'm hungry.'

I followed her to her extensive kitchen, and sat in the window nook that overlooked the tile rooftops of the lower city while she finished chopping up the vegetables for a large salad.

'Do you know this painting's history?' Freya asked, looking up from a dissected head of lettuce.

I shook my head. 'Up until now the thing has not been of overwhelming interest to me.'

'A confession of faulty aesthetics. The work was photographed at the original exhibit in 1895; Durand-Ruel photo 5828 L4451. All of the information appended to the photo fits our painting – same name, size, signature location. Then for a century it disappeared. Odd. But it turned out to have been in the estate of an Evans family, in Aylesbury, England. When the family had some conservation work done on one corner it returned to public knowledge, and was photographed for a dozen books of the twenty-first and twenty-second centuries. After that it slipped back into obscurity, but it is as well documented as any of the series belonging to private estates.'

'Exactly my point,' I said. 'How could such a history be forged?'

As Freya mixed the salad she smiled. 'I sat and thought about that for quite some time myself. But consider it freshly, Nathaniel. How do we know what we know of the past?'

'Well,' I said, somewhat at a loss. 'From data banks, I suppose. And books – documents – historians –'

'From historians!' She laughed. She provided us both with bowls and sat across from me. As I filled mine she said, 'So we want to know something of the past. We go to our library and sit at its terminal. We call up general reference works, or a bibliographic index, and we choose, if we want, books that we would like to have in our hands. We type in the appropriate code, our printer prints up the appropriate book, and the volume slides out of the computer into our waiting grasp.' She paused to fork down several mouthfuls of salad. 'So we learn about the past using computer programs. And a clever programmer, you see, can change a program. It would be possible to *insert* extra pages into these old books on Monet, and thus add the forged painting to the record of the past.'

I paused, a cherry tomato hovering before my mouth. 'But –'

'I searched for an original of *any* of these books containing photos of our painting,' Freya said. 'I called all over Mercury, and to several incunabulists in libraries on Earth – you wouldn't believe the phone bill I've run up. But the initial printings of these art volumes were very small, and although first editions probably remain *somewhere*, they are not to be found. Certainly there are no first editions of these books on Mercury, and none immediately locatable on Earth. It began to seem a very unlikely coincidence, as if these volumes contained pictures of our painting precisely because they existed only in the data banks, and thus could be altered without discovery.'

She attended to her salad, and we finished eating in silence. All the while my mind was spinning furiously, and when we were done I said, 'What about the original exhibit photo?'

She nodded, pleased with me. 'That, apparently, is genuine. But the Durand-Ruel photos include four or five of paintings that have never been seen since. In that sense the Rouen cathedral series is a good one for a faker; from the first it has never been clear how many cathedrals Monet painted. The usual number given is thirty-two, but there are more in the Durand-Ruel list, and a faker could examine the list and use one of the lost items as a prescription for his fake. Providing a later history with the aid of these obscure art books would result in a fairly complete pedigree.'

'But could such an addition to the data banks be made?'

'It would be easiest done on Earth,' Freya said. 'But there is no close security guarding the banks containing old art books. No one expects them to be tampered with.'

'It's astonishing,' I said with a wave of my fork, 'it is baroque, it is *byzantine* in its ingenuity!'

'Yes,' she said. 'Beautiful, in a way.'

'However,' I pointed out to her, 'you have no proof – only this perhaps over-complex theory. You have found no first edition of a book to confirm that the computer-generated volumes add Heidi's painting, and you have found no physical anachronism in the painting itself.'

Gloomily she clicked her fork against her empty salad bowl, then rose to refill it. 'It is a problem,' she admitted. 'Also, I have been working on the assumption that Sandor Musgrave discovered evidence of the forgery. But *I* can't find it.'

Never let it be said that Nathaniel Sebastian has not performed a vital role in Freya Grindavik's great feats of detection. I was the first to notice the anachronism of sensibility in Heidi's painting; and now I had a truly inspired idea. 'He was pointing to the patio!' I exclaimed. 'Musgrave, in his last moment, struggled to point to the patio!'

'I had observed that,' Freya said, unimpressed.

'But Heidi's patio – you know – it is formed out of blocks of the Dover cliffs! And thus Musgrave indicated

England! Is it not possible? The Monet was owned by Englishmen until Heidi purchased it – perhaps Musgrave meant to convey that the original owners were the forgers!'

Freya's mouth hung open in surprise, and her left eye was squinted shut. I leaped from the window nook in triumph. 'I've solved it! I've solved a mystery at last!'

Freya looked up at me and laughed.

'Come now, Freya, you must admit I have given you the vital clue.'

She stood up, suddenly all business. 'Yes, yes, indeed you have. Now out with you, Nathaniel, I have work to do.'

'So I did give you the vital clue?' I asked. 'Musgrave was indicating the English owners?'

As she ushered me to her door Freya laughed. 'As a detective your intuition is matched only by your confidence. Now leave me to work, and I will be in contact with you soon, I assure you.' And with that she urged me into the street, and I was left to consider the case alone.

Freya was true to her word, and only two days after our crucial luncheon she knocked on the door of my town villa. 'Come along,' she said. 'I've asked Arnold Ohman for an appointment; I want to ask him some questions about the Evans family. The city is passing the Monet museum, however, and he asked us to meet him out there.'

I readied myself quickly, and we proceeded to North Station. We arrived just in time to step across the gap between the two platforms, and then we were on the

motionless deck of one of the outlying stations that
Terminator is always passing. There we rented a car
and sped west, paralleling the dozen massive cylindrical rails along which the city slides. Soon we had left
Terminator behind, and when we were seventy or eighty
kilometres onto the nightside of Mercury we turned to
the north, to Monet Crater.

Terminator's tracks lie very close to the thirtieth
degree of latitude, in the Northern hemisphere, and
Monet Crater is not far from them. We crossed
Shakespeare Planitia rapidly, passing between craters
named after the great artists, writers, and composers of
Earth's glorious past: traversing a low pass between
Brahms and Verdi, looking down at where Degas had
crashed into the Brontës. 'I think I understand why a
modern artist on Mercury might turn to forgery,' Freya
said. 'We are dwarfed by the past as we are by this landscape.'

'But it is still a crime,' I insisted. 'If it were done
often, we would not be able to distinguish the authentic from the fake.'

Freya did not reply.

I drove our car up a short rise, and we entered the
submercurial garage of the Monet museum, which is
set deep in the southern rim of the immense crater
named after the artist. One long wall of the museum
is a window facing out over the crater floor, so that the
central knot of peaks is visible, and the curving inner
wall of the crater defines the horizon in the murky
distance. Shutters slid down to protect these windows
from the heat of Mercury's long day, but now they were
open and the black wasteland of the planet formed a

strange backdrop to the colourful paintings that filled the long rooms of the museum.

There were many Monet originals there, but the canvases of the Rouen cathedral series were almost all reproductions, set in one long gallery. As Freya and I searched for Arnold we also viewed them.

'You see, they're not just various moments of a single day,' Freya said.

'Not unless it was a very strange day for weather.' The three reproductions before us all depicted foggy days: two bluish and underwater-looking, the third a bright burning-off of yellow noontime fog. Obviously these were from a different day than the ones across the room, where a cool clear morning gave way to a midday that looked as if the sun was just a few feet above the cathedral. The museum had classified the series in colour groups: 'Blue Group', 'White Group', 'Yellow Group', and so on. To my mind that system was stupid – it told you nothing you couldn't immediately see. I myself classified them according to weather. There was a clear day that got very hot; a clear winter day, the air chill and pure; a foggy day; and a day when a rainstorm had grown and then broken. When I told Freya of my system she applauded it. 'So Heidi's painting goes from the king of the White Group to the hottest moment of the hot day.'

'Exactly. It's the most extreme as far as sunlight blasting the stone into motes of colour.'

'And thus the forger extends Monet's own thinking, you see,' she said, a bit absently. 'But I *don't* see Arnold, and I think we have visited every room.'

'Could he be late?'

'We are already quite late ourselves. I wonder if he has gone back?'

'It seems unlikely,' I said.

Purposefully we toured the museum one more time, and I ignored the colour-splashed canvases standing before the dark crater, to search closely in all the various turns of the galleries. No Arnold.

'Come along,' Freya said. 'I suspect he stayed in Terminator, and now I want to speak with him more than ever.'

So we returned to the garage, got back in our car, and drove out onto Mercury's bare, baked surface once again. Half an hour later we had Terminator's tracks in sight. They stretched before us from horizon to horizon, twelve fat silvery cylinders set five metres above the ground on narrow pylons. To the east, rolling over the flank of Wang Wei Crater so slowly that we could not perceive its movement without close attention, came the city itself, a giant clear half-egg filled with the colours of rooftops, gardens, and the grey stone of the buildings crowding the terraced Dawn Wall.

'We'll have to go west to the next station,' I said. Then I saw something, up on the city track nearest us: spread-eagled over the top of the big cylinder was a human form in a light green daysuit. I stopped the car. 'Look!'

Freya peered out her window. 'We'd better go investigate.'

We struggled quickly into the car's emergency daysuits, clamped on the helmets, and slipped through the car's lock onto the ground. A ladder led us up the nearest cylinder pylon and through a tunnel in the cylinder itself. Once on top we could stand safely on the broad hump of the rail.

The figure we had seen was only ten metres away from us, and we hurried to it.

It was Arnold, spread in cruciform fashion over the cylinder's top, secured in place by three large suction plates that had been cuffed to his wrists and ankles, and then stuck to the cylinder. Arnold turned from his contemplation of the slowly approaching city, and looked at us wide-eyed through his faceplate. Freya reached down and turned on his helmet intercom.

'– am I glad to see you!' Arnold cried, voice harsh. 'These plates won't move!'

'Tied to the tracks, eh?' Freya said.

'Yes!'

'Who put you here?'

'I don't know! I went out to meet you at the Monet museum, and the last thing I remember I was in the garage there. When I came to, I was here.'

'Does your head hurt?' I enquired.

'Yes. Like I was gassed, though, not hit. But – the city – it just came over the horizon a short time ago. Perhaps we could dispense with discussion until I am freed?'

'Relax,' Freya said, nudging one of the plates with her boot. 'Are you sure you don't know who did this, Arnold?'

'Of course! That's what I just said! Please, Freya, can't we talk after I get loose?'

'In a hurry, Arnold?' Freya asked.

'But *of course.*'

'No need to be too worried,' I assured him. 'If we

cannot free you, the cowcatchers will be out to pry you loose.' I tried lifting a plate, but could not move it. 'Surely they will find a way – it's their job, after all.'

'True,' Arnold said.

'Usually true,' said Freya. 'Arnold is probably not aware that the cowcatchers have become rather unreliable recently. Some weeks ago a murderer tied his victim to a track just as you have been, Arnold, and then somehow disengaged the cowcatchers' sensors. The unfortunate victim was shaved into molecules by one of the sleeves of the city. It was kept quiet to avoid any attempted repetitions, but since then the cowcatchers' sensors have continued to function erratically, and two or three suicides have been entirely too successful.'

'Perhaps this isn't the best moment to tell us about this,' I suggested to Freya.

Arnold choked over what I took to be his agreement.

'Well,' Freya said, 'I thought I should make the situation clear. Now listen, Arnold. We need to talk.'

'*Please*,' Arnold said. 'Free me first, *then* talk.'

'No, no –'

'But Terminator is only a kilometre away!'

'Your perspective from that angle is deceptive,' Freya told him. 'The city is at least three kilometres away.'

'More like two,' I said, as I could now make out individual rooftops under the Dawn Wall. In fact the city glowed like a big glass lamp and illuminated the entire landscape with a faint green radiance.

'And at three point four kilometres an hour,' Freya said, 'that gives us almost an hour, doesn't it. So listen to me, Arnold. The Monet cathedral that you sold to Heidi is a fake.'

'What?' Arnold cried. 'It certainly is not! And I insist this isn't the time –'

'It is a fake. Now I want you to tell me the truth, or I will leave you here to test the cowcatchers.' She leaned over to stare down at Arnold face to face. 'I know who painted the fake, as well.'

Helplessly Arnold stared up at her.

'He put you on the track here, didn't he?'

Arnold squeezed his eyes shut, nodded slowly. 'I think so.'

'So if you want to be let up, you must swear to me that you will abide by my plan for dealing with this forger. You *will* follow my instructions, understand?'

'I understand.'

'Do you agree?'

'I agree,' Arnold said, forcing the words out. 'Now let me up!'

'All right.' Freya straightened.

'How are we going to do it?' I asked.

Freya shrugged. 'I don't know.'

At this Arnold howled, he shouted recriminations, he began to wax hysterical –

'Shut up!' Freya exclaimed. 'You're beginning to sound like a man who has made too many brightside crossings. These suction plates are little different from children's darts.' She leaned down, grasped a plate, pulled up with all of her considerable strength. No movement. 'Hmm,' she said thoughtfully.

'Freya,' Arnold said.

'One moment,' she replied, and walked back down

the hump of the cylinder to the ladder tunnel, there to disappear down it.

'She's left me,' Arnold groaned. 'Left me to be crushed.'

'I don't think so,' I said. 'No doubt she has gone to the car to retrieve some useful implement.' I kicked heartily at the plate holding Arnold's feet to the cylinder, and even managed to slide it a few centimetres down the curve, which had the effect of making Arnold suddenly taller. But other than that I made no progress.

When Freya returned she carried a bar, bent at one end. 'Crowbar,' she explained to us.

'But where did you get it?'

'From the car's tool chest, naturally. Here.' She stepped over Arnold. 'If we just insinuate this end of it under your cuffs, I believe we'll have enough leverage to do the trick. The cylinder being curved, the plate's grasp should be weakened – about here.' She jammed the short end of the bar under the edge of the footplate's cuff, and pulled on the upper end of it. Over the intercom, breathless silence; her fair cheeks reddened; then suddenly Arnold's legs flew up and over his head, leaving his arms twisted and his neck at an awkward angle. At the same time Freya staggered off the cylinder, performed a neat somersault, and landed on her feet on the ground below us. While she made her way back up to us I tried to ease the weight on Arnold's neck, but by his squeaks of distress I judged he was still uncomfortable. Freya rejoined us, and quickly wedged her crowbar under Arnold's right wrist cuff, and freed it. That left Arnold hanging down the side of the cylinder by his left wrist; but with one hard crank Freya popped that plate free as well, and Arnold disappeared. By leaning over we could just see him, collapsed in a heap on the ground. 'Are you all right?' Freya asked. He groaned for an answer.

I looked up and saw that Terminator was nearly upon us. Almost involuntarily I proceeded to the ladder tunnel; Freya followed me, and we descended to the ground. 'Disturbing not to be able to trust the cowcatchers,' I remarked as my heartbeat slowed.

'Nathaniel,' Freya said, looking exasperated. 'I made all that up, you know that.'

'Ah. Yes, of course.'

As we joined Arnold he was just struggling to a seated position. 'My ankle,' he said. Then the green wash of light from Terminator disappeared, as did the night sky; the city slid over us, and we were encased in a gloom interrupted by an occasional running light. All twelve of the city's big tracks had disappeared, swallowed by the sleeves in the city's broad metallic foundation. Only the open slots that allowed passage over the pylons showed where the sleeves were; for a moment in the darkness it seemed we stood between two worlds held apart by a field of pylons.

Meanwhile the city slid over us soundlessly, propelled by the expansion of the tracks themselves. You see, the alloy composing the tracks is capable of withstanding the 425 degree centigrade heat of the Mercurial day, but the cylinders do expand just a bit in this heat. Here in the terminator is the forward edge of the cylinders' expansion, and the smooth-sided sleeves above us at that moment fit so snugly over the cylinders that as the cylinders expand, the city is pushed forward towards the cooler, thinner railing to the west; and so the city is propelled by the sun, while never being fully exposed to it. The motive force is so strong, in fact, that resistance to it arranged in the sleeves generates the enormous reserves of energy that Terminator has sold so successfully to the rest of civilization.

Though I had understood this mechanism for decades, I had never before observed it from this angle, and despite the fact that I was somewhat uneasy to be standing under our fair city, I was also fascinated to see its broad, knobby silver underside, gliding majestically westward. For a long time I did nothing but stare at it.

'We'd better get to the car,' Freya said. 'The sun will be up very soon after the city passes, and then we'll be in trouble.'

Since Arnold was still cuffed to the plates, and had at least a sprained ankle, walking with him slung between us was a slow process. While we were at it the Dawn Wall passed over us, and suddenly the twelve tracks and the stars between them were visible again. 'Now we'd better hurry,' said Freya. Above us the very top of the Dawn Wall flared a brilliant white; sunlight was striking that surface, only two hundred metres above us. Dawn was not far away. In the glare of reflected light we could see the heavily tyre-printed ground under the cylinders perfectly, and for a while our eyes were nearly overwhelmed. 'Look!' Freya cried, shielding her eyes with one hand and pointing up at the sun-washed slope of the city wall with the other. 'It's the inspiration for our Monet, don't you think?'

Despite our haste, the great Rouen cathedral of Mercury pulled away from us. 'This won't do,' Freya said. 'Only a bit more to the car, but we have to hurry. Here, Arnold, let me carry you –' and she ran, carrying Arnold piggyback, the rest of the way to the car. As we manoeuvred him through the lock, a tongue of the sun's corona licked briefly over the horizon, blinding us. I felt scorched; my throat was dry. We were now at the dawn edge of the terminator zone, and east-facing slopes burned white while west-facing slopes were still a perfect black, creating a chaotic patchwork that was utterly disorienting. We rolled into the car after Arnold, and quickly drove west, passing the city, returning to the night zone, and arriving at a station where we could make the transfer into the city again. Freya laughed at my expression as we crossed the gap. 'Well, Nathaniel,' she said, 'home again.'

The very next day Freya arranged for those concerned with the case to assemble on Heidi's patio again. Four police officials were there, and one took notes. The painting of the cathedral of Rouen was back in its place on the villa wall; George Butler and Harvey Washburn stood before it, while Arnold Ohman and Heidi paced by the patio's edge. Lucinda and Delaurence, the cook, watched from behind the patio bar.

Freya called us to order. She was wearing a severe blue dress, and her white-blond hair was drawn into a tight braid that fell down her back. Sternly she said, 'I will suggest to you an explanation for the death of Sandor Musgrave. All of you except for the police and Mr Sebastian were to one extent or another suspected of killing him, so I know this will be of great interest to you.'

Naturally there was an uneasy stir among those listening.

'Several of you had reason to hate Musgrave, or to fear him. The man was a blackmailer by profession, and on Earth he had obtained evidence of illegalities in the merger Heidi and George made five years ago, that gave him leverage over both of you. This and motives for the rest of you were well established during the initial investigation, and we need not recapitulate the details.

'It is also true, however, that subsequent investigations have revealed that all of you had alibis for the moment when Musgrave was struck down. Lucinda and Delaurence were together in the kitchen until Lucinda left to investigate the shout she heard; this was confirmed by caterers hired for the Solday party. Heidi left the patio shortly before Musgrave was found, but she was consulting with Hiu and the orchestra during the time in question. George Butler went into the house with Arnold Ohman, but they were together for most of the time they were inside. Eventually George left to go to the bathroom, but luckily for him the orchestra's first clarinetist was there to confirm his presence. And fortunately for Mr Ohman, I myself could see him from the patio, standing in the hallway until the very moment when Lucinda screamed.

'So you see' – Freya paused, eyed us one by one, ran a finger along the frame of the big painting – 'the problem took on a new aspect. It became clear that, while many had a motive to kill Musgrave, no one had the opportunity. This caused me to reconsider. How, exactly, had Musgrave been killed? He was struck on the head by the frame of one of Heidi's hall mirrors.

Though several mirrors were broken in the mêlée following Lucinda's screams, we know the one that Musgrave was struck with; it was at the bend in the hallway leading from the atrium to the patio. And it was only a couple of metres away from a step down in the hallway.'

Freya took a large house plan from a table and set it before the policemen. 'Sandor Musgrave, you will recall, was new to Mercury. He had never seen a Solday celebration. When the Great Gates opened and the reflected light filled this villa, my suggestion is that he was overwhelmed by fright. Lucinda heard him cry for help – perhaps he thought the house was burning down. He panicked, rushed out of the study, and blindly began to run for the patio. Unable to see the step down or the mirror, he must have pitched forward, and his left temple struck the frame a fatal blow. He crawled a few steps farther, then collapsed and died.'

Heidi stepped forward. 'So Musgrave died by accident?'

'This is my theory. And it explains how it was that no one had the opportunity to kill him. In fact, no one did kill him.' She turned to the police. 'I trust you will follow up on this suggestion?'

'Yes,' said the one taking notes. 'Death declared accidental by consulting investigator. Proceed from there.' He exchanged glances with his colleagues. 'We are satisfied this explains the facts of the case.'

Heidi surveyed the silent group. 'To tell you the truth, I am very relieved.' She turned to Delaurence. 'Let's open the bar. It would be morbid to celebrate an accidental death, but here we can say we are celebrating the absence of a murder.'

The others gave a small cheer of relief, and we surrounded the bartender.

A few days later Freya asked me to accompany her to North Station. 'I need your assistance.'

'Very well,' I said. 'Are you leaving Terminator?'

'Seeing someone off.'

When we entered the station's big waiting room, she inspected the crowd, then cried, 'Arnold!' and crossed the room to him. Arnold saw her and grimaced. 'Oh, Arnold,' she said, and leaned over to kiss him on each cheek. 'I'm very proud of you.'

Arnold shook his head, and greeted me mournfully. 'You're a hard woman, Freya,' he told her. 'Stop behaving so cheerfully, you make me sick. You know perfectly well this is exile of the worst sort.'

'But Arnold,' Freya said, 'Mercury is not the whole of civilization. In fact it could be considered culturally dead, an immense museum to the past that has no real life at all.'

'Which is why you choose to live here, I'm sure,' he said bitterly.

'Well of course it does have some pleasures. But the really vital centres of any civilization are on the frontier, Arnold, and that's where you're going.'

Arnold looked completely disgusted.

'But Arnold,' I said. 'Where are you going?'

'Pluto,' he said curtly.

'*Pluto*?' I exclaimed. 'But whatever for? What will you do there?'

He shrugged. 'Dig ditches, I suppose.'

Freya laughed. 'You certainly will not.' She addressed

me: 'Arnold has decided, very boldly I might add, to abandon his safe career as a dealer here on Mercury, to become a real artist on the frontier.'

'But *why?*'

Freya wagged a finger at Arnold. 'You must write us often.'

Arnold made a strangled growl. 'Damn you, Freya. I refuse. I refuse to go.'

'You don't have that option,' Freya said. 'Remember the chalk, Arnold. The chalk was your signature.'

Arnold hung his head, defeated. The city interfaced with the spaceport station. 'It isn't fair,' Arnold said. 'What am I going to do out on those barbaric outworlds?'

'You're going to live,' Freya said sternly. 'You're going to live and you're going to paint. No more hiding. Understand?'

I, at any rate, was beginning to.

'You should be thanking me profusely,' Freya went on, 'but I'll concede you're upset and wait for gratitude by mail.' She put a hand on Arnold's shoulder and pushed him affectionately towards the crossing line. 'Remember to write.'

'But,' Arnold said, a panicked expression on his face. 'But –'

'Enough!' Freya said. 'Be gone! Or else.'

Arnold sagged, and stepped across the divide between the stations. Soon the city left the spaceport station behind.

'Well,' Freya said. 'That's done.'

I stared at her. 'You just helped a murderer to escape!'

She lifted an eyebrow. 'Exile is a very severe punishment; in fact in my cultural tradition it was the usual punishment for murder committed in anger or self-defence.'

I waved a hand dismissively. 'This isn't the Iceland of Eric the Red. And it wasn't self-defence – Sandor Musgrave was outright murdered.'

'Well,' she said, '*I* never liked him.'

I told you before: she has no sense of right and wrong. It is a serious defect in a detective. I could only wave my arms in incoherent outrage; and my protests have never carried much weight with Freya, who claims not even to believe them.

We left the station. 'What's that you were saying to Arnold about chalk?' I said, curiosity getting the better of me.

'That's the clue you provided, Nathaniel – somewhat transformed. As you reminded me, Musgrave was pointing at the patio, and Heidi's patio is made of a block of the Dover cliffs. Dover cliffs, as you know, are composed of *chalk*. So I returned to the painting, and cut through the back to retrieve samples of the chalk used in the underdrawing, which had been revealed to me by infrared photography.' She turned a corner and led me uptown. 'Chalk, you see, has its own history of change. In Monet's time, chalk was made from natural sources, not from synthetics. Sure enough, the chalk I took from the canvas was a natural chalk. But natural chalk, being composed of marine ooze, is littered with the fossil remains of unicellular algae called cocoliths. These cocoliths are different depending upon the source of the chalk. Monet used Rouen chalk, appropriately enough, which was filled with the cocoliths *Maslovella barnesae* and *Cricolithus pemmatoidens*. The cocoliths in our painting, however, are *Neococcolithes dubius*. Very dubious indeed – for this is a North American chalk, first mined in Utah in 1924.'

'So Monet couldn't have used this chalk! And there you had your proof that the painting is a fake.'

'Exactly.'

I said doubtfully, 'It seems a subtle clue for the dying Musgrave to conceive of.'

'Perhaps,' Freya said cheerfully. 'Perhaps he was only pointing in the direction of the patio by the accident of his final movements. But it was sufficient that the coincidence gave me the idea. The solution of a crime often depends upon imaginary clues.'

'But how did you know Arnold was the forger?' I asked. 'And why, after taking the trouble to concoct all those paints, did he use the wrong chalk?'

'The two matters are related. It could be that Arnold only knew he needed a natural chalk, and used the first convenient supply without knowing there are differences between them. In that case it was a mistake – his only mistake. But it seems unlike Arnold to me, and I think rather that it was the forger's signature. In effect, the forger said, if you take a slide of the chalk trapped underneath the paint, and magnify it five thousand times with an electron microscope, you will find me. This chalk never used by Monet is my sign. – For on some level every forger hopes to be discovered, if only in the distant future – to receive credit for the work.

'So I knew we had a forger on Mercury, and I was already suspicious of Arnold, since he was the dealer who brought the painting to Mercury, and since he was the only guest at Heidi's party with the opportunity to kill Musgrave; he was missing during the crucial moments –'

'You *are* a liar.'

'And it seems Arnold was getting desperate; I searched among his recent bills, and found one for three suction plates. So when we found him on the track I was quite sure.'

'He stuck himself to the track?'

'Yes. The one on his right wrist was electronically controlled, so after setting the other two he tripped the third between his teeth. He hoped that we would discover him there after missing him at the museum, and think that there was someone else who wished him harm. And if not, the cowcatchers would pull him free. It was a silly plan, but he was desperate after I set up that appointment with him. When I confronted him with all this, after we rescued him from the tracks, he broke down and confessed. Sandor Musgrave had discovered that the Monet was a fake while blackmailing the Evans family in England, and after forcing Heidi to give him a job, he worked on the painting in secret until he found proof. Then he blackmailed Arnold into bankruptcy, and when on Solday he pressed Arnold for more money, Arnold lost his composure and took advantage of the confusion caused by the opening of the Great Gates to smack Musgrave on the head with one of Heidi's mirrors.'

I wagged a finger under her nose. 'And you set him free. You've gone too far this time, Freya Grindavik.'

She shook her head. 'If you consider Arnold's case a bit longer, you might change your mind. Arnold Ohman has been the most important art dealer on Mercury for over sixty years. He sold the Vermeer collection to George Butler, and the Goyas to Terminator West Gallery, and the Pissarros to the museum in Homer Crater, and those Chinese landscapes you love so much to the city park, and the Kandinskys to the Lion of the Greys. Most of the finest paintings on Mercury were brought here by Arnold Ohman.'

'So?'

'So how many of those, do you think, were painted by Arnold himself?'

I stopped dead in the street, stunned at the very idea. 'But – but that only makes it worse! Inestimably worse! It means there are fakes all over the planet!'

'Probably so. And no one wants to hear that. But it also means Arnold Ohman is a very great artist. And in our age that is no easy feat. Can you imagine the withering reception his work would have received if he had done original work? He would have ended up like Harvey Washburn and all the rest of them who wander around the galleries like dogs. The great art of the past crashes down on our artists like meteors, so that their minds resemble the blasted landscape we roll over. Now Arnold has escaped that fate, and his work is universally admired, even loved. That Monet, for instance – it isn't just that it passes for one of the cathedral series – it could be argued that it is the *best* of them. Now is this a level of greatness that Arnold could have achieved – would have been *allowed* to achieve – if he had done original work on this museum planet? Impossible. He was forced to forge old masters to be able to fully express his genius.'

'All this is no excuse, for forgery or murder.'

But Freya wasn't listening. 'Now that I've exiled him, he may go on forging old paintings, but he may begin painting something new. That possibility surely justifies ameliorating his punishment for killing such a parasite as Musgrave. And there is Mercury's reputation as art museum of the system to consider . . .'

I refused to honour her opinions with a reply, and looking around I saw that during our conversation she had led me far up the terraces. 'Where are we going?'

'To Heidi's,' she said. And she had the grace to look a little shamefaced – for a moment, anyway. 'I need your help moving something.'

'Oh, no.'

'Well,' Freya explained, 'when I told Heidi some of the facts of the case, she insisted on giving me a token of her gratitude, and she overrode all my refusals, so . . . I was forced to accept.' She rang the wall bell.

'You're joking,' I said.

'Not at all. Actually, I think Heidi preferred not to own a painting she knew to be a fake, you see. So I did her a favour by taking it off her hands.'

When Delaurence let us in, we found he had almost finished securing *Rouen Cathedral – Sun Effect* in a big plastic box. 'We'll finish this,' Freya told him.

While we completed the boxing I told Freya what I thought of her conduct. 'You've taken liberties with the *law* – you lied right and left –'

'Well boxed,' she said. 'Let's go before Heidi changes her mind.'

'And I suppose you're proud of yourself.'

'Of course. A lot of lab work went into this.'

We manoeuvred the big box through the gate and into the street, and carried it upright between us, like a short flat coffin. We reached Freya's villa, and immediately she set to work unboxing the painting. When she had freed it she set it on top of a couch, resting against the wall.

Shaking with righteous indignation, I cried, 'That *thing* isn't a product of the past! It isn't *authentic*. It is only a *fake*. Claude Monet *didn't paint it*.'

Freya looked at me with a mild frown, as if confronting a slightly dense and very stubborn child. 'So what?'

After I had lectured her on her immorality a good deal more, and heard all of her patient agreement, I ran out of steam. 'Well,' I muttered, 'you may have destroyed all my faith in you, and damaged Mercury's art heritage forever, but at least I'll get a good story out of it.' This was some small comfort. 'I believe I'll call it "The Case of the Thirty-third Cathedral of Rouen."'

'What's this?' she exclaimed. 'No, of course not!' And then she insisted that I keep everything she had told me that day a secret.

I couldn't believe it. Bitterly I said, 'You're like those forgers. You want *somebody* to witness your cleverness, and I'm the one who is stuck with it.'

She immediately agreed, but went on to list all the reasons no one else could ever learn of the affair – how so many people would be hurt – including her, I added acerbically – how so many valuable collections would be ruined, how her plan to transform Arnold into a respectable honest Plutonian artist would collapse, and so on and so forth, for nearly an hour. Finally I gave up and conceded to her wishes, so that the upshot of it was, I promised not to write down a single word concerning this particular adventure of ours, and I promised furthermore to say nothing of the entire affair, and to keep it a complete secret, forever and ever.

But I don't suppose it will do any harm to tell you.

Coming Back to Dixieland

IT FIGURES, JUST as sure as shift-start, that on our big day there'd be trouble. It's a law of physics, the one miners know best: things tend to fuck up.

I woke first out of the last of several nervous catnaps, and wandered down to the hotel bar to get something a little less heavyweight than the White Brother for my nerves. On one level I was calm as could be, but on another I was feeling a bit shaky (Shaky Barnes, that's me). Now, we drank the Brother during performances back on the rocks, of course, between sets sitting at the tables, or during the last songs when someone offered it; and Hook would make his announcement, 'We never know if this'll make us play better or worse, but it sure is fun finding out,' and then pass it around. Which was the point; we *had* to play good this day, so I wanted something soothing, with a little less pop to it than the White Brother we'd brought with us, which amplifies your every feeling, including fear.

So when I threaded my way through the hotel (which was as big as the whole operation on Hebe or Iris) back to our rooms, I expected the band to still be there sleeping. But when I'd finished stepping over all the scattered chairs, tables, mattresses and such (the remains of the previous shift's practice session) I could find only three of them, all tangled up in the fancy sheets: Fingers, Crazy, and Washboard. I wasn't surprised that my brother Hook was gone – he often was – but Sidney shouldn't have been missing; he hadn't gone off by himself since we left Ceres Central.

'Hey!' I said, still not too worried. 'Where'd they go, you slag-eaters!' They mumbled and grunted and tried to ignore me. I gave Washboard a shove with my foot. 'Where's Hook? Where's Sidney?' I said a little louder.

'Quit shouting,' Washboard said fuzzily. 'Hook's probably gone back to the Tower of Bible to visit the Jezebels again.' He buried his head in the pillow, like a snoutbit diving into bubblerock; suddenly it popped back out. '*Sidney's* gone?'

'You see him?'

Fingers propped himself up on his elbow. 'You better find Hook,' he said in his slow way. 'Hook, he'll know where Sidney gone to.'

'Well, did Hook *say* he was going to the Tower of Bible?' No one spoke. Crazy crawled over to a bed and sat up. He reached behind the bed and pulled out a tall thin bottle, still half filled with cloudy white liquid. He put it to his mouth and tilted it up; the level dropped abruptly a couple of times.

'Crazy, I never seen you hit the White Brother so early in the dayshift before,' I said.

'Shaky,' he replied, 'you never seen me get the chance.'

'You going to get us in trouble,' I said, remembering certain misadventures of the past.

'No, I'm not,' Crazy said. 'Now why don't you run down Hook, I'm pretty sure he's in Sodom and Gomorrah, he liked that place' – he took another swallow – 'and we'll hold down the fort and wait for Sidney to come back.'

'He better come back,' I said. 'Shit. Here it is the biggest day in our lives and you guys don't even have the sense to stay in one spot.'

'Don't worry,' Crazy said. 'Things'll go fine, I'll see to it.'

I took one of the slow cars through the track-webbed space between our hotel and the Tower of Bible. The Tower is one of Titania's biggest experiments in Neo-Archeo-Ritualism, sometimes called Participatory Art. Within the huge structure, set right against the wall of the Titania Gap, the setting for every chapter in the Bible is contained, which means you can participate in a wide variety of activities. The lobby of the Tower was unusually crowded for the early hours of the dayshift, but it was Performance Day, I remembered, and people were starting early. I worked from ramp to ramp, trying to make my way through the oddly assorted crowd to the elevator that would take me to Sodom and Gomorrah. Finally I slid through the closing doors and took my place in the mass of future Sodomites.

'What I want to know,' one of them said happily, 'is do they periodically sulphurize everyone in the room?'

'Every two hours,' a woman with round eyes replied, 'and does it feel real! But then they unfreeze you and you get to begin again!' She laughed.

'Oh,' said the man, blinking.

The elevator opened and the group surged past me towards Costumes. I stood and looked down some of the smoky streets of Gomorrah, hoping to see my brother in the crowd. Just as I decided to get one of the costumes and start searching, I saw him coming out of the door marked JEZEBELS, one arm wrapped around a veiled woman.

'Why, he must have just got here,' I said aloud, and took off after him. 'Hook!' I called. 'Hook!'

He heard me and quickly steered the woman into a side street. I started running. Sure enough, when I rounded the corner they had disappeared; I made a lucky guess and opened the door to a house made of sediments, and caught up with them moving up the narrow stairs. 'Hook, God damn it,' I said.

'Later,' he mumbled back at me, face buried in the Jezebel's neck.

'Hook, it's important.'

He waved his right arm back at me in a brush-away motion, and the metal rods of his hand flashed in my face. 'Not important!' he bellowed. I grabbed his arm and pulled on it.

'How can you say that?' I cried. 'Today's the day! The six bands those judges pick today get to go to Earth and everywhere –'

He finally stopped dragging us all up the stairs. 'I know

all that, Shaky, but that don't happen for a few hours yet, so why don't you go down to Psalms or Proverbs and calm down some? No reason for you to be so anxious.'

'Yes, there is,' I said, 'a real good reason. Sidney's gone.'

Hook tucked his chin into his neck. 'Sidney's gone?' he repeated.

'Nobody's seen him all shift.'

His three metal fingers waved up and down, scissoring the air; it was the same nervous sign of thought he'd made when he had his hand, and played the trumpet. 'Did you search the hotel good?' he said after a bit. 'I don't think he'd leave the hotel.'

I shook my head. 'I came here, I thought you'd know where he is.'

'Well, he's probably in the hotel somewhere, take a look why don't you?'

'What if he's not there? Come on, Hook, if we don't find him we're sunk.'

'All right,' he said. 'Shit. You're as bad as Sidney. I've been playing with that man near twenty years, and I never seen him so scared.'

'You think he's scared?' That had never occurred to me. Sidney was quiet, not too forward, but I'd never seen him scared of playing music.

'Sure he's scared.' He looked at the Jezebel, who hadn't made a sound so far. 'I got to find Sidney,' he explained. 'I'll be back to celebrate tomorrow.'

Her veiled head nodded, and I could see the flash of teeth. 'We better hurry,' Hook said. 'We're due to be turned into a pillar of salt any minute now.' We ran back and dived into the elevator, just behind the man

who had been asking questions on the way up. Down
in the lobby we dodged through a group of wide-eyed
Venusian monks and then through a stumbling crowd
of wet people from one of the aquatic scenes. Then we
made it to the exit, jumped in a car, and popped out
into the Gap.

'That Participatory Art,' Hook said, 'is really something.'

'Sidney's probably hiding in the hotel somewhere, the
bar or maybe the baggage rooms,' Hook said as we
neared our hotel.

I could see that he was as worried as I was. Despite
his easygoing speculations, his nervous trumpet fingering gave him away. Sidney's absence was a serious
matter, partly because it was so unexpected; Sidney was
never gone, never sick, never hurt; there was nothing
that could keep Sidney from playing. And how he could
play that clarinet! It was more than notes, it had to do
with what was inside the man, the strength and the
feeling; there's no way I can describe it to you but by
telling a story here; a little blues:

After the long shift's ending, when I was just a kid and
still working the sheds, I'd go down to the Heel Bar to
sip beer and listen to Sidney play his clarinet. At this
time he was playing with just Washboard and a piano
man, Christy Morton, who later got killed in the big
tunnel collapse on Troilus; and they were working out
all the old tunes he'd discovered in the Benson Curtis
tapes.

Sidney was as quiet and unassuming then as always.

It didn't matter how much stomping and shouting he stirred up, or how much Washboard and Christy sang into the tune; old Sidney would stand there, head bowed, horn cradled in his arm when he wasn't playing, as silent and bashful as a child. Then he'd raise that horn to his mouth, and when he played it was clear he had found his way of talking to the world. All the clamouring in the room channelled into him, he was transformed, and, sweat-bright with the effort, he'd wrench those songs into a sound as clean and live as a welding arc. Listening to him my cheeks would flush with blood, my heart would pound like Washboard's cowbell.

One time, late in the graveyard shift, I was joined at my front table by a Metis mute, one of the miners whose vocal cords had been ruined by the zinc blowout on Metis. Between sets Sidney sat with us, asked me how Hook was doing (this was right after his accident), and talked about Earth. He told us about New Orleans in the old times, when the jazz bands played in the streets. Telling it, he got so excited I didn't need to prod him with questions; he spoke on his own, even told us his one childhood memory of Earth: 'That ocean, it was like a flat blue plate, big as Jupiter from Io, speckled with shadows from clouds; and the horizon was straight as a rail, edge to edge cutting off a sky that was a blue I can't describe.' When he went back to play I was under the spell of Dixieland; and by the gleam in the mute's eye I could tell he felt it too. When Sidney played a good break the mute would put back his head and laugh, mouth split wide open, silent as space.

So when Sidney was done we decided to take the mute along to Sidney's place, to give the mute some

floor to sleep on; he didn't have any money or anywhere
to go. Now at this time (this was on Achilles) Sidney
lived in a cubbyhole behind one of the Supervisor's big
homes. When we got there Sidney wanted us to hold
back while he went to check if his sister-in-law was
awake – she didn't like him bringing folks home. Sidney
explained this, but the mute didn't appear to understand; he must have thought he was being left, because
every time Sidney walked a few steps and turned
around, he found the mute right behind him, grinning
and dragging me along. So there was a lot of waving
and explaining going on when the JM police suddenly
appeared; we didn't even have time to run.

'Where you going?' one of them asked.

'Home,' Sidney said.

'I suppose you live here?' the cop said, pointing at
the Supervisor's place.

'Yeah,' Sidney said, and before he had time to explain,
they were taking us off to jail.

We were hardly inside the jail door when they went
to work on the Metis mute. Kicked him and beat him
till he couldn't stand. His face was so bloody. Sidney
and I stood shaking against the wall, expecting we'd be
next, but they let us alone. Turned out one of the cops'
wives had been killed on Metis, and he'd been after the
mutes ever since. So when they were done with him
they slammed us all into the bullpen.

There's not much JM can do to make its jails any
worse than its mines, but what they can do they have
done. The cell we were in was cold and dark, like a
tunnel in a power breakdown, except for the gravity,
which felt like it was over 1.00. I crawled over the

rock floor, unable to see, and quietly called Sidney's name.

'Steve?' his voice said. 'Where you gone to?' His hand caught my arm, and he set me down beside him.

'Quit that snuffling,' he said to me. 'This is your first time in jail? Is that right? Well, it won't be your last, no, not a miner kid like you. They'll put you here many times before you're done.' He paused. 'Look at all these folks.'

A dim light gleamed through the door grating, and when my eyes adjusted I saw shapes huddled on the floor. They were gathered in knots, feet on each other's stomachs, using the survival techniques JM had taught them.

'They going to let us die?' I asked fearfully; the only times I had seen men curled together like that was when they carried the bodies, two by two, out of breakdowns.

'No, no,' he said. 'They just like us, just put in here for nothing, to be cold and hungry and heavy for a shift or two, to remind them who's boss on these rocks.' He sounded old and tired; and yet when I looked up at him, I saw that he was pulling the parts of his clarinet out of his big old coat and putting them together. He was sitting against the rock wall of the cell, with the mute propped up beside him. When his horn was together he put it to his mouth, gave the reed a lick, commenced to play.

He started soft, barely sounding the notes, and played 'Burgundy Street Blues' all the way through without raising his voice. As he played 'What Did I Do' some of the huddled figures slowly sat up and listened, backs and heads to the wall, looking up at the ceiling or the yellow squares of the grate.

Then he played the new songs, written by miners' bands and only heard in the bars scattered through their asteroids. He played 'Ceres', and 'Hidalgo', and 'Vesta Joys'; he played his 'Shaft Bucket Blues' and 'I Got Me a Feeling'. Then he played 'Don't God Live Out This Far', one of the first of the miner blues, which made it about twenty years old; and people began to join him. These were miners, men who seldom sang in the bars, seldom did more than stomp their boots or shout something between phrases; and at first their singing was an awkward sort of growl, barely in tune or time with Sidney. But he picked them up and more joined in, hesitantly, till you could make out the words of the refrain:

'Up at the shift-start,
Down in the mine shaft,
Spend my life throwing dirt on a car –
Ain't got nothing to do
But sing me the blues –
Hey don't God live out this far.'

There were about thirty verses to the song. It was about a miner who keeps getting in trouble, till JM decides to finish him: 'Super comes at shift-start for me to be hung, on account of something that I hadn't done.' The Supervisor believes he's innocent, but there's no proof. It was the same old, old thing.

When the singing got loud enough Sidney took off from the melody and floated up above it. And they sang! There was something in it that seemed to take my lungs away, so I could only breathe quick and shallow; it was what they had of the music inside themselves. Just hearing someone's voice in the dark, and knowing his life has a long way to go . . .

The light from the door just caught the plumes of breath frosting out from the men singing. I looked over at the mute. His eyes were open, staring out somewhere in space. As I watched he lifted up his hands and started a little syncopated clap, very soft, giving as much to the music as he could. When Sidney heard it he looked down at him, then looked back up; he played louder, filling the room with his sound, till the clarinet was all we heard or needed to hear, and the last verse came to its end.

'Oh yeah,' said a quiet voice.

Sidney looked at the mute, smiled, shook his head. 'A little blues for us, eh, brother?' he said. 'A little slave music.'

The mute nodded and grinned, which made his lip crack open again and spill blood down his chin.

Sidney laughed at him and wiped some of the blood from the mute's face. 'Oh yeah,' he said softly, 'a little miner music.'

We found Sidney just where Hook guessed he might be, huddled in the room where our baggage and instruments were stored. He was perched up on the box that Crazy's tuba travelled in, with his shoulders hunched and his legs crossed. When we burst into the room he jumped and then settled back, head down, staring sullenly across at us. His clarinet lay fitted in his arms. We all stood still, barred and hidden in the shadows thrown by the single bulb behind us, waiting for somebody to say something. The wisps of hair Sidney combed across his head looked thicker because of the shadows they cast on his bald pate. He looked like one of the tunnelgnomes men claim to see on Pallas; creatures who were once men maybe, who escaped JM by living in the old shafts. I had never noticed how small he was.

'You scared?' Hook asked.

Sidney raised his head to stare at Hook better. 'Yeah, I am,' he said suddenly, loud in the dim room, 'shouldn't I be?'

'Hey, Sidney,' I said, 'you don't got no reason to be scared –'

'Don't got no reason!' He pointed at me, clarinet still in hand. 'Don't you say that shit to me, Shaky. I got the best reason possible to be scared.' He jumped down from the box. 'The best reason possible. This is a contest, boy, we ain't playing to please these folks, we playing to show them that we better musicians than all them others! And if we don't show them that, if we don't win one of them grants, we gone. We back to the mines, boy, and we'll work in those shafts until JM has broke us so we can't work no more, and we'll never get to see the Earth. So don't tell me I got no reason to be scared.'

'Come on, Sidney, you can't think like that,' I said, searching for something I could say to him. 'It ain't so bad as –'

'Sidney,' Hook said, like I hadn't been talking at all (suddenly I see a picture in my head, of Sidney crouched down and shifting through a four-foot-high tunnel, Hook straddled senseless across his back, one of his hands clamped white around Hook's wrist, which ended in a tangle of bloody filaments; shouting instructions in furious fearful high voice to the men trying to get the airlock opened); I stepped back and let Hook talk to him.

'Sidney,' he said, 'you ain't thought this out. They

been putting one over on you. You're talking like this contest is a big vital thing, like we got some chance of going out there and *winning* one of them grants. Sidney, we got *no* chance, don't you realize that?'

'Hook –' I objected.

'No, you listen to me, we *got no chance*. You seen all those other musicianers here – those folks been doing nothing but play music all their *lives*, they playing all those fancy machines and doing things with music we don't even know about! And we just a bunch of miners playing some old Earth-type of music that just showed up a few years back, and only 'cause JM salvaged a ship full of band instruments and give them to us so we'd stay out of fights! And you still think we got a *chance?*'

Sidney and I stared at him.

'No way,' he continued grimly, 'no more'n there's a chance that JM will retire us at forty and send us to Mars. They got us here just so they can say they got folks from everywhere, even the rocks, and they going to give the grants to those fancy-ass musicianers, not us. So just exactly what you said is going to happen, Sidney, when this thing is over they going to send us back to the rocks to work and work, every third shift, till some equipment catches you or some tunnel collapses' – waving his hooks so they flashed silver in front of us – 'and then, if you're still alive, they'll dump you on Vesta rock and wait for you to die.

'And the only way you got to show how you feel about that, Sidney, is through that horn, through that skinny black horn of yours. When you get out there they going to be looking down on you, just like they always have, and all you can do about it is to *play* that thing! play it so hard they *got* to see you! play it and show them what kind of music a man plays when he works all his life digging in those fucking rocks!'

He stopped, gulped in some air. Sidney and I didn't make a sound. Suddenly he turned and walked over to the baggage, rummaged around a bit, then found the trunk he wanted and pulled it around so he could unstrap it and fling it open. He reached in and pulled out a long white bottle, held it high in the dim light while he unscrewed it. He turned it upside down to his mouth and took a long pull.

'*Eeeow!*' he whooped. He held it out towards Sidney. 'So what say we have a drink of the White Brother, brother, and then go play us some music.'

I looked at Sidney. I don't think I'd ever seen him indulge in the White Brother; he hardly even drank beer.

'I believe I will,' Sidney said, and swallowed near half the bottle.

Back up in our rooms Crazy was leading Fingers and Washboard in the 'Emperor Norton Stomp', running up the walls as high as he could and then diving off onto the unmade and trampled beds. He saw us standing in the doorway and from his position high on the wall he dived straight for us and bounced on the floor.

'Crazy,' Hook said cheerfully, 'you are crazy.' He stepped over him and made his way through the stuff heaped on the floor. He pulled his trombone out of the pile beside his bed.

'Let's roll,' he said.

'Wait!' Crazy cried. He poured some White Brother into cups and passed them around. When Sidney took one he didn't say a word, just grinned and pointed. Sidney paid him no attention.

We raised our cups in the air. 'To the Hot Six,' I said. 'Play that thing!' We downed the Brother; I could feel him slide into my stomach and explode there, making my blood pound and my vision jump.

We got our instruments and made our way to the lobby. When we got there we headed for the clerk's desk, bumping together and shushing each other, trying to calm down some while Hook spoke to the clerk.

'We are the Hot Six,' Hook shouted at the clerk, who stepped back quickly. 'And we playing at the Outer Planets Centre for the Performing Arts' W. H. Blakely Memorial Travelling Grant Competition' (we all threw in some 'oh yeahs!' for such virtuosity) 'and we need your fastest car right now.'

'Well sir,' the clerk said, 'all the cars have the same speed capability.'

'Oh come now, *come* now,' Hook said, 'are you telling me that you don't know of a single car that's set to go a mite faster than normal?'

'No sir, none except the cars reserved for emergencies –'

'Emergencies! Why, don't you know that's exactly what this is? An emergency!'

'An emergency,' we all echoed, and Crazy began to climb over the desk, muttering in a low voice, 'Emergency, emergency.'

'If you don't give us one of them emergency cars,' Hook continued in a lowered voice, 'then we've come over fifteen hundred million miles for no reason at all.'

The clerk looked past Hook and saw us staring at

him with the intensity that the White Brother can give you; looked at Crazy, who was clawing at the buttons on top of the counter. He shrugged. 'One of the special cars will be waiting for you at the departure gate.'

'Make it a big one,' Hook said, 'we got a lot of stuff to carry.'

We went to the departure gate and found a sixteen-person car, painted bright red, waiting for us. We threw all the instruments in the back and clambered in; Hook set the controls and fired us out into the Titania Gap.

The Gap is a long, straight canyon whose origins are unknown. It looks like it was carved into Titania some eons back by a good-sized rock (say about the size of Demeter) that nearly missed it. It's about two hundred miles long, four to ten miles wide, and nearly that deep, and almost the entire colony on Titania is set down in the skinny end of it. So when we popped out the wall of our hotel and shot down our track, we were greeted with the sight of the whole colony, covering the floor and climbing the walls of a canyon that would have swallowed most of the rocks we had lived on. There was only the fine lacing of car tracks looping through space to keep us from dropping two or three miles. Above us the swirling greens of Uranus blocked off most of the sky we could see.

'Shit, this thing *is* fast,' Hook said, after the car had taken a long drop and thrown us back in our seats. Crazy whooped and climbed over the seats back to his tuba case, from which he pulled another milky-white bottle. Fingers cheered and started singing, half-tempo like he always starts, 'I Don't Know Where I'm Going But I'm On My Way', and Hook joined him.

'I feel pretty good,' Sidney said from his window seat.

I sat back and watched the other cars slide along their strands, listening to the band keep loose. The front line, I thought, would be okay. I had been playing with Hook and Sidney since I was twelve years old – twelve years now – and Hook and Sidney had been playing together longer than that; we were the best front line there was, without a doubt, maybe the best there had ever been. And our back line was almost as good. Washboard never stopped hitting; even now he was clicking out rhythms on the side of the car, metal studs already taped to his fingers. Crazy was unreliable, we'd had to play many times without him because of his wild drinking; he didn't have the virtuoso command of the tuba that old Clarence Miles, our first tuba man, had had before he was paralysed; but nobody could pump as much air through a tuba as Crazy could, and his mad stomping and blowing was one of the trademarks of the Hot Six. Fingers – he was probably our weakest spot. He's a bit slow to understand things, and he only has eight fingers now; maybe the best thing about his playing is that all eight of those fingers hit the keys a good part of the time. That's the only way a piano man gets heard in a jazz band, especially a fine loud one like ours.

Hook slammed us into one of the track intersections without slowing down, and we dropped through it with a sickening jolt. I had visions of the whole band plummeting down the Gap like a puny imitation of the rock that had carved it.

'Goddammit Hook, what's the rush?' I asked. 'We're not that late.'

'Don't worry,' he said. 'This is just a fancy ore car here, I got it in hand.'

'Yeah, don't worry, Shaky,' Crazy chipped in. 'Why you worrying? You ain't going to get shaky again, are you, Shaky?' They all laughed, Hook hardest of all; he had named me that because I was so scared when I first played with the band that my tone had a vibrato in it.

'I feel *real* good,' said Sidney.

Then we turned a curve and were pointed right at the Performing Arts Centre. It stuck up from the canyon floor like one of the natural spires, a huge stack right at the end of the colony, the last structure before the black U of the Gap stretched out, lightless and empty. The car hit the final swoop of track up to it, and scarcely slowed down. Nobody said anything; Fingers stopped singing. As we drew closer, and the side of the building blocked out our view of the Gap, Hook finished the verse:

'And I got no place to go to
And I got no place to stay
And I don't know where I'm going
But I'm on my way.'

The waiting room backstage was crowded with a menagerie of about forty brightly dressed performers, all wandering in and out of practice rooms and talking loud, trying to work off tension. As soon as we walked in the door I could feel a heat on my cheeks, on account of all the eyes focusing on us. Everyone was happy to have something to think about besides the upcoming few hours, and as I looked at us all, standing in the doorway gawking, I could see we were good for that. Even in our best clothes (supplied by JM) we looked like exactly what we were: bulky, roughshod, unkempt, maimed, oh, we were miners, clear enough; and under the stares of that rainbow of costumes I suppose we should have quailed. But the energy we got from adrenaline and the White Brother and our wild flight down the Gap gave us a sort of momentum; and when Hook and Crazy looked at each other and burst out laughing, it was them that quailed. Glances turned away from us, and we strode into the room feeling on top of things.

I walked over to a circle of chairs that was empty and sat down. I got my trumpet out of its case and stuck my very shallowest mouthpiece into it; hit 'em high and hard, I thought. The rest of the band was doing the same around me, talking in mutters and laughing every time their eyes met. I looked around and saw that now our fellow performers were trying to watch us without looking. As my gaze swept the room it pushed eyes down and away like magic. When Washboard pulled his washboard out of his box and compulsively rippled his studded fingers down the slats to pop the cowbell, there was an attentive, amazed silence – very undeserved, I thought, considering how strange some of the other instruments in the room appeared – if that was really what they were. I walked over to the piano in a corner of the room, and nearly fell at an unexpected step down. I hit B-flat. My C was in tune with it. Hook, Sidney, and Crazy hit a variety of thirds and fifths, intending to sound as haphazard and out of tune as possible. Sidney made a series of small adjustments to his clarinet, but Hook and Crazy laid their brass down, the better to observe the show going on around them. Washboard was already moving around the room, stepping from level to level and politely asking questions about the weird machinery.

'Hey, look at this!' Hook called across to me. He was waving a square of paper. I crossed back to him.

'It's a programme,' he explained, and began to read out loud, '"Number Eighteen, the Hot Six Jazz Band, from Jupiter Metals, Pallas – an instrumental group specializing in traditional jazz, a twentieth-century style of composition and performance characterized by vigorous improvisation." Ha! Vigorous improvisation!' He laughed again. 'I'll vigorously improvise those –'

'Who's that up there?' Fingers asked, pointing with his good hand at the video screen they had up on one wall. The performer on stage at the moment was a red-robed singer, warbling out some polytonal stuff that many of the people in the room looked like they wanted to hear, judging by the way they stared at Hook. The harmonies and counterpoints the performer was singing with himself were pretty complex, but he had a box surgically implanted in one side of his neck that was clearly helping his vocal cords, so even though he was sliding from Crazy's tuning note up to the A above high C while holding a C-major chord, I wasn't much impressed.

'"Number Sixteen,"' Hook read (and my heart sledged in my chest all of a sudden; only two to go), '"Singer Roderick Flen-Jones, from Rhea, a vocalist utilizing the Sturmond Larynx-Synthesizer in four fugues of his own composition."'

'Shit,' Crazy remarked at a particularly high turn, 'he sounds like a dog whistle.'

'Pretty lightweight,' Washboard agreed.

'Lightweight? Man, he's *featherweight!*' Crazy shouted, and laughed loudly at his own joke; he was feeling pretty good. I noticed we were causing a general

exodus from the main waiting room. People were drifting into the practice chambers to get away from us, and
there was a growing empty space surrounding our group
of chairs. I caught Hook's eye and he seemed to get my
meaning. He shrugged a 'Fuck them', but he got Crazy
to pick up his tuba and go over some turns with him,
which calmed things down somewhat.

I sat down beside a guy near our chairs who was dressed
up in one of the simpler costumes in the room, a brown-
and-gold robe. He had been watching us with what seemed
like friendly interest the whole time we'd been there.

'You look like you're having fun,' he said.

'Sure,' I agreed. 'How about you?'

'I'm a little scared to be enjoying myself fully.'

'I know the feeling. What's that?' I asked, pointing
to the instrument in his lap.

'Tone-bar,' he said, running his fingers over it; without amplification it made only the ghost of a rippling
glissando.

'Is that a new thing?' I asked.

'Not this time. Last time it was.'

'You've tried this before?'

'Yes,' he said, 'I won, too.'

'You won!' I exclaimed. 'You got one of the grants?'
He nodded. 'So what are you doing back here?'

'That grant only gets you from place to place. It
doesn't guarantee you're going to make enough to keep
travelling once you're done with it.'

'Well, will these folks give a grant twice?'

'They've never done it before,' he said, and looked
up from his tone-bar to smile lopsidedly at me. 'So I've
got quite a job today, don't I.'

'I guess,' I said.

We watched the video for a while. As the singer juggled the three parts of his fugue Tone-bar shook his head. 'Amazing, isn't he,' he said.

'Oh yeah,' I said. 'The question is, do you listen to music to be amazed.'

He laughed. 'I don't know, but the audience thinks so.'

'I bet they don't,' I said.

This time he didn't laugh. 'So did I.'

Number Sixteen was leaving the stage and being replaced by Number Seventeen. That meant we wouldn't be on for an hour or so. I wished we were going on sooner; all the excitement I had felt was slowly collecting into a tense knot below my diaphragm. And I could see signs of the same thing happening to the others. Not Crazy; he was still rowdy as ever; he was marching about the room with his tuba, blasting it in the technicians' ears and annoying as many people as possible. But I had seen Fingers wandering towards the piano, undoubtedly planning to join Hook and Crazy in the phrases they were working on; some character wrapped in purple-and-blue sheets sat down just ahead of him and began to play some fast complicated stuff, classical probably, with big dramatic hand-over-hands all up and down the keys. Fingers turned around and sat back down, hands hidden in his lap, and watched the guy play; and when the guy got up Fingers just sat there, looking down at his lap like he hadn't noticed.

And Sidney got quieter and quieter. He stared up at the video and watched a quartet of people fidget around a big box that they all played together, and as he stared he sank into his chair and closed around his clarinet.

He was getting scared again. All the excitement and energy the band had generated on the trip over had disappeared, leaving only Washboard's insistent tapping and Crazy's crazy antics, which were gaining us more and more enemies among the other performers.

While I was still wondering what to do about this (because I felt like I was at least as scared as Sidney) Crazy made his way back to our corner of the room, did a quick side shuffle, and slammed into another musician.

'Hey!' Crazy yelled. 'Watch it!'

I groaned. The guy he had knocked over was dressed in some material that shifted colour when he moved; he had been making loud comments about us from the practice rooms ever since we had arrived. Now he got his footing and carefully lifted his instrument (a long many-keyed brass box that turned one arm back into itself) from the floor.

'You stupid, clumsy, drunken oaf,' he said evenly.

'Hey,' Crazy said, ignoring the description, 'what's that you got there?'

'Ignorant fool,' the musician said. 'It's a Klein synthesizer, an instrument beyond your feeble understanding.'

'Oh yeah?' Crazy said. 'Sounds a little one-sided to me.' He burst out laughing.

'It is unfortunate,' the other replied, 'that the Blakely Foundation finds it necessary to exhibit even the most *atavistic* forms of music at this circus.' He turned and stalked over to the piano.

'Atavistic!' Crazy repeated, looking at us. 'What's that mean?'

I shrugged. 'It means primitive,' said Tone-bar. Hook started to laugh.

'Primitive!' Crazy bellowed. 'I'm going to go hit that guy and let him think it over.' He turned to follow the musician, tuba still in his arms; and before anyone could move, he missed the step down and crashed to the floor, as loud as fifty cymbals all hit at once.

We leaped over and pulled the tuba off him. It was hardly dented; somehow he had twisted so it fell mostly on him.

'You okay?' Hook said anxiously, pushing back the rest of us. From somewhere in the room there was a laugh.

Crazy didn't move. We stood around him. 'God damn it,' Hook said, 'the bastard is out cold.' He looked like he wanted to kick him.

'And look!' Sidney said, lifting Crazy's left arm carefully. Right behind his hand (his fingering hand) was a bluish lump that stretched his skin tight. 'He's hurt that wrist bad,' Sidney said. 'He's out of it.'

'Fuck,' Hook said quietly. I sat down beside him, stunned by our bad luck. There was a crowd gathered around us but I didn't pay them any attention. I watched Crazy's wrist swell out to the same width as his hand; that was our whole story, right there. We'd put him on stage in a lot of strange conditions before, but a man can't play without his fingering hand . . .

'Hey, Wright is here today,' Tone-bar said. He was frowning with what looked like real concern. 'Doesn't he know some old jazz?' None of us answered him. 'No, seriously,' he said. 'This kid Wright is an absolute genius, he'll probably be able to fill in for you.' Still none of us spoke. 'Well, I know where his box is,' he finally continued. 'I'll try to find him.' He worked his way through the crowd and hurried out the door.

I sat there, feeling the knot in my stomach become a solid bar, and watched a few of the stagehands lift Crazy up and carry him out. We were beat before we began. You can play jazz without a tuba player – we had often had to – but the trombone has to take a lot of the bass line, nobody can be as free with the rhythm, the sound is tinny, there's no power to it, there's no *bottom!* Sidney looked over at Hook and said, with a sort of furtive relief, 'Well, you said we didn't have a chance,' but Hook just shook his head, eyes glistening, and said quietly, 'I wanted to show 'em.'

I sat and wondered if I was going to be sick. Crazy had crazied us right back to the rocks, and on top of my knotted stomach my heart pounded loud and slow as if saying 'ka-Doom, ka-Doom, ka-DOOM.' I thought of all the stories I'd heard of Vesta, the barren graveyard of the asteroids, and hoped I didn't live long enough to be sent there.

There was a long silence. None of us moved. The other performers circled about us quietly, making sure not to look at us. Slowly, very slowly, Sidney began to pull apart his clarinet.

'*I got him!*' came a wild voice. 'He can do it!' Tone-bar came flying in the door, pulling a skinny kid by the arm. He halted and the kid slammed into his back. With a grin Tone-bar stepped aside and waved an arm.

'Perhaps the finest musician of our –' he began, but the kid interrupted him:

'I hear you need a tuba man,' he said and stepped forward. He was a few years younger than me even, and the grin on his adolescent face looked like it was clamped over a burst of laughter. When he pushed all his long black tangles of hair back I saw that the pupils of his eyes were flinching wildly just inside the line of the irises; he was clearly spaced, probably had never seen a tuba before.

'Come on, man,' I said. 'Where did you learn to play jazz tuba?'

'Pluto,' he said, and laughed.

I stared at him. I couldn't believe it. As far as I knew, Dixieland jazz was only played in the bars on Jupiter Metals' rocks; I would have bet I knew, or knew of, every Dixieland musician alive. And this kid didn't come from the mines. He was too skinny, too sharp-edged, he didn't have the look.

'I didn't even know anyone played traditional jazz anymore,' he said. 'I thought I was the only one.'

'I don't believe it,' I said.

'We don't got a whole lot of choice, Shaky, we're running out of time,' said Hook. 'Hey kid – you know "Panama"?'

'Sure,' he said, and sang the opening bars. 'Bum-bum, da da da-da, da da-da-da da.'

'Son of a bitch,' I said.

'I can do it,' the kid said. 'I *want* to do it.'

'All right,' Hook said. 'Might as well take him.' I looked at Hook in surprise and saw that he was grinning again; clearly there was something about the kid, the intensity of those black-hole eyes perhaps, that had him convinced. He slapped the kid on the shoulder and nearly knocked him down. 'Come on!' he shouted. 'Time to go!'

'Time to go!' I cried. 'What the hell happened to Number seventeen?'

'They getting off! Let's go play!'

And the stagehands were already carrying stuff for us, watching the kid and gabbling excitedly.

'Shit,' I exclaimed, and stuck my hand out to the kid. We shook. 'Welcome to the Hot Six. Solos all sixteen bars, including yours if you want, choruses and refrains all repeated, don't worry about the tags; we'll have to stick to the old songs, do you know "St Louis Blues"? "That's a Plenty"? "Didn't He Ramble"? "Milenburg Joys"? "Mahogany Hall Stomp"? "Want a Big Butter-and-Egg Man"? "Ain't You Coming Back to Dixieland"?' and, miraculously, he kept yelling 'Yes! Yes! Yes!' as he struggled with the tuba, still almost laughing, and then we were in the hall and didn't have time for any more –

We got out on stage and it was hot as a smelting chamber. The audience was just a blue-black blur outside the lights, which were glaring down exactly like the arc lamps set around a tunnel end. I could tell seats went way up above us (*they going to be looking down on you*) and then we were all standing there set to go and a big amplified voice said, '*From Jupiter Metals, Pallas, the Hot Six,*' and suddenly we all had our horns to our mouths. I put mine down and said, '"In the Alley Blues",' which, amplified, sounded like a single word, then put the horn up and commenced playing.

We sounded horrible. They had indirect mikes on all of us, and just playing normal mezzo forte we were *booming* out into the huge cavern of the auditorium, so we could hear very clearly how bad we sounded. Hook was solid, and so was the kid, which was a relief; but my tone was quivering with just the slightest vibrato, and sometimes I couldn't hear Sidney at all. And his fear was spreading to the rest of us. We knew he had to be petrified to even miss a note.

We brought 'In the Alley' to a quick finish, and the applause was *loud*. That made me realize how big the audience was (twenty thousand, Tone-bar said) and I was more scared than ever. I could feel their eyes pressing on me, just like I can sometimes feel the vacuum when I look out a view window. I figured we'd better play one of the best songs next, so we'd get as much help from the material as possible. '"Weary Blues",' I said, meaning to say it to the band, since we had planned to play 'Ganymede'. But the mikes picked me up anyway and I heard 'Weary Blues' bounce back out of the cavern, so I just raised my horn to my lips and started; and it was probably two bars before everyone caught on and joined in. That didn't help any.

And I myself was having trouble. The more I could hear the vibrato wavering down the middle of my tone, the worse it got, and the more I could hear it . . . it began to sound like an oscilloscopic saw, and I hoped it wouldn't get out of control and break the tone completely. We got to the refrain, where 'Weary' usually starts rolling. I could tell that everyone was so scared they couldn't think about what they were playing, so the notes were coming out right by instinct, but there was no feel in them, it was like they were being played by a music box, every note made by a piece of metal springing loose.

'Weary Blues' ended and again the applause was triple forte. I stepped over to Hook and shouted, under my breath, 'Let's do "I Guess I'll Have to Change My Plans".' He couldn't hear me, so I said it louder and the mikes caught me, '"I Guess I'll Have to Change My Plans",' I announced. There was a long flurry of laughter from the audience. Hook started the intro to 'Plans', as calm as though he were playing to a crowded bar. We slid into the song and I realized how much easier it is to play fast when you're nervous. Hook was doing fine, but his backup was trembling, barely hitting the chords. With the leisure of playing accompaniment I could look up and see the silver line of boxes that held our judges, hanging high above us; and that didn't help either.

We moved quickly into 'That's a Plenty', and I could tell we'd calmed down enough to think about the music; after your body pumps full of adrenaline, soaks you in sweat, and shakes you like the ague, there's not much more it can do, you've *got* to calm down some; but that maybe wasn't helping us, since now we had to make the music ourselves, rather than leave it to instinct. I was still shaky enough that when I got to the triple-tonguing in the trumpet break, it actually seemed slow to me, and next time around I fitted in another note, hammering them with two double-tongues. This seemed to perk up the band ('Put chills down my spine,' the kid said later), but we still sounded ragged; I knew if we continued like this we were in trouble. And Sidney was still *missing phrases*. I don't think I'd ever heard him miss more than a note or two in my whole life, and here he was squeaking through bars at a time, playing like he had a crimp on his throat.

When we finished the kid waved me over to him. He raised a hand in the air and lowered it, which was apparently the signal needed to get the mike men off us. The kid was completely relaxed. He looked like he was having a good time.

'Your clarinet player is dying,' he said. 'Does he know "Burgundy Street Blues"?'

'Sure,' I said.

'Maybe you should have him play that. If he had to play a song by himself he'd be sure to calm down some.'

I turned around. 'Sidney, you ready to play "Burgundy Street"?'

He shook his head vehemently.

'Come on, Sidney,' Hook said from beside him. 'That's your song.' He turned to the audience, and the kid quickly lifted a hand. '"The Burgundy Street Blues",' Hook announced.

Now 'Burgundy Street', like 'Just a Closer Walk With Thee' or 'Bucket's Got a Hole in It', is a single-strain tune, just an eight-bar melody; and it's the variations that a clarinet player works in as he repeats it, again and again, that make the song something special. The first couple of times Sidney went through it, I could barely hear him. He was playing the melody, as simple as possible, and the sound he was making was more breath than tone. I didn't think he'd finish. He shifted towards us as if he wanted to turn his back on the audience, but Hook threw in a couple bars of harmony to bolster him, and when he started the strain a third time he took hold of himself and bore down; and that time, though the notes quivered and never got over pianissimo, he could be heard.

The kid was hopping up and down beside me as if he couldn't wait to start playing again. 'Damn that man plays fine clarinet,' he whispered to me. Suddenly I realized that if you didn't know Sidney you might think he was playing warbly on purpose, in which case it sounded all right. Apparently this occurred to Sidney too. Each time around he played a little louder, tried a few more variations, gathered a little more confidence. The fifth time around he usually played a variation filled with chromatic runs; he went ahead and tried them, and they came out sharp and well articulated. Amplified like he was, he could hear as clearly as anyone how good he sounded – he was learning what I'd already discovered, that even though you're scared, the notes come out. He began to take advantage of the new acoustics, building up till he filled the auditorium with sound, then dropping back so fast the mike men were lost, and he was as silent as piano keys pushed down.

And as he went on, I could see him begin to forget his surroundings and become what he was, a musician working on the song, putting together phrases, playing with the sounds he could make. His forehead wrinkled and smoothed as he carved an especially difficult passage; he closed his eyes, and the notes took on a life that hadn't been there before. He was lost in it now, completely lost in it, and the last time around he bent the notes like only a fine clarinet player can bend them, soaring them out into the cavern; a sound human and inhuman, music.

When he was done everyone was clapping, even me, and I realized that I had only thought the earlier applause was loud because I'd never heard that many people clap at once before. Now it was louder than when a ship takes off over a tunnel you're in . . .

We played 'Panama' next, and the difference was hard to believe. Sidney was back in form, winding about the upper registers with quick-fingered ingenuity, and as he pulled together so did the band. And the kid, as if he'd only been waiting for Sidney, began to let loose. He'd abandoned his steady *oomph-oomph-oomph-oomph* and was sliding up and down the bass clef, playing like a fourth member of the front line, and *leading* the tempo. Normally I set the tempo, and Crazy and Washboard listen to me and pick it up. But the kid wasn't paying any attention to me; his notes were hitting just a touch ahead of mine, and if there's anyone who can take the tempo away from the trumpet it's the tuba. I tried to play as fast as him but he kept ahead; by the time he let Washboard and me catch up with him we were playing 'Panama' faster than we'd *ever* played it, and excited as we were, we were equal to it. When we finished, the applause seemed to push us to the back of the stage.

We played the 'St Louis Blues', and then the 'Milenburg Joys', and then 'Sweet Georgia Brown', and each time the kid took over, pumping wildly away at the tuba, and pushed us to our limit. Sidney responded like that was the way he'd always wanted to play, arching high wails between phrases and helping the kid to drive us on. And the audience was with us! Maybe the earlier groups had been too modern, maybe too many of them had been playing to the judges; whatever the reason, the audience was with us now. An hour ago none of them had even heard of Dixieland jazz, and now they were cheering after the solos and clapping in the choruses; and we had to start 'Sweet Georgia Brown' by playing through the applause.

Then we were set for the finale. '*For all of you music lovers in the house,*' I said, knowing they wouldn't get the reference to Satchmo but saying it anyway, '*we going to beat out* "The Muskrat Ramble".'

'The Muskrat Ramble'. Our best song, maybe *the* best song. We started up the 'Ramble' and the band fell together and meshed like parts of a beautiful machine. All those years of playing in those bars: all the years of getting off work and going down and playing tired, playing with nobody listening but us, playing with nothing to keep us going but the music; all that came from inside us now, in a magic combination of fear, and anger, and the wild exhilaration of knowing we were the best there was at what we were doing. Hook was looping his part below me, Sidney leaping about above, the kid pushing us every note; and to keep up with the weave we were making I had to play hard and fast right down the middle of the song, lifting and growling and breaking my notes off, showing them all that there was a man *working* behind that horn, blowing as clear and sharp and excited as old Dipper-mouth Satchel-mouth Satchmo Louie Louis Daniel Armstrong himself. When we played the final round of the refrain everyone played their solo at once, only Fingers and Washboard held us down at all, and the old 'Muskrat Ramble' lifted up and played itself, carrying us along as if it made us and not the other way around. Hook played the trombone coda and we tagged it; then the kid surprised us and repeated the coda, and we barely got our horns back up to tag it again; then we all played the coda and popped it solid, the end.

I motioned the band off. We were done; there was no way we could top that. We started for the wings and the roar of the audience soared up to a gooseflesh howl. We hurried off, waving our arms and shouting as loud as anyone there, jumping up and down and slapping each other on the back, chased by a wall of sound that shook the building.

*   *   *

We waited; tired, happy, tense, we waited:

And God damn me if we didn't win one of those grants, a four-year tour of the Solar System; oh, we leaped about that waiting room and shouted and hit each other; Fingers and Washboard marched about singing and smashing out rhythms on the walls and furniture; Hook stood on a table and sprayed champagne on us; the kid rolled on the floor and laughed and laughed, 'Now you're in for it,' he choked out, 'you're in for it now!' but we didn't know what he meant then, we just poured champagne on his head and laughed at him, even old Sidney was jumping up and down, wisps of hair flying over his ears, singing (I'd never heard him sing) a scat solo he was making up as he went along, shouting it out while tears and champagne ran down his face:

'bo bo de zed,
we leaving the tunnels!
woppity bip,
we going to see Earth!
yes we (la da de dip)
going (ze be de be dop)
home!'

Stone Eggs

TOM FINN GOT on the Greyhound bus intending never to get off. He had purchased a month pass in Chicago and gotten on bus 782. He planned to take the southern route to California, go up the Pacific coast, back to the Great Lakes, and on to New England. Or wherever. When he bought the next pass he would think about it.

In the bus it was cool. The air from the vent played on his arm. All the windows except the windshield were tinted dark green, polarizing the light and reducing the outside world to a wash of greys. Tom liked it that way.

They stopped in the run-down parts of towns where the bus depots were, to change passengers and eat meals. Joplin, Missouri; Tulsa, Oklahoma; Amarillo, Texas. Half an hour for lunch, an hour for dinner. He fell into the routine with relief.

He got on a New York-to-Los Angeles bus, and a

group of passengers stayed on it for two or three days. He watched them as they lived their lives on the bus, talking and getting to know each other. Finn never introduced himself to anyone, or talked. At night people slumped in their seats, unselfconsciously sleeping. Some kept on their little overhead lights and talked all night long. Tom Finn could not sleep in a sitting position, so at night he unobtrusively crawled under his seat and slept curled on the floor, using his tennis shoes for a pillow. It was comfortable enough. In the mornings he scrambled up onto his seat and stared back at the few bleary-eyed strangers who were awake at dawn. A thin-faced young black man. A girl with stringy hair and dirty clothes. An old couple. The poor, in all their variety . . . Then back to the little toilet room, which grew more fetid by the hour.

As they crossed New Mexico he looked out at the parched grey land, dozed, observed the occupants of the seat ahead of him. A fat young woman struggled vainly to control her four sons, slapping them and threatening them with worse. The boys – aged eight, seven, four, and one, Finn guessed – ignored her, except for the infant, who cried or slept or sucked a bottle. The mother had scarcely slept in the three days Finn had sat behind her. He watched the oldest son, who tormented the four-year-old incessantly, and wondered if the boy was naturally evil or if his meanness was the result of his upbringing. Naturally evil? . . . The boy would grow up to be a runaway, he thought. Finn was a runaway.

That evening the bus pulled off Highway 8, in the south Arizona desert, for a dinner stop. The offramp circled down to a road that stretched off into the desert to the north and extended to the south no farther than a small group of buildings just off the freeway. Approaching the group of buildings, Tom read a sign: DATELAND RESTAURANT, POST OFFICE, AND CURIO SHOP.

He joined the file of people getting off the bus. 'One hour, now,' the bus driver said. Although it was nearly dusk the air was still hot and dry. Finn walked across the gravel parking lot to the door of the café. There were two middle-aged men sitting at the counter. All the booths were empty. The waitresses were talking to each other. Tom saw that it was yet another restaurant that could not survive without its Greyhound concession. He sat in one of the booths, and a waitress took his order. He ordered a hamburger, fries, and a Coke. While he waited he flipped through the selections listed in his table jukebox console. Country-western, old rock and roll, songs in Spanish. Behind him sat the mother and her four boys. 'Stop that. Stop that or I'll hit you in front of everybody.' When his food came he ate quickly, paid his bill and left.

The main building was in the shape of an L; the long side was the café, the short side was the curio shop. Finn walked over to the curio shop, thinking to get out of the heat. Beside the door was a thermometer in an old tin Coca-Cola sign. It read 104 degrees. He went into the shop.

Quite a few people from the bus were already there, wandering about. Tom did the same. The curio shop offered for sale string ties with clasps made of clear plastic that held embalmed scorpions; cactus-growing kits; postcards with pictures of donkeys and cactus flowers and Jackalopes; turquoise rings, the turquoise white and cracked; candy in yellowed cellophane; and stone eggs. Everything in the shop had obviously been there for years and years; all those chill airconditioned days and long hot nights had desiccated every item. No one from the bus was buying anything. The cashier stared out the window. It reminded Finn of things he could not afford to think of, and feeling that he might scream, or start to cry, he left the shop.

The heat outside relaxed him. The sun was about to set. Behind Dateland there was an old road leading off over a hill to the east. Finn began to walk on it. He was fascinated by the thin roads, asphalt or gravel or dirt, that crisscrossed the great American desert. He had seen a lot of them from the bus. Who had built them, and when? It was easy to imagine Interstate 8 being built: hundreds of men, huge yellow bulldozers and earthmovers, a whole community, moving along through the desert and excreting the highway behind it. But what about these little roads, stretching from nowhere to nowhere under the broiling sun? Finn couldn't imagine their construction. He stared down at the faded, cracked asphalt as he walked. Sand silted over the edges of the road. It could have been built a thousand years ago. These are the ruins of the twentieth century, he thought. Already here.

The road ended in a settlement of foundations. Rectangles of cement, half covered by sand, with fixture pipes rusting through at one corner of each foundation. The sun was below the hill now, and the settlement was in shadow. It was still very hot. Finn walked around the area, looking at the cement and the dry grass that had overgrown it and died. Wind gusted through the shadows, rustling the grass. In the east the sky was a deep blue.

Eventually he sat down on a concrete block and let the desert fill him. Occasionally the faint diesel roar of a truck wafted over from the interstate to the north. In the western sky the evening star appeared. This was his life, Tom Finn thought, this desert, this community in ruins before it had ever been occupied . . . Through his tears it seemed the homes that somebody had planned to put there did indeed stand, as clear glass houses that revealed everything about their owners, brittle things that could be shattered with a blink of the eye. And each blink brought the houses crashing to the ground, and the faint stars with them so that they should have been great pyres burning around him on the desert floor.

Then the evening star dropped like a stone over the western horizon, and it didn't come back no matter how hard Finn blinked. As if it had been a meteor. Just a shooting star, Finn thought. But fear rustled through him like the wind, and he got up and walked quickly back over the old abandoned road. Something had happened . . .

From the hill he could see the back of Dateland. The parking lot was empty. Finn cursed out loud. He had missed the bus! Sitting out there thinking about his mess of a life he had missed his bus. He hurried down the hill, cursing still. He would have to wait in that café for the next bus, and call ahead to get the Greyhound people to recover his suitcase. Damn it! Hadn't the bus driver counted his passengers? Had no one noticed his absence?

But when he got to the building, he forgot his anger.

Dateland was empty. Boarded up, faded, sand-drifted, empty.

The sun had been down for a while now, and Finn

found himself shivering. Absently he walked over to look at the thermometer by the curio-shop door; it was broken. He turned the doorknob and pushed the door in; a gust of wind pulled it out of his hand, and it hit the counter inside with a wooden *thwack*. Finn stuck his head in the door and looked around, afraid to enter. Everything in the curio shop was the same, except dustier. A handful of Jackalope postcards tumbled to the floor, caught by the wind, and Finn jumped back with his heart racing.

It took all his courage to open the door to the café. It too was deserted. Parts of it had been removed: the jukeboxes, the kitchen fixtures, the drink machines. The vinyl booth seats were cracked like dried mud. Overcome by sudden terror, Finn rushed out of the café to the safety of the gravel parking lot. But it was getting dark; the vast network of stars revealed itself; Dateland stood behind him dark and empty, like a house in a child's nightmare. He shivered uncontrollably. The dry wind made little noises against the building. A loose plank somewhere slapped woodenly a few times. He was afraid. 'What's going on here?' he cried out miserably. No answer but wind.

He ran up the road to the freeway onramp. The spare concrete of Interstate 8 was tremendously reassuring. Nothing there had changed. The highway was empty in both directions, but that was not unusual. He walked up the onramp until he was out on the westbound lanes, ready to stop the next car that came by. He could just see Dateland over the shoulder of the eastbound lanes, a dark mass in the starlit desert sand.

Hours passed, and no cars drove by. He was frightened again. It got colder, and he sat on the blacktop edging the white concrete of the lanes, where it was still warm with the day's heat.

Then to the east he saw headlights approaching, and he jumped up stiffly, adrenaline pumping up his heartbeat. 'Now stop,' he muttered, 'please stop, please stop, please stop . . .'

Just before they would have reached him the lights slowed, turned on the big circular offramp leading down to Dateland. It was a Greyhound bus.

He ran down the onramp and along the road back to Dateland. Another bus! His pass was still in his pocket . . .

The bus was pulling back out of the parking lot when he ran up. '*Wait*,' he screamed, the word torn out of him like no other had ever been in his life. The headlights caught him for a moment, the bus stopped, the door at the front *whooshed* open.

He jumped onto the first step, grabbed the chrome handrail and pulled himself up the steps to the main aisle. There was only one passenger on the bus, an old woman sitting in the seat behind the driver. The driver looked up at him. 'Sit down,' he said. 'Can't go until you sit down.'

Finn sat in the front seat, across from the old woman and the driver. He felt his bus pass in his pocket; but the driver was turning onto the onramp, oblivious to him. He sat back, happy to be leaving Dateland. Yet he was afraid to ask the two people across from him what they knew of it.

'So you found a new doctor, eh?' the driver said when they were on the freeway and up to speed. He was looking in his mirror at the old woman.

'Yes, I did,' she replied. 'The best you can find, these days anyway. A Jack Mathewson, from Gila Bend. Trained by Westinghouse. He says he'll replace the pivot in my lower back with a new part made by G.E.'

'That might work,' the driver said. 'Got a G.E. pivot myself.'

Tom Finn, pressed back against his window, stared at the two people across from him. The old woman . . . her eyes were glass. The bus passed under a light over the freeway, and he saw that her skin was some kind of plastic. He tried to control his breathing . . .

'The plain fact is,' the old woman-thing said, 'it's hell to grow old. Nothing to be done about it.'

'Nope,' the driver agreed.

'Forty-seven years as a librarian, and me with a bad back. Sometimes you wonder why we were designed to feel pain at all.'

'Keeps us alive.'

'*I* think it was because people didn't want us to have any advantages,' she said, looking for an instant at Finn. 'Ah, well. All of my typemates dead and gone for years now. And Westinghouse has no more parts for my type, they say.'

'G.E. parts are just as good. But I know what you mean. All my typemates are gone too. Last century was the good one for simulacra.'

'Don't you know it!'

Tom Finn got up unsteadily and walked down the aisle to the back of the bus, thinking that he might throw up in the toilet. But when he got to the door, he couldn't bring himself to open it; he imagined looking into the coppery mirror and seeing his reflection grin at him with steel teeth – imagined unzipping, and finding only smooth metal. Had he always been a machine, and only dreamed, out there in the desert, of being something else? For a long time he stood there swaying with the bus. A part of his mind noticed that the bus's engine didn't sound like the old piston-driven ones used to. The *old* piston-driven ones? Furtively he looked up the bus at the two figures, still talking in low tones. Something had happened, back there at Dateland . . . he couldn't bear to look down at himself. After a while he forced himself (for the sake of appearances! he thought) to return to the front of the bus. He watched the simulacra talking to each other, and listened to their words for a long time, wondering how to ask what year it was. Finally exhaustion overcame him and he was lulled to sleep by their voices and the hum of the bus.

He was awakened by the sound of the bus downshifting. They were on the curve of another offramp. He jerked up and looked around. They were still in the desert; it was light, just before sunrise. Just off the freeway was their destination, another little isolated café. Finn saw the sign on the building and felt faint; DATELAND RESTAURANT, POST OFFICE, AND CURIO SHOP.

'Isn't this where I got on?' he croaked, his mouth dry with sleep and fear. They were the first words he had spoken since getting on the bus.

The driver turned his plastic head (it was obvious in the dawn) to glance at him, and laugh. 'You think I drive this bus in circles? We're west of Yuma now. There's lots of places that look like that in this desert.'

The old woman was asleep, or turned off, still upright in her seat across from Finn. Finn felt his own pump hammering the fluids through him, and all of a sudden it was too much. He gave in to it.

Without thinking he got off the bus when it stopped. Walked over to the door of the curio shop. Without surprise he registered the fact that the bus was driving off, back to the freeway. The thermometer by the door was still broken, the paint on the tin almost gone. It still read 104. He opened the door and walked inside the curio shop. All the goods were still there, safe and untouched, covered with dust. Finn swallowed hard. There was something about the place, something he had sensed when he first entered it so many years ago . . .

The sun broke over the horizon, flooding the shop with dusty white light. Behind the cashier's booth there was a closet. In it he found a broom and a feather duster, and he went to work cleaning up. All of the arrowheads, the turquoise and onyx and malachite rings, the cactus-growing kits, the postcards, the stone eggs. All as clean as new.

A couple of hours later he stood, sweaty and grimy, in a clean and orderly curio shop. White dust motes like talcum swirled in the air, made bright and palpable by the low morning sun. He walked outside into the fresh air, which was still cool. Glancing in the café door, he shook his head; he'd have to attend to that later.

Another Greyhound swooped down the circular offramp. He hurried back to the curio-shop door. Maybe somebody would buy something. Nervously he watched as people stepped down from the bus. Some of them walked towards cars that Finn had assumed were wrecks, on the other side of the gravel lot; they drove away to the north, under the freeway and out of sight.

But several more, observing him standing in the shop doorway, approached the shop. Finn stepped back inside, to clear the entrance.

One by one they filed past. 'Opening the old place up again, eh?' a man said.

'Yes,' Finn replied, and cleared his throat. 'I'm going to give it a try.' He stared at the man. In the klieg-light glare of the horizontal sun the man's blue eyes were quite clearly glass. But that look on his face, that curiosity . . . Finn blinked and the man blinked too, and Finn saw the film of tears and the tiny red veins. An iris could look like crystal from some angles, he knew that . . . Eventually Finn shook himself and followed the man in. He couldn't tell. He didn't care.

'Oh, look,' a young woman said to her companion, an older woman.

'That would look nice in your room,' the older woman said. Finn could hear the years in her voice, and he was reminded of the old woman on his bus.

'I want this,' the young woman said to Finn. 'How much is it?'

She held out one of the stone eggs. He took it from her cool hand. It was smooth and brown, mottled by black cracking deep in the stone. Finn looked around: no cash register.

'Um,' he said, feeling in his pockets for change. 'A dollar.'

'Sold,' she said, and laughed. The old woman smiled. While the young woman fumbled in her pocketbook, Finn cleaned the egg one last time with a rag he had found under a counter.

'You have to be careful with these,' he warned her.

'They're lighter than they look. And fragile? They'd break like glass if you dropped one.'

'I'll remember.' She handed him a dollar. George Washington still on the front, he saw. 'Where are you living?'

'Well . . .' The men examining the postcards swivelled their heads to hear his answer. 'There's some old foundations over the hill to the east. I'm going to set up out there.'

'We live on the other side of the freeway; you should come visit.'

'I will.'

Then they trailed out of the shop, talking and leaving great swirls in the mote-coned morning air. Finn watched them from the doorway; they all balanced with unnatural carefulness across the gravel. He shrugged. When they were all gone, out of sight under the freeway, he went back inside. He would have to find a cash register, and start the air conditioner up again. He straightened up the postcards. Rearranged the stone eggs. After breakfast he would walk up the narrow road to the north.

Ridge Running

T HREE MEN SIT on a rock. The rock is wet granite, a bouldertop surrounded by snow that has melted just enough to reveal it. Snow extends away from the rock in every direction. To the east it drops to treeline, to the west it rises to a rock wall that points up and ends at sky. The boulder the three men are on is the only break in the snow from the treeline to rock wall. Snowshoe tracks lead to the rock, coming from the north on a traverse across the slope. The men sit sunning like marmots.

One man chews snow. He is short and broad-chested, with thick arms and legs. He adjusts blue nylon gaiters that cover his boots and lower legs. His thighs are bare, he wears grey gym shorts. He leans over to strap a boot into an orange plastic snowshoe.

The man sitting beside him says, 'Brian, I thought

we were going to eat lunch.' This second man is big, and he wears sunglasses that clip onto prescription wire-rims.

'Pe-ter,' Brian drawls. 'We can't eat here comfortably, there's barely room to sit. As soon as we get around that shoulder' – he points south – 'the traverse will be done and we'll be at the pass.'

Peter takes in a deep breath, lets it out. 'I need to rest.'

'OK,' Brian says, 'do it. I'm just going to go around to the pass, I'm tired of sitting.' He picks up the other orange snowshoe, sticks his boot in the binding.

The third man, who is medium height and very thin, has been staring at the snow granules on his boot. Now he picks up a yellow snowshoe and kicks into it. Peter sees him do it, sighs, bends over to yank his aluminium-and-cord snowshoes out of the snow they are stuck in.

'Look at that hummingbird,' the third man says with pleasure and points.

He is pointing at blank snow. His two companions look where he is pointing, then glance at each other uncomfortably. Peter shakes his head, looks at his boots.

'I didn't know there were hummingbirds in the Sierras,' the third man says. 'What a beauty!' He looks at Brian uncertainly. '*Are* there hummingbirds in the Sierras?'

'Well,' Brian says, 'actually, I think there are. But . . .'

'But not this time, Joe,' Peter finishes.

'Ah,' Joe says, and stares at the spot in the snow. 'I could have sworn . . .' Peter looks at Brian, his face squinched up in distress. 'Maybe the light breaking on that clump of snow,' Joe says, mystified. 'Oh, well.'

Brian stands and hoists a compact blue pack onto his shoulders, and steps off the boulder onto the snow. He leans over to adjust a binding. 'Let's get going, Joe,' he says. 'Don't worry about it.' And to Peter: 'This spring snow is great.'

'If you're a goddamn polar bear,' Peter says.

Brian shakes his head, and his silvered sunglasses flash reflections of snow and Peter. 'This is the best time to be up here. If you would ever come with us in January or February you'd know that.'

'Summer!' Peter says as he picks up his long frame pack. 'Summer's what I like – catch the rays, see the flowers, walk around without these damn flippers on –' He swings his pack onto his back, steps back quickly (clatter of aluminium on granite) to keep his balance. He buckles his waistbelt awkwardly, looks at the sun. It is near midday. He wipes his forehead.

'You don't even come up with us in the summer anymore,' Brian points out. 'What has it been, four years?'

'Time,' Peter says. 'I don't have any time, and that's a fact.'

'Just all your life,' Brian scoffs. Peter shakes off the remark with an irritated scowl, and steps onto the snow.

They turn to look at Joe, who is still inspecting the snow with a fierce squint.

'Hey, Joe!' Brian says.

Joe starts and looks up.

'Time to hike, remember?'

'Oh, yeah, just a second.' Joe readies himself.

Three men snowshoeing.

Brian leads. He sinks about a foot into the snow with every step. Joe follows, placing his yellow snowshoes carefully in the prints of Brian's, so that he sinks hardly at all. Peter pays no attention to prints, and his snowshoes crash into and across the holes. His snowshoes slide left, downhill, and he slips frequently.

The slope steepens. The three men sweat. Brian slips left one time too often and stops to remove his snowshoes. They can no longer see the rock wall above them, the slope is so steep. Brian ties his snowshoes to his pack, puts the pack back on. He puts a glove on his right hand and walks canted over so he can punch into the slope with his fist.

Joe and Peter stop where Brian stops, to make the same changes. Joe points ahead to Brian, who is now crossing a section of slope steeper than forty-five degrees.

'Strange three-legged hill animal,' says Joe, and laughs. 'Snoweater.'

Peter looks in his pack for his glove. 'Why don't we go down into the trees and avoid this damn traverse?'

'The view isn't as good.'

Peter sighs. Joe waits, scuffs snow, looks at Peter curiously. Pete has put suntan oil on his face, and the sweat has poured from his forehead, so that his stubbled cheeks shine with reflected light.

He says, 'Am I imagining this, or are we working really hard?'

'We're working very hard,' Joe says. 'Traverses are difficult.'

They watch Brian, who is near the middle of the steepest section. 'You guys do this snow stuff for *fun?*' Peter says.

After a moment Joe starts. 'I'm sorry,' he says. 'What were we talking about?'

Peter shrugs, examines Joe closely. 'You OK?' he asks, putting his gloved hand to Joe's arm.

'Yeah, yeah. I just . . . *forgot*. Again!'

'Everyone forgets sometimes.'

'I know, I know.' With a discouraged sigh Joe steps off into Brian's prints. Peter follows.

From above they appear little dots, the only moving objects in a sea of white and black. Snow blazes white and prisms flash from sunglasses. They wipe their foreheads, stop now and then to catch their breath. Brian pulls ahead, Pete falls behind. Joe steps out the traverse with care, talking to himself in undertones. Their gloves get wet, there are ice bracelets around their wrists. Below them solitary trees at treeline wave in a breeze, but on the slope it is windless and hot.

The slope lessens, and they are past the shoulder. Brian pulls off his pack and gets out his groundpad, sits on it. He roots in the pack. After a while Joe joins him. 'Whew!' Joe says. 'That was a hard traverse.'

'Not really hard,' Brian replies. 'Just boring.' He eats some M and M's, waves a handful up at the ridge above. 'I'm tired of traversing, though, that's for sure. I'm going up to the ridge so I can walk down it to the pass.'

Joe looks at the wall of snow leading up to the ridge. 'Yeah, well, I think Pete and I will continue around the corner here and go past Lake Doris to the pass. It's almost level from here on.'

'True. I'm going to go up there anyway.'

'All right. We'll see you in the pass in a while.'

Brian looks at Joe. 'You'll be all right?'

'Sure.'

Brian gets his pack on, turns and begins walking up the slope, bending forward to take big slow strides. Watching him, Joe says to himself, 'Humped splayfoot pack beast, yes. House-backed creature. Giant snow snail. Yo ho for the mountains. Rum de dum. Rum de dum de dum.'

Peter appears around the shoulder, walking slowly and carelessly. He spreads his groundpad, sits beside Joe. After a time his breathing slows. 'Where's Brian?'

'He went up there.'

'Is that where we're going?'

'I thought we might go around to the pass the way the trail goes.'

'Thank God.'

'We'll get to go by Lake Doris.'

'The renowned Lake Doris,' Peter scoffs.

Joe waves a finger to scold. 'It is nice, you know.'

Joe and Peter walk. Soon their breathing hits a regular rhythm. They cross a meadow tucked into the side of the range like a terrace. It is covered with suncones, small melt depressions in the snow, and the walking is uneven.

'My feet are freezing,' Pete says from several yards behind Joe.

Joe looks back to reply. 'It's a cooling system. Most of my blood is hot – so hot I can hold snow in my hand and my hand won't get cold. But my feet are chilled. It cools the blood. I figure there's a spot around my knees that's perfect. My knees feel great. I live there and everything's comfortable.'

'My knees hurt.'

'Hmm,' Joe says. 'Now that is a problem.'

After a silence filled by the squeak of snow and the crick of boot against snowshoe, Pete says, 'I don't understand why I'm getting so tired. I've been playing full-court basketball all winter.'

'Mountains aren't as flat as basketball courts.'

Joe's pace is a bit faster than Pete's, and slowly he pulls ahead. He looks left, to the tree-filled valley, but slips a few times and turns his gaze back to the snow in front of him. His breaths rasp in his throat. He wipes sweat from an eyebrow. He hums unmusically, then starts a breath-chant, muttering a word for each step: *animal, animal, animal, animal, animal.* He watches his snowshoes crush patterns onto the points and ridges of the pocked, glaring snow. White light blasts around the sides of his sunglasses. He stops to tighten a binding, looks up when he is done. There is a tree a few score yards ahead – he adjusts his course for it, and walks again.

After a while he reaches the tree. He looks at it; a gnarled old Sierra juniper, thick and not very tall. Around it hundreds of black pine needles are scattered, each sunk in its own tiny pocket in the snow. Joe opens his mouth several times, says 'Lugwump?' He shakes his head, walks up to the tree, puts a hand on it. 'I don't know who you are?' He leans in, his nose is inches from bark. The bark peels away from the tree like papery sheets of filo dough. He puts his arms out, hugs the trunk. 'Tr-eeeee,' he says. 'Tr-eeeeeeee.'

He is still saying it when Peter, puffing hard, joins him. Joe steps around the tree, gestures at a drop beyond the tree, a small bowl notched high in the side of the range.

'That's Lake Doris,' he says, and laughs.

Blankly Peter looks at the small circle of flat snow in the centre of the bowl. 'Mostly a summer phenomenon,' Joe says. Peter purses his lips and nods. 'But not the pass,' Joe adds, and points west.

West of the lake bowl the range – a row of black peaks emerging from the snow – drops a bit, in a deep, symmetrical U, an almost perfect semicircle, a glacier road filled with blue sky. Joe smiles. 'That's Rockbound Pass. There's no way you could forget a sight like that. I think I see Brian up there. I'm going to go up and join him.'

He takes off west, walking around the side of the lake until he can go straight up the slope rising from the lake to the pass. The snow thins on the slope, and his plastic snowshoes grate on stretches of exposed granite. He moves quickly, takes big steps and deep breaths. The slope levels and he can see the spine of the pass. Wind blows in his face, growing stronger with every stride. When he reaches the flat of the saddle in mid-pass it is a full gale. His shirt is blown cold against him, his eyes water. He can feel sweat drying on his face. Brian is higher in the pass, descending the north spine. His high shouts are blown past Joe. Joe takes off his pack and swings his arms around, stretches them out to the west. He is in the pass.

* * *

Below him to the west is the curving bowl of a cirque, one dug by the glacier that carved the pass. The cirque's walls are nearly free of snow, and great tiers of granite gleam in the sun. A string of lakes – flat white spots – mark the valley that extends westward out of the cirque. Lower ranges lie in rows out to the haze-fuzzed horizon.

Behind him Lake Doris's bowl blocks the view of the deep valley they have left behind. Joe looks back to the west; wind slams his face again. Brian hops down the saddle to him, and Joe whoops. 'It's windy again,' he calls.

'It's always windy in this pass,' Brian says. He strips off his pack, whoops himself. He approaches Joe, looks around. 'Man, for a while there about a year ago I thought we'd never be here again.' He claps Joe on the back. 'I'm sure glad you're here,' he says, voice full.

Joe nods. 'Me, too. Me, too.'

Peter joins them. 'Look at this,' calls Brian, waving west. 'Isn't this amazing?' Peter looks at the cirque for a moment and nods. He takes off his pack and sits behind a rock, out of the wind.

'It's cold,' he says. His hands quiver as he opens his pack.

'Put on a sweatshirt,' Brian says sharply. 'Eat some food.'

Joe removes his snowshoes, wanders around the pass away from Brian and Peter. The exposed rock is shattered tan granite, covered with splotches of lichen, red and black and green. Joe squats to inspect a crack, picks up a triangular plate of rock. He tosses it west. It falls in a long arc.

*   *   *

Brian and Peter eat lunch, leaning against a boulder that protects them from the wind. Where they are sitting it is fairly warm. Brian eats slices of cheese cut from a big block of it. Peter puts a tortilla in his lap, squeezes peanut butter out of a plastic tube onto it. He picks up a bottle of liquid butter and squirts a stream of it over the peanut butter.

Brian looks at the concoction and squints. 'That looks like shit.'

'Hey,' Peter says. 'Food is food. I thought you were the big pragmatist.'

'Yeah, but . . .'

Pete wolfs down the tortilla, Brian works on the block of cheese.

'So how did you like the morning's hike?' Brian asks.

Pete says, 'I read that snowshoes were invented by Plains Indians, for level places. In the mountains, those traverses' – he takes a bite – 'those traverses were terrible.'

'You used to love it up here.'

'That was in the summers.'

'It's better now, there's no one else up here. And you can go anywhere you want over snow.'

'I've noticed you think so. But I don't like the snow. Too much work.'

'Work,' Brian scoffs. 'The old law office is warping your conception of work, Peter.'

Peter chomps irritably, looking offended. They continue to eat. One of Joe's nonsense songs floats by.

'Speaking of warped brains,' Peter says.

'Yeah. You keeping an eye on him?'

'I guess so. I don't know what to do when he loses it, though.'

Brian arches back and turns to look over the boulder. 'Hey, Joe!' he shouts. 'Come eat some lunch!' They both watch Joe jerk at the sound of Brian's voice. But after a moment's glance around, Joe returns to playing with the rocks.

'He's out again,' says Brian.

'That,' Peter says, 'is one sick boy. Those doctors really did it to him.'

'That *crash* did it to him. The doctors saved his life. You didn't see him at the hospital like I did. Man, ten or twenty years ago an injury like that would have left him a vegetable for sure. When I saw him I thought he was a goner.'

'Yeah, I know, I know. The man who flew through his windshield.'

'But you don't know what they *did* to him.'

'So what did they do to him?'

'Well, they stimulated what they call axonal sprouting in the areas where neuronal connections were busted up – which means, basically, that they grew his brain back!'

'*Grew* it?'

'Yeah! Well some parts of it – the broken connections, you know. Like the arm of a starfish. You know?'

'No. But I'll take your word for it.' Peter looks over the boulder at Joe. 'I hope they grew back everything, yuk yuk. He might have one of his forgetting spells and walk over the edge there.'

'Nah. He just forgets how to talk, as far as I can tell.

Part of the reorganization, I think. It doesn't matter much up here.' Brian arches up. 'Hey, JOE! FOOD!'

'It does too matter,' Peter says. 'Say he forgets the word *cliff*. He forgets the concept, he says to himself I'm just going to step down to that lake there, and whoops, over the edge he goes.'

'Nah,' Brian says. 'It doesn't work that way. Concepts don't need language.'

'What?' Peter cries. 'Concepts don't need language? Are you kidding? Man I thought Joe was the crazy one around here.'

'No seriously,' Brian says, shifting rapidly from his usual reserve to interested animation. 'Sensory input is already a thought, and the way we field it is conceptual. Enough to keep you from walking off cliffs anyway.' Despite this assertion he looks over his shoulder again. There stands Joe nodding as if in agreement with him.

'Yes, language is a contact lens,' Joe says.

Peter and Brian look at each other.

'A contact lens at the back of the eyeball. Colour filters into this lens, which is made of nameglass, and its reflected to the correct corner of the brain, tree corner or rock corner.'

Peter and Brian chew that one over.

'So you lose your contact lenses?' Brian ventures.

'Yeah!' Joe looks at him with an appreciative glance. 'Sort of.'

'So what's in your mind then?'

Joe shrugs. 'I wish I knew.' After a while, struggling for expression: 'I feel things. I feel that something's not right. Maybe I have another language then, but I'm not sure. Nothing looks right, it's all just . . . colour. The names are gone. You know?'

Brian shakes his head, involuntarily grinning.

'Hmm,' Peter says. 'It sounds like you might have some trouble getting your driver's licence renewed.' All three of them laugh.

Brian stands, stuffs plastic bags into his pack. 'Ready for some ridge running?' he says to the other two.

'Wait a second,' Peter says, 'we just got here. Why don't you kick back for a while? This pass is supposed to be the high point of the trip, and we've only been here half an hour.'

'Longer than that,' says Brian.

'Not long enough. I'm tired!'

'We've only hiked about four miles today,' Brian replies impatiently. 'All of us worked equally hard. Now we can walk down a ridge all afternoon, it'll be great!'

Peter sucks air between his teeth, holds it in, decides not to speak. He begins jamming bags into his pack.

They stand ready to leave the pass, packs and snow-shoes on their backs. Brian makes a final adjustment to hipbelt – Pete looks up the spine they are about to ascend – Joe stares down at the huge bowl of rock and snow to the west. Afternoon sun glares. The shadow of a cloud hurries across the cirque towards them, jumps up the west side of the pass and they are in it, for a moment.

'Look!' Joe cries. He points at the south wall of the pass. Brian and Pete look –

A flash of brown. A pair of horns, blur of legs, the distant *clacks* of rock falling.

'Mountain goat!' says Brian. 'Wow!' He hurries across the saddle of the pass to the south spine, looking up frequently. 'There it is again! Come on!'

Joe and Pete hurry after him. 'You guys will never catch that thing,' says Peter.

The south wall is faulted and boulderish, and they zig and zag from one small shelf of snow to the next. They grab outcroppings and stick fists in cracks, and strain to push themselves up steps that are waist-high. The wind peels across the spine of the wall and keeps them cool. They breathe in gasps, stop frequently. Brian pulls ahead, Peter falls behind. Brian and Joe call to each other about the goat.

Brian and Joe top the spine, scramble up the decreasing slope. The ridge edge – a hump of shattered rock, twenty or twenty-five feet wide, like a high road – is nearly level, but still rises enough to block their view south. They hurry up to the point where the ridge levels, and suddenly they can see south for miles.

They stop to look. The range rises and falls in even swoops to a tall peak. Beyond the peak it drops abruptly and rises again, up and down and up, culminating in a huge knot of black peaks. To the east the steep snowy slope drops to the valley paralleling the range. To the west a series of spurs and cirques alternate, making a broken desert of rock and snow. The range cuts down the middle of it all, high above everything else that can be seen. Joe taps his boot on solid rock. 'Fossil backbone, primeval earth being,' he says.

'I think I still see that goat,' says Brian, pointing. 'Where's Peter?'

Peter appears, face haggard. He stumbles on a rock, steps quickly to keep his balance. When he reaches Brian and Joe he lets his pack thump to the ground.

'This is ridiculous,' he says. 'I have to rest.'

'We can't exactly camp here,' Brian says sarcastically, and gestures at the jumble of rock they are sitting on.

'I don't care,' Peter says, and sits down.

'We've only been hiking an hour since lunch,' Brian objects, 'and we're trying to close in on that goat!'

'Tired,' Peter says. 'I have to rest.'

'You get tired pretty fast these days!'

An angry silence.

Joe says in a mild voice. 'You guys sure are bitching at each other a lot.'

A long silence. Brian and Peter look in different directions.

Joe points down at the first dip in the ridge, where there is a small flat of granite slabs and corners filled with sand. 'Why don't we camp there? Brian and I can drop our packs and go on up the ridge for a walk. Pete can rest and maybe start a fire later. If you can find wood.'

Brian and Pete both agree to the plan, and they descend to the saddle campsite.

Two men ridge running. They make swift progress up the smooth rise, along the jumbled road at the top of the range. The bare rock they cross is smashed into fragments, splintered by ice and lightning. Breaking out of the blackish granite are knobs of tan rock, crushed into concentric rings of shards. They marvel at boulders which look like they have sat on the range since it began to rise. They jump from rock to rock, flexing freed shoulders. Brian points ahead and calls out when he sees the goat. 'Do you see it?'

'Sure do,' Joe says, but without looking up. Brian notices this and snorts disgustedly.

Shadows of the range darken the valley to the east. Joe hops from foothold to foothold, babbling at Brian all the while from several yards behind him. 'Name it, name it. You name it. Naammme. What an idea. I've got three blisters on my feet. I named the one on the left heel Amos.' Pause to climb a shoulder-high slab of granite. 'I named the one on the right heel Crouch. Then I've got one on the front of my right ankle, and I named that one Achilles. That way when I feel it it's not like pain, it's like a little joke. Twinges in my heel' – panting so he can talk – 'are little hellos, hellos with every step. Amos here, hi, Joe; Crouch here, hi, Joe. It's amazing. The way I feel I probably don't need boots at all. I should take them off!'

'You'd probably better keep them on,' Brian says seriously.

Joe grins.

The incline becomes steeper and the edge of the ridge narrows. They slow down, step more carefully. The shattered rock gives way to great faulted blocks of solid mountain. They find themselves straddling the ridge on all fours, left feet on the east slope and right feet on the west. Both sides drop sharply away, especially the west. Sun gilds this steeper slope. Joe runs his hand down the edge of the range.

* * *

The ridge widens out, and they can walk again. The rock is shattered, all brittle plated angular splinters, covered with lichen. 'Great granite,' Joe says.

'This is actually diorite,' Brian says. 'Diorite or gabbro. Made of feldspar and darker stuff.'

'Oh, don't give me that,' Joe says. 'I'm doing well just to remember granite. Besides, this stuff has been granite for a lot longer than geologists have been naming things. They can't go messing with a name like that.' Still, he looks more closely at the rock. 'Gabbro, gabbro . . . sounds like one of my words.'

They wind between boulders, spring up escarpments. They come upon a knob of quartz that rises out of the black granite. The knob is infinitely cracked, as if struck on top by a giant sledgehammer. 'Rose quartz,' says Brian, and moves on. Joe stares at the knob, mouth open. He kneels to pick up chunks of the quartz, peers at them. He sees that Brian is moving on. Rising, he says to himself, 'I wish I knew everything.'

Suddenly they are at the top. Everything is below them. Beside Brian, Joe stops short. They stand silently, inches apart. Wind whips around them. To the south the range drops and rises yet again, to the giant knob of peaks they saw when they first topped the ridge. At every point of the compass mountains drop away, white folds crumpling to every horizon. Nothing moves but the wind. Brian says, 'I wonder where that goat went to.'

Two men sitting on a mountaintop. Brian digs into a pile of rocks, pulls out a rusty tin box. 'Aha,' he says.

'The goat left us a clue.' He takes a piece of paper from the box. 'Here's its name – Diane Hunter.'

'Oh, bullshit!' cries Joe. 'That's no name. Let me see that.' He grabs the box out of Brian's hand and the top falls off. A shower of paper, ten or twenty pieces of it, pops out of the box and floats down to the east, spun by the wind. Joe pulls out a piece still wedged in the box. He reads, 'Robert Spencer, July 20th, 2014. It's a name box. It's for people who want to leave a record of their climb.'

Brian laughs. 'How could anyone get into something like that? Especially on a peak you can just walk right up to.' He laughs again.

'I suppose I should try to recover as many as I can,' Joe says dubiously, looking down the steep side of the peak.

'What for? It's not going to erase their experience.'

'You never know,' says Joe, laughing to himself. 'It very well might. Just think, all over the United States the memory of this peak has popped right out of twenty people's heads.' He waves to the east. 'Bye-bye . . .'

They sit in silence. Wind blows. Clouds pass by. The sun closes on the horizon. Joe talks in short bursts, waves his arms. Brian listens, watches the clouds. At one point he says, 'You're a new being, Joseph.' Joe cocks his head at this.

Then they just sit and watch. It gets cold.

'Hawk,' says Brian in a quiet voice. They watch the black dot soar on the updraught of the range.

'It's the goat,' says Joe. 'It's a shapechanger.'

'Nah. Doesn't even move the same.'

'I say it is.'

The dot turns in the wind and rises, circling higher

and higher above the world, coasting along the updraught with minute wing adjustments, until it hovers over the giant, angular knotpeak. Suddenly it plummets towards the peaks, stooping faster than objects fall. It disappears behind the jagged black teeth. 'Hawk,' Joe breathes. 'Hawuck divvve.'

They look at each other.

Brian says, 'That's where we'll go tomorrow.'

Glissading down the snow expanse, skidding five or ten feet with each stiff-legged step, the two of them make rapid progress back to camp. The walking is dreamlike as they pump left . . . right . . . left . . . right down the slope.

'So what about that goat?' says Joe. 'I never did see any prints.'

'Maybe we shared a hallucination,' says Brian. 'What do they call that?'

'A folie à deux.'

'I don't like the sound of that.' A pause while they skid down a steep bank of snow, straight-legged as if they are skiing. 'I hope Pete got a fire going. Damn cold up here.'

'A feature of the psychic landscape,' Joe says, talking to himself again. 'Sure, why not? It looks about like what I'd expect, I'll tell you that. No wonder I'm getting things confused. What you saw was probably a fugitive thought of mine, escaping off across the waste. Bighorn sheep, sure.'

After a while they can see the saddle where they left Peter, far below them in the rocky expanse. There is a spark of yellow. They howl and shout. 'Fire! FIRE!'

*　　*　　*

In the sandy camp, situated in a dip between slabs of granite, they greet Pete and root through their packs with the speed of hungry men. Joe takes his pot, jams it with snow, puts it on the fire. He sits down beside Peter.

'You guys were gone a long time,' Peter says. 'Did you find that goat?'

Joe shakes his head. 'It turned into a hawk.' He moves his pot to a bigger flame. 'Sure am glad you got this fire going,' he says. 'It must have been a bitch to start in this wind.' He starts to pull off his boots.

'There wasn't much wood, either,' Pete says. 'But I found a dead tree down there a ways.'

Joe prods a burning branch, frowns. 'Juniper,' he says with satisfaction. 'Good wood.'

Brian appears, dressed in down jacket, down pants, and down booties. Pete falls silent. Glancing at Pete, Joe notices this, and frowns again. He gets up stiffly to go to his pack and get his own down booties. He returns to the fire, finishes taking off his boots. His feet are white and wrinkled, with red blisters.

'Those look sore,' says Pete.

'Nah.' Joe gulps down the melted snow in his pot, starts melting more. He puts his booties on.

They watch the fire in silence.

Joe says, 'Remember that time you guys wrestled in the living room of our apartment?'

'Yeah, we got all those carpet burns.'

'And broke the lamp that never worked anyway –'

'And then you went berserk!' Brian laughs. 'You went berserk and tried to bite my ear off!' They all laugh, and Pete nods, grinning with embarrassed pride.

'Pete won that one,' Joe says.

'That's right,' says Brian. 'Put my shoulders to the mat, or to the carpet in that case. A victory for maniacs everywhere.'

Ponderously Peter nods, imitating official approval. 'But I couldn't beat you tonight,' he admits. 'I'm exhausted. I guess I'm not up to this snow camping.'

'You were strong in those days,' Brian tells him. 'But you hiked a radical trail with us today, I'll tell you. I don't know too many people who would have come with us, actually.'

'What about Joe here? He was on his back most of last year.'

'Yeah, but he's crazy now.'

'I was crazy before!' Joe protests, and they laugh.

Brian pours macaroni into his pot, shifts to a rock seat beside Peter so he can tend the pot better. They begin to talk about the days when they all lived together as students. Joe grins to hear them. He nearly overturns his pot, and they call out at him. Pete says, 'The black thing is the pot, Joseph, the yellow stuff is fire – try to remember that.' Joe grins. Steam rises from the pots and is whipped east by the evening breeze.

Three men sitting round a fire. Joe gets up, very slowly, and steps carefully to his pack. He unrolls his groundcloth, pulls out his sleeping bag. He straightens up. The evening star hangs in the west. It's getting darker. Behind him his old friends laugh at something Pete has said.

In the east there are stars. Part of the sky is still a light velvet blue. The wind whistles softly. Joe picks up a rock, looks at it closely. 'Rock,' he says. He clenches the rock in his fist, shakes it at the evening star, lofts it skyward. 'Rock!' A tear gleams in his eyes. He looks down the range: *black dragon back breaking out of blue-white*, like consciousness from chaos, an unbroken range of peaks –

'Hey, Joseph! You lamebrain!'

'Space case!'

'– come take care of your pot before it puts the fire out.'

Joe walks to the woodpile grinning, puts more wood on the fire, until it blazes up yellow in the dusk.

Black Air

THEY SAILED OUT of Lisbon harbour with the flags snapping and the brass culverins gleaming under a high white sun, priests proclaiming in sonorous Latin the blessing of the Pope, soldiers in armour jammed on the castles fore and aft, and sailors spiderlike in the rigging, waving at the citizens of the town who had left their work to come out on the hills and watch the ships crowd out the sunbeaten roads, for this was the Armada, the Most Fortunate Invincible Armada, off to subjugate the heretic English to the will of God. There would never be another departure like it.

Unfortunately, the wind blew out of the northeast for a month after they left without shifting even a point on the compass, and at the end of that month the Armada was no closer to England than Iberia itself. Not only that, but the hard-pressed coopers of Portugal had made many of the Armada's casks of green wood, and when the ship's cooks opened them the meat was rotten and the water stank. So they trailed into the port of Corunna, where several hundred soldiers and sailors swam to the shores of Spain and were never seen again. A few hundred more had already died of disease, so from his sickbed on the flagship Don Alonso Perez de Guzman el Bueno, seventh Duke of Medina Sidonia and Admiral of the Armada, interrupted the composition of his daily complaint to Philip the Second, and instructed his soldiers to go out into the countryside and collect peasants to help man the ships.

One squad of these soldiers stopped at a Franciscan monastery on the outskirts of Corunna, to impress all the boys who lived there and helped the monks, waiting to join the order themselves. Although they did not like it the monks could not object to the proposal, and off the boys went to join the fleet.

Among these boys, who were each taken to a different ship, was Manuel Carlos Agadir Tetuan. He was seventeen years old; he had been born in Morocco, the son of West Africans who had been captured and enslaved by Arabs. In his short life he had already lived in the Moroccan coastal town of Tetuan, in Gibraltar, the Balearics, Sicily, and Lisbon. He had worked in fields and cleaned stables, he had helped make rope and later cloth, and he had served food in inns. After his mother died of the pox and his father drowned, he had begged in the streets and alleys of Corunna, the last port his father had sailed out of, until in his fifteenth year a Franciscan had tripped over him sleeping in an alley, enquired after him, and taken him to the refuge of the monastery.

Manuel was still weeping when the soldiers took him aboard *La Lavia*, a Levantine galleon of nearly a thousand tons. The sailing master of the ship, one Laeghr, took him in charge and led him below decks. Laeghr was an Irishman, who had left his country principally to practise his trade, but also out of hatred of the English who ruled Ireland. He was a huge man with a torso like a boar's, and arms as thick as the yardarms of the ship. When he saw Manuel's distress he showed that he was not without kindness; clapping a callused hand to the back of Manuel's neck he said, in accented but fluent Spanish, 'Stop your snivelling, boy, we're off to conquer the damned English, and when we do your fathers at the monastery will make you their abbot. And before that happens a dozen English girls will fall at your feet and ask for the touch of those black hands, no doubt. Come on, stop it. I'll show you your berth first, and wait till we're at sea to show you your station. I'm going to put you in the main top, all our blacks are good topmen.'

Laeghr slipped through a door half his height with the ease of a weasel ducking into one of its tiny holes in the earth. A hand half as wide as the doorway reemerged and pulled Manuel into the gloom. The terrified boy nearly fell down a broad-stepped ladder, but caught himself before falling onto Laeghr. Far below several soldiers laughed at him. Manuel had never been on anything larger than a Sicilian pataches, and most of his fairly extensive seagoing experience was of coastal carracks, so the broad deck under him, cut by bands of yellow sunlight that flowed in at open ports big as church windows, crowded with barrels and bales of hay and tubs of rope, and a hundred busy men, was a marvel. 'Saint Anna save me,' he said, scarcely able to believe he was on a ship. Why, the monastery itself had no room as large as the one he descended into now. 'Get down here,' Laeghr said in an encouraging way.

Once on the deck of that giant room they descended again, to a stuffy chamber a quarter the size, illuminated by narrow fans of sunlight that were let in by ports that were mere slits in the hull. 'Here's where you sleep,' Laeghr said, pointing at a dark corner of the deck, against one massive oak wall of the ship. Forms there shifted, eyes appeared as lids lifted, a dull voice said, 'Another one you'll never find again in this dark, eh master?'

'Shut up, Juan. See boy, there are beams dividing your berth from the rest, that will keep you from rolling around when we get to sea.'

'Just like a coffin, with the lid up there.'

'Shut up, Juan.'

After the sailing master had made clear which slot in particular was Manuel's, Manuel collapsed in it and began to cry again. The slot was shorter than he was, and the dividing boards set in the deck were cracked and splintered. The men around him slept, or talked among themselves, ignoring Manuel's presence. His medallion cord choked him, and he shifted it on his neck and remembered to pray.

His guardian saint, the monks had decided, was Anne, mother of the Virgin Mary and grandmother of Jesus. He owned a small wooden medallion with her face painted on it, which Abbot Alonso had given to him. Now he took the medallion between his fingers, and looked in the tiny brown dots that were the face's eyes. 'Please, Mother Anna,' he prayed silently, 'take me from this ship to my home. Take me home.' He clenched the tag in his fist so tightly that the back of it, carved so that a cross of wood stood out from its surface, left an imprinted red cross in his palm. Many hours passed before he fell asleep.

Two days later the Most Fortunate Invincible Armada left Corunna, this time without the flags, or the crowds of spectators, or the clouds of priestly incense trailing downwind. This time God favoured them with a westerly wind, and they sailed north at good speed. The ships were arranged in a formation devised by the soldiers, orderly phalanxes rising and falling on the swells: the galleasses in front, the supply hulks in the centre, and the big galleons on either flank. The thousands of sails stacked on hundreds of masts made a grand and startling sight, like a copse of white trees on a broad blue plain.

Manuel was as impressed by the sight as the rest of the men. There were four hundred men on *La Lavia*, and only thirty were needed at any one time to sail the ship, so all of the three hundred soldiers stood on the sterncastle observing the fleet, and the sailors who were not on duty or sleeping did the same on the slightly lower forecastle.

Manuel's duties as a sailor were simple. He was stationed at the port midships taffrail, to which were tied the sheets for the port side of the mainmast's sails, and the sheets for the big lateen-rigged sail of the foremast. Manuel helped five other men pull these ropes in or let them out, following Laeghr's instructions; the other men took care of the belaying knots, so Manuel's job came down to pulling on a rope when told to. It could have been more difficult, but Laeghr's plan to make him a topman like the other Africans aboard had come to grief. Not that Leaghr hadn't tried. 'God made you Africans with a better head for heights, so you can climb trees to keep from being eaten by lions, isn't that right?' But when Manuel had followed a Moroccan named Habedeen up the halyard ladder to the main top, he found himself plunging about space, nearly scraping low foggy clouds, and the sea, embroidered with the wakes of the ships ahead, was more often than not *directly below him*. He had clamped, arms and legs, around a stanchion of the main top, and it had taken five men, laughing and cursing, to prise him loose and pull him down. With rich disgust, but no real physical force, Laeghr had pounded him with his cane and shoved him to the port taffrail. 'You must be a Sicilian with a sunburn.' And so he had been assigned his station.

Despite this incident he got on well with the rest of the crew. Not with the soldiers; they were rude and arrogant to the sailors, who stayed out of their way to avoid a curse or a blow. So three-quarters of the men aboard were of a different class, and remained strangers. The sailors therefore hung together. They were a mongrel lot, drawn from all over the Mediterranean, and Manuel was not unusual because of his recent arrival. They were united only in their dislike and resentment of the soldiers. 'Those heroes wouldn't be able to conquer the Isle of Wight if we didn't sail them there,' Juan said.

Manuel became acquainted first with the men at his post, and then with the men in his berth. As he spoke Spanish and Portuguese, and fair amounts of Arabic, Sicilian, Latin, and a Moroccan dialect, he could converse with everyone in his corner of the lower foredeck. Occasionally he was asked to translate for the Moroccans; more than once this meant he was the arbiter of a dispute, and he thought fast and mistranslated whenever it would help make peace. Juan, the one who had made the bitter comments to Laeghr on Manuel's arrival, was the only pure Spaniard in the berth. He loved to talk, and complained to Manuel and the others continuously. 'I've fought *El Draco* before, in the Indies,' he boasted. 'We'll be lucky to get past that devil. You mark my words, we'll never do it.'

Manuel's mates at the main taffrail were more cheerful, and he enjoyed his watches with them and the drills under Laeghr's demanding instruction. These men called him Topman or Climber, and made jokes about his knots around the belaying pins, which defied quick untying. This inability earned Manuel quite a few swats from Laeghr's cane, but there were worse sailors aboard, and the sailing master seemed to bear him no ill will.

A life of perpetual change had made Manuel adaptable, and shipboard routine became for him the natural course of existence. Laeghr or Pietro, the leader at Manuel's station, would wake him with a shout. Up to the gundeck, which was the domain of the soldiers, and from there up the big ladder that led to fresh air. Only then could Manuel be sure of the time of day. For the first week it was an inexpressible delight to get out of the gloom of the lower decks and under the sky, in the wind and clean salt air; but as they proceeded north, it began to get too cold for comfort. After their watches were over, Manuel and his mates would retire to the galley and be given their biscuits, water and wine. Sometimes the cooks killed some of the goats and chickens and made soup. Usually, though, it was just biscuits, biscuits that had not yet hardened in their barrels. The men complained grievously about this.

'The biscuits are best when they're hard as wood, and bored through by worms,' Habedeen told Manuel.

'How do you eat it then?' Manuel asked.

'You bang pieces of biscuit against the table until the worms fall out. You eat the worms if you want.' The men laughed, and Manuel assumed Habedeen was joking, but he wasn't certain.

'I despise this doughy shit,' Pietro said in Portuguese. Manuel translated into Moroccan Arabic for the two silent Africans, and agreed in Spanish that it was hard to stomach. 'The worst part,' he offered, 'is that some parts are stale while others are still fresh.'

'The fresh part was never cooked.'

'No, that's the worms.'

As the voyage progressed, Manuel's berthmates became more intimate. Farther north the Moroccans suffered terribly from the cold. They came belowdecks after a watch with their dark skins completely goose-pimpled, like little fields of stubble after a harvest. Their lips and fingernails were blue, and they shivered an hour before falling asleep, teeth chattering like the castanets in a fiesta band. Not only that, but the swells of the Atlantic were getting bigger, and the men, since they were forced to wear every scrap of clothing they owned,

rolled in their wooden berths unpadded and unpro-
tected. So the Moroccans, and then everyone in the
lower foredeck, slept three to a berth, taking turns in
the middle, huddling together like spoons. Crowded
together like that the pitching of the ship could press
them against the beams, but it couldn't roll them
around. Manuel's willingness to join these bundlings,
and to lie against the beams, made him well-liked.
Everyone agreed he made a good cushion.

Perhaps it was because of his hands that he fell ill.
Though his spirit had been reconciled to the crusade
north, his flesh was slower. Hauling on the coarse hemp
ropes every day had ripped the skin from his palms, and
salt, splinters, belaying pins and the odd boot had all
left their marks as well, so that after the first week he
had wrapped his hands in strips of cloth torn from the
bottom of his shirt. When he became feverish, his hands
pulsed painfully at every nudge from his heart, and he
assumed that the fever had entered him through the
wounds in his palms.

Then his stomach rebelled, and he could keep nothing down. The sight of biscuits or soup revolted him;
his fever worsened, and he became parched and weak;
he spent a lot of time in the head, wracked by dysentery. 'You've been poisoned by the biscuits,' Juan told
him. 'Just like I was in the Indies. That's what comes
of boxing fresh biscuits. They might as well have put
fresh dough in those barrels.'

Manuel's berthmates told Laeghr of his condition,
and Laeghr had him moved to the hospital, which was
at the stern of the ship on a lower deck, in a wide room

that the sick shared with the rudder post, a large
smoothed tree trunk thrusting through floor and ceiling. All of the other men were gravely ill. Manuel was
miserable as they laid him down on his pallet, wretched
with nausea and in great fear of the hospital, which
smelled of putrefaction. The man on the pallet next to
him was insensible, and rolled with the sway of the
ship. Three candle lanterns lit the low chamber and
filled it with shadows. One of the Dominican friars, a
Friar Lucien, gave him hot water and wiped his face.
They talked for a while, and the friar heard Manuel's
confession, which only a proper priest should have done.
Neither of them cared. The priests on board avoided
the hospital, and tended to serve only the officers and
the soldiers. Friar Lucien was known to be willing to
minister to the sailors, and he was popular among them.

Manuel's fever got worse, and he could not eat. Days
passed, and when he woke up the men around him were
not the same men who had been there when he fell
asleep. He became convinced he was going to die, and
once again he felt despair that he had been made a
member of the Most Fortunate Invincible Armada. 'Why
are we here?' he demanded of the friar in a cracked
voice. 'Why shouldn't we let the English go to hell if
they please?'

'The purpose of the Armada is not only to smite the
heretic English,' said Lucien. He held a candle closer to
his book, which was not a Bible, but a slender little
thing which he kept hidden in his robes. Shadows leaped
on the blackened beams and planks over them, and the
rudder post squeaked as it turned against the leather
collar in the floor. 'God also sent us as a test. Listen:

'"I assume the appearance of a refiner's fire, purging the dross of forms outworn. This is mine aspect of severity; I am as one who testeth gold in a furnace. Yet when thou hast been tried as by fire, the gold of thy soul shall be cleansed, and visible as fire: then the vision of thy Lord shall be granted unto thee, and seeing Him shall thou behold the shining one, who is thine own true self."

'Remember that, and be strong. Drink this water here – come on, do you want to fail your God? This is part of the test.'

Manuel drank, threw up. His body was no more than a tongue of flame contained by his skin, except where it burst out of his palms. He lost track of the days, and forgot the existence of anyone beyond himself and Friar Lucien. 'I never wanted to leave the monastery,' he told the friar, 'yet I never thought I would stay there long. I've never stayed long any place yet. It was my home but I knew it wasn't. I haven't found my home yet. They say there is ice in England – I saw the snow in the Catalonian mountains, once, Father, will we go home? I only want to return to the monastery and be a father like you.'

'We will go home. What you will become, only God knows. He has a place for you. Sleep now. Sleep, now.'

By the time his fever broke his ribs stood out from his chest as clearly as the fingers of a fist. He could barely walk. Lucien's narrow face appeared out of the gloom clear as a memory. 'Try this soup. Apparently God has seen fit to keep you here.'

'Thank you Saint Anna for your intercession,'

Manuel croaked. He drank the soup eagerly. 'I want to return to my berth.'

'Soon.'

They took him up to the deck. Walking was like floating, as long as he held on to railings and stanchions. Laeghr greeted him with pleasure, as did his station-mates. The world was a riot of blues; waves hissed past, low clouds jostled together in their rush east, tumbling between them shafts of sunlight that spilled onto the water. He was excused from active duty, but he spent as many hours as he could at his station. He found it hard to believe that he had survived his illness. Of course, he was not entirely recovered; he could not yet eat any solids, particularly biscuit, so that his diet consisted of soup and wine. He felt weak, and perpet-ually light-headed. But when he was on deck in the wind he was sure that he was getting better, so he stayed there as much as possible. He was on deck, in fact, when they first caught sight of England. The soldiers pointed and shouted in great excitement, as the point Laeghr called The Lizard bounced over the horizon. Manuel had grown so used to the sea that the low head-land rising off their port bow seemed unnatural, an intrusion into a marine world, as if the deluge was just now receding and these drowned hillsides were just now shouldering up out of the waves, soaking wet and covered by green seaweed that had not yet died. And that was England.

A few days after that they met the first English ships – faster than the Spanish galleons, but much smaller. They could no more impede the progress of the Armada than flies could slow a herd of cows. The swells became steeper and followed each other more closely, and the changed pitching of *La Lavia* made it difficult for Manuel to stand. He banged his head once, and another time ripped away a palmful of scabs, trying to keep his balance in the violent yawing caused by the chop. Unable to stand one morning, he lay in the dark of his berth, and his mates brought him cups of soup. That went on for a long time. Again he worried that he was going to die. Finally Laeghr and Lucien came below together.

'You must get up now,' Laeghr declared. 'We fight within the hour, and you're needed. We've arranged easy work for you.'

'You have only to provide the gunners with slow match,' said Friar Lucien as he helped Manuel to his feet. 'God will help you.'

'God will have to help me,' Manuel said. He could see the two men's souls flickering above their heads: little triple knots of transparent flame that flew up out of their hair and lit the features of their faces. 'The gold of thy soul shall be cleansed, and visible as fire,' Manuel recalled. 'Hush,' said Lucien with a frown, and Manuel realized that what Lucien had read to him was a secret.

Amidships Manuel noticed that now he was also able to see the air, which was tinged red. They were on the bottom of an ocean of red air, just as they were on top of an ocean of blue water. When they breathed they turned the air a darker red; men expelled plumes of air like horses breathing out clouds of steam on a frosty morning, only the steam was red. Manuel stared and stared, marvelling at the new abilities God had given his sight.

'Here,' Laeghr said, roughly directing him across the deck. 'This tub of punk is yours. This is slow match, understand?' Against the bulkhead was a tub full of coils of closely braided cord. One end of the cord was hanging over the edge of the tub burning, fizzing the air around it to deep crimson. Manuel nodded: 'Slow match.'

'Here's your knife. Cut sections about this long, and light them with a piece of it that you keep beside you. Then give sections of it to the gunners who come by, or take it to them if they call for it. But don't give away all your lit pieces. Understand?'

Manuel nodded that he understood and sat down dizzily beside the tub. One of the largest cannon poked through a port in the bulkhead just a few feet from him. Its crew greeted him. Across the deck his stationmates stood at their taffrail. The soldiers were ranked on the fore- and sterncastles, shouting with excitement, gleaming like shellfish in the sun. Through the port Manuel could see some of the English coast.

Laeghr came over to see how he was doing. 'Hey, don't you lop your fingers off there, boy. See out there? That's the Isle of Wight. We're going to circle and conquer it, I've no doubt, and use it as our base for our attack on the mainland. With these soldiers and ships they'll *never* get us off that island. It's a good plan.'

But things did not progress according to Laeghr's plan. The Armada swung around the east shore of the Isle of Wight, in a large crescent made of five distinct phalanxes of ships. Rounding the island, however, the forward galleasses encountered the stiffest English resistance they had met so far. White puffs of smoke appeared out of the ships and were quickly stained red, and the noise was tremendous.

Then the ships of *El Draco* swept around the southern point of the island onto their flank, and suddenly *La Lavia* was in the action. The soldiers roared and shot off their arquebuses, and the big cannon beside Manuel leaped back in its truck with a bang that knocked him into the bulkhead. After that he could barely hear. His slow match was suddenly in demand; he cut the cord and held the lit tip to unlit tips, igniting them with his red breath. Cannonballs passing overhead left rippling wakes in the blood air. Grimy men snatched the slow match and dashed to their guns, dodging tackle blocks that thumped to the deck. Manuel could see the cannonballs, big as grapefruit, flying at them from the English ships and passing with a whistle. And he could see the transparent knots of flame, swirling higher than ever about the men's heads.

Then a cannonball burst through the porthole and knocked the cannon off its truck, the men to the deck. Manuel rose to his feet and noticed with horror that the knots of flame on the scattered gunners were gone; he could see their heads clearly now, and they were just men, just broken flesh draped over the ploughed surface of the deck. He tried, sobbing, to lift a gunner who was bleeding only from the ears. Laeghr's cane lashed across his shoulders: 'Keep cutting match! There's others to attend to these men!' So Manuel cut lengths of cord and lit them with desperate puffs and shaking hands, while the guns roared, and the exposed soldiers on the castles shrieked under a hail of iron, and the red air was ripped by passing shot.

*   *   *

The next few days saw several battles like that as the Armada was forced past the Isle of Wight and up the Channel. His fever kept him from sleeping, and at night Manuel helped the wounded on his deck, holding them down and wiping the sweat from their faces, nearly as delirious as they were. At dawn he ate biscuits and drank his cup of wine and went to his tub of slow match to await the next engagement. *La Lavia*, being the largest ship on the left flank, always took the brunt of the English attack. It was on the third day that *La Lavia*'s mainmast topgallant yard fell on his old taffrail crew, crushing Hanan and Pietro. Manuel rushed across the deck to help them, shouting his anguish. He got a dazed Juan down to their berth and returned amidships. Around him men were being dashed to the deck, but he didn't care. He hopped through the red mist that nearly obscured his sight, carrying lengths of match to the gun crews, who were now so depleted that they couldn't afford to send men to him. He helped the wounded below to the hospital, which had truly become an antechamber of hell; he helped toss the dead over the side, croaking a short prayer in every case; he ministered to the soldiers hiding behind the bulwarks of the bulkheads, waiting vainly for the English to get within range of their arquebuses. Now the cry amidships was 'Manuel, match here! Manuel, some water! Help, Manuel!' In a dry fever of energy Manuel hurried to their aid.

He was in such perpetual haste that in the middle of a furious engagement he nearly ran into his patroness, Saint Anna, who was suddenly standing there in the corner of his tub. He was startled to see her.

'Grandmother!' he cried. 'You shouldn't be here, it's dangerous.'

'As you have helped others, I am here to help you,' she replied. She pointed across the purplish chop to one of the English ships. Manuel saw a puff of smoke appear from its side, and out of the puff came a cannonball, floating in an arc over the water. He could see it as clearly as he could have seen an olive tossed at him from across a room: a round black ball, spinning lazily, growing bigger as it got closer. Now Manuel could tell that it was coming at him, *directly* at him, so that its trajectory would intersect his heart. 'Um, blessed Anna,' he said, hoping to bring this to his saint's attention. But she had already seen it, and with a brief touch to his forehead she floated up into the maintop, among the unseeing soldiers. Manuel watched her, eyeing the approaching cannonball at the same time. At the touch of her hand a rigging block fell away from the end of the main yard; it intercepted the cannonball's flight, knocking the ball downward into the hull where it stuck, half embedded in the thick wood. Manuel stared at the black half sphere, mouth open. He waved up at Saint Anna, who waved back and flew up into the red clouds towards heaven. Manuel kneeled and said a prayer of thanks to her and to Jesus for sending her and went back to cutting match.

A night or two later – Manuel himself was not sure, as the passage of time had become for him something plastic and elusive and, more than anything else, meaningless – the Armada anchored at Calais Roads, just off the Flemish coast. For the first time since they had left

371

Corunna *La Lavia* lay still, and listening at night Manuel realized how much the constant chorus of wooden squeaks and groans was the voice of the crew, and not of the ship. He drank his ration of wine and water quickly, and walked the length of the lower deck, talking with the wounded and helping when he could to remove splinters. Many of the men wanted him to touch them, for his safe passage through some of the worst scenes of carnage had not gone unnoticed. He touched them, and when they wanted, said a prayer. Afterwards he went up on deck. There was a fair breeze from the southwest, and the ship rocked ever so gently on the tide. For the first time in a week the air was not suffused red: Manuel could see stars, and distant bonfires on the Flemish shore, like stars that had fallen and now burnt out their life on the land.

Laeghr was limping up and down amidships, detouring from his usual path to avoid a bit of shattered decking.

'Are you hurt, Laeghr?' Manuel enquired.

For answer Laeghr growled. Manuel walked beside him. After a bit Laeghr stopped and said, 'They're saying you're a holy man now because you were running all over the deck these last few days, acting like the shot we were taking was hail and never getting hit for it. But I say you're just too foolish to know any better. Fools dance where angels would hide. It's part of the curse laid on us. Those who learn the rules and play things right end up getting hurt – sometimes from doing just the things that will protect them the most. While the blind fools who wander right into the thick of things are never touched.'

Manuel watched Laeghr's stride. 'Your foot?'

Laeghr shrugged. 'I don't know what will happen to it.'

Under a lantern Manuel stopped and looked Laeghr in the eye. 'Saint Anna appeared and plucked a cannonball that was heading for me right out of the sky. She saved my life for a purpose.'

'No.' Laeghr thumped his cane on the deck. 'Your fever has made you mad, boy.'

'I can show you the shot!' Manuel said. 'It stuck in the hull!' Laeghr stumped away.

Manuel looked across the water at Flanders, distressed by Laeghr's words, and by his hobbled walk. He saw something he didn't comprehend.

'Laeghr?'

'What?' came Laeghr's voice from across midships.

'Something bright . . . the souls of all the English at once, maybe . . .' His voice shook.

'What?'

'Something coming at us. Come here, master.'

Thump, thump, thump. Manuel heard the hiss of Laeghr's indrawn breath, the muttered curse.

'Fireships,' Laeghr bellowed at the top of his lungs. 'Fireships! Awake!'

In a minute the ship was bedlam, soldiers running everywhere. 'Come with me,' Laeghr told Manuel, who followed the sailing master to the forecastle, where the anchor hawser descended into the water. Somewhere along the way Laeghr had gotten a halberd, and he gave it to Manuel. 'Cut the line.'

'But master, we'll lose the anchor.'

'Those fireships are too big to stop, and if they're hellburners they'll explode and kill us all. Cut it.'

Manuel began chopping at the thick hawser, which was very like the trunk of a small tree. He chopped and chopped, but only one strand of the huge rope was cut when Laeghr seized the halberd and began chopping himself, awkwardly to avoid putting his weight on his bad foot. They heard the voice of the ship's captain – 'Cut the anchor cable!' And Laeghr laughed.

The rope snapped, and they were floating free. But the fireships were right behind them. In the hellish light Manuel could see English sailors walking about on their burning decks, passing through the flames like salamanders or demons. No doubt they were devils. The fires towering above the eight fireships shared the demonic life of the English; each tongue of yellow flame contained an English demon eye looking for the Armada, and some of these leaped free of the blaze that twisted above the fireships, in vain attempts to float onto *La Lavia* and incinerate it. Manuel held off these embers with his wooden medallion, and the gesture that in his boyhood in Sicily had warded off the evil eye. Meanwhile, the ships of the fleet were cut loose and drifting on the tide, colliding in the rush to avoid the fireships. Captains and officers screamed furiously at their colleagues on other ships, but to no avail. In the dark and without anchors the ships could not be regathered, and as the night progressed most were blown out into the North Sea. For the first time the neat phalanxes of the Armada were broken, and they were never to be reformed again.

When it was all over *La Lavia* held its position in the North Sea by sail, while the officers attempted to identify the ships around them, and find out what Medina Sidonia's orders were. Manuel and Juan stood amidships with the rest of their berthmates. Juan shook his head. 'I used to make corks in Portugal. We were like a cork back there in the Channel, being pushed into the neck of a bottle. As long as we were stuck in the neck we were all right – the neck got narrower and narrower, and they might never have gotten us out. Now the English have pushed us right down into the bottle itself. We're floating about in our own dregs. And we'll never get out of the bottle again.'

'Not through the neck, anyway,' one of the others agreed.

'Not any way.'

'God will see us home,' Manuel said.

Juan shook his head.

Rather than try to force the Channel, Admiral Medina Sidonia decided that the Armada should sail around Scotland, and then home. Laeghr was taken to the flagship for a day to help chart a course, for he was familiar with the north as none of the Spanish pilots were.

The battered fleet headed away from the sun, ever higher into the cold North Sea. After the night of the fireships Medina Sidonia had restored discipline with a vengeance. One day the survivors of the many Channel battles were witness to the hanging from the yardarm of a captain who had let his ship get ahead of the Admiral's flagship, a position which was now forbidden. A carrack sailed through the fleet again and again so every crew could see the corpse of the disobedient captain, swinging freely from its spar.

Manuel observed the sight with distaste. Once dead, a man was only a bag of bones; nowhere in the clouds overhead could he spot the captain's soul. Perhaps it had plummeted into the sea, on its way to hell. It was an odd transition, death. Curious that God did not make more explicit the aftermath.

So *La Lavia* faithfully trailed the Admiral's flagship, as did the rest of the fleet. They were led farther and farther north, into the domain of cold. Some mornings when they came on deck in the raw yellow of the dawn the riggings would be rimed with icicles, so that they seemed strings of diamonds. Some days it seemed they sailed across a sea of milk, under a silver sky. Other days the ocean was the colour of a bruise, and the sky a fresh pale blue so clear that Manuel gasped with the desire to survive this voyage and live. Yet he was as cold as death. He remembered the burning nights of his fever as fondly as if he were remembering his first home on the coast of North Africa.

All the men were suffering from the cold. The livestock was dead, so the galley closed down: no hot soup. The Admiral imposed rationing on everyone, including himself; the deprivation kept him in his bed for the rest of the voyage. For the sailors, who had to haul wet or frozen rope, it was worse. Manuel watched the grim faces, in line for their two biscuits and one large cup of wine and water – their daily ration – and concluded that they would continue sailing north until the sun was under the horizon and they were in the icy realm of death, the north pole where God's dominion was weak, and there they would give up and die all at once. Indeed, the winds drove them nearly to Norway, and it was with great difficulty that they brought the shot-peppered hulks around to a westerly heading.

When they did, they discovered a score of new leaks in La Lavia's hull, and the men, already exhausted by the effort of bringing the ship about, were forced to man the pumps around the clock. A pint of wine and a pint of water a day were not enough. Men died. Dysentery, colds, the slightest injury; all were quickly fatal.

Once again Manuel could see the air. Now it was a thick blue, distinctly darker where men breathed it out, so that they all were shrouded in dark blue air that obscured the burning crowns of their souls. All of the wounded men in the hospital had died. Many of them had called for Manuel in their last moments; he had held their hands or touched their foreheads, and as their souls had flickered away from their heads like the last pops of flame out of the coals of a dying fire, he had prayed for them. Now other men too weak to leave their berths called for him, and he went and stood by them in their distress. Two of these men recovered from dysentery, so his presence was requested even more frequently. The captain himself asked for Manuel's touch when he fell sick; but he died anyway, like most of the rest.

One morning Manuel was standing with Laeghr at the midships bulkhead. It was chill and cloudy, the sea was the colour of flint. The soldiers were bringing their horses up and forcing them over the side, to save water.

'That should have been done as soon as we were forced out of the Sleeve,' Laeghr said. 'Waste of water.'

'I didn't even know we had horses aboard,' Manuel said.

Laeghr laughed briefly. 'Boy, you are a prize of a fool. One surprise after another.'

They watched the horses' awkward falls, their rolling eyes, their flared nostrils expelling clouds of blue air. Their brief attempts to swim.

'On the other hand, we should probably be eating some of those,' Laeghr said.

'Horse meat?'

'It can't be that bad.'

The horses all disappeared, exchanging blue air for flint water. 'It's cruel,' Manuel said.

'In the horse latitudes they swim for an hour,' Laeghr said. 'This is better.' He pointed to the west. 'See those tall clouds?'

'Yes.'

'They stand over the Orkneys. The Orkneys or the Shetlands, I can't be sure anymore. It will be interesting to see if these fools can get this wreck through the islands safely.' Looking around, Manuel could only spot a dozen or so ships; presumably the rest of the Armada lay over the horizon ahead of them. He stopped to wonder about what Laeghr had just said, for it would naturally be Laeghr's task to navigate them through the northernmost of the British Isles; at that very moment Laeghr's eyes rolled like the horses' had, and he collapsed on the deck. Manuel and some other sailors carried him down to the hospital.

'It's his foot,' said Friar Lucien. 'His foot is crushed and his leg has putrefied. He should have let me amputate.'

Around noon Laeghr regained consciousness. Manuel, who had not left his side, held his hand, but Laeghr frowned and pulled it away.

'Listen,' Laeghr said with difficulty. His soul was no more than a blue cap covering his tangled salt-and-pepper hair. 'I'm going to teach you some words that may be useful to you later.' Slowly he said, '*Tor conaloc an dhia*,' and Manuel repeated it. 'Say it again.' Manuel repeated the syllables over and over, like a Latin prayer. Laeghr nodded. '*Tor conaloc an naom dhia*. Good. Remember the words always.' After that he stared at the deckbeams above, and would answer none of Manuel's questions. Emotions played over his face like shadows, one after another. Finally he took his gaze from the infinite and looked at Manuel. 'Touch me, boy.'

Manuel touched his forehead, and with a sardonic smile Laeghr closed his eyes: his blue crown of flame flickered up through the deck above and disappeared.

They buried him that evening, in a smoky, hellish brown sunset. Friar Lucien said the shortened Mass, mumbling in a voice that no one could hear, and Manuel pressed the back of his medallion against the cold flesh of Laeghr's arm, until the impression of the cross remained. Then they tossed him overboard. Manuel watched with a serenity that surprised him. Just weeks ago he had shouted with rage and pain as his companions had been torn apart; now he watched with a peace he did not understand as the man who had taught him and protected him sank into the iron water and disappeared.

A couple of nights after that Manuel sat apart from his remaining berthmates, who slept in one pile like a litter of kittens. He watched the blue flames wandering over

379

the exhausted flesh, watched without reason or feeling. He was tired.

Friar Lucien looked in the narrow doorway and hissed. 'Manuel! Are you there?'

'I'm here.'

'Come with me.'

Manuel got up and followed him. 'Where are we going?'

Friar Lucien shook his head. 'It's time.' Everything else he said was in Greek. He had a little candle lantern with three sides shuttered, and by its illumination they made their way to the hatch that led to the lower decks.

Manuel's berth, though it was below the gun deck, was not on the lowest deck of the ship. *La Lavia* was very much bigger than that. Below the berth deck were three more decks that had no ports, as they were beneath the waterline. Here in perpetual gloom were stored the barrels of water and biscuit, the cannonballs and rope and other supplies. They passed by the powder room, where the armourer wore felt slippers so that a spark from his boots might not blow up the ship. They found a hatchway that held a ladder leading to an even lower deck. At each level the passages became narrower, and they were forced to stoop. Manuel was astounded when they descended yet again, for he would have imagined them already on the keel, or in some strange chamber suspended beneath it; but Lucien knew better. Down they went, through a labyrinth of dank black wooden passageways. Manuel was long lost, and held Lucien's arm for fear of being separated from him, and becoming hopelessly trapped in the bowels of the ship. Finally they came to a door that made their narrow hallway a dead end. Lucien rapped on the door and hissed something, and the door opened, letting out enough light to dazzle Manuel.

After the passageways, the chamber they entered seemed very large. It was the cable tier, located in the bow of the ship just over the keel. Since the encounter with the fireships, *La Lavia* had little cable, and what was left lay in the corners of the room. Now it was lit by candles set in small iron candelabra that had been nailed to the side beams. The floor was covered by an inch of water, which reflected each of the candle flames as a small spot of white light. The curving walls dripped and gleamed. In the centre of the room a box had been set on end, and covered with a bit of cloth. Around the box stood several men: a soldier, one of the petty officers, and some sailors Manuel knew only by sight. The transparent knots of cobalt flame on their heads added a bluish cast to the light in the room.

'We're ready, Father,' one of the men said to Lucien. The friar led Manuel to a spot near the upturned box, and the others arranged themselves in a circle around him. Against the aft wall, near gaps where floor met wall imperfectly, Manuel spotted two big rats with shiny brown fur, all ablink and twitch-whiskered at the unusual activity. Manuel frowned and one of the rats plopped into the water covering the floor and swam under the wall, its tail swishing back and forth like a small snake, revealing to Manuel its true nature. The other rat stood its ground and blinked its bright little round eyes as it brazenly returned Manuel's unwelcoming gaze.

From behind the box Lucien looked at each man in

turn, and read in Latin. Manuel understood the first part: 'I believe in God the Father Almighty, maker of heaven and earth, and of all things visible and invisible ...' From there Lucien read on, in a voice powerful yet soothing, entreatful yet proud. After finishing the creed he took up another book, the little one he always carried with him, and read in Spanish:

'"Know ye, O Israel, that what men call life and death are as beads of white and black strung upon a thread; and this thread of perpetual change is mine own changeless life, which bindeth together the unending string of little lives and little deaths.

'"The wind turns a ship from its course upon the deep: the wandering winds of the senses cast man's mind adrift on the deep.

'"But lo! That day shall come when the light that *is* shall still all winds, and bind every hideous liquid darkness; and all thy habitations shall be blest by the white brilliance which descendeth from the crown."'

While Lucien read this, the soldier moved slowly about the chamber. First he set on the top of the box a plate of sliced biscuit; the bread was hard, as it became after months at sea, and someone had taken the trouble to cut slices, and then polish them into wafers so thin that they were translucent, and the colour of honey. Occasional wormholes gave them the look of old coins, that had been beaten flat and holed for use as jewellery.

Next the soldier brought forth from behind the box an empty glass bottle with its top cut off so that it was a sort of bowl. Taking a flask in his other hand, he filled the bowl to the midway point with *La Lavia*'s awful wine. Putting the flask down, he circled the group while the friar finished reading. Every man there had cuts on his hands that more or less continuously leaked blood, and each man pulled a cut open over the bottle held to him, allowing a drop to splash in, until the wine was so dark that to Manuel, aware of the blue light, it was a deep violet.

The soldier replaced the bottle beside the plate of wafers on the box. Friar Lucien finished his reading, looked at the box, and recited one final sentence: 'O lamps of fire! Make bright the deep caverns of sense; with strange brightness give heat and light together to your beloved, that we may be one with you.' Taking the plate in hand, he circled the chamber, putting a wafer in the mouths of the men. 'The body of Christ, given for you. The body of Christ, given for you.'

Manuel snapped the wafer of biscuit between his teeth and chewed it. At last he understood what they were doing. This was a communion for the dead: a service for Laeghr, a service for all of them, for they were all doomed. Beyond the damp curved wall of their chamber was the deep sea, pressing against the timbers, pressing in on them. Eventually they would all be swallowed, and would sink down to become food for the fishes, after which their bones would decorate the floor of the ocean, where God seldom visited. Manuel could scarcely get the chewed biscuit past the lump in his throat. When Friar Lucien lifted the half bottle and put it to his lips, saying first, 'The blood of Christ, shed for you,' Manuel stopped him. He took the bottle from the friar's hand. The soldier stepped forward, but Lucien waved him away. Then the friar kneeled before Manuel and crossed himself, but backwards as Greeks did, left to right rather than the proper way. Manuel said, 'You are the blood of Christ,' and held the half bottle to Lucien's lips, tilting it so he could drink.

He did the same for each of the men, the soldier included. 'You are the Christ.' This was the first time any of them had partaken of this part of the communion, and some of them could barely swallow. When they had all drunk, Manuel put the bottle to his lips and drained it to the dregs. 'Friar Lucien's book says, all thy habitations shall be blest by the white brilliance that is the crown of fire, and we shall all be made the Christ. And so it is. We drank, and now we are the Christ. See' – he pointed at the remaining rat, which was now on its hind legs, washing its forepaws so that it appeared to pray, its bright round eyes fixed on Manuel – 'even the beasts know it.' He broke off a piece of biscuit wafer, and leaned down to offer it to the rat. The rat accepted the fragment in its paws, and ate it. It submitted to Manuel's touch. Standing back up, Manuel felt the blood rush to his head. The crowns of fire blazed on every head, reaching far above them to lick the beams of the ceiling, filling the room with light – 'He is here!' Manuel cried, 'He has touched us with light, see it!' He touched each of their foreheads in turn, and saw their eyes widen as they perceived the others' burning souls in wonder, pointing at each other's heads; then they were all embracing in the clear white light, hugging one another with the tears running down their cheeks and giant grins splitting their beards. Reflected candlelight danced in a thousand parts on the watery floor. The rat, startled, splashed under the gap in the wall, and they laughed and laughed and laughed.

Manuel put his arm around the friar, whose eyes shone with joy. 'It is good,' Manuel said when they were all quiet again. 'God will see us home.'

They made their way back to the upper decks like boys playing in a cave they know very well.

The Armada made it through the Orkneys without Laeghr, though it was a close thing for some ships. Then they were out in the North Atlantic, where the swells were broader, their troughs deeper, and their tops as high as the castles of *La Lavia*, and then higher than that.

Winds came out of the southwest, bitter gales that never ceased, and three weeks later they were no closer to Spain than they had been when they slipped through the Orkneys. The situation on *La Lavia* was desperate, as it was all through the fleet. Men on *La Lavia* died every day, and were thrown overboard with no ceremony except the impression of Manuel's medallion into their arms. The deaths made the food and water shortage less acute, but it was still serious. *La Lavia* was now manned by a ghost crew, composed mostly of soldiers. There weren't enough of them to properly man the pumps, and the Atlantic was springing new leaks every day in the already broken hull. The ship began taking on water in such quantities that the acting captain of the ship – who had started the voyage as third mate – decided that they must make straight for Spain, making no spare leeway for the imperfectly known west coast of Ireland. This decision was shared by the captains of several other damaged ships, and they conveyed their decision to the main body of the fleet, which was reaching farther west before turning south to Spain. From his sickbed Medina Sidonia gave his consent, and *La Lavia* sailed due south.

Unfortunately, a storm struck from just north of west soon after they had turned homeward. They were helpless before it. *La Lavia* wallowed in the troughs and was slammed by crest after crest, until the poor hulk lay just off the lee shore, Ireland.

It was the end, and everyone knew it. Manuel knew it because the air had turned black. The clouds were like thousands of black English cannonballs, rolling ten deep over a clear floor set just above the masts, and spitting lightning into the sea whenever two of them banged together hard enough. The air beneath them was black as well, just less thick: the wind as tangible as the waves, and swirling around the masts with smoky fury. Other men caught glimpses of the lee shore, but Manuel couldn't see it for the blackness. These men called out in fear; apparently the western coast of Ireland was sheer cliff. It was the end.

Manuel had nothing but admiration for the third-mate-now-captain, who took the helm and shouted to the lookout in the top to find a bay in the cliffs they were drifting towards. But Manuel, like many of the men, ignored the mate's commands to stay at post, as they were clearly pointless. Men embraced each other on the castles, saying their farewells; others cowered in fear against the bulkheads. Many of them approached Manuel and asked for a touch, and Manuel brushed their foreheads as he angrily marched about the forecastle. As soon as Manuel touched them, some of the men flew directly up towards heaven while others dove over the side of the ship and became porpoises the moment they struck the water, but Manuel scarcely noticed these occurrences, as he was busy praying, praying at the top of his lungs.

'*Why* this storm, Lord, *why?* First there were winds from the north holding us back, which is the only reason I'm here in the first place. So you wanted me here, but why why why? Juan is dead and Laeghr is dead and Pietro is dead and Habedeen is dead and soon we will all be dead, and why? It isn't just. You promised you would take us home.' In a fury he took his slow match knife, climbed down to the swamped midships, and went to the mainmast. He thrust the knife deep into the wood, stabbing with the grain. 'There! I say *that* to your storm!'

'Now, that's blasphemy,' Laeghr said as he pulled the knife from the mast and threw it over the side. 'You know what stabbing the mast means. To do it in a storm like this – you'll offend gods a lot older than Jesus, and more powerful, too.'

'Talk about blasphemy,' Manuel replied. 'And you wonder why you're still wandering the seas a ghost, when you say things like that. You should take more care.' He looked up and saw Saint Anna, in the maintop giving directions to the third mate. 'Did you hear what Laeghr said?' he shouted up to her. She didn't hear him.

'Do you remember the words I taught you?' Laeghr enquired.

'Of course. Don't bother me now, Laeghr, I'll be a ghost with you soon enough.' Laeghr stepped back, but

Manuel changed his mind, and said, 'Laeghr, why are we being punished like this? We were on a crusade for God, weren't we? I don't understand.'

Laeghr smiled and turned around, and Manuel saw then that he had wings, wings with feathers intensely white in the black murk of the air. He clasped Manuel's arm. 'You know all that I know.' With some hard flaps he was off, tumbling east swiftly in the black air, like a gull.

With the help of Saint Anna the third mate had actually found a break in the cliffs, a quite considerable bay. Other ships of the Armada had found it as well, and they were already breaking up on a wide beach as *La Lavia* limped nearer shore. The keel grounded and immediately things began breaking. Soupy waves crashed over the canted midships, and Manuel leaped up the ladder to the forecastle, which was now under a tangle of rigging from the broken foremast. The mainmast went over the side, and the lee flank of the ship splintered like a match tub and flooded, right before their eyes. Among the floating timbers Manuel saw one that held a black cannonball embedded in it, undoubtedly the very one that Saint Anna had deflected from its course towards him. Reminded that she had saved his life before, Manuel grew calmer and waited for her to appear. The beach was only a few shiplengths away, scarcely visible in the thick air; like most of the men, Manuel could not swim, and he was searching with some urgency for a sight of Saint Anna when Friar Lucien appeared at his side, in his black robes. Over the shriek of the dark wind Lucien shouted, 'If we hold on to a plank we'll float ashore.'

'You go ahead,' Manuel shouted back. 'I'm waiting for Saint Anna.' The friar shrugged. The wind caught his robes and Manuel saw that Lucien was attempting to save the ship's liturgical gold, which was in the form of chains that were now wrapped around the friar's middle. Lucien made his way to the rail and jumped over it, onto a spar that a wave was carrying away from the ship. He missed his hold on the rounded spar, however, and sank instantly.

The forecastle was now awash, and soon the foaming breakers would tear it loose from the keel. Most of the men had already left the wreck, trusting to one bit of flotsam or other. But Manuel still waited. Just as he was beginning to worry he saw the blessed grandmother of God, standing among figures on the beach that he perceived but dimly, gesturing to him. She walked out onto the white water, and he understood. 'We are the Christ, of course! I will walk to shore as He once did.' He tested the surface with one shoe; it seemed a little, well, infirm, but surely it would serve – it would be like the floor of their now-demolished chapel, a sheet of water covering one of God's good solids. So Manuel walked out onto the next wave that passed at the level of the forecastle, and plunged deep into the brine.

'Hey!' he spluttered as he struggled back to the surface. 'Hey!' No answer from Saint Anna this time; just cold salt water. He began the laborious process of drowning, remembering as he struggled a time when he was a child, and his father had taken him down to the beach in Morocco, to see the galley of the pilgrims to Mecca rowing away. Nothing could have been less like the Irish coast than that serene, hot, tawny beach, and he and his father had gone out into the shallows to splash around in the warm water, chasing lemons. His father would toss the lemons out into the deeper water, where they bobbed just under the surface, and then Manuel would paddle out to retrieve them, laughing and choking on water.

Manuel could picture those lemons perfectly, as he snorted and coughed and thrashed to get his head back above the freezing soup one more time. Lemons bobbing in the green sea, lemons oblong and bumpy, the colour of the sun when the sun is its own width above the horizon at dawn . . . bobbing gently just under the surface, with a knob showing here or there. Manuel pretended he was a lemon, at the same time that he tried to remember the primitive dog paddle that had gotten him around in the shallows. Arms, pushing downward. It wasn't working. Waves tumbled him, lemonlike, in towards the strand. He bumped on the bottom and stood up. The water was only waist deep. Another wave smashed him from behind and he couldn't find the bottom again. Not fair! he thought. His elbow ran into sand, and he twisted around and stood. Knee deep, this time. He kept an eye on the treacherous waves as they came out of the black, and trudged through them up to a beach made of coarse sand, covered by a mat of loose seaweed.

Down on the beach a distance were sailors, companions, survivors of the wrecks offshore. But there among them – soldiers on horses. English soldiers, on horses and on foot – Manuel groaned to see it – wielding swords and clubs on the exhausted men strewn across the seaweed. 'No!' Manuel cried, 'No!' But it was true. 'Ah,

God,' he said, and sank till he was sitting. Down the
strand soldiers clubbed his brothers, splitting their fragile eggshell skulls so that the yolk of their brains ran
into the kelp. Manuel beat his insensible fists against
the sand. Filled with horror at the sight, he watched
horses rear in the murk, giant and shadowy. They were
coming down the beach towards him. 'I'll make myself
invisible,' he decided. 'Saint Anna will make me invisible.' But remembering his plan to walk on the water,
he determined to help the miracle by staggering up the
beach and burrowing under a particularly tall pile of
seaweed. He was invisible without it, of course, but the
cover of kelp would help keep him warm. Thinking
such thoughts, he shivered and shivered and on the still
land fell insensible as his hands.

When he woke up, the soldiers were gone. His fellows
lay up and down the beach like white driftwood; ravens
and wolves already converged on them. He couldn't
move very well. It took him half an hour to move his
head to survey the beach, and another half hour to free
himself from his pile of seaweed. And then he had to
lie down again.

When he regained consciousness, he found himself
behind a large log, an old piece of driftwood that had
been polished silver by its years of rolling in sand. The
air was clear again. He could feel it filling him and leaving him, but he could no longer see it. The sun was
out; it was morning, and the storm was over. Each
movement of Manuel's body was a complete effort, a
complete experience. He could see quite deeply into his
skin, which appeared pickled. He had lost all of his

clothes, except for a tattered shred of trousers around his middle. With all his will he made his arm move his hand, and with his stiff forefinger he touched the drift-wood. He could feel it. He was still alive.

His hand fell away in the sand. The wood touched by his finger was changing, becoming a bright green spot in the surrounding silver. A thin green sprig bulged from the spot, and grew up towards the sun; leaves unfolded from this sprout as it thickened, and beneath Manuel's fascinated gaze a bud appeared and burst open: a white rose, gleaming wetly in the white morning light.

He had managed to stand, and cover himself with kelp, and walk a full quarter of a mile inland, when he came upon people. Three of them to be exact, two men and a woman. Wilder looking people Manuel couldn't imagine: the men had beards that had never been cut, and arms like Laeghr's. The woman looked exactly like his miniature portrait of Saint Anna, until she got closer and he saw that she was dirty and her teeth were broken and her skin was brindled like a dog's belly. He had never seen such freckling before, and he stared at it, and her, every bit as much as she and her companions stared at him. He was afraid of them.

'Hide me from the English, please,' he said. At the word *English* the men frowned and cocked their heads. They jabbered at him in a tongue he did not know. 'Help me,' he said. 'I don't know what you're saying. Help me.' He tried Spanish and Portuguese and Sicilian and Arabic. The men were looking angry. He tried Latin, and they stepped back. 'I believe in God the Father Almighty, Maker of Heaven and Earth, and in all things visible and invisible.' He laughed, a bit hysterically.

'Especially invisible.' He grabbed his medallion and showed them the cross. They studied him, clearly at a loss.

'*Tor conaloc an dhia*,' he said without thinking. All four of them jumped. Then the two men moved to his sides to hold him steady. They chattered at him, waving their free arms. The woman smiled, and Manuel saw that she was young. He said the syllables again, and they chattered at him some more. 'Thank you, Laeghr,' he said. 'Thank you, Anna. Anna,' he said to the girl, and reached for her. She squealed and stepped back. He said the phrase again. The men lifted him, for he could no longer walk, and carried him across the heather. He smiled and kissed both men on the cheek, which made them laugh, and he said the magic phrase again and started to fall asleep and smiled and said the phrase. *Tor conaloc an dhia*. The girl brushed his wet hair out of his eyes; Manuel recognized the touch, and he could feel the flowering begin inside him.

– *give mercy for God's sake* –

Muir on Shasta

'YOUR GOODNESS MUST have an edge to it,'
Emerson had said to him, as if a single week's
acquaintanceship in euphoric Yosemite could
reveal any of the edges in a man. Still it had been valuable advice, for Muir's edges lay buried under sunny
meadows and brook babble, and it could be that the old
philosopher had only meant to say You should let your
edges show, or It is all right to have edges. A valuable
lesson indeed.

Shasta was an Emersonian mountain, it occurred to
Muir as he sat on its summit pinnacle. In its youth it
had leaped towards heaven, rising ten thousand feet
above the surrounding plains; now it was ancient,
glacier-cloaked, its broad peak rounded and craterless,
its creative fires banked. And yet there were still sharp
outcroppings of lava on the ridges, and enough fire rising
from the depths to boil a muddy spring near the summit;

and there was in the end the massive snowy fact of the mountain itself, isolate, powerful, brooding, godlike. Emerson had been just like that.

Muir hefted a brass barometer. He and an acquaintance, Jerome Bixby, had ascended Shasta that morning to take readings, although really the readings were no more than an excuse to climb the mountain and have a look around. From the peak, one saw mountains everywhere – the Coast Range, the Siskiyous, the Trinity Alps, the northern Sierra, snowy flat-topped Lassen – mountains to every point of the compass, a wild tangle of ridges and peaks.

As he sat and watched, clouds rose out of the valleys and over the ridges, until everything except Shasta was submerged. He stood on a snow island in an ocean of cloud. To the west a thunderhead billowed up, its bright lobes as solid as marble. He gazed at it with a connoisseur's eye, feeling the wind yank his beard, feeling it rake through the weave of his coat, rapt with his usual peak exaltation –

But there was Bixby, plodding across the white summit plain, looking like a black ant. He had been waiting below the ultimate peak, but now he huffed up the small remnant of the crater wall that was the mountain's highest point, and once at Muir's side said, 'We should go down – a storm is coming!'

'One more reading,' Muir said, irritated. He didn't care about the reading, but he didn't want to descend.

So they stayed on the peak, and the wind freshened, and then the clear air overhead was suddenly marred by streams of mist like carded wool. Just as he completed the last reading they were enveloped in cloud, and the wind grew stronger; and as he followed Bixby down the knob and onto the summit plain, six-faceted hailstones clattered onto the tortured red rock, and thumped into the packed snow, and onto their backs.

Then as they forced their way west, past the hissing fumaroles of the hot spring and over big chunks of black lava, snow began to fall in waves so thick that at times they were unable to see even their own feet. Blasts of wind slapped them on the ear, snow crystals stung their faces, and it got so cold so fast that Muir became curious, and stopped to read his thermometer; the temperature had dropped twenty-two degrees in ten minutes, and was now below zero.

Lightning flicked, dim in the clouds, and thunder began to bang around them, in explosions so violent that they vibrated one's whole body. 'Wow!' Muir shouted, inaudible in the barrage. He was grinning. The truth was, he loved storms in the mountains. He had been in them so many times that he was confident no storm could harm him, if he continued to walk in it; the heat engendered by exertion was always enough to counter even the wildest assaults. And so he struggled on through the crashing, howling vortex of snow and wind and thunder, head down, thrusting forward as if wrestling some herculean elder brother, whooping at the storm's high drama and spectacle, its brute strength and godlike grandeur – laughing at its sheer excess –

But he had entirely forgotten to think of Bixby. Who, in fact, had fallen behind, and was out of sight. Muir crouched in the shelter of a giant lava block that marked the route along their ridge, and waited. After a while Bixby appeared out of the snow, and one look made it clear that he was not having the same sort of fun that Muir was.

The two men huddled together in the lee of the block. Weird light illuminated them in flashes, and it was almost too noisy to hold a conversation. 'We can't go on!' Bixby shouted.

'What?' Muir said, astonished.

'We can't go on!'

'But we must! We have no choice!'

'We'll be killed!'

'No, no – we'll stay on the ridge, I know the way!'

'It's too exposed!'

This was the very reason that they must take the ridge. The slopes to either side would be swept by avalanches, and even if they escaped these, they would be likely to wander onto a glacier. The ridge, on the other hand, would be blown clear of snow, providing a rocky road down to safety. It would be windy, but no wind could blow a man from a rock; if gusts threatened to do so, one could always lie flat till they were over.

Irritably he tried to explain this, but Bixby would have none of it. He just shook his head and shouted again, 'We can't go down!' He looked the same as always, face calm, his shouts in a reasonable tone of voice; but there was a stubbornness in him, and when Muir shouted, 'I memorized the way down the ridge,' he stared at Muir as if confronted with a madman. And the thunder crashed, and the hurtling air roared across the ridge, catching on a million jagged lava teeth and shrieking, keening, howling, drowning out mere human voices.

'We must go down!' Muir shouted again. 'We have no choice!'

'We can't go down! It's impossible! We'll be killed!'

'It's stopping will kill us!' Muir replied, getting angry. Stupid man, did he think this block's feeble shelter would be enough to protect them? 'We have no choice!' he repeated.

Bixby shook his head. For an instant he looked like Muir's father, insisting on a point of Bible doctrine. 'I won't go on!'

'We must go on!'

'I won't go on!'

And that was that. There is a stubbornness in fear that will balk at even the most perfect logic. Muir tugged furiously at his beard. 'What do you propose to do!' he shouted.

Bixby wiped the snow from his face and looked around, blinking cowlike. 'The fumaroles are warm,' he said.

'The fumaroles are *boiling!*' Muir shouted. Anger spiked through him, he wanted to grab the man by the coat and shake his courage back into him. 'Superheated poison gas!'

But Bixby was trudging back towards the fumaroles, hunched into the wind, staggering as gusts shoved him from side to side.

'Fool!' Muir cried, and cursed him roundly.

He stayed by the block, searching the clouds for a break that he could use as argument to convince Bixby to continue. But none came; the storm raged on; and suddenly he realized that his anger at Bixby was a transitive expression of his own fear. He could not leave his companion behind; and so now they were both in very great danger.

*　　*　　*

The fumaroles near the peak were among the last small vestiges of Shasta's volcanic glory. Superheated gases rose through cracks in the long throat, and emerged in a small depression on the western side of the summit, where they heated a mixture of snowmelt, volcanic ash, and sand, creating a patch of boiling black mud.

Muir approached it. In the storm's cold air the patch steamed heavily, making it look like the clouds were pouring out of the mountain as well as rushing over it: an eerie sight. Bixby was already crouched at the mud's edge. Muir stomped to his side.

Bixby looked up. 'This will keep us safe from frost!'

'Oh yes, safe from frost!' Muir said sarcastically. 'But how will we keep from scalding ourselves? And how will we protect our lungs from the acid gases? And how will we get off the mountain once we soak our clothes? Storm or clear, we'll freeze on our way down! We'll have to stay until morning, and who knows what kind of day it will be!'

Bixby shivered miserably.

Muir held his breath, let out a long sigh. There was nothing for it. They were there. He crouched and looked over the roiling snow-rimmed pit. Wind whipped any warmth coming off the mud directly away; their zone of safety was about a quarter of an acre in extent, but only an eighth of an inch thick. Scylla and Charybdis, embracing.

Muir sighed again and tromped into the mud, sinking immediately to his knees and feeling the heat burn his legs. Jetting bubbles of gas made the mud look like molten lava. But on the windward side of the pool they would probably be safe from the gas. As long as the wind held steady. And it seemed it would; it roared out of the west, cutting through clothing; they couldn't stand in it long. Growling, Muir finished sitting in the shallows of the pool. Hot water seeped out of the mud into his pants, then his shirt and coat. He lay back, his head against the windward snowbank, his body outstretched in the mud. Spindrift ran across his face. His nose, which had no feeling to it, still conveyed to him the stench of sulphur. The warmth of the mud burned his skin, but he had to admit it was a relief from the fierce wind. A laugh burst from him like gas from the mud; then a jet of rising bubbles scalded his back and he yelped, rolled hastily to the side. He elbowed a snow and mud poultice over the hot spot, dizzy with the carbonic stink. Now he was covered with mud, his coat and trousers completely soaked. Bixby was the same. Standing up would have turned them into ice statues of themselves. They were committed.

It was necessary to shift position frequently, to immerse an exposed limb, or expose a boiled one. The passage of time was marked by pain. The storm continued unabated, and the two men lay isolated by the shrieking wind, so that each might have been there alone except that occasionally Muir would raise his head and cry out, and Bixby would shout something back, and both would subside into solitude again. Snow fell so thickly that they breathed it. It settled on the exposed parts of them, and packed to a rime so hard that they crackled when they shifted.

The sun had apparently set, and it was dark. Muir could see nothing but blackness. At times the mud seemed blacker than the sky; then the sky would seem blacker than the mud. As black as the world had been during his episode of blindness, so many years before. He saw the file leaping into his eye, the aqueous humour draining into his hand, the swift darkening in his sight on the wounded side, and then, that night as he lay trembling in a strange bed, the relentless darkening on the other. Until he was left in total darkness. That fear had been the worst of his life; this was nothing to it, a natural darkness, a storm in its fury to be watched and loved. I will lift up mine eyes unto the hills, and *see*. He had been blind for three weeks, three full weeks of doctor's assurances and secret terror; and when his sight had returned he had walked out of his life and never returned, never looked back, tossing away the destiny that his father and country had thought proper for him, farming, inventing machinery, all that; he abandoned all that and gave himself to the wilderness. So that, properly speaking, it was in fact a blessing to be here boiling in a volcano's caldera with a blizzard thick about his ears. Part of nature's bounty –

Groans from Bixby broke his thought. He saw the lump of the man, rolling to escape a fumarole, struggling to keep from sinking. In some places the mud was viscid clay, in others black tea, whistling in its pot. Lumps of something, perhaps soaked pumice, floated under the surface, and he tried arranging a bed of the lumps under him to protect him from rising gas jets, but they kept slipping away. The wind still howled, but the clouds were thinning; the snow blowing across their bodies must have been spindrift, for he saw a star. If you can see one star, press on! as the saying had it. But not tonight.

Soon the clouds scudded off east, and starlight bathed the scene. The familiar patterns sparked the night sky, drawing around him all the other nights he had lain out in the world. The eye is a flower that sees the stars. If they had continued their descent, they would now be down on the snow slopes, where starlight would have made darkness visible, and guided them home. Instead, soaked as they were, and with a mile of wind-ripped ridge to negotiate, they were going to have to spend the night. But he said nothing. It was done. And his fault really, for staying on the peak so long. Besides, the sight of the stars brought it to him that whatever the discomfort, they were likely to survive; so it did not signify. He had spent many a cold night on a mountain. It could even be said that the boiling mud made this night less miserable than some, though – the skin of his back suddenly flaring – none other had been so purely painful. Still, he was used to pain, accustomed to it. He had grown up with it, working a hardscrabble farm for his father, a mean, small-minded man, a lesson in how not to be a Christian, all those days spent studying the Bible while his boys worked to get his bread, and then beating them with switch, belt –

His leg was on fire. He pulled his knee up into the icy wind, and for an instant smelled the gas. Once his father had set him to digging wells, and seventy feet down seeping gas had overwhelmed him, he had swooned and had only just come to, only just dragged himself far enough up the rope ladder to breathe good air, and live. He lifted his head and shouted at Bixby. 'Still there, Jerome?'

A croak. Something about the cold. Still there. Muir

settled back into the mud. Forget that whole world, that whole life, the way it could make his stomach knot. Look at the stars. The eye is a flower that sees the stars, immersed in primal cold and heat. His left foot squelched in its boot, propped on the snowbank. Wiggle the toes against wet leather, make sure they were still there. No. They were cold past feeling, only a certain vague numbness; while his right foot burned, scalded so that he nearly shouted, and certainly groaned. Leg yanked up; the wind wrapped the wet trouser to his leg and froze his thigh, while the foot still throbbed with the pain of the burn.

'Are you suffering much?' Bixby called.

'Yes!' Fool, what did he think? 'Frozen and burned! But never mind, it won't kill us!' As long as they weren't overcome by gas. A jet of bubbles pushed at his backbone, he rolled and shoved mud over the scalding spot, hitting at it furiously with a fist gone numb with frostbite.

Each hour was a year. The stars were in the same places they had been when they first became visible; so not many years could have passed. Concentrating on the stars near the horizon, he tried to see them creep west. That one, nearly occluded by a low wall of lava: focus on it, watch it, watch it, watch it . . . had it moved? No. Time had stopped. They had continued the descent, perhaps, and died in the attempt, and now they lay in some well-bottom hell of his father's stripe, or in a circle of Dante's inferno, in which heat and cold mingled without moderating the other, creating a pain unfamiliar to those in the simpler circles. He could hear their moans –

Ah, that star was occluded. Half an hour had jumped

past all at once. As if time were a matter of instantaneous jumps, from one eternal moment to the next – which in fact it often seemed to him to be, as during those sunny warm afternoons when he would lie in a Sierra meadow by a chuckling stream and watch the clouds, dreaming of nothing, until with a jerk he would return to the meadow and the shadows would be stretching twice as long as before, over perfectly sculpted patches of meadow grass, the larks singing 'wé-ero, spé-ero, wé-eo, wé-erlo, wé-it.'

Drifting in and out. A call to Bixby got a feeble response. Still alive if nothing else. A bubble burst, splashed hot mud over his face, and he spluttered and wiped his nose clear. He couldn't feel his left arm, or make it move; he wasn't sure when that had happened. That was his windward side, so presumably it was benumbed in the onslaught of air. He tried to dip the arm further under the mud, to bury it. Not a process one would want to carry too far, descending limb by limb into black muck. Now the arm seemed to be burning; was that a fumarole bubbling up? No. In fact he had accidentally plunged the arm into the snowbank; his right hand confirmed it. But how the skin burned!

Then a gas bubble lifted his knee, and the back of his leg felt like glacier melt had been poured over it; it ached with cold, the knee joint creaked with it! He groaned. Cold now scalded and heat froze, and he didn't know which was which!

Perhaps it didn't matter. Caught between cold reason and hot passion, ignorant flesh always paid the price. One could never tell which was which. Outrageous pain! Better to leave all that behind.

A solution occurred to him. He stood up. He looked back down and saw his body lying there, stretched out in the mud, mostly submerged. A sponge, soaked in immortality. A mass of eternal atoms, bound together in just that particular way, to witness the beauty of the universe.

Yes: he stood there gazing down at his boiled and frozen body. Somewhat bemused, he tried a few steps; circled the mud patch; then took off across the windswept snow, towards an exposed rock outcropping. There was a building there, a small square cabin, white in the starlight. As he approached he saw that its walls were made of pure white quartz. Its door and windows were edged with quartz crystals. The door and the roof were made of slate, all dotted with lichen. The windows were thin smooth sheets of water.

He opened the door and walked in. The table was a slab of glacier-polished granite. The benches around it were fallen logs. The bed was made of spruce boughs. The carpet was green moss.

It was his home. He sat on one of the logs, and put his hand on the table. His hand sank into the granite. His body sank into the log, and then into the moss, and then into the quartz.

He felt himself dissolving out into the great mass of the mountain, tumbling slowly down through the rock. He had melted into Shasta. The mountain mumbled in his ear 'I am.' With a puff of its cheeks it blew him aloft, threw his atoms out into the sky. They tumbled off on the wind and dispersed to every point of the compass, then fell and steeped into the fabric of the land, one atom in every rock, in every grain of sand and soil, like gas in mud, or water in sponge, until his body and California were contiguous, united, one. Only his vision remained separate, his precious sight, the landscape's consciousness soaring like a hawk over the long sand beaches, the great valley, the primeval sequoias, the range of light – but the mountains were different – blinding glaciers covered all but the highest peaks, fingered down through the hills, and cut Yosemite's walls. Then they retreated, dried up and ran away.

He tumbled, soared west. It was night, now, and below lay the bay like a sparkling black map, the black water criss-crossed with bridges of light, the surrounding hills dotted with millions of white points like stars, defining towers, roadways, docks, arenas, monuments; a bay-circling city, impossibly beautiful. But so many people! It had to be thousands of years in the future, as glaciers were thousands of years in the past. He was soaring through time, out of the knife-edge present, back to glaciers and forward to supercities, perhaps ten thousand years each way. An eyeblink in the life of stones, and the Sierra would stand throughout; but chewed at by the future city as much as by the ancient glaciers, perhaps. Sheep cropped meadows to dust in a single summer; and the shepherds were worse. And if so many came to live by the bay . . .

Curious, fearful, he tilted in his flight, soared east over the great valley, through the gold-choked foothills, up among the peaks. He rose in a gyre and stared down at starlit granite. There a valley had been drowned, a shocking sight. Wheel, turn, soar, take heart: for all was dark. Not a light to be seen, the whole length of the range. The backbone of California, gleaming in moonlight.

This much beauty would always be in danger, there was no avoiding that. Its animals must defend it. All its animals. He soared over the highest peaks, and then looked back; a full moon bathed the great eastern escarpment with white light. Death Valley burned, Whitney froze –

His ankle was in a fumarole, his head in the muddy snowbank. He shifted, saw that the wheel of stars had turned nearly a quarter turn. He took several long deep breaths. His vision cleared with the cold air, he returned to the moment and his bed in the mud. He could feel his lungs and his mind; beyond that, he and the mountain still seemed one undifferentiated mass, which he felt only in a distant, seismic way. But now he knew where he was. For a while he had soared on a great wind through time; but now he was just John again, flat on his back, and numb with cold.

Still, he remembered the vision perfectly. That was quite a voyage great Shasta had sent him on! Perhaps visions like that were why the Indians worshipped it.

As for what he had seen . . . well, the habitable zone was never thick. Caught between the past and future, we squirm in a dangerous eighth of an inch. Perhaps it was like that always. The atmosphere, for instance, was frighteningly thin; hike for a day and you could ascend the larger part of it, as when climbing Shasta itself. The landscape was tightly wrapped in a thin skin of gas.

And the earth itself rolled in a thin temperate sphere around the sun, a zone of heat that neither boiled the seas nor allowed them to freeze solid; that shell might only be a few feet thick, or an eighth of an inch, who knew? It was a miracle the earth rolled within that sphere! Delicate, precious dewdrop of a world, hung in the light with the nicest precision, like every dewdrop in every morning's spider-web . . .

The wheel of stars had turned again. Bixby was shifting, muttering as in a dream. The sky in the east was the black nearest blue. And then the blue nearest black. Light seeped into the world as if vision were a new faculty, a sense born instant by instant, to creatures formerly blind. The stars began to slip away; he watched a dim one grow fainter and then wink out of visibility, a strange moment. The eyes are flowers that see the stars.

Bixby croaked something about leaving. But they were on the western side of the peak, and it would be hours before the sun appeared. Meanwhile it was cold beyond movement. When they shifted their coats crackled as if made of thin glass.

The sky, though cloudless, was a dull and frosty blue. He could see nothing of the earth but their mud patch, and the snow and lava bordering it. He still felt part of the mountain, with no discernible break between his skin and the mud. As the morning light blossomed it seemed to fill him, pouring through his eyes and down into the rock; he felt himself a conduit in a vast interconnected totality, an organism pulsing with its own universal breath. The heat at his core caught and burned, so that he was warm enough to melt his coat's sheath of ice; that was heat displaced from the volcano, which was heat displaced from the sun; which was heat displaced from the heart of the Milky Way; which was heat displaced from the heart of the universe, from that original heart's diastolic expansion. No dualism was significant in the face of this essential unity: he was an atom of God's great body, and he knew it. The landscape and his mind were two expressions of the same miracle.

On the lonely peak of a nearly extinct volcano, two black specks of consciousness observed the morning light.

The time came at last to try a descent. Imagination over reason, action over contemplation; thus he had always believed, and never more than now! It was time to think two thoughts down the mountain.

Spindrift sparked overhead like chips of mica, and then the sun cracked the mountaintop. They stood like golems new-made of clay, ice shattering from their chests, mud sluicing off their backs. They slapped their arms together and the world burned in their fingertips. Nature was the greatest teacher, for those who listened; and Muir had learned long ago that there was a reserve of energy at the end of any long period of suffering. It was something mountaineers often had the chance to discover.

They staggered crazy-legged over the long ridge. They reached the snow slopes and descended more rapidly, swimming through drifts, glissading at the top of little avalanches, falling on their faces; but all downwards, and so of use, their weakness only speeding the descent.

Then the clean smell of pinesap cut through the sulphur stench in their hair, and they were at treeline. Bixby sat against a tree and rested, while Muir went on, in search of their host Sisson. Godlike he strode through a meadow, its wildflowers exploding in his sight, dot after dot of pure drenched colour. And then he saw Sisson's horses through the trees, and smelled his coffee on the fire. Smoke rose through slanting sunbeams. He was home; and now he was home.